Keeper of Dreams

Keeper of Dreams

ANNA RAEBURN

THE BODLEY HEAD

LONDON

A CIP catalogue record for this book is available from the British Library.

ISBN 0 370 31291 0

© Anna Raeburn 1989

Printed in Great Britain for
The Bodley Head Ltd,
31 Bedford Square, London WC1B 3SG
BY
Mackays of Chatham PLC

First published 1989

In the middle of every onion is a tear.

Yiddish proverb

1   *Mercer*

The drive down to my sister's is ugly. It's the sort of countryside that's only called country because there aren't enough houses close together for it to be called town. And they're grey and unexciting and the gardens are lumpy and the pretty ones don't look as nice as they'd look in another place.

I don't know if it's always grey when we're going down there, but it always seems grey. And it always takes longer to get there than forever, as though by beginning the journey you'd entered a tunnel in which everything was weightless and suspended, without clocks. Josh has always travelled everywhere with patience but now he's getting to the stage where you have to ask him to stop asking how much longer it's going to take to get there. It's a pretty enough day in summer 1986 and I'm already dreading what driving down to my sister's on Boxing Day will be like.

Two or three years ago we began to go down to my sister Lindsay's house on Boxing Day to see my mother Joan. I used to call my mother Midge. It was an adult nickname for her because I began to feel funny about calling her Mummy and for some reason recoil from calling or being called Mum. But I don't call her Midge any more. On more than one occasion recently I have heard myself call her Mother in that formal, chilly, middle-class British way we're all so easily parodied for and when I'm referring to her I call her Joan. It's part of my freedom. She calls me by my name and I call her by hers. But I don't want to call her Joan. She isn't Joan. That sounds like the name of one of my friends. I wish she were. She's my mother.

You can tell when I'm getting ready to go down to see my mother. I want everything to be right. Once I used to ask what I could bring for her since I live in the gilded city and she's out there in the country. She lives about thirty miles from Lindsay in a house they shared before Lindsay's marriage. That should tell you quite a bit about my sister and my mother. When my father died, my sister moved in with my mother. I couldn't have done that. One of the best things my mother and I ever did was to acknowledge that I had to be off out of it.

I don't ask what to bring so much now, although I still offer occasionally. But I usually make her a cake. She had me late, she's very old and she can't stand the cake-baking action any more. Her failing eyesight precludes the use of a blender. So I make her a cake.

For a long time, I took clothes I'd bought to show her. I took magazines and books, articles I thought would interest her. And of course I can't do all those things any more because of her blindness. Sometimes she asks me to choose a lipstick or to bring a sauce or relish I've introduced her to, that she's grown fond of, to put on the endless bits of chicken and chops she consumes.

Going down to see my mother means I want everything to be right. I want it with childish fervour. I want me to be right and Con, my husband, to be just so and Josh to be neat and clean and charming. Somewhere in my head I want to give her the best I've got. I used to dress up for going down there, even apologise for coming home in informal clothes. After all, she had years of me in jeans when I was married to my first husband, David, and I know I didn't offer her my best then because I was too busy giving him everything I'd got, including several kinds of energy I couldn't really spare. But I always gave her things. I always loved her.

She won't or can't come to spend Christmas with Con and Josh and me. We have a more or less open-plan flat and an active small boy, so an old lady with her very possessive little dog at her heels isn't on. She came for the first two Christmases we lived there, once when there was no Josh and once when he was small and manageable. But she didn't come for the next because she felt that Lindsay was feeling left out and, she reminded me, 'After all, I do have two daughters.' And once she came after that but she was carsick and refused to acknowledge how deaf she was so then we came up with this compromise, this mature arrangement which theoretically

2

takes everyone's needs into consideration. Joan spends Christmas with Lindsay and her husband Bob, and then Con and I go down to see them all on Boxing Day with Josh.

Christmas is very loaded for us. My mother's wedding anniversary is on Christmas Eve, my father died just before Christmas and my sister's first great love was killed in a car crash at Christmas, the year before they were going to get married. Christmas is quiet and loyal and low-key.

I never understand why people don't like Christmas. I do. I used to because I remembered it at home, the decorations which were kept from one year to the next and the tree with the spun-glass peacock propped up underneath because the loop to hang him from had broken. He was old and he came from my mother's home. And I liked turkey and the family rule which was that at Christmas you were given what you needed whilst for your birthday you could have what you wanted, within modest limits.

I like it now that I've a home of my own and a man to make Christmas for, a man and a child I love. Most of the year I can get through going down to see my mother. For years I wanted to, but not so much now, less and less in fact, and the reason why not swims round and round like something threatening you can't define in a murky pool. And this has been building up.

The energy that went into trying to get everything right before we left backfired upon Con and me. We'd rub each other up the wrong way and wind up shouting. For months, I'd always forget something – at my home, not my mother's – now, wouldn't your friendly neighbourhood psychiatrist have fun with that little tangle? The child would cry, the car would splutter. Last year I began to sense that something was indissolubly wrong. It had to do with my mother and sister and me. And it was a great shock to me.

I was brought up to believe in family love and my family lived it. It wasn't cosy and sweet or blameless. But it worked. I always thought it had worked. I had known for a long time that my mother thought and felt differently about Lindsay from the way she did about me but I'd accepted her rationalisation.

Lindsay is twelve years older than me. She was born into a different world; my mother was a different woman when she had her from the woman she was when she had me. My father was a different man. I knew something about the differences but I'd never thought about whether they should count or not. They were just differences. I was brought up to believe in the sanctity of the

3

differences, individualism, but nobody bothered to teach me that there might be a price put on it. Or that the price might be to do with different definitions of love.

There had been rumblings about the will Lindsay wanted my mother to leave. There had been rumblings over my mother's wish to stay in the house she had shared with my sister instead of going to live with Lindsay and Bob as Lindsay suggested. My mother would say that she knew that Bob had some very good points but she couldn't live with him. Let's face it, she didn't want to live with anybody, although I felt at one stage not inconsiderable guilt because by not buying a suitable house at the right moment, I forfeited the right to offer her an alternative. However, she assured me with some force that she didn't want to live in the city and she didn't want to live with anybody. That was round one.

Round two was that my sister pressed quite firmly for my mother to go and live with her, in a 'granny annexe' to be built on her house, and she leaned sufficiently heavily for my mother to give in and accept an estate agent's coming out to value the property. My mother sounded sad. I said into the telephone, 'Why are you doing this? Why put yourself through this? If you don't want to move, you don't want to move.'

My mother's voice became querulous. 'You don't seem to realise,' she said, 'that I have to make a decision in everybody's best interests. I can't just think of myself.'

I argued with her. I told her that at eighty odd she could do whatever she wanted, she'd earned the right to.

'I have to take into account,' she said, 'Lindsay's wishes.'

'Damn Lindsay and her wishes,' I said. 'Look, Midge, I'll make it easy for you. I have a share in the house, don't I?'

She said 'Yes' very quietly.

'OK' I said. 'Then tell Lindsay I refuse to sell. She can't do anything without me, can she? Blame me. Say I'm just being difficult.'

'Oh darling, thank you' she said from the end of the phone.

Lindsay and I are very different. She's tall and I'm small. She locks off and I explode. She fights with rectitude, my sister the good daughter, the hard worker. My mother's house is thirty miles away from her own home and at least once a week she drives over to see my mother. She assembles shopping for her, not all of it to be sure, but the heavy and occasional stuff my mother can't manage. When she first arrives, she fixes the sink or folds the blankets or does bits of gardening – whatever my mother, Joan, wants her to do.

Lindsay has to do things. She can't just sit and she can't not do. Give her time and she may think, but she's afraid of her thoughts. In the winter she stacks logs by the outhouse and fills the coal bucket. In summer she washes the clothes my mother sometimes finds too heavy to deal with. She telephones my mother every day to dictate to her a word game she can no longer pick out of the paper without great difficulty and using her magnifying glass. My mother doesn't like to use her magnifying glass or her hearing aid.

Lindsay also uses the house and my mother as a refuge from Bob. I don't know if either one of them acknowledges this and, if they do, there's no guarantee they'd talk about it, but my mother is the affair Lindsay isn't having, the permanent other which keeps the marriage going. Bob is insecure and lazy and dependent, always coming up with schemes to make money. He hasn't worked for a couple of years, though he does grow superb vegetables. I suppose he has good points but I never see them. What I most remember about Bob is that when I was pregnant with Josh, he stood beside me at the kitchen sink and said 'You'll see this one through, won't you?' I never told Con. He'd have killed him.

So I've always known that my mother and sister had a relationship I could not share.

They had twelve years of each other before I was born. Things happened during the last section of that, and even before. It's funny discovering that you've really begun to grow up inside your head, rather than the external key-of-the-door stuff people make such a fuss about. Joan thought independence was important for me, very important, as important as breathing, and as a child I fought for breath. She says she thought independence was important for Lindsay too but if we were maps, you'd find mine was unmarked whereas on Lindsay's, all roads lead back to my mother.

Joan and Paul had been married for seven or eight years before they had Lindsay, so when I start looking at Lindsay and what she is or isn't I'm forced to think as I've been taught and wonder what she came into as well as what straws I drew. Seven years is a long time to be together before you're prepared to share your life with a child but Joan's reasoning was impeccable.

'Your father,' she told me, 'was away and I got scared, the way you do. I thought something would happen to him and he'd never come back and I'd be left with nothing. So when he came home, I told him I wanted a baby.' And Paul was delighted, after seven years of being told no when he wanted children. After seven years of a large washable rubber contraceptive because Joan hardly knew what contraception was and had decided it was something men did. (She told me herself about seeing it and what she thought.)

Thinking about Joan from this distance is not as I'd planned it at all. I don't feel sorry for her. It doesn't restore the perspective, it changes it again.

Last year was full of warning signs. Whatever the weather was doing on the outside where it belongs, there were storm clouds rolling up in banks inside my head. Lindsay's voice grew ever louder to deal with my mother's deafness and she developed a series of arch verbal mannerisms like an ageing celebrity holding the audience more by familiarity than charm. Whenever Con and I took Josh to see my mother, Lindsay arrived with Bob and the atmosphere would become stiff with everybody's self-control, because I am embarrassed by him and Con loathes him and Con's loathing is like a thing to be negotiated all on its own, its possibilities stupefying.

Whenever Lindsay arrived, whatever else had been happening stopped. And my nerves would begin their second spiral, the pattern of the first having been pointed out by Con so that I'd try to contain it. Josh would cope because he's a child and has a lovely nature, but the crossing of conversational lines, the mishearings, the volume of everything and the unspoken underpinnings would screw tighter and tighter, as if some giant hand was trying to wring us all out in the wash. Eventually we'd make our farewells and leave and I'd begin the litany of complaint and confusion which would blur into tears. I'd cry for a few miles and then sleep or get Con to talk about something else because you run out of things to say when everything is so unclear and so sad.

Or I'd manage in the car and we'd get home and I'd bath Josh and he'd go to bed and then I'd sit on our bed and cry, or the tears would begin trickling over the salad. And I can't tell whether I cried for pain or loss, for remembrance or bewilderment. I can't remember when it began – when Lindsay married Bob, when I married Con, when I had the baby, events viewed inevitably under the distorting lens of my mother's age? One day I woke up knowing that this was not a dream I could shake off, not a bad taste in my mouth I could get rid of with toothpaste and sunshine. And even then I thought it was all to do with me. Just me.

Because I was the second and felt like the second, the after-thought. Because I was the younger. Because I didn't see as much of my mother as Lindsay did. Because dealing with them all made me tired and I was tired anyway, to start with. Because Con wasn't conventional or easy, being truthful and willing to observe conventions only insofar as he could point out that that's what he was doing, though I didn't want him to do anything else.

And then one night Con said that he didn't think he could watch my sister and my mother at me any more. And I froze where I stood. When I turned back to him, he didn't look as though he'd taken leave of his senses. He was sitting by the window studying the glass into which he'd poured his drink and he looked as he always looked. He raised his eyes to meet mine.

'I shall have to say something if it's going to go on' he said.

'It's not my imagination then is it?' I asked, beginning to try to break out of the pack ice which threatened my knees.

He shook his head.

'What's it about then, Con? What is it?'

He looked at me. 'They're jealous.'

'Jealous? Jealous of what?'

'You and me, your life, Josh, the writing, everything.'

'But that's what my mother wanted for me. They wanted me to be happy, to be good at what I did.'

He nodded again.

'Then what are you saying? I don't understand.'

But I did. Wanting for people, wishing them success and luck and love and happiness – that's fine. That's right. It's only proper. But how do you feel when they get it? Get it all, or so very much of it in comparison with the not very nice deal fortune has dealt you? Get it all and it's so far away from what you understand, with different prices and different rewards?

We didn't talk about it any more but I suppose we both became more aware – Con because he is aware, it's how he is, like a machine recording all that passes, how it plays. Once a watcher, always a watcher. And I became more aware because for the first time I had a witness.

It wasn't to do with my being difficult or not fitting in. Something was going on, over and above my emotions and my personality. Con had said so and he wouldn't lie. And because I had a witness I recorded the matter of the house and the matter of the will, which it seemed that I alone could bear to raise, and began to think about them.

The will was not a great matter. Joan doesn't have very much, though she has more now – through Lindsay's efforts and mine, Lindsay's when she lived there and mine ever since, this purely in the sense of money-more – than she had when Paul died. My accountants and solicitors, the ones I've had dealings with down the years, were defeated by my wish not to treat my family as a business proposition. But I remembered Paul's death; I shall never forget it and what it meant to me, never mind Joan or Lindsay. And the memento I'd set my heart on was given to Lindsay and the sweater of his that Joan gave me, she sent first to the cleaners.

I knew Lindsay's house wouldn't be improved by what she absorbed from my mother's and I ceased feeling pious and generous and other-worldly. I knew the things I wanted out of my mother's house, mostly books and old photographs and a vase or a chair, and though Lindsay is quite another person when apart from my mother, so she is another yet again if Bob's around or his latest scheme needs backing.

When we went away that summer, after Con had first indicated something was amiss, I gave Lindsay all the directions about how to get hold of us. I used to do this with some unhappiness because I deeply wanted to be there when my mother died, to see her out. And I noted, curiously, that this time the wish did not come so readily to my mind. So off we went for sun and sand and sea, to ring Joan when we came home and answer the questions and explain why we hadn't rung but we had sent postcards. They hadn't arrived yet? Well, they would – that's the trouble with the post in those places . . .

In the autumn my sister and her husband went on a late holiday, she having left me with all the same details about how to get hold of her, check the flights and so on. She rang my mother when she arrived. She rang her the next night but one. And two days later my mother rang to ask me to ring Lindsay because it would be cheaper and easier for me to do it from London, and then I could ring her back and tell her how everything was. So I did, slightly stunned because it was, until then, all so out of character. Everything was wrong, wrong, wrong. Even the voice on the telephone was different. Something had moved and changed in what I had thought was the architecture of my family and I had not been warned that it might. And I was frightened by how annoyed I felt. Lindsay didn't seem surprised. She was having a good time and relaying it was part of the pleasure.

Some days later we were speaking on the telephone and

somebody called to see Joan. She asked me to ring her back. An hour and a half later she rang me to say that she had rung me back because, yes, she knew she'd asked me to ring her but she couldn't wait any longer because Lindsay was due back that night and was going to ring her when she got home and Joan didn't want my call to interfere with her call from Lindsay. And my eyes filled.

But then the series I was writing got into trouble so we couldn't go down for several weeks and when we next did, it was the long, grey drive down on Boxing Day, during which Josh got bored and Con withdrew into as severe a form of control as I'd ever seen on him.

Con has a long pale face and black hair. When it is necessary, it seems that every cell of his being moves imperceptibly back, retrenches, waits, is called in and gathered for whatever may follow. I was puzzled. Yes, all right, it was my sister's house on Boxing Day, and Lindsay and Joan had been strange this year, but it was Christmas, wasn't it? There were things about Christmas which could never be relied upon in Con's home but always held true in mine. He says I'm the only person who ever made him like Christmas. Perhaps I depended too much upon those old memories but this was halfway back to where I learned to make Christmas. Wasn't it?

Joan walked past me to Josh. Con walked away from me to Bob. Bob's grown-up son was visiting and my sister had that tight look round her mouth which announced louder than a warcry that she was coping. We exchanged our presents and I was stuck with a frilly box of tissues and a shoulder bag when I'd spent a year with massage and physiotherapy, not allowed to carry anything on my shoulder. And frilled tissue boxes come under the same heading in my mind as toilet-roll covers. I'm a snob, an ungenerous unthinking egotistical selfish snob.

Con and I took Lindsay and Josh out for a walk after lunch, leaving my mother to watch Bob and his son devour a bowl of nuts. When we came home, Joan and Lindsay both tried to make tea and Joan could be heard asking where things were, not hearing and asking again, while Linday, speaking too quietly for her to hear, complained. I played with Josh, I sat very still, I listened to Con talk about thrillers with Bob. And the sky began to darken at Christmas two years ago. The darkness filled the room and when my mother and sister came in from the kitchen, they seemed more threatening than I'd ever seen them, as if they'd been turned inside out and all the unspoken, unforgotten, disappointed bits were sticking out of

9

them, like disagreeable hedgehogs. We made our goodbyes. I didn't dare look at Con. For Con is sometimes the light I shine in dark places and when I had looked in the beam, expecting to see the reflection of my own misfittedness, what I saw were two sharks dancing a private gavotte.

2 *Joan*

Joan loved her father. He smelt of the sun. His face was dark brown and pointed like the face of an elf in her storybook, or like something that might appear out of the fire she loved to lie in front of, watching pictures in the flames. Her father Edward taught her to dry the peel of oranges in the fireplace and then to throw the crisp remnants into the grate where they were consumed in a puff of coloured gas and pungent sweetness. No matter how late he came in, she would settle deeper into her sleep once he was inside the door. He was her special weapon against her brother's indifference and her sister's twitterings.

'Weren't you close to your mother?' I asked.

Her hands were up to the wrists in washing. I was sitting on a chair beside her aged six. She paused and looked at me carefully.

'My mother got tired' she said. 'There were twins before me and they died.'

I thought that was awful.

Joan shook her head without explaining.

'But then there was you,' I said consolingly.

She raised her eyebrows wryly. 'That's right, and my mother gave me to my father.'

I didn't understand.

'After I was born,' she said. 'He came in to see her and she just scooped up the baby and held it out to him saying, "Here, you take care of this one." And he did.'

'Was he a tall man?' I asked, thinking of my own father, thinking too of his father whom she loathed, her father-in-law, the Old Man whom she always described as a good-looking little man as though the second took totally from the first.

'Not so tall, but square shoulders, a good shape and a beautiful smile. I've got a picture somewhere I should show you.'

But when I asked her about her mother, her face became composed, carefully non-committal. She said her mother was pretty and added, 'Poor old Mum.'

My mother's father Edward and Charlotte his wife lived in a small house at the unfashionable end of Holland Park, just beyond where Holland Park stops. The house was on a corner so there were only neighbours on one side and there was a bit of a tree in the garden and room for some pansies and delphiniums.

The first thing Joan ever noticed about the house was that nothing felt as it looked. The cloth on the table was not only dark bronze with flowers and fringes, but made of chenille which clung to her fingers. The curtains were not just dark red, they were velvet, fat and lined; the windows were draped with cotton lace. The piano was carved, the banisters like wooden doilies, and even the aspidistra stood on a table with twisted legs. Joan longed for the surfaces to be smoother, easier for her fingers to negotiate. As it was she rarely managed to put her hand down without touching something else: a vase, a plate, an ornament, her mother's sewing box braced for the next intake of socks and stockings, buttons and hems.

'Mother kept it all very clean, I'll give her that,' said Joan to me, looking down the avenue of her memory fifty years later. Joan didn't clear things up, she shoved them out of sight. Handkerchiefs down the sides of the chairs or under the pillows, broken locks into the dresser drawer on the left, string and brown paper into the drawer on the right. She liked things to look tidy but she didn't really deal with them. And she wasn't interested in housework either.

But I knew that my mother hated clutter, longed for smooth surfaces and light bright colours. I couldn't understand how her mother could have been so different and so I asked her about it. 'It was the fashion of the day,' she said. 'It was a long time ago, before the First War. You must remember I was born in 1901.'

That sounded like something too long ago to imagine to me. I wanted to ask more but I didn't know where to begin.

'Did you have electric light?' I said, and she answered thoughtfully, 'Not in the first house, I don't think so.'

'Why did you move?'

'There just wasn't enough room for us all.'

And that was the second thing she noticed about the house.

When there was just Guy and Cecily and Joan, as the baby she had her own room, but by the time she was four, Winifred was born, and Joan had to share Cecily's room and make the best of it. But the best of it was going out with her father.

Edward took her for walks, in the park to look at the trees and the squirrels, in the West End to look at the shops. She wondered why it was just her, she didn't know about her mother 'giving' her to him, but it was delicious to have something she didn't have to share, or make the best of.

One day she saw a woman with very heavy make-up on her face, like a mask. She pulled at his sleeve. He bent down to her.

'Dad,' she whispered, 'did you see that woman? She had all different colours on her face.'

'That's right,' he said gently.

'But why, Dad?' she asked. 'She looked horrible.'

'She's painted because she's working, Joan. She is a streetwalker and that make-up is her advertising.'

Fancy having to walk the streets for your living. It sounded lonely. 'Is she – is she not a nice person?' Mother divided the world into nice and not nice, it was the ultimate deciding factor about everything.

'Joanjoan,' he said quietly, 'we're not likely to know. She lives her life and we live ours.'

'And how does the paint work?' she wanted to know.

'It brings her her trade and her trade is men. You see, when you're older you might find that make-up means something to you that it doesn't mean now.'

Joan wondered if he was cross. Her mother often got cross when Joan asked a string of questions or simply a question Charlotte would prefer not to have to answer. But to Edward no question was out of bounds. She shot a quick look at him but he was looking at where they were up to on the journey, because today he had decided to take her to the Zoo.

To begin with he let her wander up and down the paths and peer in at different things, but then he took her off to see the seals and watch the penguins dive. She came back to the penguins three times

13

until he refused to return again and, consulting his watch, took her to the lion house which smelt harsh and acidic. There were men in boots feeding the animals great lumps of meat, and watching that was so exciting she forgot to be scared.

Joan noticed that her mother really didn't mind if she went off alone with her father, that she seemed almost relieved at the thought of his absence and, when he was there, increasingly displeased with him, though Joan didn't know why. One day she saw her father put his arms round her mother and heard her say sharply, 'No Edward, thank you. I'm too old for that sort of thing.' And he stood there for a moment with an odd look on his face and then moved away to pick up his newspaper. When Joan came forward, he immediately put it down and asked if she'd like a walk before tea.

The Zoo became their preferred territory. They could spend a long time together discussing the colours and shapes of all the animals, where they came from, and then he could sit and she could walk away and come back for him. He took her there at unexpected times, early in the morning, last thing in the evening. It wasn't until years later that she wondered how he had managed to arrange that, whether he knew one of the doormen or one of the keepers. It was on one of their special trips that he took her to see the snakes being fed and she confided in him that she envied the snakes.

'Why?' he asked, smiling.

'They're so neat and clean,' she said. 'Nobody could ever get cross with them for making a mess when they ate.'

'Did you get into trouble for that?'

She hung her head. 'Yes. Mummy said I eat like a guttersnipe.'

He said nothing. She looked up at him. He was still watching the snakes swallowing white mice. 'Look,' he said. 'You must try not to make such a mess and then you can be anything you want. What would you be if you could be anything at all that you wanted?'

'I'd like to be a dancer,' she said. 'My friend Lizzie Collett at school goes to a dance class, and they play at being moonbeams to lovely music. I think I'd like that.'

He nodded thoughtfully.

'Could I have dancing lessons, too?'

He didn't reply. She pulled gently at his sleeve.

'Hm?'

'Dancing lessons. Like Lizzie Collett?'

The keeper was shutting the doors at the back of the snakes' enclosures. Her father straightened up.

She waited.

'I don't know that we can afford it just now. But we could try. I'll talk to your mother. Why dancing? Do you know why you want to dance?'

She nodded. 'Because it makes me feel free and pretty.'

He smiled at her and took her hand.

'Well certainly, that's a good reason for wanting something. But you don't have to dance to feel that. You are pretty and you are free – free to choose what you want and what to make of your life. Free and pretty, that's my girl.'

And he dropped her off at school, charming her teacher into forgiving her for being a few minutes late.

But her mother refused to hear of such nonsense.

'I don't know what you think we're made of' she said, folding her mouth as she folded her laundry, 'but there's not enough money in this house as it is and if there's any to spare it will be for proper education, first for Guy and then for Cecily, before we start wasting money on silk shoes and moonbeams.'

So Joan had to content herself with dancing about in her shared room when Cecily was out, or twirling round the front room when she had it to herself and after she'd dusted the aspidistra. If Joan didn't like the dusting and polishing which were her weekly tasks, apart from daily errands and abjurations to be more helpful, Cecily was old enough to remember when they'd had a maid. Not for very long, it's true, but the extra pair of hands she represented was sorely missed. She went just after Joan was born and the coming of Winifred made it clear that help in the house was a thing of the past.

Joan welcomed school, which was a tall red-brick building attended by all the local children, the farthest hall and its surrounding classrooms being reserved for the youngest. She liked the stories and the singing and the books. And before long school was more than another place to go. It was a refuge from the anger that seemed to occupy her home as fiercely and personally as if someone else had moved in.

Charlotte and Edward were the kind of parents who believed that their disagreements should not take place in front of the children. But the children sensed the disharmony long before it became overt. Charlotte fell into speaking to her husband through the children. He withdrew more and more into his paper, his walks with Joan, his work. At least, his work was what he said he did, and their mother made no comment.

15

As a peace offering, Edward offered to move them all into a larger house.

'We can't afford it,' said Charlotte, as if that was the end of the matter.

'Yes, we can, if we go a bit further out,' he rejoined.

Charlotte snorted, her fingers busy at the pastry board.

Joan stood, ready to make leaves and trimmings from the leftovers when her mother had the pie case cut.

'Such as where?' asked Charlotte, still disbelieving.

'Ealing, I thought. I went and had a look and I talked to agents about the rent.'

'And where will the children go to school?'

'Locally, I expect,' he said, patting his pockets for his pipe.

'Don't smoke that thing in here, Edward – not while I'm cooking.'

He apologised.

'Wouldn't a bigger house be easier, now, with the four children?'

Charlotte shrugged. 'Sounds like more work to me.'

Joan watched her father. He remained calm.

'Cecily and the boy are big enough now to take care of their own rooms, Joan too, if we asked her – wouldn't you, Joanjoan – and even help out with Winifred?'

Anything, thought Joan, anything, if only they'll stop.

She nodded.

'Well, I suppose we could look,' said Charlotte grudgingly, 'but moving will cost money, Edward, and I don't have a penny left over from what you give me.'

'Never mind,' said her father, almost cheerfully. 'I've a bit put by and I'll talk to Charlie Hedges at the office. I'm due for a bit more, I'd say, with all the little extras he's had me working on recently.'

'Don't go and upset him,' said Charlotte. 'Joan, stop fiddling with that lump of dough and get on with it, if you're making the decorations. I can't stand here all day. And I'm not promising, Edward. I only said we'd look.'

Her father rose and made to kiss her mother's cheek as she bustled by, but she went past him so that he missed and Joan thought he looked hurt. She went to him quickly and put her arms round his waist and a few minutes later he was making up silly rhymes and teasing her.

Not only had Edward looked at houses, he had found a house for them and, although she grumbled, it was much more what Charlotte wanted in that it was less cramped and they could all eat in the kitchen together which saved a great deal of time. So somehow the money was found and the arrangements were made and the van came to move them but even the sunlight and the roses in the garden didn't please her mother, who began to complain immediately about how much work moving was and wondered why she'd ever let herself be talked into this, refusing to be mollified by everyone trying to help or even by a neighbour bringing tea and cake to welcome them.

There were more rooms in this house, and the garden was a little bigger, but they bought nothing new, the furnishings remained the same and after a short time everything looked the same and felt the same and the house felt almost as confined as the old one. Far from easing, the arguments escalated. To begin with, it was always their mother who was sharp and their father who fielded the verbal rocks she hurled at him, but then he began to answer back and not even solid walls and her hands over her ears could prevent Joan from hearing them.

Charlotte's complaints began and ended with lack of money, as if money would put right everything that was wrong, but in between she bemoaned her efforts, the unceasing battle with the house, food and the children, and even said that they should never have moved, because all it had done was cause her more work. To Joan, happily settled into a new school barely two streets away, and with a large black cat called Nero, this was awful. Cecily now worked for a modiste and Guy had a job with an insurance firm. They both enjoyed the new-found privacy of their own rooms and Joan and Winifred had the attic all to themselves. They ate the same things, did the same things – how could it be costing more? Edward's answer both to his own distress at the domestic friction and Charlotte's upbraiding was to work harder. He spent less time with Joan and she missed him, but she had made friends at school in whose gardens and kitchens she played, she had her little sister and she had the cat. Her mother cleaned the house over and over again, as if it were some lamp which if she scoured hard enough would produce a genie to grant her a wish, and Joan wondered what she'd wish for.

When her father came home from work her mother spoke to him formally for as long as she could but sooner or later her tongue would catch fire and she would shout at him and rattle the poker or the saucepans. Now he began to answer back, in low tones but with no less anger. He was pale and there were terrible rings round his fine eyes and Joan thought he looked different somehow.

One day, as she came home from school, she thought she saw him putting a suitcase into a taxi. She called to him but he was too far away to hear her and, although she ran, the cab pulled away, so she hurried home.

Her mother was not in the kitchen. Joan rushed upstairs. Her parents' bedroom door was closed. She hesitated. Then she knocked.

'What is it, Joan?' Her mother had come down from the attic and stood holding a cup.

'I thought I saw Dad getting into a taxi and I wondered where he was going.' She didn't know why she felt unnerved but she did, as if something had happened and she had discovered it.

'He's going away on business for a few days.'

Joan started to ask when he would be back but her mother cut her short.

'Win is in bed with a cold, she was sent home halfway through the day and I have the most terrible headache. Please let me lie down for half an hour and read to your sister, keep her amused.'

Joan climbed to the room she shared with Win and found her small sister heavy-eyed and dozy. She read her *The Tailor of Gloucester* and hoped everything would be all right.

At dusk her mother called. Joan jumped up and ran to her but her mother just asked her to send Cecily up when she came in and to leave her alone, she was feeling awful. So Joan went back upstairs but Win had dropped off to sleep. She crept past her mother's door down to the kitchen and lit the gas lamp, to wait for Cecily. Time moved more slowly than she'd ever known it. She'd never known her father to take a bag with him before, or to leave in a taxi. He had taken a taxi once or twice, once she remembered when they were all going to a concert and he was afraid they'd be late, but her mother was most upset about the extravagance. And why did her mother have her headache today? The house was so still she could hear the clock ticking and her heart beating and, far from reassuring her, it began to sound like a drum in her head, beating out bad news, bad news, and she wondered what, why . . .

The cat patted the window and she jumped up to let him in and held him on her knee, beginning to cry and not knowing why. Cecily arrived, went up to see her mother and returned to tell Joan that there was nothing to cry about, Dad would be back soon. Joan looked at her.

'Well, don't look at me like that. I'm telling you what Mother told me,' said Cecily crossly. 'I'm to make supper as soon as Guy gets home.'

Her mother did not come down to supper. Her brother and sister ate, exchanging few words, and Joan ate because she was hungry. Cecily asked her to make sure Win was all right and she took soup up to her and bread and helped her eat it. Everybody seemed to be doing what they would usually and normally have done but Joan couldn't get rid of the feeling that something was wrong. She was at the kitchen door – she'd been trying to read and had decided she wanted to go to bed – when she heard Guy.

'What's the point of not telling her? You know Joan, she's probably already sensed it. That's what she was crying about.'

'But Mother said,' protested Cecily.

'Well, Mother's wrong.' In spite of herself Joan was quite impressed to hear Guy say this, and so firmly. 'Tell her the truth and she'll deal with it.'

Joan opened the door. 'Tell me what?' she asked.

Guy and Cecily turned to her and Cecily explained. 'Dad isn't going to live here any more. Well, not for a bit, anyway. He and Mother have some talking to do.'

'Will he be coming back?' Joan heard herself ask.

Cecily looked uncomfortable.

'From time to time to see us all,' said Guy smoothly.

Joan looked at him.

She went past them up the stairs. Winifred was asleep and she cried very quietly so as not to wake her. He must be coming back, she thought, because he didn't say goodbye, not even to me, and he says that I'm his special girl. How special is that if he goes without saying goodbye? I knew it, I knew it, she thought. I knew there was something. Where will he go? If this was a story, something would happen. Flowers for him would grow out of my tears or he'd know that like an arrow in the heart I missed him and he'd come back. Maybe Mother told him to go and that's why her head hurts. And the tears got thicker and she went out on to the landing and stood in the darkness and waited for something to happen but it didn't, so she went to bed.

For the next few days their mother said very little. On Sunday their father came for tea. They were all pleased to see him, and he them, but they were wary in front of their mother who poured the tea and passed the bread and butter, saying as little as possible. Joan decided she too would say as little as possible so she answered his questions and thanked him for the book he had brought her and waited. When he left, Joan and Cecily washed the tea things, her mother took Winifred for a walk and Guy filled the coal buckets and read a book.

There were several months of such Sundays. In that time, Joan's mother remained sharp-tongued – it was her way – but they all felt the easing of her temper. Although she missed her father, Joan would not risk disturbing this relative calm by asking questions her mother felt were best left unasked. Once when she was particularly unhappy she wrote him a letter – she had found the office address to send it to in the newspaper which was still delivered (she was surprised it hadn't been stopped when he had left home) but she decided not to send it. Her mother would be angry if she knew.

She didn't know why her mother would be angry but she knew that she would be.

And now the fiction of 'talking things over' could not be maintained. He was not coming back, her mother said, and on the next Sunday he had asked to speak to Guy and Cecily privately. He saw them one after the other in the living room. Guy affected not to care and Cecily sniffed a bit but thought it was for the best and then he asked to see Joan.

'She's still a child,' said her mother from where she sat in the kitchen, mending. 'I'd have thought you'd want to spare the young ones . . . ' Her father looked at her mother patiently, with all the good humour and charm of earlier days. Joan watched them both. 'You gave her to me, Charlotte, don't you remember? You said "Here you are, you take care of this one!" I'll be tactful, I just want to talk to her myself.' Her mother shrugged her displeasure and Joan was permitted to follow her father from the kitchen into the front room. He sat in his usual chair, she perched on the settee.

'I'm going away Joan' he said. 'I mean, I'm not coming back this time.' She nodded. 'So I thought you might like to come with me, being my special girl and all, and we could make a home together, the two of us?'

She stared at him. His face was still very handsome, though it had begun to get pale and puffy if you saw it in the wrong light. And she thought of the Zoo and the walks and the talks and the snakes.

'Well,' he said. 'What do you think?'

She didn't move. He leaned forward to the fire, to rub his hands.

'I couldn't,' she said. 'I couldn't leave. I don't want to.'

He looked at her.

'I'm sorry,' she whispered.

He nodded. They sat in silence for a few minutes. Then he smiled his lovely smile at her and said 'All right, little one.'

She never saw him again.

3   Mercer

Seeing your nearest and dearest as maneaters may be shocking, but life goes on. I did not deem confrontation with Lindsay or Joan to be much use and anyway it was not what I wanted to do. I felt like a kid with a kaleidoscope. I wanted to wait until the pieces moved round and see if I saw the situation between us any differently. And as if to keep my mind on other things, Con and I yielded to a friend, had the flat we'd lived in for ten years valued and discovered we could afford a house.

But first we had to sell what we'd got.

The estate agents came and wrote inaccuracies about the maisonette we lived in because it wasn't like everything else they had to sell. So we kept seeing people who wanted what we didn't have and I'd have to call the agents again day after day. In the meantime we started looking at houses.

I'm not good at looking at houses when they've got other people's things in them. They're always too tangible to overlook. Con can walk in somewhere and envisage this wall down and that one arched, the whole smoothly painted and waiting for the treasured things we've accumulated together. I become agitated. I cannot see how it would be because how it is fills my vision.

There was one particular house he went out to see on his own because we didn't want to drag Josh around with us to all these places over the weekend. The day was damp and warm and I was stung by a sleepy wasp as I stood in the grocer's. It bit my neck and, when I flipped a hand at it, fell down the front of my dress and stung my breast. Con came back looking quite pleased and said he thought he'd found it, would I come and look at the house that afternoon, and I told him about the stings. He helped me put stuff on them and then looking gently into my face he said, 'That was a wasp with taste,' and we smiled and hugged and Josh came to get into the middle, shouting 'Me too! Me too!' So at three o'clock we drove to the house.

The street was pretty enough, with trees and flowers in the gardens. I was working very hard at trying to suspend my judgement, to clear my mind of what I would see first so that I could imagine what could be done with it.

The agent showed us the garden and led us round the rooms. I could hear myself nodding and moving and walking, giving what was said thought, even going up into the roof to see what a lovely workroom the attic could be made into for me. I volunteered nothing.

I was thinking about everything Con said, everything the agent said and wondering why, why am I filled with this absolute blind panic like a rat in a trap? That's how I feel – trapped – but I'm still wondering why, what is it? We were there for half an hour and Con asked as we passed on the stairs, 'What do you think?'

'I don't know,' I said. 'I'm thinking.'

It was the right money, it would be an investment, it was a pleasant street.

I know I responded. I could hear myself being reasonable and asking sensible questions but feeling wary and light-headed, and thinking, it's the stings. When we got into the car, Con drove in silence, very carefully. A tear slithered down my face, the side away from him. He was watching the road. I was so glad he hadn't noticed the tear. It was like special pleading.

'What do you think of it?' he asked.

'I think,' I said carefully, 'that the street is all right and that the house has great possibilities and provided we do all the things you say we've got to do straight away, I'll manage in it. But I can't tell you I'm thrilled.'

He asked me what I didn't like about it and I told him – the shape of the rooms, the size of the garden, the grey tiles in the kitchen which reminded me of a reformatory or a public lavatory, and the pinched bathroom.

'Did you like anything?' he asked ironically.

'Yes,' I said. 'I liked the pantry and the airing cupboard and the drying rack in the kitchen.'

'How odd,' he said. 'I liked it all, I wonder what it was.'

'Oh, I don't know,' I said. 'I don't know. Except that it's cold and it's wet and the stings shook me and the thought of moving, the packing and the upheaval into more packing and upheaval while walls come down and rewiring is done and the roof is transformed and there's no light and where do I write, when do I write? Josh goes to school and you go to work and I'm stuck in it. The idea of being ill in that house makes me physically sick.'

Poor Con. So attractive to neurotic women.

'Then we won't offer for it,' he said philosophically.

'Yes we will,' I said. 'You said it was a good investment for what we have to spend.'

'Yes, it is,' he said, 'but if you feel like that about it . . . '

'Forget it,' I said. 'I'll come round.'

But that house rose up at intervals behind my eyes and haunted my dreams. A white house that wasn't white because every surface was grubby and uncared for. A house full of mirrors, mirrors with no shape and lots of sides. A house with rooms full of wire-backed chairs and pink plastic walls, an ugly house with a mean cold bathroom. It was the idea of being alone in it I hated and I couldn't think why. The next day was Sunday and as I was putting on a kettle, I knew.

I'm forty-two and supposed to be grown up, forty being the magic age of maturity. But from the time I left home at seventeen until I married David at twenty-five and from the time I left him until I met Con, which was another four years or so, I lived in rooms in other people's houses and other people's flats. I know everybody is entitled to their own taste but I rarely found any echo of mine and living among unchosen ugliness, something you have very limited power to alter or improve, is very souring for the spirit.

When I was with David, my first husband, through the tailend of the spiritual Sixties, I was supposed to be above these things. He certainly was. So it was I who put together whatever items we had which constituted a home. David believed in having the floor washed but he wouldn't dream of washing it, whether because he was a genius or just a man I was never sure.

Anyway, he thought I was mad to campaign for a tablecloth, to save up for steak knives, to want to enhance where we lived, when all I had to do was rise above it. And I could not explain to him that nothing made me feel less inspired than the lack of colour, the charmlessness of the places in which we lived. I wasn't unwilling to rise above it but I found that easier to do when what I left behind me was cleaner and prettier. I was, he told me repeatedly, inescapably bourgeois. And I was duly ashamed. His attitude added to my impression that he was more gifted than I, but it didn't stop me. For my own sanity, I had to continue to conform to the way I wanted to live and that very neatly excused him from having anything whatever to do with the maintenance of our lives but to enjoy every possible benefit of it.

He may have mocked my weekly trip to the laundrette, my fastidious bedmaking (he called it 'doing a Sophia Loren on the bed'), but he was happy to have clean clothes to turn to and a smooth bed to sleep in. When my work failed – I ceased to be able to write for a long time after an initial success with a play – and his anticipated dreams of success as a film-maker foundered, it was he who kept on working at projects, developing ideas, writing scripts. I took up secretarial work to tide us over.

Joan didn't like David and him being the covert reason that I went back into secretarial work was just the cherry on the poisoned cake. He didn't like her, either, though he never said so. He just criticised her politically. She represented all sorts of snobberies he couldn't respect. Of course his own mother had them too, but much more so. Joan confused him. He couldn't see why she wanted him to get a job and earn some money teaching when he was a creative professional.

But if, like his mother, she had sat in her immaculately kept house, drinking tea from fine china in between firing the latest unsatisfactory maid and going to concerts and dinners and lunches with her women friends, all manicured and coiffed with not a thought between them, he could have put it down to her middle-class mentality. But coming from Joan's tired little cottage which hadn't a decent picture in it but was full of books not quite light enough to dismiss, where classical music was not venerated but neither was double damask napery – it didn't add up. Which on reflection proves that good old flexible David found these material considerations a damn sight harder to ignore than he'd ever freely have admitted.

When David was married to me, he looked like a brigand. He wore waistcoats made of animal hides and boots with high heels and great tongues. But not because this was what weekend bohemians wore. Rather, because it was what he could afford, what he liked, even what was practical. He would not debate taste and he affected not to care. This meant too that he pretended not to know that what he wore oddly became him because he swaggered in it and exuded extreme confidence, almost bravado. The only people he was ever tender with were actors, and then only as a last resort, because it was the only way to get what he wanted from them. He had left South Africa carrying with him one of those films which come into being as an act of will, with no money, black and white working together clandestinely, about the coming of the revolution which still hasn't come.

I met him just after the first of the two plays I wrote before we married began to be successful. I had not meant to write a play. I'd meant to write something and it came out that way. I had failed at being an actress but then I wrote a play about pregnancy and abortion which was very 'in' that year and it was not only accepted by an agent, it was sold, produced and well received. I was twenty-five. It was too soon. It was more catharsis than craft but I didn't know that then.

He had not come to see the play but to talk to one of the names attached to that theatre about certain actors he'd seen in another play or one of the other man's films. We were introduced and I left shortly afterwards to go somewhere else. He drew up in the van beside me as I walked along the street and asked if I wanted a lift.

We went to have lunch in a café and he talked about his film with a mixture of deprecation and absorption which made it clear how important it was to him. He did not ask about me or my play. He told me about himself. At the end of the lunch, he had another appointment. We parted. It was cold, October or so.

I went home, read a bit, thought a bit, had a bath, went out to dinner with a friend, came home to bed and got on with my life. I was in a highly positive phase. The bad times were behind me. When you're up you think you'll never be down again. I was writing. But I talked about him. Joan my mother picked up something in my voice when I'd only seen him three or four times. He didn't play delaying games with me, he had other things to do too. But he was interested, he came back. Joan said she thought it would be good for me to be married. Anyway, when he asked me to marry him, I said yes and she was delighted. She said she was delighted.

I do not know why I fell in love with David. Perhaps I was easily impressed. His background seemed exciting. He spoke faultless

French. He had a wonderful smile. We agreed about *The Battle of Algiers*. Are these reasons to fall in love? I remember the first time after we went to bed together, thinking quite clearly as I got up, oh well, you can't have everything. I remember sitting with him in a restaurant talking about friendship. I was talking about my friends and he said, 'What happens when one of these friends falls in love with you?'

'It doesn't happen,' I said coldly.

'But it must have happened some time,' he insisted. But it had not. So we were clearly not going to be friends and I don't think we ever were.

David lived in a smallish room in a ratty flat with a bed, a wardrobe and a tin trunk he used as a bedside table. He had use of the bathroom and the kitchen, obviously, and the flat was owned by another émigré, two generations on, who occasionally invited us to watch television in his room. Almost at once I found I could not write and I did not care. I was married. It was fun and the euphoria was so powerful it lit up the flat and heated the bathroom. He was still finishing his film. It became clear that we must have money. I saw his need as greater than mine. Now I'm not so sure. But then I hardly hesitated. This was going to be the marriage which finally brought me into the human race as a grown-up person, the woman I longed to be. I earned, I kept house and he created. I believed in him, in me with him. It was going to be fine.

It took me about a year and a half to begin to recognise that admiration is a thin diet. And another year or so to face the fact that I was emotionally malnourished to the point that I'd try anything, first of all to help me to continue in my rarefied union and secondly to console me for having failed at it. The price of the marriage was too high for me to pay. I had wanted it, had got it and had discovered that I should have settled for something else.

I never felt that about Con. Con presumed we had to have somewhere to live and set about organising it. He accepted every effort I made towards what he called nesting with pleasure and pride. I sometimes wonder if I know what he thinks of me but if I ask him, he answers and is willing to discuss it. It is my insecurity to wonder whether, having kept his own counsel for so long, he tells me the truth or what I want to hear. But there is much less time for negative cerebration than there was with David. Con likes living, encourages me to like it too, and we have interests to share and room to give each other which does not require sacrifice or self-chastisement.

When we found a house, it had a room in it for me. There were other things to recommend it but the main thing was that it provided me with somewhere to work. Waiting for it to be ready, I did all the things I'd always done – writing amid the packing cases, getting up at five o'clock in the morning to finish things off before the workmen arrived. But walls were painted the colour we wanted them and shelves were fitted and carpets laid. It was ordinary enough to all sorts of people but to me it was special because it meant that I was being cherished for what I was instead of what I could be shaped into being. All I had to do was get on with living in it and enjoying it. The house was shaped for me.

4 *Joan*

It was a source of some embarrassment to Joan that she had fewer special memories about the years of war between 1914 and 1918 than about the period immediately before and afterwards. She knew that war was a terrible thing in the same way that she knew if she put her hand in the fire, it would burn. But she had never put her hand in the fire and her response to the war was similarly at one remove.

Just after her father left, a family moved in next door with five sons. They were Scots, freethinkers, and after an exchange of politeness, the younger children began to visit for tea and to play. They liked to play mad games, chasing each other through the house in a savage version of tag or dancing wildly to music improvised upon piano, drum, pipes and saucepan lids. But Joan liked Robert best. He was seventeen to her nearly thirteen, as slight as his brothers but taller and gentler. She did not have to worry about him noticing her because she knew that he did.

After years in the shadow of her older sister's pink-and-white prettiness, topped with thick chestnut hair which twisted effortlessly into a chignon, leaving curly tendrils clinging to nape and temples, Joan too had become pretty. Her nondescript brown skin took on a warmer, more apricot tone against which her eyes seemed startlingly blue and her hair, long confined to plaits which were pressed between sheets of brown paper to make artificial wavelets for special occasions, was cut shorter and shone a rich, honey brown. She held herself well – her father had insisted that deportment was important for them all – and her unselfconsciousness set off her physical blossoming.

There had been a time when she thought her father's absence would break her heart. She cried frequently while observing that nobody else did, or if they did, she never saw them. She found herself remembering with longing not only the things they used to do together but what they all did as a family and how her father's presence had coloured outings, special occasions and holidays. She remembered the smell of the sea and the seaweed at the beach, the kippers or home-cured ham for tea at the guest house. They had gone away every summer that she could remember, though her mother had already said there would be no holiday this year. She remembered too her father bringing in the tree for Christmas and the year he gave her the peacock to hang at the top of it, just under the star. And the year before, when he took them all to *The Mikado* and *Chu Chin Chow* and bought Cecily the sheet music for 'The Cobbler's Song' which they sang together. And she felt that she was not saying goodbye to him so much as goodbye to an aspect of herself; that life would change now and she was lost in the middle of the change. She felt more lost, too, because everybody else was following her mother's example and making the best of it.

She tried very hard to please her mother but she soon realised that this was an unattainable goal. She had best settle for not displeasing her. And she realised that she felt a dependence upon her mother that she would never have noticed as long as her father was there, because all sorts of pleasures were tied up with him. Her mother provided a continuity she needed without ever knowing that she needed it. But the trouble was that she found it so hard to talk to her mother, though she was conscious of desperately wanting to be able to. She knew that she had to be careful with her mother, but not because her mother was frail. And she realised one night, as the watery moon shone blearily into the room she shared with Win, that she was deeply afraid of her mother's anger and dreaded equally how easily she incurred it.

She would not think of telling her mother that she wanted to be an actress, indeed she couldn't think of anybody with whom she could share this secret. She hadn't the slightest idea of how to go about it and she suspected, even at that stage, that this was more a delicious dream than a serious ambition. She knew that dreams, like bulbs, had to be kept in the dark if they were ever to bloom, even briefly. In fact she knew more about dreams than she did about reality, through which she sleepwalked, simultaneously trying to learn without upsetting anybody.

She had graduated from the lower school hall and classrooms into the main body of the school and continued to enjoy her lessons, though she wished she were better at French. The French master was young and handsome – surely he could see how much she was attracted to him? She had, however, no ear for languages, unlike her friend Dorothy whom young Mr Phillips encouraged to read far more sophisticated texts than the ones they used at school. He brought books to school for her and kept her behind after class to discuss them.

One Monday morning Dorothy was absent. When her absence continued, Joan was asked if she knew anything about it. She said that she did not but at break came upon a group of girls whispering, which they stopped hastily at her approach. Mr Phillips appeared rather tired and pale, and perhaps not quite so dashing, and without the sparkle Dorothy's ability put into it French was just another lesson. As they left the class Joan heard one girl remark to another that she wondered if all he'd taught Dorothy was French, and the sniggered rejoinder. She blushed. They were just jealous. But her blush was spotted.

'Maybe Dorothy told Joan and Joan promised never to tell?' There were smirks and nudges.

Joan glared at her tormentor. 'Dorothy wouldn't – she isn't like that, she – '

'And you still think you make a baby by falling under a gooseberry bush!'

Looking into their faces, Joan recognised that her schoolmates possessed knowledge she lacked and she was torn between trying to find out more and indignation at the attack on her friend's name. But logic told her that Dorothy had done something she shouldn't have and a phrase emerged which lodged in her mind and irritated by its lack of definition.

That night as she laid the table for supper she asked her mother, 'What's a bad girl?' Her mother, whose continuing war with kitchen utensils made a subtle approach nearly impossible, cried, 'What's that?' Joan went over to where she stood and faced her. 'A bad girl. I want to know what it means. That's what they're saying about Dorothy at school, that she was bad.' Her mother looked at her grimly. Then she shrugged and turned back to the stove.

31

'Don't you know?' persisted Joan. Her mother had not exploded so far.

'Well,' said her mother, 'there are only two kinds of girls in the world, my dear, good and bad – and cynics would say that a girl is only bad when she's found out doing something wrong.'

Joan thought fast. 'Does this have something to do with Mr Phillips?' she asked.

Her mother looked at her. 'Certainly. Men have their fun and women are left holding the baby. In marriage or out of it. And,' as Joan opened her mouth to say more, 'the less said about the whole matter, the better, as far as I'm concerned. Now go and call Guy and Cecily. I don't want this to spoil.' She turned back to the stove.

Joan thought very hard that night as she lay in bed. She didn't see how Dorothy, who had always been so nice and bright and winning, could possibly have turned into a bad person overnight. Bad people stole money and beat their children. Joan was sure that Dorothy had never stolen anything. So being bad in the sense that the girls had used the phrase at school and which her mother seemed to understand had something to do with Mr Phillips. Well, supposing Dorothy did spend too much time with him, supposing they did something they weren't supposed to do? Joan knew there was something men and women did, but what was a mystery to her. It was all right to do it if you were married but quite wrong if you weren't and this revolved around having or not having babies. She thought that Dorothy must be having one because otherwise there wouldn't have been such a fuss. But why was she blamed for all this when Mr Phillips was still there and nobody blamed him? She remembered the woman with the painted face she'd seen with her father long ago. Where did she fit in? She wondered if streetwalkers were only for unmarried men and if they ever had babies. She recalled her father's voice, quite level and willing to explain. He could have told her what was really going on with Dorothy and Mr Phillips. Perhaps she could write to him – she fell asleep.

The summer was long and hot. Joan wondered why she had never noticed the dust before. Her mother said that the horse-drawn buses had made the streets smell but the new motor buses caused all this dust, and she was always flicking over the furniture or asking Joan to, sending her here and there with a dustpan and brush or asking her to give the hall a once-over where the dust had got in from the front door. Several times when the boys next door had invited her to join them in a game or expedition, she had had to refuse because her mother wanted her to do something about the house. Joan couldn't see the point of cleaning the house. It just got dirty again. But she knew better than to argue with her mother.

It was particularly unfair when Win could trot off next door or across the road to her friends and Cecily spent all her spare time walking out with Harry. The only person who worked as she did, thought Joan, feeling particularly put out on this occasion, was Guy. Guy went to the office he worked in and came home and went again, whatever the weather, the next morning. Since their father left, Guy had assumed the mantle of chief support to the household, though money still came from time to time from their father. Joan had seen her mother open an envelope and, muttering, stuff the contents into her bag. Joan had recognised his writing. Once she asked her mother if she knew his address and her mother had had a headache for two days. Another time she had persuaded Win to ask for it but her mother just answered, 'I'm sure I don't know, leave me in peace.'

But nobody told Guy what to do, thought Joan. He was a man. He could go out when and wherever he pleased. He was the one person their mother always greeted and waved farewell to with a smiling face. But he never brought home a girl. When Cecily began walking out with Harry, Joan had heard her mother trying to suggest to Guy that the next thing he needed was a nice young lady and Guy rebutting her in perfect good humour, saying he didn't have time and anyway, it wasn't his sort of thing. How could it not be his sort of thing? Joan wondered. If men and women didn't get on very well, they certainly didn't get on any better without each other. Even her mother was always complaining how difficult life was without a man in the house and she didn't know how she'd ever manage if it weren't for Guy. Men without women became lonely and old like Mr Morgan down the street, or else – was there an alternative? There were men who were terribly good friends like . . . like Dr Watson and Sherlock Holmes. Perhaps Guy would prefer that? She hoped he would have somebody soon. She didn't like to think of him being lonely and alone.

But he didn't seem either.

Increasingly in conversation he referred to Bingham, Bingham this and Bingham that. 'Bingham and I are off on Saturday for a little jaunt down the river.' 'Bingham and I are dining out tonight – so I won't be in for supper, Mother.' Bingham Hinde was not a colleague where Guy worked but a client, a senior client whose attention had been drawn to Guy when Guy saved him some money. Nobody in the family knew how long they'd been friends before his name began to be mentioned. Their mother tried to ask her usual questions but Guy was adept at keeping his mother at arm's length, playing on her pride in his judgement and her guilt at his contribution to the family purse. Soon it seemed that Bingham wanted to offer Guy a job.

'I expect it's a very good opportunity,' said Joan's mother, turning the hem on one of Joan's dresses for Win to wear. From the slight frown on her forehead and the set of her lips, Joan divined that her mother was not entirely happy about the projected move. But Guy knew better than to approach his mother by argument. He brought Bingham Hinde home the night Cecily announced her engagement, together with four bottles of champagne.

Cecily was excited. 'Oh you are kind! Isn't he kind, Mother?' Joan looked at her mother.

'Most kind,' agreed her mother, with a smile that never reached her eyes.

Then Harry came forward, Guy presented 'the lucky fellow' to Mr Hinde and Cecily drew them into the room.

Mr Hinde was slightly shorter than Guy, with pale, expensive-looking clothes, smelling strongly of eau-de-cologne, and some twenty years his senior. Once the introductions were made, he devoted his attention to their mother who never lost her watchful look. But he was able to set her mind sufficiently at ease about the security of the position he was offering Guy. It wasn't his work that interested Joan but the way that he took charge of her mother's misgivings and reversed them, without once raising his voice, in the middle of a family gathering. He was perfectly courteous to Cecily and Harry, if not very interested, and his eyes rested on Guy's face like a caress. Joan thought it quite odd. Men looked at Cecily, she was the acknowledged beauty of the family. Lately people had looked at Joan. But Mr Hinde looked at her brother like that.

When they dispersed, Guy left to walk Mr Hinde to a taxi. Joan watched them go. They paused in the darkness and Joan thought she saw Mr Hinde put his hand on Guy's cheek and Guy incline his head towards the older man. She pulled back into the doorway sharply and closed the door. She did not know what it meant but she knew that her mother sensed something and was unwilling to talk about it. Win was too young, and Cecily only in love with Harry. The only person she could discuss what she had seen with was Guy.

34

It took her several days to find a way to be alone with her brother. He came in to change, their mother was out shopping and he came looking for Joan to ask if she would press a tie for him. She went to heat up the iron at the back of the stove and he followed her down to the kitchen.

'Why do you have to have this tie?' she asked.

'It's my favourite,' he replied with a grin. 'And we're going out.'

She didn't need to ask who 'we' were.

'Somewhere nice?'

'It usually is with Bingham. He's very generous.'

She nodded. She did not know how to frame the questions she wanted to ask.

'Are you all right?' he asked. 'Getting on a bit better with Mother?'

She looked at him, startled. 'I think so,' she said. 'Are you looking forward to working for him?'

Her brother agreed easily that he was.

'Is it very important to you?'

He considered her question. 'It is time for a change, yes.'

She went on doing things with her hands, spreading the ironing blanket, smoothing the tie, testing the iron.

'Is that why it's important?'

In the silence which lay between them, the iron hissed faintly. She kept her eyes down till the tie was finished, held it across her outstretched palm to him, eyes still downcast.

He took the tie.

'Thanks,' he said and turned away, but immediately turned back. 'You're sharp enough to see, Joan. Don't let anybody cloud that for you. We can't choose who we love.'

5 *Mercer*

I am being driven through the autumnal dark to a party, full of all sorts of people I know and don't know. There are actors and celebrities and personalities and models and all sorts of other people who must be with them because they're all talking together in that seamless, pointless way that people do when they take each other's frame of reference for granted. It's a graceful room with lots of flowers and lights, but the lights are mellow and everybody looks warm and pretty. I'm going to that party. I've been invited. At least I think I have. I get out of the car, somebody opens the door for me. I smile, I'm greeted by somebody else who smiles, I'm waved in. I put down my coat, I touch my hair – a silly touch, it doesn't need anything doing to it – and I enter that room which I've already 'seen', knowing I've got the timing right, I'm right to be there. And one by one these people, all these pretty people, turn away from me.

In my dream I can't ask why. I can't hear any sound in that dream now, just breathing and rustle as their clothes move. And they all turn away.

I wake up. Con lies on the other side of the bed sleeping quietly. I lie looking at the room, our bedroom for three months since we moved in, and I wonder where the room in my dream was. Not that it matters. It's a compendium of interiors in magazines, images from films. A room of perfect proportion, lighting, shadow, temperature. I put my hand to the base of my throat. Sweaty. I do not put on the light. It's a matter of honour with me not to disturb people when they're sleeping. I hate having to wake Con when he has to be off early, or getting Josh up for school. I don't want to wake Con anyway. What would I tell him?

It's been a long time since I thought that if he really loved me, he'd wake as I wake, feel my trouble, I wouldn't have to explain. He'd know. Why did I dream about being an actress? Was it about being an actress? That was so long ago and anyway, it didn't work. I won't ask Con. If I do, he'll say it was what I was reading before I went to sleep. I bend down into the half-darkness to inspect the book title. There wasn't anything in that. Why did they turn away from me? If David were here, he'd tell me it's my breath. David was the only person, the only man in my whole life to tell me I had bad breath.

By the time we broke up I had got to the stage where I felt like a leper. I put my hand up to cover my mouth before I was introduced to anybody. I cleaned my teeth six times a day and gulped down chlorophyl tablets and even sucked mints, though I hate them.

Bad breath is awful. I'm always meeting nice men with bad breath. One day I went to see Mara, an actress friend, and she whisked me off to lunch with two interesting men. All men were interesting to Mara. Anyway, one of them was a psychiatrist and remarkably sweet of breath. He was a roly-poly sort of man with a bit of a jowl and a habit of talking as if to a crowd of little boys he wanted to be friends with. The conversation somehow came to marriage and thence to mine, which was all too familiar to Mara. I talked about it all the time.

Suddenly I put my hand in front of my mouth and said, 'I'm sorry.'

'What's the matter?' asked Rolypoly.

'My breath,' I said. 'I'm sorry.'

'What's the matter with your breath?'

'It's bad, I'm sorry.'

He asked me to take my hand away. I could feel the heat of the blush on my face. I took my hand down but still half-averted my face. He asked me to look at him. Mara and her friend were now watching.

'Open your mouth,' he said. He cut short my protest with 'Good heavens, girl, it's only a mouth. I work in the Health Service, you know, quite used to worse things than mouths being offered to me.' I breathed out, he sniffed, I watched him. 'Nothing wrong with your breath,' he said. 'Classic rejection game, bad breath.'

37

I'm no good with my own dreams. I can work out quite a bit from other people's but my own are rare or rarely remembered and they're always about fear and rejection or war or pestilence and more fear. One day I should make a list of my fears and burn it. Very cleansing stuff, fire. But if I could make such a list, I'd be halfway to being free of the fear because it would be defined, I'd have managed to give it a name. The few times I've tried to write dreams down, they've become blurred, slipped away from me. I should have a pad at the bedside, one of those little lights insomniacs are supposed to use to read and not disturb anyone, a pencil at the ready, and then I'd be afraid all over again, afraid of taking myself too seriously.

When David dreamed, he dreamed of Africa, the veldt, the faces, the music, the animals. Or he dreamed of Paris, where he lived and taught when he first left Africa, before he went back and made the film. But eventually I learned that wherever David was, somewhere else was better. He offered himself as one who wanted a home but he had no use for it except that it kept him serviced and ready for the next adventure.

In the first year of our hasty marriage, he discovered that the kind of films he wanted to make were unheard of in England and that even television, which in those days had money, was not interested in what he had to offer. So he went abroad to look for a producer sympathetic to his ideas. He went away four times in twelve months – to Paris, to Sweden, to Cannes and to Sweden again. He had been happy in Paris, had studied near Cannes, and his first love was Swedish, but it seemed ignoble to concentrate upon the seductive possibilities of all this when he was cast in my mind as a tortured artist in the most expensive medium and was looking for a backer.

Every time he left, I thought I would never see him again. And I looked round the small room in which we lived and I could understand why he wouldn't come back. What was there to come back to?

During the first two trips, I decided that my insecurity was as plain as the nose on my face and if I'd known him better, I might not have felt so stranded. And I kept my mouth shut about it, partly because there wasn't anybody to tell and secondly because our marriage was suspect enough, to those on my side strange in its swiftness and lack of ceremonial and to those on his side – comrades from here and there, artists of one kind or another, one or two academics – it had no point. They did not understand why we had married at all. It was a bourgeois institution, irrelevant if not despised.

But at the third of these partings, none of my rationalisations worked. Brave best foot forward, head held up, I too am a person – none of it held. I range Midge. I had always rung her regularly. Now I rang her often. Talking about my trouble wasn't the only reason for calling her. I just wanted her to confirm by the apparent order of her world that the turbulence of mine was temporary and as such bearable.

I don't remember what we talked about until she asked me if I'd heard from David and then it was like a cork coming out of a bottle. No, I said, no, I hadn't heard. He's moving about so much, there's no time and no money to spare for telephone calls, and anyway, why should he write? Plainly puzzled, she asked what I meant. What I meant, I said, was that he probably wouldn't be coming back. What did I mean, she asked. 'Why should he come back?' I gasped as the jets of water began from my eyes. 'What is there to come back to?'

'Oh darling' she said, 'darling, don't be silly. Of course he's coming back. It's just very tough on you, that's all.' And even now, I don't know whether she meant to address me as if I were a child with dogmuck on my shoe, whether she felt my capacity for being what she called highly strung must be braced against the realities of married life as she knew it, or whether she implied that I should count my blessings. Trouble, huh? said her voice. You ain't seen nothin' yet.

And every time he came back, he was further away. And I learned to move away in my own direction because that was the only way I could avoid drowning, by moving nearer to the higher ground of my selfdom. Or selfishdom. I did not mind that David had other women. I think I expected it, for lots of reasons which had to do with distance and me and his work and my image of love at the time. But I was uncomfortable and so, naturally, I took my comfort where I found it. One old lover, a couple of new ones and the fulfilment of long-promised blandishment with a much older painter whose work I still occasionally see exhibited and laugh at how expensive it's got and how the girl in the picture might have been me.

What, then, held David and me together? He wished to be different from his parents, who divorced when he was thirteen, and I wished to be one part of a repeat performance of my mother and father as I then preferred to perceive them. Also I was tired of pretending that I could manage on my own when I didn't really feel that I could and when you get to that stage, which is by no means the bottom of the pit, you'd rather have what you've got, what you said you wanted, than face up to why that isn't going to work either.

I can't say I was dazzled by his involvement in films. But I felt he had a real talent whereas mine was just a come-and-gone. I was a shot in the dark; David was going to be acknowledged as a film-maker. He certainly worked at it. I once rang Joan from a cultural institute where we had spent five hours viewing unintelligible Third World underground movies. It was a wet Sunday afternoon and I would really rather have seen some old favourite that never dates. She made some joke about 'suffering for your art' and it took another two years before I began to see that I was suffering, yes, for art, yes – but not for mine.

It was five o'clock in the morning when that thought hit me, the pre-dawn punctuation of the lonely, when I had got up and gone into the living room of the flat where we then lived to try to do some writing, only to discover that David had moved all my papers. Again.

He could not bring himself to say that he felt that we should concentrate on one of us at a time, that there was one law for him and his behaviour, another for me, that I was politically, artistically, socially irredeemable but that he loved me anyway and if I would just take up my seat at the back of the bus, the show could roll. I am enormously grateful to David for one thing. He taught me, by illustration, more vividly than he could ever know, the law of paradox, for the harder I tried to back him, the more I got under his feet. The more careful I was to be unobtrusive, the more obvious and disturbing I became. And when our arguments ceased to be cleansing domestic trifles and became verbal trench warfare, he threw plates at the wall and glass at the floor. It was catching. I almost got him once.

And then one night we met a friend of his with an old friend of mine. In the pub our conversation became quite lively. He talked to his friend, I to mine, and I was immensely cheered just by encountering the two of them together. When we left the pub, he drove the car too fast, sloughing it from side to side, until we reached a traffic light at which I ripped open the door and leapt out. He pulled over and chased me, caught me, dragged me back to the vehicle. I wasn't screaming, I hadn't the guts. He accused me of flirting with my friend, pushed me into the house. I tried to answer, he hustled me into the living room. He yelled at me, I tried to yell back. But I croaked. He threw books at me, he flung vases and bottles, and when I tried to leave the room he pushed me aside, slammed the door and heaved a chair at it. He raged, I can't remember the words, only the quality of the sound, and he picked up my papers, my poor pathetic look-I-can-still-do-it, look-how-hard-I'm-trying papers and flung them at me. I grabbed for them, he clouted my face and threw a teapot. Cold, fortunately. And I sank to my knees and gibbered. All of which interests me only now to know if the scar still hurts when I press it. And it does. Probe, probe – ouch!

I ceased to want him although we still went to bed together. He lectured me about who I was and what I was. He would ring me and ask if there was anyone else there. If I said there was, he'd scream and call me names. If I said no, he'd scream at me and tell me I was lying.

During our four years together, he made four documentaries – absolutely not what he wanted to do – which kept us in a vehicle of sorts, but everything else he earned, he expected to plough into his own endeavour. I went to work, kept house, fed the people he invited home, typed his endless scripts and script ideas.

One night he told me he couldn't stand me any more, he'd have to get out, and he stood there packing his files and clothes while I begged him not to go. I don't know why I wanted him to stay, probably I just couldn't think of how to explain that I was so unbearable that he'd left me. He took his passport, he said he'd send for anything else he wanted when he was ready. Four days later I came back home after a bad movie and found myself starring in another. He was in bed, his back towards me when I came in. He didn't speak. I crept into a corner of the bed. He told the darkness, with me listening, that he had had to come home because he didn't have enough money to go away.

He went abroad to make ready for a film. It was what he wanted to do. Even if the film wasn't what he wanted, doing something akin to that made him feel happier. I packed my belongings and put them in storage. When he came back, he tried to call me at the office where I'd worked but I had moved on to be a secretary in a PR consultancy, so he had to ask around to find me.

When he caught up with me, he railed and stormed, then he wept and asked me to have lunch. It was awful. He looked so ill, he must have loved me. To begin with, I let him know where I was and he called at all times of the day and night. He turned up where I worked, at a rather grand office just off Park Lane where they wrote promotions for pickles and arranged press launches for new biscuits. The people I worked with weren't at all put out when he shouted, they were used to people shouting so, sooner or later, they'd ask him to calm down and the endless telephone calls through which they did their business would continue.

I offered to leave. My boss smiled. 'No need,' he said, 'no need at all. He'll get over it, you know,' implying, 'and so will you.' Within three months he was gone, next heard of having an affair with a politically acceptable American star who was to be the main attraction in his version of a well-known author's early work. Not a big film, but a very definite step on the way. Which I thought must be how he viewed me, if he thought of me at all, until years later when Con spotted the actress at the gym where he works out and introduced himself, mentioning in his matter-of-fact way how he came to be curious about her. 'You're married to Mercer! My God, when I was with David, that's all he ever talked about. Mercer, and his mother.' Both of us weeping at the foot of the crucifixion of his ambition, his mother stuck in Kaffirkopje with a gun under her pillow and half the house shuttered in mourning because he'd gone away and me in a rented room with a bathroom down the hall, a typewriter I couldn't use on a table and the scent of failure on my skin so clearly, I thought everybody could smell it.

6 *Joan*

My father used to tell me stories about what he called 'his war'. He spent from 1914 to 1918 stationed in India and Mesopotamia. He enlisted before his eighteenth birthday and was presumed drowned off a troop ship coming home four years later through the Bay of Biscay.

Although the contrast between what he had expected and what happened was harsh, it was also adventurous and interesting. Joan was fond of saying that it seemed to her he went away a boy and came back a man. He knew it was a miracle that he had lived to tell about it when so many died, and he loved to talk about it. Joan must have known these stories backwards, she'd heard them so many times before, but I don't remember her stopping him, or pulling faces and trying to avert them in any way. Indeed I remember her laughing again and again at the funny ones and joining in the discussion which would follow the others. Paul was a great storyteller.

In marked contrast, Joan told me only three things about her war. Her sister's fiancé was killed. Joan was very grateful not to have anyone else close to her in it to lose. And thirdly that she would never forget the sheets and sheets of names of those missing, presumed dead, which were published day after day in the papers, on black-bordered pages, like invitations to a funeral. But it was nothing to do with Joan.

Her brother Guy was being trained by Mr Hinde in the development of his business, the spin-off of which was the lucrative manufacture of dressings. Her mother told her that her father was too old to be called up. She didn't add that in his ill-health – he had kidney disease – they wouldn't have taken him even if he'd been a much younger man. And although the oldest son of the family next door, Robert, wanted to enlist in the army, he was initially refused.

Joan could see that Robert wanted to join up. To describe patriotism as a wave was to sell it short. Young men wanted to fight for their country as naturally as they drew breath. And as they went on breathing, so they went on enlisting. Robert was the eldest of a family of boys with a father too old to fight. He felt the family honour rested on his shoulders. Joan knew that she should be proud of him but all she felt was a sense of hopelessness at being unable to hold him. For Robert was the first boy who had ever kissed her and he did it very well.

His position with regard to his brothers gave him a degree of privacy which was mercifully unquestioned. Joan joined all of them in their games from time to time but mostly she and Robert met at the gate in the wall between their two houses and slipped from there to a deserted attic high at the back of his house where they sat close together, talked and stroked each other with the absorption of the young who think they have invented such pleasures.

He had told her he wanted to be a doctor. 'But if there's a war – ' he said, not finishing his sentence.

'There won't be, will there?' she asked.

'My father thinks it's highly likely. I shall volunteer.'

'Will it last long?' Joan concentrated fiercely on the darn in the knee of her stocking.

'I don't know,' said Robert. 'Let's hope not. Everyone seems to think it will be over in a few months.'

War was declared on a Tuesday in August and Joan went scurrying home from school. Within weeks, Harry, who was engaged to her sister Cecily, had joined the navy and Robert had tried to join the army and been rejected. Mrs Boyle told Joan's mother on one of the rare occasions when they exchanged more than an undemonstrative greeting when shopping.

'Too young and a bit weak in the chest,' said Mrs Boyle, her placid face frowning. 'His father is so relieved he's not to go but I was horrified he'd even tried. He added a few years to his age, you know, and anyway I thought that chest of his had cleared up long ago. Perhaps you'd send Joan over tonight to cheer him up a bit?'

44

Joan's mother graciously conceded, noting that while it was right and proper for a young man to want to serve his country, she was sure Mrs Boyle would be happier to have him safe at home. She would have moved on then but Mrs Boyle asked her, 'What about your boy?'

Joan's mother paused before replying. 'No, I don't think Guy will be going. Some of the businesses are exempted, I believe.'

When Joan went to tea at the Boyles that night, Robert was very quiet and there was no opportunity to slip away. In general conversation she couldn't say or do very much. His brothers seemed to have agreed that for Robert's sake, the less said about his failed enlistment the better. Joan excused herself to wash her hands and lingered in the hall, hoping that Robert would follow her. Just when it seemed she couldn't wait a minute more, he came out and looked at her, waiting at the bottom of the stairs. He looked so bleak that she didn't know what to say. Then she said she was sorry. He shrugged. 'But I'm glad too,' she said. 'I'll feel so much better if you're staying.'

He said nothing, turned away and went into the kitchen. She didn't like to follow him, so she continued upstairs. There wasn't another chance to speak privately all evening and she lingered until Mrs Boyle came in and said kindly, 'Hadn't you better be getting off now, Joan? Your mother will be wondering where you are.' This was silly because her mother knew perfectly well where she was and had for once encouraged her to be there, but Joan felt after that, she must leave, so she said she was going. Robert regarded her carefully, his brothers ranged about him.

To begin with, the war changed nothing. Cecily went down by train to see Harry off from Portsmouth. Sometimes her mother complained about the price of this or that but then she had always done so.

Joan and Win went to school and spent more time together, for the Boyles' house was not as welcoming as it used to be and the father of the little girl across the street whom Win used to play with joined up, so her mother took her and went home to their people in Essex. Sometimes Joan saw one or other of Robert's brothers but he didn't come looking for her and there wasn't much she found to say to them. She only wanted to know about Robert.

The memory of his face began to blur and she missed his hands stroking her and his kisses and even the hot awkward moments when she sensed he wanted something more. She thought she had

45

dreaded these moments but now she remembered that he was always gentle with her and that any difficulties were always navigated with dignity. She saw boys look at her and sometimes she looked at them but there were few opportunities to meet them. Her mother kept her quite busy when she was out of school. And so she alternated between pushing away memories of her time with Robert and clinging to them. She took Win for walks, helped her mother as much as she could and life went on, until the telegram came.

When she came home from school, her mother told her not to disturb Cecily, who was upstairs lying down.

'She had a telegram,' said her mother, filling the kettle.

Joan stared at her. 'Is something the matter with Harry?'

Her mother shook her head and, straightening up, she turned to face her. 'Harry is dead.' Joan felt her eyes fill. She fumbled for her handkerchief. Her mother patted her shoulder.

'Poor Cecily,' sniffed Joan.

Her mother did not respond.

As the war dragged on, Joan noticed there were fewer men in the streets when she went out walking and if there were they were hardly men at all, or very old. Every man who could went to fight. It was expected of them. She saw the hoardings: 'Men of Britain – women expect you to fight'. There were sometimes Zeppelins in the sky and the mother of every second girl at school was working in a way which was unheard of before the war – in factories and offices, as clerical staff in hospitals and auxiliary nurses. At school they were asked to collect money for comforts 'for our fighting men' and to knit, and encourage those round them to knit, socks, mufflers and balaclavas. Joan's mother complained that she had never a minute to herself but she too knitted one or two items.

When she read of the cold and the mud endured by the troops, Joan found herself wondering if any of the things they knitted were any use. What good could they be in the face of conditions beyond understanding? What was the point of woollen socks to keep your feet warm when your feet were never to be dry, much less warm, and the wool soaked into the skin, became imbedded and infected and had to be picked out with tweezers and needles, while to clear the infection you had to immerse the feet, already miserably cold, in Condé's fluid? And the numbers haunted her. She couldn't imagine such numbers of anything, of eggs or apples, let alone dead or wounded. She wanted to tell Robert not to go, that it was useless, so many had already gone and would never come back or would come back wounded so badly it would be better for everybody that they didn't return. But she did not. Instead she wondered if Harry and Cecily would have become engaged if war hadn't been in the air. The good thing about Harry was that their mother had approved of him. She clearly didn't approve of Mr Hinde even though Guy was doing famously in his employ and making very good money.

One morning her mother received a letter which she opened and read. Within those few lines, her face became a mask. Cecily and Guy had already left for work. Win and Joan observed their mother, exchanged glances and said nothing. They cleared and washed the breakfast dishes, got ready for school and left with only a muffled farewell from upstairs.

When Joan came home that night, later than usual because she was helping with costumes for the school play, the living-room door stood open and her mother's voice could clearly be heard.

'You may not leave this house, not to go and live with that man!'

And her brother's voice, less harsh but equally emphatic.

'I shall be leaving within the next couple of weeks and I shall make my own arrangements.'

'Don't think I don't know what's going on!'

And Guy's voice, almost mocking. 'Nothing is going on, except that I have certain business opportunities which will be best pursued if I am independent and nearer the office.'

'Fine talk, fine talk. Words and stuff, that's all that is.'

'Mother, I suggest you lower your voice. I work for Bingham Hinde and he has made me a proposition – '

Her mother made some remark too low for her to hear.

'What you think is not important. What is important is that I will continue to support you financially and in the light of my father's last letter – '

'Don't you sneer, don't you dare sneer at him – '

Guy sounded very patient now, he knew how to handle this.

'I'm not sneering. I'm just being practical. I will make you a proper allowance so that between what Cec gives you and I send, you'll be able to manage. Obviously Dad will do his best.'

Joan stood in the kitchen shadows, only half understanding what she had heard, and listened to her brother go upstairs. The stillness after the explosion was full of small electric particles which pricked her skin and she felt terribly sorry for her mother.

Almost shyly, she pushed open the living-room door. Her mother stood staring without seeing at the closed curtains. Feeling she was not alone, she turned to face Joan.

'Are you all right?' The words sounded foolish.

Her mother nodded. 'Yes, thank you, Joan.' They looked at each other. 'It's quite late, isn't it? You should be getting along.'

Joan hesitated.

'Oh, go away.' And Joan fled.

The next morning was surprisingly like the one before. Guy and Cecily left early. Win and Joan ate breakfast and their mother went upstairs to begin her chores. It was Joan's job to empty the rubbish into the bin and in the living-room waste-paper basket she found the letter her mother had scrumpled up. It said that her father had lost his job, was now working as a freelance and would send whatever money he could. Joan had hoped he would send an address. She had continued to try to find out where he was but her mother either ignored her enquiries or evaded them through one of her headaches. But the letter was written from his old office. So she scrumpled it up again.

Joan thought about Guy leaving to go and live with Mr Hinde. She wondered whether their love took the form of long embraces which left them smiling and happy. She knew that long embraces were part of it but she suspected there must be more to it if people made such a fuss about it. And whatever it was, it was supposed to make people happy. Was Guy happy? She supposed he was. But Mother wasn't happy about Guy's presumed happiness. Had Mother ever been happy? Joan thought about it. Long ago, when she was quite small, she remembered her mother laughing and happy, even pleased and laughing with her father. But very soon she didn't like him to touch her and then that got worse and the fights began.

She wondered what the difference was between Cecily and her Harry and Guy and Bingham Hinde. Could you be in love with somebody you worked for? It might be difficult. But then Joan remembered the look she had seen pass between her brother and Mr Hinde, and the touch, and what her brother had said to her ages ago.

Whatever it was, this love business, it was very important – must be, or people wouldn't get so upset about it. But it was awfully hard to find out about. The girls at school sniggered in corners but you only told your best friend if you knew anything and she didn't really have anyone close like that. And love seemed to be to do with knowledge, Joan thought. People in love or people who had been in love knew something that other people didn't know and that special knowledge gave them power. She wondered what it would be like to feel that you could do something risky, like fall in love, and not get caught out. She wondered if she would ever be sure, like Guy, who was sure enough of himself to leave home and attempt the next task Mr Hinde set him. But then Guy was a man and men were different after all. And Joan wondered what the differences were and if it was only in comparing men to women that they were so different, or whether one kind of man could be different from another.

The war was more than half over when one day, on her way home from school, she saw Robert coming towards her. As they drew level, he smiled his old charming smile and asked how she was. She was well, she said, and asked about him. 'I'm going overseas next week,' he said. 'They're not so particular now and I'm that much older. Wish me luck!'

'Oh, I do,' she said. 'I do.'

'By the time I come home you'll be quite the young lady,' he said, 'and have forgotten all our times together.' She shook her head and, remembering Harry, she said, 'You will be careful, won't you?'

He smiled at her and asked her for a kiss to set him on his way. She glanced in the direction of her mother's house and pecked his cheek nervously.

'Little Joan,' he murmured. They stood for a moment then he touched his forelock in salute and walked on.

In her final year at school she made friends with one of Harry's sisters. She'd gone once or twice with Cecily to Harry's mother's for tea and found Mary most vivacious. She sang and danced and sewed theatrical costumes for the local amateur dramatic society, though she confided to Joan that really, she was going to go on the stage properly. Looking at her pretty face and bright ways, listening to her sing naughty songs and dance about, Joan could not tell her they shared an ambition. She felt quite dull in comparison.

'I sing in a restaurant,' said Mary, 'and I'm trying to get a job understudying in one of the theatres.'

Joan was fascinated. When the subject of her future employment was mooted at home, her mother always silenced her with, 'Get an education first, and then we'll see.' Mary was doing what Joan dared not try.

They agreed to meet again, for tea, and while Joan stared at Mary's well-powdered face, the talk turned to boyfriends. 'Do you go out with anyone?' asked Mary. 'I mean, it can't all be school-books?' Joan, excited by the warmth of the teashop, her friend's enthusiasm and an unaccustomed confidence, told her all about Robert.

'So you're one of us!' exclaimed Mary triumphantly. 'Not as green as you look, hey?'

Joan stopped, with tea in her mouth and swallowed it hastily. 'Oh, but –' she stammered. 'No, well, you see – I mean, we never did anything. It was quite childish really, I suppose – '

Mary looked puzzled. 'But you said he went overseas,' she said.

'Yes,' said Joan. 'Yes, he did, eventually, but I hadn't seen him for some time then and we weren't as close as we'd been when we were younger.'

'And he didn't get any little going-away present, any souvenir from you?'

'No,' said Joan. 'You mean – no. No.'

'Well,' said Mary, patting her lips with her napkin. 'I must say I think that's a bit mean. He'd been there since you were quite young, you're a jolly pretty kid and you never offered him a lock of hair or a picture, let alone anything more comforting.'

Joan looked at Mary. 'My mother says there's only two kinds of girls, good girls and bad girls. When Robert and I – we – '

'And nice girls do what their mothers tell them,' said Mary. 'Or at least keep it looking that way for the sake of family peace and quiet. Poor little Joan. I can see you've got a lot to learn, about what makes the world go round. How old are you now?' Joan told her, 'Seventeen.' 'A good age to begin, I'd say,' said Mary, skilfully turning the conversation to birthdays and fashion. On the omnibus home Joan reflected she wasn't even sure of what she said. Mary clearly wasn't a 'nice girl' though Joan thought she was one of the nicest girls she'd ever met. Obviously she knew a good deal more than Joan so a little detective work was called for.

That night she tried to sound out Cecily but her elder sister, clad most becomingly in mauve and grey, was more interested in getting her hair just right before she went out to a concert with a friend. 'You've got plenty of time before you need to know all that,' said she with a dismissive wave of her hairbrush, 'and when you do, I should think you'd speak to Mother, not me.'

Joan turned back to her book. She couldn't imagine how to ask her mother what she wanted to know.

The next day her mother was short and snappish, angry with

everything and everybody. When Joan tried to help, her mother grumbled at her and when she hung back, she complained that she had to do everything herself. That night Joan asked if she might go out. It was a Friday, she had the weekend for any schoolwork and Mary had asked her to a party given by friends. Grudgingly her mother gave permission, admonishing her not to be late. Even her mother's temper couldn't damp Joan's enthusiasm for a party where, Mary said, there would be real theatricals, actresses and even an actor or two. But the party was not what she'd hoped at all. It was a far cry from the romance of the picture palace or Robert's gentle sensuality. The women were heavily made-up, laughing and smoking, the men laughed louder and tried to kiss everybody. And they all drank a great deal, more than Joan had ever seen before. She left for the last bus, having pushed away a little fat man half a dozen times, with his words ringing in her ears.

'M-my, my, M-m-m-mary,' he said, pretending to stammer, 'wherever did you find such a n-n-nice girl?' But he didn't make it sound nice at all, and Joan saw Mary shrug in an irritated way.

Joan stared out of the bus window at the London streets sliding by. They weren't actors, well – not real actors, the way she'd thought they'd be. By the time she got off she'd decided that if those were Mary's friends, then perhaps Mary wasn't as nice as she'd thought. She put the key in the lock. Without thinking she hung up her coat and, entering the kitchen, she asked her mother, 'What's a nice girl?'

'Oh, Joan, not now. It's late and I'm tired.'

'But I want to know.'

'Well, I don't think Mary's a nice girl from what you say about her, running with a fast crowd, smoking and drinking.'

'But all sorts of people drink and smoke. That's not it. Mother, what makes a bad girl?'

Her mother stood up and said, 'That's enough, Joan. I'm not going to stand here and discuss this with you.'

Joan shut the kitchen door, locked it and put the key in her pocket. 'Mother, I want to go on the stage.'

'No.'

'Why not?'

'Because it's no suitable place for a nice girl.'

'Mother, what's the difference between a nice girl and any other kind of girl?'

'You should know. I always made sure that you and your sisters had a good home. Now, stop being difficult. Open the door and let's go to bed.'

Joan drew a deep breath. 'I'm not going to open the door until you answer my questions. Why can't I go on the stage? What's a good girl or a bad girl or whatever it is? Why won't you tell me? I tried asking Cecily the other night and she won't tell me. Maybe she doesn't know either. But you must know. You're always talking about it –' She seemed unaware that she was talking very loud and very fast. Her mother, who had risen, stood her ground.

'You may not go on the stage because it is an uncertain way to earn a living, unreliable in terms of work and the company you'd have to keep. We have existed on less and less since your father lost his job and without Guy –' her tongue wet her lips briefly – 'things would have been even harder. Guy and Cecily made it possible for us to go on much as before so that you and Win have had some time to be children, and schooling. It could have been much worse. Your teachers say you're bright. Then you should become a teacher. Plenty of work, money to be earned and money buys security. A good girl is one who behaves herself and a bad girl is one who does not. Now –'

'I don't understand,' said Joan. 'Behaves herself how?'

'In the company of men,' said her mother fiercely. 'In the company of men.'

Joan stared at her. 'Is it something to do with being married?'

Her mother drew herself up. 'You do not have to be married to go to bed with a man but it is only permissible for nice people to do so after they are married. A fast girl, a bad girl, a girl who is not nice are polite ways of describing a girl who has been with a man before she's married.'

'What if he goes to war?' asked Joan, thinking guiltily of what she and Robert hadn't done.

'Joan, please,' said her mother with evident distaste. 'Harry is dead and Cecily and I have agreed that all that is best left unsaid. Now please, open the door and let's put an end to this unpleasant conversation.'

Joan felt for the key and unlocked the door.

'Mother, where is Dad?'

Her mother gritted her teeth so violently that in the harsh hall light, it looked as though her cheeks had fallen in.

'I don't know,' she said levelly.

Joan wanted to ask if she missed him but her mother swept past her, up the stairs, and it was only in thinking about it afterwards that Joan realised that as well as the knowledge she'd sought, she'd gained a little more.

7 *Joan*

Joan could never remember deciding to be a teacher. Her mother thought she was suited to it and she supposed that, in some way, it was her last great effort to please her mother, by doing what she wished. She couldn't think of anything better to do and her mother made it clear that she should be trained for something. By the last of her schooldays she was firmly aimed at teacher-training college with a small grant helpfully provided by the local authority, probably principally aiming at shepherding young men returning from war towards a useful and rewarding occupation.

When she thought of it, a teacher was a long way from being an actress, but she knew that she was not prepared to have that fight with her mother, she didn't want it enough. She cast longing sideways glances at her dreams and addressed herself to reality.

The war and school ended within months of one another. By the second week of January in 1919 she was working as a kennel maid for a woman who bred Samoyeds, great white fluffy dogs, in shape reminiscent of Huskies. She mucked out and swept up and groomed them incessantly as their long fur and their mistress's pride in them dictated. The pay was low but it was something and she proudly made her contribution to the family kitty, while saving up for college in September.

The college was in South London, a series of large Victorian buildings including several halls of residence. She had applied to live in without much hope and was delighted to be accepted. It was unarguably impractical to be spending money going to and from her place of study and this presented her with the chance to put distance between herself and her family painlessly. She was somewhat daunted by the awfulness of the food but this faded when she came in contact, easy, expected contact, with young men as well as young women. She remained rather serious about her work but the chance to discuss personalities and reactions with her contemporaries along the corridor was as good as an unexpected present. She was among the first to shorten her skirts, the last to bob her hair and she never managed to smoke with any conviction. Still she was asked out and not knowing how to say 'no', she accepted.

He was quite an ordinary young man who took her to the local cinema, bought her a poached egg and suggested a detour on the way back to the college, to call in at a friend's flat. When the friend wasn't home, though the door was open, a more sophisticated young woman might have taken the hint. But Joan suspected nothing until he drew closer to her on the sofa ('We'll just give it a couple of minutes and see if he turns up, shall we?') and, stroking the hand nearest to him, commented on the length of her eyelashes. She turned to face him. 'I say,' he said, 'you know, you're jolly pretty.'

'Am I?' she murmured.

He started to tell her how pretty, but sidetracked into kissing her which she thoroughly enjoyed until the hand that was on her shoulder reached for her breast and the hand that rested at her waist moved lower. She stood up, brushing him aside, and said she thought they should be going. He stared at her.

'Must we?' he asked.

She drew a deep breath and thought of every heroine she'd ever admired.

'Well, yes, I think so,' she said. 'It's rather late and I would like to look at my history before the lecture tomorrow. I don't know much about Edward the First.' She even remembered, she recalled to her delighted circle in recounting the tale, to smile sweetly and look him straight in the eye.

He rose reluctantly.

'And anyway,' she went on, still perfectly good-humouredly, 'your friend isn't going to come back.'

Without waiting for another moment, she walked towards the door, opened it and began to descend the stairs. She was at the corner when he caught her up and escorted her back through the dark streets, on the bus and into college.

Joan liked kissing. She particularly liked men and kissing when she had the support and agreement of several other girls of similar age and background who also liked kissing but didn't intend to do anything else.

'I would,' said her best friend Maisie Dunlop, who not only kissed and refused to go further but, to add insult to injury, couldn't be coerced through alcohol as she had a harder head than many of the slightly faster sporting set. 'But there's always the baby thing.'

'I had a friend at school who had to leave because of that,' said Joan. '*He* didn't, though.'

'Who was he?'

'The French master.' She sighed. 'I thought it was so unfair.'

Maisie squinted at the silk stocking she was mending.

'If it wasn't for that, would you?'

Joan thought about it for a moment. 'I don't think so,' she said. 'The trouble with men is that they can always leave you.'

She thought a lot about her father. She wished he could somehow know that she had left home on her own reasonable terms to go on to the next stage of her life. He would have been proud of her, she felt sure, and the idea of how she could have pleased him made her remember how she used to please him and then she missed him all over again. Funnily enough, although there were all sorts of demands on her time, both of work and recreation, there seemed to be more opportunity to think than there had been at home and so, having considered her father's role in the past, she began to consider her mother's from the time that he had left.

She could see that her mother worked and tried but she could also see how shut off she was. Her mother did not want to discuss, she wanted to decide. She was proud of Guy in her own way but she resented his bid for independence. Cecily was all right, she was much like Mother and would marry suitably and that would be all right. And Win was little Win. But the sort of pride that had made her mother tell her once that she was bright and should go in for teaching had not expanded once Joan decided to follow her suggestion. Joan had done as was expected. That was not a matter of praise but of propriety. And far from bringing them closer, now that Joan's feet were set on an appropriate path, her mother was less interested in her than ever.

Sometimes she'd take a friend home with her for tea and arrive full of sparkle and chat, to hug Win and stroke the family cat and tell stories of how Maisie Dunlop said she could drink anything if only she could eat half a pound of butter first and how the PT instructor made them all laugh because he would explain everything in long, long sentences even though he had this terrible stutter. But within ten minutes she was sitting nervously in her chair, her friend similarly silenced, her mother was doling out tea and cake and the family catechism had begun.

Had she heard from Guy? Well, it wasn't surprising if she hadn't. He was doing awfully well. Don't forget to write to him. And Cecily had been appointed a trainee buyer in Lockwoods. Not exactly Debenhams, of course, but you never knew, with hard work and will-power, what could be achieved. Was she paying proper attention to her work? She and Win didn't know how lucky they'd been. She must make a go of teaching, she'd never regret it. More tea? And within two cups of tea and a round-up of family news, Joan was quite glad to take her friend for a tramp through the streets and rush back for supper in hall.

But she never took Katherine Canning home for tea. Katherine was far too different for Joan to face familial awkwardnesses over the teatray with her. And yet she couldn't work out why. Katherine wasn't rich. Her clothes, like Joan's own, were frequently made over. She was a solid student, as was Joan, and she wasn't a leader, an extrovert or a flirt. But she was beautiful. She was dark, with large hazel eyes and skin like old ivory, golden green in its shadows, with a slightly curved nose and a full, almost heavy mouth. Joan loved looking at Katherine, they had conversations and shared tables and sat together with others in a group at various lectures, but somehow Joan felt that such a beautiful person should be spared the sullenness she had come to associate with the house in Ealing.

One day Katherine fell into step beside her and asked if she was going to the party the drama society was giving after the last night of *Androcles and the Lion.*

'I'd like to,' said Joan, 'if I can find a pair of shoes. My present ones have just about given up the ghost.'

Katherine looked at her as if she were about to share a secret of great importance. 'Meet me at the main gate this afternoon. I know where you can buy some shoes.' Joan agreed and that afternoon Katherine took her arm earnestly.

'My parents have a school in Kent,' she said. 'But there are four of us and there really isn't much money. My mother's still got the two younger ones to think of so I try to make do.' Joan, aware that she was being accepted into a confidence, nodded. 'But I found this place which has odd good things, especially shoes, and I thought you might like to know about it too. You won't tell everyone about it, will you?' Joan, flattered, insisted that she would not. 'My brother is coming to the dance tonight,' Katherine went on. 'You must meet him.'

All thought of pleasure about Katherine and the shoes flew out of Joan's head when she met Paul.

To begin with, he was bigger than any man she'd ever known. She couldn't understand after she had met him how she could have missed seeing him before, but came to learn that his interests were predominantly on the sporting side of the courses and that, as he was considered a remarkable athlete and was taking this degree after having been in the army, he was part of a different group within the college. The impression of his size was emphasised by his colour for he was naturally as dark as his sister and was burned to the colour of polished wood after spending four war years in India. He was slightly bandy from riding and his hair was already thinning on top. His dark eyes regarded her carefully and he held her gently when they danced in large clean dry hands. They became inseparable.

Swathed in scarves she cheered him on the rugby pitch, shrieking the college yell. Hands balled into fists to do the hitting for him, she watched him box. And she sat very straight with pride in her back while he led and arranged gymnastic displays and helped his fellow students. But best of all she liked to dance with him. His bulk was not fat but his body was big and strong, like sun-warmed stone, and as is often the bonus for big people, his movements were light and he danced with grace. Dancing with Paul gave her the kind of thrill she used to think she'd get from acting, except now that she reflected, she saw that acting was never as important to her as being a star and that's how she felt when people cleared the floor and stood back to watch them dance together.

But there was something more than that. In Paul she found a friend, a man she thought she could trust. She talked to him as she had talked to no one, not even her father, who had left before she had come to the stage of defining a lot of what she now longed to discuss.

58

She told him about her father and mother. He was not shocked, but said simply, 'Nobody on the outside ever understands why a marriage works or doesn't.'

'But my parents disagreed about everything,' said Joan.

'So do mine,' Paul acknowledged. 'The difference is that my father will never leave my mother because he knows he can't manage without her. She holds him up.'

Joan thought for a minute. 'Does it have to be like that?'

He looked at her.

'I hope not,' he said, his face straight but his eyes merry.

She looked at him quickly, saw the kindness of the tease and relaxed.

'I wish I could like my mother more,' she said thoughtfully.

'I wish I could like my father more,' he said, 'but I can't.'

'Can't you try?'

'Liking has to be mutual. My father doesn't like me.'

'Why ever not?'

'I grew too tall and made him feel even smaller.' He stood up and helped her up.

'Don't you worry about it?'

He tucked her hand into his arm and answered her. 'No. I worry about all sorts of things but not that. That's just the way it is. And it must be better to admit it than to pretend.'

Another time she leaned against him as they sat on a wall and stroked his fingers while he told her about Katherine and Sylvia and Julie, all of whom were younger than he, so much so that when he came home from India, after he was supposed to have been drowned so they weren't expecting him anyway, his mother had to tell his baby sister Julie who he was. She thought he was just some big brown man, a stranger who had appeared out of the night.

'I got the last train from London and the tram had gone so I walked up to the village. The house has no back garden, only a front one which faces a wall, and there's a door set in it. I opened the door quietly and there were lights in three rooms in the house – it was like a tableau. There was Ma in the kitchen, working away; my father reading something in his study and my sisters upstairs, the two younger ones, with Katherine reading to them. And then I rang the bell and my father came to answer it and he called my mother. The girls came to hug me, except Julie who thought I was funny and not to be trusted because I smelt of tobacco and salt and leather. But she soon got over it, cuddled up on my knee and made a great fuss when

59

she had to go to bed.'

Joan said thoughtfully, 'My brother didn't go away during the war, at least not the way you did. He was exempted because the man he used to work for – he's his partner now – owned all sorts of businesses, including factories for making dressings.'

Paul lit a cigarette. 'Lucky for him.'

Joan shot him a quick look. 'Was it very bad?'

'It's never pretty. There were at least some pretty bits, where I was, as long as you didn't get shot or taken ill, but the war in Europe was another thing, the end of everything that went before. Logical extension of modern warfare beginning with the American Civil War. Simply hell on earth.'

There was silence for a minute.

'I don't think Guy wanted to avoid it,' offered Joan. 'It just worked out that way.'

'Was he always in that line?'

'Well, no. He worked in insurance to begin with and Mr Hinde was a client, but Guy saved him some money somehow, I don't think I ever knew the details. Anyway, they became friends and he offered Guy a job with him and it went on from there. Of course, once the war broke out, everybody did everything they could and Guy moved out to be nearer where he worked.'

'Conscientious of him,' observed Paul quietly.

'He and Cecily did a lot for Mother regarding money after Dad left. Guy was very good to us.'

'You're very fond of him.'

Joan looked away a little.

'And now he's in partnership with this chap – whatyoucallhim, Hinde?'

She nodded.

'Hope he's as involved with the business as your brother sounds as if he is.'

'Oh he is,' said Joan quickly. 'Mr Hinde would never let Guy down and anyway, they live together.' She heard the words go out of her mouth, she could not recall them, she wished very hard that he would understand, would not dismiss or question them, would hear what she really meant. He looked at her carefully, put his cigarette packet into the pocket of his battered jacket, held out his hand to her and she stood beside him. Five steps she counted, stopped and looked at him clearly. 'Do you understand?' she asked.

He nodded, beginning to Walk again. 'Some fellas are like that.'

One morning she got up and one of her friends called to her as she went to breakfast that she had a letter. She thought it might be a note from Paul, she couldn't think of anything else, and so mindful of how long the morning often seemed till lunch she gulped down tea and toast before she went to the desk to ask for it. It was from her mother, telling her briefly that she had heard that her father was dead. She thought Joan would want to know, although there were as yet no details. Joan stood in the hall and stared unseeingly ahead of her. She saw herself and her sisters dancing on the sand and the soft sandals he made them every summer so their feet would be comfortable – how silly that seemed, for her mother had insisted that every other pair of shoes should be worn until it was worn out, irrespective of how much the foot grew and was cramped. She looked down to her feet, already misshapen, and saw only a blur through her tears. She thought of his face calmly watching the snake while it was fed and of his hands smoothing her hair before he took her on one of their outings to see what they would see. She saw again the curves and lines of his handsome face and the darkness of his eyes, before they became swollen and strained. She did not go to lectures; she lay on her bed, reading and rereading the note. Katherine came to look for her to tell her Paul was asking for her. She combed her hair and put on her coat. She was cold. He took her to a teashop and told her she was pale. 'My father died,' she said.

He said he was sorry. 'Will you go home for the funeral?'

'I don't know, I don't think so. He may have been dead for a while. Mother's only just heard. I told you, they haven't been together for some time.'

When tea was over, they walked back to college, his arm round her, in silence. At the gates, he turned to her and asked her if she would marry him at the end of the course. She agreed. She supposed they must have kissed but when she thought back to it, she could not remember. It didn't matter.

Her father's death was like a bruise to the bone. It continued to hurt when it was brushed against but was covered by the daily events around her. She ended her first year successfully, so did Paul, and they were both sent out on teaching practice. She went to a northern town where the streets were damp and the school was cold and ate so badly she developed whitlows on her fingers. She made her mother a grey silk blouse with faggoting and a fine finish but her mother reproved her for wasting money. Paul's school was just as unprepossessing but he was near enough to his home that with an effort he could ride over once or twice and he invited her down to meet his family.

He lived in a village, seventy miles out of London and into Kent. She took a train into London and another out to get there. The house was set back from a narrow lane with a garden before it. There were apple trees and lavender bushes. His mother was tiny, with a lined face and a sweet smile. His sisters were, like Katherine, all tall and striking and ebullient. Although she'd never known such a noisy lot, she enjoyed the games and the talk until Paul's father arrived, bringing with him the cold wind of self-control, and they had a fairly formal supper. Suddenly she understood why Paul was so measured about her father, for he hardly spoke to his own.

Once the Old Man, as all his children called him, had retired to his study, the girls and Joan washed up and then they all sat talking and drinking tea till quite late with Paul's mother. The next morning the young people walked to the sea and came back tired and hungry to eat an enormous lunch, a meal once again inhibited by the appearance of Paul's father. There were two lives in that house, she decided, just as there had been in her own – one with the father and one without. One with a man and one without, she thought wryly, thinking of Guy. Paul kissed her goodbye at the train, while his younger sisters smiled and whispered among themselves and Katherine bore herself gravely, like the family duenna.

Throughout the second year, she and Paul continued to meet when they could. He came to meet her mother, she spent one or two more weekends with his family in the country, but their marriage was never mentioned. Joan enjoyed a successful flirtation with a rather richer young man, the son of a successful solicitor, but he faded away and she found that she took Paul's presence as much for granted as he took hers. They were a couple.

At the beginning of a winter day she went with Paul to see him off with the team for a rugby match far away and he told her he thought they should wait until they had jobs before they married. She agreed, feeling suddenly better about it all. She didn't know why. She waved to him as the bus left and decided she could brave her mother for tea that afternoon.

When she arrived Win told her excitedly that Guy was there, and Mr Hinde. She pushed her hair into place, tidied herself and walked into the room with her head up. Her brother got up to greet her, kissed her perfunctorily and she turned to shake hands with Mr Hinde. Her mother came in with the teapot, for once quite flushed and amiable, so Joan sat with Win on the settee and listened while Guy told office stories and made jokes and Mr Hinde smiled his careful smile.

'Well,' said her mother, 'and what's your news, young lady?' And Joan heard herself saying that she thought she would be marrying at the end of the course, once she and Paul had jobs.

Her mother looked at her for a moment, her face hardening a little. 'I see,' she said. 'Now there's something. What do you think of that, Guy?' And Guy smiled easily and came to kiss Joan's cheek again and murmur congratulations, while Mr Hinde smiled more broadly and, inclining his head in her direction, remarked, 'How nice.'

The conversation resumed, Win was sent to buy something they'd forgotten for supper and, for once, Joan felt she did not have to wait to be dismissed. She rose and, as she did so, Mr Hinde stood too and knocked over the milk jug which was at the edge of the tray. Guy bent to right it, spreading his large handkerchief over the liquid while Mr Hinde apologised. Joan heard herself say, 'I'll get a cloth,' and as she left the room, half-turned back to see Guy's hand almost comfortingly on Mr Hinde's sleeve and Mr Hinde's dismissive smile into her mother's face which looked in an instant as if it had been wiped of expression in the effort of control. And in that instant Joan was immeasurably glad that Guy had told her he loved Mr Hinde and she could accept it, as Paul apparently accepted it, even if she didn't understand. That her mother rejected it so totally pushed her in the other direction. It wasn't that it was right, she supposed, but it was and therefore it must be accepted for what it was. She was pleased with the effort and clarity of this thought.

Once the tray was tidied away, coats were fetched and Joan was left with Guy and Mr Hinde.

'You mustn't mind her too much, you know,' said Guy. 'Things haven't been easy since Dad left and Mother always wanted everything her way. I expect she rather hoped to see me married before you and Ceci.' Joan looked at him. 'But it doesn't appeal to me and it does to you two so she'll have to make the best of it. You'll be all right if you marry, won't you?' His tone implied money. Joan nodded with determination.

'Good girl. Because I can always manage a few pounds if it would help – by way of a wedding gift.'

63

She shook her head.

'Oh don't be silly, Joan, money's only money. Don't be like Mother and forever worrying about it.'

She realised that this was the longest conversation she'd had with her godlike brother for many years, since she was much younger and he the apple of his adoring mother's eye, and wondered what had brought it on.

'A gift's a gift,' she heard herself say, 'that's what Dad always said.' To her confusion her eyes filled. Guy turned her gently to face him.

'Handkerchief?' he offered. She grabbed it, much embarrassed.

'Blow,' he advised. 'Poor Dad. I can't find out much about that. Sorry. You were always closest to him. And of course he may as well be in the sea for all Mother knows. He ratted on her when he left and ratted on her again when he died. Twice betrayed and forever disappointed, that's my mother. Still, each to his own, eh? Don't forget, I'm always good for a few pounds.'

Mr Hinde had hailed a taxi, they were leaving. Joan caught his arm.

'Are you all right?' she asked, putting every inference she couldn't frame into the innocuous words.

Guy patted her hand, oddly paternal. 'Yes thank you, sister mine. Where the gold grows, there stay I.' And he was gone. Joan walked alone to the station.

She did not discuss all this with Paul. Men did what they had to do, and since keeping the family flag flying was what was expected of sons, she would have been surprised to hear her own behaviour interpreted as more of the same. Guy was obviously another person who might be able to explain things to her but he was always preoccupied with his own life and, after all, they had never been close, though she rather wished they had been, were still, and then she could confide in him. But there wasn't anyone to confide in. Her mother made it clear that she wasn't really interested in a wedding which had been decided without the discussion and deference she felt were her due, so Joan took refuge in Mother Canning who sewed her dress and gave Paul money for them to have a few days in the Lake District with other friends from college before they all commenced work, a holiday which was also to serve as their honeymoon.

Paul got a job as a housemaster at a small school near his parents' home, but the wedding was to be in London. His father would come to London and so, knowing Paul's feelings on that score, his mother decided she must stay away and Joan's mother declined to attend. 'I'm so busy and anyway, you don't need me there to hold your hand,' she said. And Joan was surprised at herself for feeling more relieved than hurt. In spite of this, or maybe because of it, she wanted to fulfil all the wedding traditions – 'something old, something new/something borrowed, something blue' – so to this end, her dress was new and blue, she borrowed a fine handkerchief from Maisie Dunlop and old was her handbag, the only good-quality one she'd ever owned, lovingly polished for the occasion. And for the same superstitious reasons she wanted to spend the last night of her single life in her old home. Her mother agreed with a shrug and made up a bed for Paul in Guy's old room.

That night they sat up late, talking, long after her mother had gone to bed. There was a small cottage in the grounds to begin in and they'd collected a few things together. They talked about clothes for the holiday.

'I hope the family won't be grand,' said Joan.

'They may be but we won't be,' said Paul.

'I had to buy some shoes, you can't go walking in thin things with the soles through, but if they dress for dinner – '

'You'll put your brogues under your best dress and let them know which is most important,' Paul finished for her, his brow furrowed in mocking imitation of her own. She swiped at him playfully with a cushion and he pulled her to him.

'I thought we'd go and see my folks when we come back, just to show we did it all properly,' he said above her head.

She lay against his shoulder, looking at the fire.

'That would be nice,' she agreed. 'My brother was quite forthcoming, kissed my cheek and wished me well. He even offered us some money if we were short. But I thought not. I wasn't sure whether it was a gift or a loan but I thought I didn't want to start off like Mother, ever under Guy's protection, even if it was well intentioned.'

'I'm glad you didn't take it,' he said. 'We can manage without that.'

'I thought so.' She nodded. 'So now it's all settled except – what do we do?' She sat up and looked at him. He was puzzled. 'I mean, do after we're married.' He could see that she was serious. 'You see, I've never gone in for that sort of thing and I don't want to be a nuisance on the night.' She thought she might be blushing but hoped he wouldn't notice in the fire's glow.

'You mean intercourse?'

She nodded firmly.

'Well, it begins like this,' he said, reaching for her again with a smile, first to kiss and then to stroke her. He explored the back of her neck, the tops of her shoulders and, lowering his hands, rested them against her breasts. Their eyes met.

'I can't – ' she began. 'I'll just put the light off.'

When she came back to the sofa beside him, he continued to caress her. His stroking was quite different from Robert's, quite different from anybody else's really, much more decided. He moved her back on the sofa and put her hand between his legs. 'That's an erection,' he said. 'Your breasts rise up and heat and your vagina opens. My penis becomes hard. I put my penis inside your vagina and we make love.'

She began to laugh, partly from nervousness and partly because he sounded so grave, but he silenced her with kisses.

'You know what you're doing,' she said. It was more of a statement than a question.

'It's to be hoped so,' he said, his eyes twinkling again.

She screwed up her courage to say the next bit.

'And there won't be any mistakes?'

'You mean babies?' She nodded. He shook his head.

'Don't you have to do something to make sure?'

'No,' he said kindly. 'Not the first time. Every other time, but not the first time.'

'Oh.' And he began to kiss her again. He found the way into her, moved upon her, kissed her some more and time passed. She stroked his head and enjoyed his hands upon her, felt troubled, but massaged and soothed at the same time. He moved faster, gasped and was still. It could be nice, she decided, once she was used to it. Very nice. But she couldn't see what the fuss was about except for the babies. Paul leaned back from her, tidying himself unobtrusively.

'So?' he said with a smile. 'Do you think you'll be able to live with that?'

'Yes,' she told him, looking into his eyes. He was big and strong and reliable. He didn't seem to wish to go away, hadn't for two years, and it was a small price to pay.

8 *Mercer*

I am small, very young, curled up in my bed. At least, it isn't my bed, it's the bed Lindsay sleeps in when she's at home and I like to sleep in it after she's gone, before the sheets are changed, because it smells friendly like woodsmoke. I have my hands between my legs and I am massaging myself into the sweet nod-out which always eventually comes. It sends me to sleep. I have done it ever since I can remember.

The covers are pulled back and Joan says, 'Come on, darling. You're always doing that. Leave yourself alone now, and let's get you to sleep.' But before she says that, I see her face, which unlike her voice is neither gentle nor reasonable. Her face is fierce with something I don't understand.

When I recreate that memory, many years later, what I see on my mother's face is envy, longing. How can it be so easy for her, asks her face, when it wasn't/isn't for me? I'm not sure of the tense of the expression but I am sure of how it looked.

I don't think I would have thought about my mother so hard if I hadn't wanted to understand myself and I only wanted to do that when life became good and I got lucky and I didn't want the bad times any more. Not that the bad times were always that bad, you understand, but rather they just didn't lead anywhere, though many of them were all right while they were going on. I don't know where I wanted them to go, though of course I thought I did at the time. I did want to be loved, most terribly, to the point that I began to think it was more than being loved which I wanted, rather an unconditional love which is rarely available.

If you're lucky, your mother loves you unconditionally. I think Joan did, but most mothers only love you like that for a certain period, whilst you're at a certain age, and what I couldn't come to terms with was finding the love had changed. I should have expected it, reasonably speaking; I did accept it but I went on looking for that unconditional love from somebody else and being disappointed over and over again because I never found it. Isn't that what other women, older women, call setting your sights too high, so that no matter what rich and wonderful emotional wares a man offers you, it's not what you're looking for – because what you're looking for doesn't exist?

When I wanted to be an actress, Joan encouraged me. She took me to see plays and films and discussed the texts with me. My father did that, too, though I don't think he knew he was feeding my desire to perform. But the performing meant something else, too, which I only came to realise when it was over. It meant a chance to be the centre of attention, to give out and be good at something. I used to dance and sing and act, mimic voices and tell stories. I drew and wrote as well but what I wanted was stardom. I wanted my name on the marquee because if it was there big enough then surely there must be enough love to go round. Thinking about it was one thing, realising it was another. When I read about so-and-so who starved in a garret to pay for her acting lessons, I had no knowledge of starvation or garrets. It became another set in my head, another costume call, another script to learn. I had no more realistic idea of becoming an actress than Joan had had before me, but I dreamed less rosily.

When I was fifteen and helping backstage in the theatre, there was a man who directed an occasional production. He wasn't a director proper but he had some talent and the occasional opportunity to exercise it with some filler, and apart from that, he was over thirty, had money and a car. Talking to him made my hands nervous. I couldn't look at him and I couldn't not look at him. And one night he drove me home, parked the car under some trees and kissed me violently. And I felt the invisible string which drew close my thighs and belly and everything in between open like a sea anemone, the labia both petals and antennae.

He kissed me very thoroughly. I don't remember feeling like a pupil, more that I'd been waiting for this, and then he sat back in the darkness of the car and felt in his pocket for a cigarette. After a minute or two he put out his hand to touch my face and I rubbed against it like a cat. He drove me home. And I thought about his face and imagined him touching my breasts and came with even more honeyed satisfaction than usual.

He did not discuss how he was going to proceed and he did not touch me when anyone else was around. Was I a teenage seductress? Strictly limited to eyelashes and repartee, because I didn't touch him first. But a couple of times a week, he drove me home. Sometimes we detoured to look at a beauty spot on the way where we could get out of the car. He would hold me against him and I would bury my nose in his neck and feel his friendly erection pushing through his trousers and lean my meagre breasts into his hands. Did he want to make love to me? I didn't ask. He said he did. What stopped him? He was careful, Alexander, very careful. I was under age and he wanted it to be right. Perhaps he wanted it to be right more than I did, perhaps he was more careful than romantic, but I was content to be led. And I loved the caresses, the kissing, the stroking and excitement.

I don't know what he told Joan but he never hid from her. He must have convinced her that he would behave because twice he was allowed to take me to the nearest city to the theatre, driving fifty miles each way, taking me out to dinner and home to his house before home to mine, and still he regarded me as something he'd like but not yet. Maybe he got as much or more out of the anticipation than he would have from taking me to bed.

When I went away into repertory, he made light of it. I was still young, just over sixteen, and he knew I'd be back to see my parents. But I did not come back. I went to secretarial school in London, in between engagements as I thought, and it was a year or so before I came back to the town where my parents lived.

When I returned I made friends immediately with a young reporter who was tall and plain but who wanted me with terrible urgency and clarity, a great relief after a year of wanting to do it but not wanting to make the first move in case it was the wrong one. And I could never tell with actors. I'd got fond of a boy in the theatre company until he told me gently one night that he was awfully sorry but he was more interested in the barman and I felt a fool. Hugh the reporter lived in a miserable little flat with a surprisingly large clean bed in it. I don't remember how we met but I can still see myself lying back on the carpet, still tasting instant coffee as he kissed me.

He began to undo buttons and I protested that it was only afternoon, at which he grinned with sudden vivacity and reminded me that there's no rule to say you only make love in the dark. And he was wonderful. He was like finishing the jigsaw and winning the prize.

So we had a very simple relationship which involved minimal exchange of views and maximum exchange of body fluids. I walked in and we embraced and removed each other's clothes. He thought it was stunning and I thought it was something which, if I practised, I might be good at, although I knew it wouldn't get me anywhere with him but where we were. It came to an end suddenly when he took a new job at the other end of the country. He hadn't told me he was applying for it, though I wasn't surprised. He hadn't asked me what I was doing at home if I was supposed to be an actress. He didn't ask me to go with him and I didn't ask why not but I went from what I thought of as the real thing back to fantasy land and found it a bit like going on a diet.

Joan looked at me wisely one day and asked if I were missing Hugh. I tried to answer both lightly and carefully, wondering how much she knew, making some mumble which could be interpreted either way, without direct answer.

A couple of days later, she asked me what I was going to do and I pointed out that I wasn't going to get anywhere unless I went up to London so I thought I'd go and start looking. I'd been on the telephone and arranged to stay with friends, I'd checked into a temporary secretarial agency to keep body and soul together. She asked if I had heard from Hugh. I said I had not. 'I thought you were quite – involved' she said. I said we hadn't actually talked about what the score was. 'I mean, he hadn't made me any promises or anything – it was just that – ' and I stopped. She looked at me, her eyes wise, her mouth tight.

'It's very easy to get used to it,' she said. And I blushed.

I promised myself after that that I would not be used to it, would not just do it, but I liked it. I was good at it. I had no hobbies and it was the only reliable talent I had. I did go back to London and got some bits and pieces of work, mostly with a fringe group with whom I performed for quite long periods of time in between stints in offices to pay for the rent and the tuition I thought I should have. But I was quite haphazard about everything to do with the fur- therance of acting. Now I think that I liked the idea of acting but not the reality of trying to make it happen. I didn't go to the places where other actors met, I never found a worthwhile agent – they all wanted to explore my other talent – and I hated having my picture taken.

So somewhere in there I fell into the habit of not making a commitment to anything at all. I wasn't committed to acting because I was worried about money. I wasn't committed to any one man because he might expect more from me than I felt I wanted to give. I wasn't committed to being a secretary because I still dreamed of being a star. And I wasn't committed to that, I came to realise, because it involved disciplines and sacrifices which may seem very small in the human scale of things but which nevertheless indicate that the progenitor is serious in his/her endeavour. I was never serious about anything at this stage, except myself and not getting cornered.

Joan watched this manoeuvring carefully. Having sought her route through a man, she was fascinated to observe me trying to find my own way towards something she too had wanted. I continued to drift like this for some years. At intervals I would talk about acting or singing or movement or speech. I took classes, evening courses, in all of them. Or I would speak with equal enthusiasm – in preparation perhaps for another role? – about work, the office I was in and the people I shared it with. During all of this time I did not confide that I was writing but wrote songs, poems, essays, drafts and a whole novel which I tore up one New Year's Eve, drinking ginger ale and a miniature of brandy. And then I got pregnant.

I don't know who the father was. I had been having a rather comradely affair with an advertising copywriter who was trying to write a play. We went to pubs together and occasionally to dinner or parties. Going home to bed together was a polite thing to do, like saying thank you for dinner. Though I didn't go to bed with him solely out of gratitude but more because to have refused would have disturbed the otherwise comfortable shape of the evening. I didn't have to, I wanted to. I preferred being with somebody, not quite anybody, and the occasional awkwardness of maintaining both proximity and distance seemed inexpensive compared with being alone.

But I did meet somebody else, a Russian ballet dancer whose wife had left him. She too was in the ballet, quite well known and probably the better dancer, but I was touched by his predicament and found the idea of a Russian ballet dancer appealing. So I let him take me easily from the chair to the bed and stay the night and forget the Pill. When the period was missed, I had no contact with the dancer (though I do remember his name) and the copywriter was touchingly concerned. I tried to ignore it but almost immediately I began to feel queasy and my waist to thicken so I asked the questions not unfamiliar in my circle about who and where and how much.

In my mind at the time, I did not so much kill a child as submit to a procedure which cut away the badness in me. It was physically lowering, not so much painful as uncomfortable, but emotionally it cleared the decks. Nothing I had been doing had any more meaning for me and as I sat in my bedsitter waiting to feel better, I began to write. Writing things down in order to feel better is a fairly primitive form of therapy and writing things down in order to send them to somebody else and get rid of them is hardly original, but for once I had nothing else to think about and so I thought with ferocious clarity. And it seemed to me quite awful that having an abortion or an unwanted child was the same for a woman as having a woman is for a man. So many women only stop being girls and begin to grow up through pain. I can't talk about it too much now, it makes me cry. But it seemed that the men I had tried to be with, all that experience to which I had been exposed, did not serve to get me past the mental age of about twelve. Only death does it for so many of us. And it's not even a death, it's a killing.

Not only did I write it all down but my timing was right. I sent it to the right agent at the right time and it was bought, mounted and put on at a prestigious theatre to which my mother and father came one night and I lied, saying it was what had happened to a friend which started me thinking about it. Joan accepted all that but she was hurt that I had never told her about my writing. For years, she had only to show the slightest interest and I told her anything she wanted to know but now I felt I could not, should not, must not because it would lead me into explanations I knew I could not offer for fear they'd disturb the new-found central mystery of my life. I do not know if I wanted to punish her because she so willingly accepted my version of how the play came to be and so made it impossible for me to confess the awful thing I had done and feel better. But I do know that I felt more careful about writing than I felt about anything that so far had been a part of my life and I could not give that up, even for my mother's approbation.

9 *Joan*

Nobody took a picture of my parents on their wedding day. I knew that they married at Christmas, in a church near the college, which Paul had managed to arrange by persuading Joan to attend morning service with him as often as he could, as well as coaching the boys' club football team.

'Why aren't there any pictures?' I demanded one Saturday morning, surrounded once again by snapshots of time past, in and out of folders, through which I loved to look.

Joan shrugged uninterestedly. 'I suppose nobody had a camera,' she said.

'But what did you wear?'

'Brown shoes, beige coat, blue dress. Very refined.'

'What did it look like?' She straightened up.

'The dress was wool georgette with a round neck – ' she indicated – 'and long sleeves. A bit baggy, that's how we wore them at the time.'

'When?'

'Christmas Eve, 1921.'

'Was it nice?'

'I suppose it was. It was a long time ago.'

'Was there snow?'

She shook her head, smiling. 'No. There was fog and frost and it was freezing. I never took my coat off.'

'Tell me about the coat.'

73

'One of the girls along the corridor at college lent it to me. It was a good one, with a big fur collar, a lovely thing. And I had new shoes and silk stockings and a hat, down over my eyes of course, with cockades at the side.'

I asked what cockades were. She tried to describe them but I didn't understand. 'I've still got them upstairs somewhere. I'll show them to you later.'

But when she did, I was disappointed by the quasi-military look of them and thought how odd they must have looked attached to the side of her hat. And I didn't like to ask what colour that was because the cockades themselves were black and red. I couldn't think that they 'went' with anything and I thought that it was very important that things matched or contrasted. A near miss just wasn't good enough, even if the shoes were very dark brown so's you could get away with the black, and the red was supposed to lend a spot of colour.

I asked about flowers. She said she thought she had some.

'I've never been to a wedding,' I said thoughtfully. She was on her way back downstairs by now, to do the next thing.

'Neither had I,' she said.

All she knew was that the interior of the little church looked much as it always did except for some boughs of holly arranged in a copper jug on a table near the door. There were no special flowers, the fog shut out the pale light, already fading fast in the late afternoon. And it was cold. Joan shivered in the borrowed coat, squared her shoulders and clasped her hands more firmly together. Then Paul arrived with the ring and they went in to meet the vicar, a little man with a voice usually as dry as autumn leaves, now moistened and made husky by a heavy cold. Katherine came with her cousin Wilfred, whom Joan had met at Paul's home a couple of times. He was nice enough, if shy. Cecily arrived with Guy. This was unexpected and Joan blushed with pleasure. When the service began, she felt uncomfortably like an unprepared student caught in a demanding oral exam. It was very important not to rush, not to pause, to stand still and promise. The insides of her legs felt cold. Paul's hand, brushing the back of hers, felt warm. '... man and wife,' she heard. And Paul's dark face filled her vision as he kissed her. When he stood back, she looked up briefly into the darkness of the high roof, at the faces round them, and as she thanked the vicar, saw Guy whispering to Paul, who nodded gravely.

A car loomed up, summoned by Guy's proprietorial wave, and he shepherded them all into it.

'Mother's for a sherry and then out for a meal, all right?'

Joan looked at Paul, who nodded. 'Most kind,' said Katherine gravely, the personification of the groom's family. 'Good old Guy!' said Cecily, hugging his arm and rallying them all with what the family called her 'social' voice.

Joan's mother was waiting in her best blouse to pour the sherry. And as they went in and Joan submitted to her formally brief kiss, she realised that she no longer saw her as the most important person in every group. She was just a woman who might have been pretty had she not been so discontent, in a fine grey silk blouse which echoed the colour of her hair. Today she was happier than usual because Guy was there without Bingham Hinde. Joan went to take off her hat but Paul stopped her.

'Leave it, I like it,' he said and Joan thought afterwards that maybe it was the hat which boosted her confidence in dealing with her mother, that and the knowledge that she'd never have to share a house with her again.

Guy marshalled them out before the atmosphere had time to flag from silly jokes and pleasantries, leaving her mother waving, and drove them all to a road house for what he called 'something nourishing'. He insisted on champagne so that Wilfred could toast the bride and Guy the groom. Katherine and Wilfred came to see Joan and Paul off to their walking holiday in the Lake District, while Guy drove Cecily home.

As Katherine and Wilfred faded into the steam and fog at Euston, Joan was almost afraid to remove her hat. But she did so, and examined the nature of her feelings. Was it, she asked herself, the hat or the champagne or the two of them together? Was it Guy appearing out of nowhere like that and being so sweet? Was this how people felt when they got married? She smiled and thought that if that was so, she could see a reason for it. Paul took her hand and asked her how she felt.

'Fine.' A draught hit her knees, not much protected by silk stockings, and she shivered. He drew her closer.

'It went off quite well, didn't it?' he said. 'Though I'm sorry my mother wasn't there.'

She looked at him. 'I'm not sorry my mother wasn't there.' He patted her hand comfortingly. She wanted to go on and he didn't indicate that she should not. 'The only one of us she really loves is

Guy – and she doesn't approve of him.'

'But it wasn't a bad business, was it?' he asked.

'No.' She shook her head. 'Better than I expected, to tell the truth.'

He patted his pocket for the inevitable cigarette and disengaged himself briefly to light it, then settled himself back to hold her with one hand and smoke with the other.

'I'm glad it was in a church,' he remarked. She wanted to know why.

'I always liked the church at home and if we couldn't be married there, I'm glad we found another one.'

'What did you like about it?'

He thought for a minute. 'It's very old, built near where Augustine landed, and it has a certain peace about it. I sang in the choir, of course, and the organ was a hand-pump job so we had to take it in turns to work the bellows.' His eyes began to twinkle. 'What we discovered was that if you pumped like hell and then took a breather, the organ would wind down, sounding more like the drone on bagpipes, and the organist would be embarrassed. So we used to try and get it just right. Pump like mad, let it run down but catch it and begin to pump again, just as it began to fade.'

She smiled.

'And you could spit from the organ loft and see whose head you could hit.' She wrinkled her nose. 'And then get out of there and into your place in the choir like lightning so you couldn't be blamed for it.'

'Did you like singing?'

'I liked doing it and I liked how it sounded. I just didn't understand a lot of what we sang. I remember I once asked my father what "wooden stone" was and when he found out the line was "wood and stone", he was furious and lectured me about not being able to worship unless you understood what you were saying.'

'But did you want to worship?' she asked.

'Not particularly. I wanted to get out of the house.'

'Is that why you joined the army?'

'I suppose partly, yes.' He stretched his legs before him. 'I must have wanted something pretty badly because joining up was nothing like I'd imagined. My mother was crushed, my father tight-lipped. The camp was cold and we drilled in blue canvas slops, like prison overalls, with walking sticks. There were no uniforms and no weapons.'

76

'Were you frightened?'

'No time to be. They worked us pretty hard trying to get us into shape. And then they took us down to Chatham to board the troop ship. First thing issued was two sodden blankets. Last thing my mother said to me was "don't get your feet wet". I was seasick almost as soon as we began to move and when the weather worsened crossing the Bay of Biscay, I thought I'd die. Eventually I crawled up and was greeted by an enormous seaman, much bigger than me, who watched me as I clung to the rail and brought me thick ship's cocoa and seaman's biscuits. When I smelled it, I retched, but thank God, it stayed down. I'll never forget him. He had hands – ' he regarded his own briefly, the first two fingers of the right curved and stained from holding cigarettes – 'twice the size of mine.'

Twice as big as Paul's big hands and I could creep inside and be safe forever, thought Joan, surprised to find that he had warmed her like a dog and that she felt sleepy.

'Where did you dock?' she asked. She wasn't being polite, she was interested, Paul was always interesting, but it was warm and she was tired and his voice, at once deep and ironic, was very soothing.

'Calcutta. And moved supplies up the line by mule train.'

The cold countryside slid past the darkened windows, he talked, she asked and punctuated as she could until they arrived, to be greeted enthusiastically by the friends they were staying with, who loaded their bags into the car. Paul exclaimed at their kindness. The bed was more than kind, it was caressing, and as she climbed in, Joan yawned. When Paul returned from the bathroom she was asleep.

When she awoke the next morning, she was alone. Teeth brushed and glowing all over from a brisk wash in a cold bathroom, she pulled on a thick sweater, tweed skirt and the sensible shoes Paul had ribbed her about. Their friends' mother told her that Paul had gone riding. Burying her nose in a welcome cup of tea, Joan reflected. I went to sleep and he went riding. And it's Christmas Day. 'Oh,' she gasped. 'H-happy Christmas!'

Her hostess smiled broadly.

'The season's not supposed to be the foremost thing on your minds at the moment, dear. Anyway, I expect we'll muster for a late lunch. Now do have another cup of tea, it's no trouble, and fresh toast is on the way.'

That night, warm with food and wine and laughter and silly games, when everybody including the cat had been kissed under the mistletoe, Joan tugged Paul's hand. 'Shall we go up?' she whispered. The first walk was organised for the next day. They'd have breakfast and make sandwiches. Goodnight, goodnight.

They walked up the stairs.

'You go first in the bathroom,' said Joan. 'You take ages.'

Paul was back in five minutes, smiling smugly, and slithered into bed. It was true that no matter how friendly the downstairs, the upper passages of the house were not to linger in. Joan rushed back, tripped on her dressing gown and fell against the bed. She was drawn in unceremoniously with great speed, the light switched out, kissed with some enthusiasm and entered. She had been looking forward to it. Perhaps it was not being in her mother's house, perhaps it was the bed or the wine, but it was definitely different from the first time. It hurt a bit and Paul moved much more, but before she had time to examine her sensations, he stopped. She heard the crackle of paper in the darkness, then a small scuffling sound while Paul supported himself above her and then tried to push back into her again. It was more difficult but they managed it, the movement began to flow again until suddenly he exclaimed into the pillow, lay as if caught for a moment and then relaxed. She stroked his shoulder and wondered if she ought to be doing something. And what was that noise? He was very still and heavy, with most of the bedclothes wrapped underneath him. Perhaps she'd hurt him? Should she ask? Funny to think of how easy it was to ask him things when she'd found it so difficult to talk to her mother. Paul moved gently away, murmuring goodnight, and they both slept.

For the next few days they tramped through the countryside, sustained by large packets of sandwiches and much banter. Then it was time to start work. The school was called Brivett House, a long, low building, functional rather than elegant, undistinguished except for the agreeable colour of its weathered brick, and set in its own grounds. Paul was to teach games, gymnastics and English – this last the subject of their respective matriculations, though there wasn't a job for Joan initially. And far from wanting one, she was quite delighted to be concentrating on being Paul's wife. Besides the headmaster's house, which had been built on grounds purchased for the school when the main house was acquired for that purpose, there were four cottages in the adjacent lane. The smallest of these was allotted to them, it being explained that housemasters

78

and their families had apartments in the main block while those teaching throughout the school had the separate accommodations. They had two bedrooms, though one was so tiny it rapidly became the room where anything not in immediate use was housed, a main room on the ground floor with a tiny kitchen and bathroom at the back.

They were expected to eat most of their meals at the masters' table in the main hall, though this was not rigidly required in the first few days while they settled in. Joan meant to apply all her skills and taste to those rooms. She was used to not having money, to having to make do with what furniture there was, but she felt sure she ought to be able to make it into an attractive place for Paul to spend time with her in the evenings.

She had just changed the position of the two chairs in the little living room for the third time when the headmaster's wife called. She was not at all what Joan expected, being tall, forthright and friendly, so friendly that Joan found her initial bashfulness almost immediately eased. And the warmth of this impression was further enhanced by a brief conversation with the headmaster when they went to the school hall for supper that evening.

'Think you'll like it here?' asked Robert Bower. He'd met her once before when they first arrived but as yet had had no time to form an opinion. Newlyweds in his experience were usually absorbed in each other but Canning seemed a level-headed sort of young chap and his little wife was pretty and rather quiet. Joan said she thought so.

'A bit far from everything, if you like the bright lights, but the sea is just down the road and the air here is wonderful and we've a nice bunch of people – ' he indicated his staff with a wave. Joan agreed. 'I hear my wife made her call this afternoon? You must let us know if there's anything we can do to make you more comfortable.' And they went in to supper.

For three years at Brivett House, Joan lived in a rather pleasant limbo. It was almost as if she had been excused from having to work. Although the school was on the borders of West Sussex and Hampshire, and so theoretically within reach of Paul's home, the journey involved either a car or two train journeys – one into London and another out again to the Kent coast. But they had neither a car nor access to one and although they weren't in want, there wasn't cash to spare for train fares very often. So Paul put distance between himself and his father, whilst writing to his mother, and Joan wrote cards, mostly to her older or younger sisters. Friends came to visit them from time to time and they lived in the world of the school. Paul had told her from the beginning that this was a very good start to his teaching career and, trusted with his confidence to make what tactful contribution she could without treading on the toes of housemasters' wives, Joan fitted in well. The Bowers came to approve of the Cannings.

Freed from the grind of classes, unable to get away from the feeling that she was playing house, she discovered how much she liked to walk in the country and be by herself. It was true that lovemaking remained perfunctory rather than idyllic but she bathed in the reflected glow of Paul's popularity and drifted along, admired by the senior boys, happy in her surroundings. She did not know how long she would have been content, but the next stage came as a shock.

She knew the school would be bigger. It was not only bigger but further north, in what was like another country. She knew that the commensurate demand upon Paul would be greater and that he saw the training and coaching and organising he did as what he should do if he didn't want to remain a teacher. She knew all that. What she did not know was what that involved. For an increasing proportion of their lives, Paul was absent, and worse, if he wasn't absent he was careful to keep her at arm's length.

'You can't,' he explained, 'do everything and play sport to this standard.' 'Everything' didn't mean food. He had always been a modest eater in spite of his great size. It didn't mean drink. He drank in celebration or defeat equally deeply though as an ordinary social drinker, he was circumspect. 'Everything', she discovered, meant that he was alone with her less than he'd ever been, that he expected her to socialise with him, reflecting in her good sportsmanship what a good sport he was, and he expected that he would not have to excuse or explain himself when he declined to do more than hold her hand the night before an important sporting event.

At first she went along with it. She supposed it would have to be. Whenever she appeared in the homes and schools of Hennington or the towns surrounding, she was always being told how wonderful he was, how he brought new life to this or that, rearranged so-and-so and now it was a winner. But she became tired of being his mirror. He was still kind and affectionate but she found the chaste kisses more reminiscent of courtship than marriage. It wasn't that anything wonderful happened in bed but the act suggested a focussing of attention. Without it she wasn't sure how much he noticed her.

She became restless and angry, irritable with everything. Paul asked her if she was feeling all right.

'Oh yes,' she said sourly. 'I feel all right, I feel fine. How kind of you to enquire. In between matches, are we? Isn't there a fixture on Saturday?'

He shrugged his big shoulders carefully.

'It seems to me I have to put the work in now,' he said, 'if I'm going to do anything with it from an administrative point of view.'

'I'm sure you do,' said Joan, 'but do you have to be doing something every night? And does whatever you're doing that happens every night have to be more important than us?'

'It's not more important than us,' said Paul, watching her.

'Well, it certainly feels as if it is. It's you and one team of boys or another, with me put to one side.'

He looked down at her. 'I don't mean you to feel pushed aside,' he said uncomfortably 'but you don't always want to stand in the cold and watch either. What do you want, darling?'

Joan moved away from him and began to straighten cushions and pile things up. 'I don't know, I don't know.' Why didn't anybody ever tell you how embarrassing all this was? Shouldn't he know what was wrong? Why should she have to spell it out for him?

'Are you ready – would you like to start a baby?'

'No, thank you' said Joan. 'I've told you before, I'm not keen on that just yet. And anyway, I don't see much chance of it at the present moment.'

He went on looking at her and she went on spitting out words.

'I mean, don't we have to do something in order to get pregnant? Something we don't do an awful lot at the moment because sometimes you're too tired and sometimes you're training and sometimes too you probably think I might not like it. But I would, Paul, I would. I'd like a little more attention from you.'

'You'll get it' he said gravely.

She went with him to the rugby club dance because she always did, and he said it would be a very nice one and it was. It was rather boozy but there was a great deal of laughter and dancing. Quite late in the evening, she went into the powder room and stopped dead. Checking her appearance with the solemnity of the very drunk was a pretty woman, stark naked.

'Are you all right?' asked Joan, not knowing quite what to do.

' 'Course.' She smiled at Joan. 'I'm with John Riker and he bet me that I was too drunk to undress and dress again without help, so you'd really be a dear if you could just sit there and act as a witness. O K?' And she bent unsteadily but firmly to a pile of slippery garments on the floor. A bit bewildered, Joan sat down and watched the prettily curved white body being stuffed into suspenders, stockings and very decorative underwear.

'I'm Ann Shand, by the way. Who're you?'

'Joan Canning.'

The dark wavy head bent over the dress fastening looked up.

'Hello, Joan Canning,' she said into the mirror. 'Canning? Isn't that the name of the big new boy on the team?'

Joan nodded.

'Very nice, too. You must come and meet John, though we're only calling him John tonight because we're both pie-eyed. Usually he's Jack.'

She looked at herself in the glass, grimaced at the circles under her hazel eyes and powdered her nose very carefully. In spite of herself, Joan said, 'Very good. Except for the earrings.'

Ann Shand picked them up and said, 'Will you do 'em for me?'

Joan thought that was cheating but the dark girl's charm, like her scent, was pretty convincing. 'And who but you,' she smiled invitingly, 'will ever know?' Joan fastened the earrings.

They left the powder room together. Ann held her arm quite firmly, pushing happily through the crowd and waving at a tall figure in the corner.

'Treasure trove, Jackie boy, treasure trove! Look who I found in the most unexpected place? John Riker, Joan Canning. Shall we have a drink? John, could you – '

John was still staring at Joan. 'Where did you say you found her?' Joan was staring, too.

'Hello,' said John and put out his hand.

'Hello,' said Joan, and shook it.

'Drinks,' said Ann.

'I'll get them,' said John.

'There's a sweetie,' said Ann, hitching herself into a chair. 'John's such a nice man.'

'Is he your husband?' asked Joan.

'No. I'm married to a fellow called Bernie Wootton but he just won't come out to play. I've known Jack since I was four or five, he's like a sort of brother.'

'He's very – attractive.' Joan looked in the direction in which he'd gone.

'Mmm. How long have you been here?' asked Ann.

Jack reappeared with three drinks and the evening blurred. She saw Paul drinking and laughing so she did the same, to be driven home hours later, singing and laughing with everybody else, and dropped off at the small house they'd rented to which she felt no attachment whatsoever. She wandered in and fell asleep on the sofa.

The next morning she woke up under a blanket Paul must have put over her to the sound of knocking at the door. Drowsy, her hair on end, she answered the door to her neighbour, who looked a bit taken aback but said there was a message from school, that she should meet a Mrs Wootton at the Blue Bird Hotel for lunch. There was a number if there was any difficulty, and she proffered a piece of paper. Joan thanked her and shut the door. Her first thought was what shall I wear? That made her smile wryly. She hadn't anything smart enough for Ann or the Blue Bird. Oh well, she could at least be clean, and she went upstairs, wondering what it was all about. It did not occur to her not to go.

10 *Mercer*

Often the world seems like a giant puffball mushroom, sealed against me, and I can gain entry if I can just find the little tag which leads to the dotted line which magically begins to unzip the mushroom. I know it's not the most elegant image. I could have called it a maze or a puzzle but to define a maze or a puzzle you have to be able to see it and very often I felt that I saw nothing. That is, I saw the teapot and the kettle and the tap to draw the water but I could not see how the structures everybody worked through worked. Worse, I could not see how they had come into being or were made. The mushroom is solid but light, filling but bland, and you can't do anything with it until you have peeled it. Mine is not a magic mushroom. It doesn't transform itself from or into anything. It is just a sealed world I scrabble around at the foot of, occasionally going for walks round the perimeter and looking for an unlocked gate which will at least take me into the outer courts. From there, I sometimes stray into a garden or on to a lawn. Other people may be there and for a few moments I stop feeling locked out.

You only have three ways to go when you experience exclusion as tangibly as I do. You can ignore the whole thing and build your own world. You can try harder to find ways in but you'll wind up rubbing your hands until they bleed against the bare brick of the outer garden wall. There is no hidden spring which will make them open and lead you further inside. They need a password and you

84

don't know it. Or you can bide your time and wait for the occasional invitations which thoughtfully and unfailingly include a key. Building your own world or waiting to be summoned to the other requires enormous strength, emotional musculature. Maybe that's why I like elephants. Sometimes I should like to feel that when I put my forehead against the section of the wall I'm trying to crack, it would move and give way, scattering the immovable bricks as if they were gravel. It's easy to see why people like animals, even love them and prefer them to human kind. Animals have simpler rules to live by than we do. To them an action is instinctively right or wrong. They either perform or refuse. With humans, it's the built-in and accepted levels of manipulation which are so tiring.

When I'd written that first piece, *The Cradle*, it did not occur to me that I might be in fashion or in favour, in or out. I was working. I appeared on television, made some radio broadcasts, spoke at a seminar or two. When you were working at something people see, these things were likely to happen. But I soon learned that you could not just 'do' them and that even if you did, whatever you did was open to interpretation. If I did not prepare, wore the clothes I'd been working in all day – this meant one thing. If I dressed up a bit, changed my hair, wore some make-up – that meant something else. It doesn't matter, I discovered, whether you're playing the game or not. *They* are playing the game with you. So I gave up. I did what I did and I said what I said and this led me to be further outside, because it seemed that I was not respectful of the game and the game was all to the many. I talked to Harry Dent at the theatre which put on my play. 'Keep writing,' he said. 'Fame is a bastard thing. It's like fog. It looks misty and dramatic when you're not in the middle of it but when it surrounds you, you cough like a bronchitic and find that your hands and face are smeared with something you never even knew you were walking through. You're very young, kid. Keep writing.' It didn't seem important that he had described me as famous, much more that he had acknowledged my difficulty and told me how to go about dealing with it. I went on writing.

I came up with something else and he introduced me to two other young writers he was mentor to, Linda Silva and Fin Quilty. He suggested the idea of a workshop to the three of us, put up subjects, tore our puny dramas to pieces with great humour and kept us alive on a bursary and endless cups of tea until we produced *Scenes from the Murder of a State* in his theatre club. The night we opened,

Linda was pacing about in the bar, muttering, and Fin was nowhere to be found. When the piece ended, there was a total silence and then enthusiastic applause. I looked at Linda and she at me.

'Where's Fin?' I asked her.

'Don't know. Sounds all right,' she said, jerking her head towards the source of the sound. 'Want a drink?'

'No thanks.'

I took the shortest way through the building and came full on into the first people leaving the club. I didn't wait to see if they recognised me, I ran. I ran round the corner of the building, ducked into the side door and asked for Harry. They said he was out front. Fin. I asked if I could use the house phone to Harry's office. Of course he didn't answer. I ran up the stairs. I waited ten minutes there, was just about to leave when he came in, grinning.

'Mercer! Good tidings. They liked it. Let's – '

'Harry, where's Fin?'

'I dunno. Isn't he with you?'

'No, Linda was up in the bar, I went to meet them but he isn't up there.'

'Well, all right, love – he's around somewhere, probably be by later on. You know, funny how first nights take you. Probably drunk under a table somewhere. Come on now, come and have a drink and let me boast about you – '

I shook my head. 'I'll see you later. Harry, look, thanks and I'll see you – I've just – I – '

He caught my arm. 'You think something's wrong with Fin?'

I looked at him and nodded.

'Wait a minute, I'll ring him at home and then there are a couple of bars we can try.'

His landlady found Fin, dead of alcoholic poisoning, on the floor of the landing between his flat and the bathroom. Naturally that got us a lot of publicity, until Linda and I began to feel like a pair of crows and to be embarrassed by the sight of each other. Harry played wise man and counsel very well but we couldn't get over it. Would we work together again, he asked us. Well, we could but we would rather not, we said. OK, he said, he'd have a think about it. He rang me a week later.

In his office he suggested an idea for a play, handing me typewritten notes on a couple of sheets of paper. When I looked bewildered, he whipped me in and said, 'Stop looking dumbstruck. Can you start thinking about that?' I said I could. 'Then have a go,' he said, putting his glasses back on his nose, his hands straying to some papers.

'Alone?' I asked.

'Certainly alone. Why not alone?' he said.

'What about Linda?'

He looked at me patiently.

'Forget that,' he said. 'We tried it, it worked once, I don't think it would work again. You did most of the guts of the last job, you know. Shame about Fin, nice boy, but he hadn't got it.'

'And Linda?'

'Why do you keep going on about Linda, Mercer? You're not in this business for Linda, are you? You're in it for you. Never mind about Linda.'

I began to do up my coat. 'No, I just thought that Linda might – that you might – '

'Mercer, Linda's out, you're in. OK? Plain enough?' He bent to his papers. I walked to the door. 'Let's speak next week. See how it's going.' I looked at him.

'What about the money?' I asked.

'Same as before,' he said, frowning. 'OK?'

'No,' I said.

'You expect me to raise it a little?' His eyes were cool and thoughtful.

'You were paying three. Now you're paying one. I expect you to raise it quite a bit.'

'Got representation, Mercer?'

'Yes' I said clearly. 'I have.'

'Then get somebody to call me.'

'Right,' I said. I called the office of the agency who had dealt with *The Cradle* and asked to speak to somebody about a new play. The answering voice asked lots of questions, cheered when I said I'd asked for more money and sounded more friendly than I had expected. She got the point. I had representation. She told me her name was Judith Chase. Now all I had to do was write.

When I was writing, the idea of the sealed world would not have occurred to me. Writing was like mining. The hours were long, the heat intense, I assumed odd positions to get at the seam. Every bit of me ached and when the shift was done, the only muscles still working were in my head. And they were only fluttering.

When I couldn't write, when it, the magic 'it', jammed, I comforted myself in the same way that I always had. But I hadn't quite the courage to walk out of the room and lie down on the bed in the other room, or at least not very often. It seemed a bit disrespectful, like sticking two fingers in the air at the effort of what I was doing. I did use the bed sometimes but most of the time, I checked that the door was locked, slithered down on the floor, put my hands between my legs and ran again the private films from my very limited collection of effective fantasies, climaxed, went to sleep for a few minutes, got up, washed my hands, made a cup of tea and went back to work.

Going to bed with somebody was something I occasionally contemplated, almost wistfully, because it hadn't happened for so long, but getting involved with anybody was strictly out of bounds. If I had a second bite at the apple all on my own, over poor Fin's dead body and across Linda Silva's disappointed face, then I wasn't going to risk a wasted day over anybody I could think of in the romantic department. My agent, Judith, says I was so switched off that I wouldn't have noticed a pass if it were made at me.

In a rare mood of wanting to explain myself to her and thus extend our relationship from a purely commercial one into something a little more personal, I said that I thought commitment to anything other than writing got in the way.

Judith adjusted her earrings, her hair and her cuffs and asked, 'And what did it get in the way of before you wrote?'

'Wanting to act.'

She looked at me carefully.

'How badly did you want to act?'

I had the grace to look a little less highly motivated.

'Not badly enough.'

Judith poured two glasses of white wine, remembered I don't like it, found she had no red and came up with orange juice.

'Strikes me,' she said, 'that any excuse is a good one for not making a commitment. What's so frightening about commitment?'

'It makes me feel trapped.'

'Ever thought about talking to anybody about it?'

'Why should I want to talk to anyone about it – it's not as if it's a problem.'

'Isn't it?' I looked at her. In spite of her silk shirt and superficial gloss, she didn't sound as if she was making small talk. The trouble is, I can never tell. I looked at her and said nothing. She went on sipping her wine and watching me.

'Judith,' I began.

'Jud,' she interrupted me. 'Rhymes with mud. Daddy wanted a son.' She shrugged. 'Call me Jud. Friends do.'

'Jud,' I said, thinking what's all that about friends? 'Look, if this is the thin end of the wedge and you're working up to telling me that I am exceedingly pale and beginning to walk with a curious lurch and people are talking – I think I'd rather have it straight. I'm writing. Harry's happy, you're happy, the deal is good. What's the problem?'

'Did you hear what you just said?' She had a low, clear voice, faintly inflected transatlantic. I put my glass down because annoyingly my hand was beginning to shake. 'Did you? You said, "I'm writing, Harry's happy, you're happy, and the deal's good." Aren't you supposed to be happy some of the time?'

I stood up and reached for my coat which was over the back of the next chair.

'Mercer, I'm not trying to be unkind, but you are very switched off. You have been ever since I've known you and it seems rather late in the day to be talking as if it were a good thing.'

'What do you suggest I do?'

'Well, becoming a bit more aware about it can't hurt. And take a break from yourself. Go to the country, have a week off, maybe see somebody – '

'Do you mean on a date or is that a euphemism for seeing a psychiatrist?'

She looked levelly at me. I couldn't have got this far if I hadn't sensed that she was trying to be kind.

'Yes, yes, I suppose it is.'

My back was sweating now. 'Jud, if there's something wrong with the work – has Harry said something because, honestly, I'd much rather know – '

'The work is fine. Harry is as happy as a clam. I'm worried about you.'

'Why? Why do you have to choose now to worry?'

'Because you're so cut off and getting more so. I used to think it was because of the abortion but now I'm not sure. I just think you'd be happier if you had a break from yourself – '

'You mean, as in go out and get laid?'

She sighed. 'No, Mercer, that's not what I mean. I've said what I mean.'

'Just one question, Judith.' Using her full name was deliberate.

'Why did you have to choose now to raise this?'

She shrugged. 'I don't see you that often, things aren't getting better, maybe even a little worse. I thought I must say that, as a friend, I'm worried.'

I was fastening my coat now, chewing my mouth.

'I appreciate your concern. I can't help but be aware that you'd be a whole lot more concerned if I stopped writing. Happy comes second, Judith, a long long way second. I have work to do and happy comes second.'

And I left.

But by then I'd met David who introduced me to what I thought my real life was going to be. So I dropped out of this third effort and into the marriage I thought I needed. And promptly ceased to write.

11 *Joan*

The Blue Bird Hotel was at Garslake, a bus ride away, and it did not occur to Joan what steps she had taken until she was on the way. She had bathed and tidied and put on her better clothes and left the house without even trying to get a message to Paul, to explain that she would be home late, or do more than make sure that there was food to eat. She had never done any of this before.

She pulled a mirror out of her handbag and pushed wisps of hair into place, whilst determinedly avoiding looking at herself. Paul would manage, she told herself, and she knew that however attracted she was to Ann Shand, it wasn't just that that made her run so fast to meet her.

Ann was in the bar, her dark face framed by a becoming felt hat, a silver fox cape over her expensive tweeds. The air around Joan seemed to grow cold for an instant before Ann's face lit up and she turned to the barman to order a drink for her guest and got up, hands extended.

'I thought you'd never get here!'

'Sorry.' Joan went a bit pink. 'I had to take the bus and walk through.'

'The bus? Oh Lord, how boring. I'm sorry, it never occurred to me. I just thought this would be a nice place for lunch. Sherry all right?'

Joan took it and they walked through to the dining room. The waitress left them to consider food, Ann suggested and Joan agreed, and it was all ordered before Joan realised with consternation that she probably wouldn't have enough money. She couldn't very well ask for the menu back and work out her bill so she looked at her hands.

Ann asked if she had enjoyed the dance the night before. Joan said that she had. 'Didn't we drive you home?' asked Ann. Joan said she thought so. The soup came.

Ann chattered on and stopped, realising that Joan hadn't touched her soup.

'What's the matter?'

'I haven't got enough money.'

Ann looked at her for a moment and then laughed. 'Just as well I have then, isn't it? Oh, do eat up, it'll be cold. Cold soup's miserable.'

Joan opened her mouth and Ann cut her short.

'Eat up, I said. I've got more money than sense, anyone'll tell you. Mind you, you shouldn't need telling, having found me in the lavatory, drunk as a fiddler's, trying to put my clothes back on for a bet.'

Joan said, 'But it won't ever be different. I haven't got it and you have.'

Ann sipped her drink and looked at her steadily.

'Joan, you may not yet have noticed it but this place is a hole. Not the hotel, not even Garslake, which is pretty enough, but the area. What makes it bearable is money. I have it, more than enough, and fortunately I have friends who are loaded too. We get it from our fathers or their fathers, not usually much further back, or our marriage partners who aren't so stupid that they don't know that's why we stay. One thing money can do is make living in a hole a lot more bearable but even then, you have to have people to enjoy it with you. I never lend, I only give, and I won't give if I don't want to.' She smiled dazzlingly at the waitress and, when the girl went away with their soup plates, continued. 'Everything all right with the Moving Mountain?'

'I'm sorry, I don't – ' Joan shook her head in bewilderment.

'Sorry, my nickname for your very presentable husband. You see, there's a real advantage in a presentable husband. It means at least you can put on a show from time to time. Are things all right at 'ome?'

'Yes. Yes, of course,' said Joan, feeling uncertain.

'That's part of the trouble with Bernie, Bernard to whom I'm married. Nice enough, kind, quite funny even, and frantically generous, but not what you'd call dazzling in company. Which is where Jack comes in.'

Their meal arrived. Joan thought of the white skin, the body she'd seen the night before. She shot a quick look at the face opposite, becomingly made up but not to conceal anything. Ann must be about the same age as herself, maybe a year or two older. But she was a lot more worldly wise.

Ann said nothing more until they were alone again. 'Do you understand?'

Joan said, 'I think so. You're telling me how your marriage works, checking to see if mine's the same and warning me that I should stay away from Jack.'

Ann raised her eyes to heaven. 'Oh, Lord, child, you sound like a vicar's daughter. I want to be friends, I'm always short of new friends and last night was a good start. You don't faint at the sight of nudity, you're pretty as paint and a little bird tells me that the Big Boy's here, there and everywhere but not at your side as much as you'd like. So you're sort of spoken for but spare, like me. You probably know what you will and won't do, that's fine, so do I. But there's no harm in a bit of fun while we're waiting, is there? We might do well together.' Involuntarily, Joan had begun to smile. 'Now don't laugh. It's just my way to talk a mile a minute. I thought you'd like a bit of background. As for Jack, he's free, white and well over twenty-one. He'll do what he does. What I'm saying is that you're a bit of a baby and I wouldn't want the responsibility of dealing you into to play too fast too soon. Hm?'

Through this speech, Joan discovered that it was impossible to be insulted by Ann. She talked like a gunfighter and smiled like a film star. She would make living a lot more entertaining. She knew who she was and where she was, she could drive, she had a talent for pleasure.

Joan smiled and relaxed. Ann smiled too.

She felt a bit nervous when she approached her house later that afternoon, dropped off by Ann's long low fast car, but she needn't have worried. Paul wasn't there. He was coaching and had left her a note on the kitchen table, saying he'd have supper with the Carsons and be back late. There was no displeasure she could discern. He had accepted her right to independent activity. Joan didn't want to upset him but she didn't want to continue to sit around and wait for him and grow miserable doing it.

93

If he would accept her friendship with Ann without feeling he lost by it, they could be very civilised and very grown-up. He could do what he wanted to do and she could do what she wanted to do. And there would be no recriminations on either side. Knowing that she could get out of the house to a world different from his cheered her up tremendously. She went to find a duster and found herself humming. She did some washing, sorted some laundry and promised herself to buy flowers for the living room in the morning. 'Silly not to make the best of things,' she muttered briskly to herself before she went upstairs and ran a bath. While the bath was running she fingered the clothes in the wardrobe, admired how a colour suited her in the mirror. Of course, Ann had lovely clothes, she reflected. And Ann had lovely money. But at that moment, although she remarked it, she didn't envy her any of it. She was just pleased to have been extended an invitation in her own right. She had a bath, read a bit and was asleep before Paul came in.

In the next few months, Joan's life began to move much faster. As a wealthy woman with time on her hands, Ann would often turn up and sweep her off for lunch or tea. In spite of her apparent chic, Joan discovered too that Ann liked to walk and was happy enough to don boots and a headscarf, if there was someone to walk with. They drove further afield than Joan could have got under her own steam and went somewhere for tea on the way home.

Joan waited for Paul to complain but he did not. They lived separately in the same house. The dances and celebrations and nights out to which he and his friends went occasionally were items on the calendar to Ann and her circle, for whom enjoying themselves was a full-time exercise. If Joan had hoped that by being less available to Paul she would become more desirable, she was disappointed. They still didn't make love as often as Joan would have liked them to and, when they did, she continued to feel that there was something missing. But she found that Paul was no slouch when it came to drinking and dancing and fooling about when she was in his company.

They didn't discuss a child again, perhaps because Paul was waiting for her to bring the subject up and she was having far too much fun. Besides, they had very little money and their resources were strained to breaking point. She had always kept house on the allowance Paul gave her and asked for a bit more if she needed it but now, he told her regretfully, the margins were very tight. 'There are family difficulties,' he told her, knowing that the word family was still a red flag against her further questioning. Sure enough, she grimaced but didn't press him. And they went on with the implicit understanding that they would enjoy their time together and make the best of it in their very separate ways when they were apart. And if Paul wasn't around, there was always Jack Riker.

Before she knew Ann, Joan thought flirting was what other people did. She didn't know that she could. But observing Ann's mixture of breathless talk and salty stories and remembering the power of the direct gaze, she soon began to try her own wings in this direction. It was almost expected to flirt in Ann's circle. Flirting was part of pretending and they were all pretending things were better or worse or different from what they were. One couple was very happy together but that was boring so they were always sniping at each other and pretending to look for consolation elsewhere, before going home happily arm-in-arm. The lonely pretended to be extrovert, the extrovert pretended to be heartless, the married pretended to be single and, unlike Cinderella, they were all very careful to be out of the ballroom before the clock struck twelve. They all had money, except one or two outsiders like Joan who added something to the proceedings and so were taken along for the ride, and they all had cars. And as they all drank quite a lot, nobody sat in judgement on anybody else for the odd alcoholic excess or occasional absence because of a hangover.

One weekend when Paul was away visiting his family – he wanted to go alone and so Joan let him – Ann rang.

'Are you free this evening? You are? Joan, be a love. There's a party I promised I'd go to with Jack and some bloody business people of Bernie's have just shown up and we've got to give them dinner. Jack would love to take you – do say you can go?'

'But what party – where? Ann, you know I can't dress for anything like that –' Joan held the telephone unnecessarily tightly.

'Oh, do stop, I'll send over a fur and you'll be fine.'

So Joan agreed.

She looked at herself in her old familiar best dress, put perfume on every pulse spot for the third time and flung on the coat. Jack duly arrived and whistled appreciatively. He drove very fast and answered her questions about the party they were going to, frightening her more and more with each bit of information he provided. By the time he took her arm to lead her in, she was shaking and white and far too scared to do more than sip her drink.

In spite of her initial misgivings, the evening passed in a pleasant enough haze. Clearly everybody knew Jack and she found that quite a few people knew or knew of Paul as well. Determined not to make a fool of herself, and feeling a lot more vulnerable without the borrowed fur, she found herself watching Jack. Long of leg, merry of eye, he was never without a drink in his hand. It was the first time she noticed how much he drank, though she had to admit it seemed to have remarkably little effect. By the time they left, it was late and cold, and he felt for a flask in his car.

She looked at his hands on the steering wheel and wondered how they'd feel. She shook herself. She'd felt them, hadn't she? After all, they'd danced together often enough. Yes, her mind insisted, but I wasn't thinking of dancing. Speeding through the night, he turned to her. 'You're very quiet,' he said. 'You all right?' She must say something, something to make it clear to him that she was ready, that he had only to make a move and she would respond, but even as she thought about the words, he continued to look at her, the car still roaring forward. And then other lights came up out of the darkness equally fast, a horn blared, she cried out, he looked round and pulled the wheel so hard that they came to an abrupt halt quite a way off the road. They sat for a moment and he began to laugh.

'Not quite what you had in mind, princess?' he said merrily, fishing about for his flask again. 'Here – ' and he offered her the bottle. She was staring at him. 'Not frightened, were you? Not with Uncle Jack? Just damn lucky there are no walls along this stretch of the road.' He gulped from the flask and offered it to her again. She sat staring at him. He screwed the lid back on the flask and put it in his pocket, then turned back to her. He put his hand round her face, stroked the brow, nose, cheek and neck with the other. She gave a little sigh and her lips parted. He got out of the car. Several minutes passed.

'Come on, Joan,' he called. 'Give me a hand – we've got to get this baby back on the road.' She took off the fur and pushed as he directed. They had to turn it round to go back down a little hill to get the engine going, then he reversed, came back up the hill and she got in quickly, pulling the coat about her. He began to talk as if nothing had happened but she sat very still and replied monosyllabically.

She slept most of the next morning and rising late discovered that, while her thoughtfulness had saved her friend's coat, it had not done her dress much kindness. She looked at her other dance dresses and, choosing two and fishing about for patterns and ideas, she settled into a quietly restorative sewing afternoon. Ann didn't call, it was raining and grey so she wasn't tempted to go walking, and she refused to think about how foolish she might have been the night before. She made a pie for supper and waited for Paul to come in. He looked terribly tired when he arrived and she was surprised at how glad she was to see him. After supper he said that he wanted her to know that from now on things would be better.

'I should have told you before but it's all so detestable. My mother was being dunned by my father's creditors.'

Joan came back from the doorway and looked down at him. 'How dreadful!'

'I couldn't let it go on,' he said looking into her face. 'My mother appealed to me for help so I gave the Old Man an ultimatum. I told him I'd pay them off but I never want to see him again. And that's where the money's been going for the last three years. That's why I was so glad you made friends with Ann Shand and had good times because I couldn't do anything except keep going.'

She noticed that, broad as he was, he seemed stooped, as if he was afraid she would be angry. And she was suddenly terribly grateful that it was in her power to do the right thing, to give him something that he needed.

'Come and sit down in the front room,' she said. 'Would you like tea or coffee?' She made him the tea he requested and sat beside him on the settee while he talked about his mother working to keep his father, and the debts and the shame of it, and how his father had beaten him as a boy, and Joan held his arm and stroked him until he finished. 'I don't see that you could have done it any other way,' she said. And he put his great head on her shoulder and closed his eyes as if that was the benediction he sought.

Within five minutes he was asleep, so she sat there while her shoulder grew stiff and her back began to ache. At one, he stirred, stared at her and began to apologise. She smiled it away, touched by his genuine confusion, and they went peacefully to bed. He fell asleep holding her hand.

Almost a year later, he went away on a course and Ann decided to have a party. Actually Ann and Bernard decided to have a party which made it a little unusual although Ann was quite matter-of-fact about it. 'Everybody keeps asking why but since when do you need a reason for having a party? It'll be fun to have a big do at the house, we haven't for ages. Is Paul around? Oh, well, you know us all so well, you can come on your own can't you? I'll get Jack to pick you up.'

Joan had not been alone with Jack Riker since the evening when, in her own mind, she offered herself to him. But since that was long ago and far away – a year and a half to be precise – and as things between Paul and herself were warmer, if not more passionate, she polished her self-possession and climbed into the car in control of the situation.

They had several drinks on the way there and picked up another couple, the wife of whom particularly wanted to drive Jack's car. Jack let her and he sat in the back of the car with Joan. At the next stop they picked up another friend of Ann's temporarily without a vehicle. There wasn't a great deal of room in the back of Jack's car anyway, and the seat was certainly not designed for three. Joan was terribly aware of Jack's closeness. He had to have one arm round her for them all to fit in but she could feel his warmth and when he reached across her to throw a cigarette out of the window, his hand brushed against her breast.

Ann greeted everyone with open arms, champagne bottles in each hand. 'Coats in the hall, ladies to the right, gentlemen to the left. Joan, my lamb, champagne for you?'

'Yes please,' said Joan. Ann progressed through the house, talking and laughing and pouring. The house was large and warm, brilliantly lit and full of people. Music came from a small band in one room and a friendly young man whisked Joan away to dance. Dancing was very absorbing. She loved to dance. It took her mind off the unease she'd been feeling in the car. She flung back her head and laughed, she drank whatever she was handed and was suddenly confronted by Jack Riker.

'Are you avoiding me?' he said, smiling meaningfully.

'Perish the thought,' she said, smiling back, and held out her hands.

Jack was a wonderful dancer, almost as good as Paul, and a tease and a flirt and a total delight, if only, if only, my smile will stay on and my hands don't shake. If only we can stick to dancing, if he doesn't touch me in that way I have to think about, oh damn, they're playing a slow number and my head's spinning and, 'Excuse me,' she said, and almost ran up the stairs, opened a door – a room, a room, any room! – a window, air – he turned her round and kissed her hard. She looked at him. He closed the door, came back

98

to her, held her head and looked at her. She started to say something. 'Shhh,' he said and kissed her again. His kisses were not like Paul's or even her memories of Robert. They were not cheerful exchanges between friends.

He seemed to be tasting her – her mouth, her skin – feeling her with his lips and the tip of his tongue. And she was kissing him back as if he were water and she was dying of thirst. She wanted to pull off his clothes, pull off her own. She wasn't sure of the rest of it, surely it would follow, but he had his own speed and she accepted it. His hands rested on her breasts with the greatest delicacy, it made her want to scream, then his caresses changed as if he were trying to tell her something but she couldn't understand, only knew one way forward, one way to proceed. And suddenly he broke away quite white, his eyes darker than she had ever seen them, and took her hands. 'Sit down,' he whispered, 'sit here. I want to tell you – ' But she silenced him with a kiss and he embraced her again and they fell back on the convenient bed and her body moved against him, begging him, and still he kissed her. Breathless they lay, staring at each other, then he struggled to sit up. He went to the door. Unlocking it he looked at her. 'Sorry,' he said, and went out, closing it behind him.

Joan dragged herself up and looked in the mirror. You shouldn't look in a mirror when you're drunk, she remembered someone saying, because when you're drunk you don't see what you really look like. She thought she looked very attractive. She straightened her hair and her dress as well as she could and then she sat in a chair. Her head swam and she wanted to go home. She thought she ought to be able to behave with dignity but that she wanted to go home. Downstairs she found a couple leaving and asked if they could drop her off. They agreed good-humouredly and she hurried to retrieve her coat from the crowded racks. She would ring Ann in the morning.

The couple who gave her the lift were mercifully self-absorbed and much of their conversation excluded her. As she sat in the back of the car, she examined how she felt and she felt foolish. Your trouble is that you can't keep from going too far, she thought. All that drink and then acting like an idiot. But she was too honest not to admit that what she had felt was more than drink or excitement. She had felt different, unlike anything she'd felt before. If it had been anybody else but Jack she could have talked to Ann about it. One of the things she had enjoyed about her friendship with Ann was that Ann knew about all sorts of things and, as the years had passed, she had felt more free about asking for information. The trouble was that if she didn't discuss it with Ann, she didn't know who she *was* going to discuss it with. The small house she shared with Paul had never appeared shabbier or more soothing. She dropped down gratefully on a chair and sat for a long time before she went to bed.

The next morning she went on a quiet snoop through the library to see if she could find out anything from there but the books she found had drawings that quite repelled her and were couched in language which left her more bewildered than before. She left and as she crossed the main street she saw a familiar figure wave . . . 'Hey!' Joan walked quickly to the car door.

'Ann, I'm so sorry about last night. I didn't feel well and you had other guests so I . . . '

'Am I giving you coffee or are you giving me coffee?'

Joan had known Ann too long to mistake the determined timbre in her voice. 'Let's have coffee at home,' she said.

Ann nodded. 'Get in.' They drove in silence.

When Joan brought the coffee, she was suddenly aware of how rarely Ann had been inside her home and that she, Joan, had only been once or twice to Ann's. Ann's clothes looked out of place against the down-at-heel furnishings.

'What happened last night?' Ann asked.

'I told you,' said Joan. 'I drank too much, didn't feel too good and made a dash for home.'

Ann sipped her coffee.

'Jack was quite worried about you.'

Joan made no comment.

'He could have driven you.'

'But why should he?' asked Joan. 'There was no need to make a fuss —'

'Somebody made a pass at somebody,' said Ann levelly, eyes lowered as she put her coffee cup safely aside. 'Somebody got unusually excited and hitched a ride home on the nearest broomstick.'

Joan didn't move.

'You were interested in Jack from the first, you always have been. Jack is very interesting. But Jack is strictly for looking at, friend.'

Joan stayed still.

'Oh, I know you think this is all possessiveness on my part but before you get really hurt – or more to the point Jack does – I'll make it very clear. Jack just can't. He never has been able to. Heaven knows why.'

Joan wet her lips. 'Is that why he drinks?'

Ann looked at her sharply. 'Either still waters run deep or you've learned a lot since I first met you. I don't know whether it's because he drinks or he drinks because – and so on. What I'm trying to say is, it's nothing personal. It's not you he's rejecting. It's – ' she gave a bitter little smile – 'more like all of us.'

'Is that why you keep him around?' asked Joan.

'What a horrid thing to say! I don't keep him around. He's a friend, one of my oldest friends, and I accept him for what he is. And so does Bernie. And I'd like you to, too.'

'How very well organised,' said Joan softly.

Ann didn't stay long.

When she had gone, Joan sat down and for the first time looked at Ann, Ann's marriage, Ann's husband and friends, Ann's drinking and partying, and saw it as more like fever and less like fun. It was all right, she thought, as long as you went along with it and didn't ask questions or step out from the convention of having a good time. Once you did, you stopped being one of the gang and became an outsider again. She wondered why it had taken her so long to understand. She wondered why she had persisted in the idea that she was something special to Jack Riker. She had had a lot of fun, she reflected, and although she knew she would see Ann in the future, she knew she wouldn't ever see her again in quite the same way. People always talk about affairs with men but I had a sort of affair with Ann. And now it's over. She put on her oldest coat and went for a walk.

It was dark and she was tired when she came in, feeling a bit shaken as though she'd had a fall. She had a bath and a boiled egg and wondered if Paul would ring, but he didn't. She went to bed and fell asleep almost straight away. Suddenly she saw her father bending over her, his eyes sad and his face tired. And as she reached up for him he drew away and away until she could only see him in the distance getting into a taxi. She felt rather than heard someone behind her and it was Robert, but he was naked and she was so taken aback, she just stared. And as she looked, there was a great explosion and the whole of one side of his body caved in and he collapsed, bleeding, calling her name and she ran, to her horror, not towards him but away from him. On and on she ran until she came to a river by which Paul sat smoking and talking to his mother and she fell into his arms. His mother smiled and Joan looked up into his face and he smiled. Joan smiled. And then the smile became something else and his eyes looked sad and he began to pull away from her and she looked and he was being swallowed into the ground and there were dirty old banknotes blowing about in the wind, like dead leaves, and she clung to him and clung to him but it was no use and she begged him, 'Paul – please Paul – please stay!' but his hands were slipping out of hers. And she woke with a terrible start.

The house was still. She put on the light. She touched her wedding ring. She went downstairs and stood by the telephone, willing it to sound. It remained silent. She looked round the curtain, out into the street, but there was nothing and no one. She sat on the sofa until it was light and when she awoke properly she knew what she would do. So that, when Paul returned home, she said she had something to tell him. 'I dreamed you were gone,' she said, 'and I had nothing left of you. It was awful. Let's have a family. I'm ready now.' And he enfolded her with his great warm arms and smiled his tenderest smile and told her she had made him very, very happy.

12 *Joan*

Once Joan had decided she would have a child, she waited with impatience for it to happen. And so of course it didn't. She found that she spent more time alone, seeing Ann Shand occasionally for coffee if they met by chance or having a drink together with other people. Ann was no longer a frequent caller or visitor and Joan was content to mix with the other masters' wives more often or walk on her own if Paul was busy.

She had thought that babies came ever so quickly, like a flash, her mother always said they did, but this one seemed to be taking its time. She thought about it a lot but that's all she did. She didn't buy toys or knit clothes, she didn't moon around over other people's children. Indeed, she quite startled herself at how very indifferent she felt towards the idea of anybody's baby but her own. And Paul's, of course.

After a few months she began to watch herself to see if there was any change, not a change occasioned by pregnancy, but a change because she wasn't yet pregnant. She listened to her voice – was it sharp? Was she tense? She was not. She was much as she'd been before, perhaps a little less discontent. Was she sleeping? Yes, quite soundly. You can't wait for it, she decided. Waiting for it is sure to make it decide not to come. And you can't trick it, either, which is why it is important to know how you feel. You can't pretend to be calm about it if your heart's in a fever of impatience. Was her heart in a fever of impatience? She thought about it. It wasn't. She went for a walk.

She supposed she would feel something different. She didn't know what, just a difference. She felt her body experimentally, she watched herself attentively. It was no good, she didn't feel different. She peeled the potatoes. She looked out of the kitchen window to where the birds played on the small square of grass at the back of the house. When she next looked it was raining and cold and the leaves were falling and scudding about. And then it was dark almost all day, as if the sky were sulking. And the only flowers were in frost on the glass before she got the stove going in the morning. She went out in her boots and dressing gown to feed the birds. Gradually the snow melted and the earth lay, sodden and dark. She sat at the kitchen table writing a shopping list and she realised that she felt different. Her mind examined the thought. For how long had she been feeling different? She didn't know. She went shopping.

It was market day and the little stalls were piled with vegetables and apples and farmhouse cheese. She was standing in a shaft of sunshine looking at a pile of oranges when she decided to go and see Dr Moffatt. She walked determinedly to his surgery, was asked to wait a moment and saw him within twenty minutes. But he'd nothing to tell her. It wasn't a baby that had made her feel different, it must have been the spring.

Paul bought her a terrier she called Beauty, joined shortly afterwards, to save its neck, by a little sister of remarkable ugliness, known as the Beast. Taking the dogs out gave a new zest to the endless miles Joan walked with the wind in her face. She had now thrust the whole matter of having a baby away from her. It was taking so long that she didn't want to have to consider it in case it didn't happen, so that it came as quite a surprise when she stood up at the end of a concert in the town hall at the end of September and fainted. When she came round, Paul was looking concerned and Dr Moffatt was holding her hand and murmuring. 'Is it . . .?' she asked. 'In the summer,' replied the old man, smiling at her. 'Just what you've been wanting.'

Paul took her home and helped her to bed with a large cup of tea. He didn't say much but she thought he was pleased. He'd always been the one who wanted the baby – and then she did and now, well, she wasn't sure how she felt. But that was silly, she reminded herself, because it was on the way.

The months passed like pebbles, smooth and round and incurious. Paul accepted her changing shape, she accepted it herself.

A month before the baby was born, she bought a dozen nappies, and then a week later, another. Her next-door neighbour presented her with a little knitted coat and her mother-in-law sent a parcel of old silk petticoats and a soft shawl. She ate, she walked, she played with the dogs and she seemed to herself to have turned in, as if she was looking inside herself, waiting, watching a pool of water, shadowed in half light, waiting for something to happen to the water, for the surface to begin to move.

She went to London on a whim and wandered round the Zoo. She couldn't face the snake house but she enjoyed the sense of visiting something from so long ago. Her eyes filled at the memory of her father and cleared again when the bus came and took her to Selfridges, where she bought a beautiful christening dress.

She kept it in her top drawer and took it out to touch and rewrap as if it were a relic or a symbol, something she couldn't quite believe she'd got. It was hard to believe that babies fitted into baby clothes – they were so very small. She did not ask herself how she would manage. She assumed that she would. She had a girl from the village now, who came to do heavy work like making fires and laundry. It was pleasant to have a companion whose sole aim was to please you and make things easy and comfortable for you. Meggy was very plain, her bones blurred over with an outer casing of sweet white unhealthy fat. She was the youngest of a family of nine and she expected to work from the moment she arrived until just before she put her coat on, always ready to spend an extra hour or so if it was necessary or helpful.

Paul had not discussed the child very much with Joan except to say that he thought if she liked, they might spend the summer with his mother, who lived further south. It would be warmer there, better for the child, and she could have a rest. She wrote to her mother across years of silence broken only by Christmas cards to tell her about the baby.

They both carefully referred to the expected baby as the child, without allusion to which sex it might be. She didn't know what Paul thought about it and she was convinced that he wanted a boy. In some way, she admitted to herself, she felt she had let him down by spending so much time with Ann Shand and Jack Riker. But she was disinclined to further examine what might have happened and soon her memories of them became unreal, like something vaguely uncomfortable she had dreamed. What she embarked upon now was much more important. He didn't know it, but the baby was a gift for Paul and if her gift was to be perfect, she hoped for a boy too. But in her innermost heart she didn't care, as long as it was well, what it was, and sometimes she felt this so hard that it seemed that Paul must feel it from her and hear it too, and see it as a kind of disloyalty to him. But they didn't discuss this either.

One day in May, she left Meggy hanging out the washing and went off to buy some ribbon she'd set her heart on to trim a bedjacket. She went the long way round through the churchyard and sat for a time with the warm sunshine on her face, before she went into town. She wondered how her mother had felt with Guy. She must have felt something special about him because he was the first and the first is always special. Perhaps she had not been so busy then but quieter, easier with herself. Perhaps she too had gone for walks and sat in the sun on a gravestone. The idea of her mother's face, warmed and softened, made her smile. Her mother had been truly pretty. She remembered her once long, long ago, in a big straw hat with every kind of violet on it, white and purple and pink and almost black. Her collar had little bones in it and her bodice fitted with many seams. But the memory was distant, the picture fuzzy, and it didn't linger. She got up to go and felt the child move, almost stretching inside her. It wasn't unpleasant but it was very powerful and she felt suddenly aware of another person living within. It made her wary for a moment, and then almost unconsciously, she braced herself and walked on towards the haberdasher's shop.

On the way home the child shifted again and her body began to feel tight, like a fine skin on a frame with the light behind it. She felt that everybody could see what was going on but this idea soon faded for she saw few people and they only smiled their ordinary smiles and went on their way. She had not thought about how far away the house was until today. The distance seemed completely different. When she saw the door of the house, she was absurdly relieved, as though now she could at least be private. She stood in the kitchen. She could hear Meggy singing upstairs. Soon she would come down. She waited. She took off her coat in the hall and went into the front room. She perched on the end of the couch, waiting for things to move again, and when they did she stood up hastily, and began to pace. People talk about waiting for a baby, but how do you wait for a baby? She wondered if there was a proper way to do it.

Meggy came down and Joan asked her to make some tea. By the time the girl brought the tray in, Joan was standing braced against the fireplace, feet slightly apart and the fingers of one hand spread wide on the bulge of her stomach. Meggy poured the tea and accepted Joan's offer of a cup with gratitude. She confided that everything was nice and tidy upstairs, she'd had a good dust round, just to be getting ready . . . Joan asked her how she knew. 'Oh I don't,' said Meggy with a sunny smile. 'It's just that with my mam and all her little ones, she always said it was better to be prepared for quite a while because you never know when they're comin'.'

For Joan the afternoon was shapeless, bits of chat when Meggy was in the room and silences while she went away again. Joan walked, talked, stood and sat with a profound sense of unease. By the time evening came, Meggy had persuaded her to try to rest and had her lying like a lady in a magazine, draped across her bed. But no sooner had the door shut behind Meggy than Joan got off the bed and began to pace again.

The pains – she now realised that these were they – became stronger. She grabbed at the corners of furniture for support. She kept urging herself on, promising herself that it would be all right if she could just live through the next one. When the contractions came, they seemed as dark and primeval as the sea. They blotted out the cheerful rooms and the bits and pieces that she knew. All she could see in front of her eyes was pain and darkness, like the pressure she had always imagined on the head of a diver with all of those tons of water on his head. The source of her pressure was the child and, when the pain clawed, it seemed to pull in her vision with its force, rendering her unable to see anything but the edges of the pain as it swelled up and ebbed away.

How long this went on she did not know. Time ceased to mean anything. She had forgotten to time the period between the contractions and she dragged herself back to the bedroom to wait for the next one.

All at once, there was a banging on the back door. She couldn't move – yes, she could. She crawled down the stairs as Meggy and her mother came in through to the hall. Mrs Winterham looked at her briefly and said, 'Get the doctor, Meggy – quick as you can. You come back up with me, Mrs. Doctor'll be here soon.' And when he came back it was with something in a cylinder, something for her to sniff to ease the pain. But it didn't ease it. When she sniffed she had no pain and saw herself floating above the bed and when she didn't sniff, the pain dug into the small of her back and the doctor was thanking Mrs Winterham and shooing her and Meggy away and the District Nurse arrived and the room spun and she heard the doctor say, 'She's tired out, poor girl. It's rough on her.' Rough on me, rough on me. Breathe and float, breathe and float, breathe and – she whimpered. And she heard them muttering about forceps. She wanted to ask the doctor but her tongue was thick and she had great difficulty in getting the words to the end of her tongue. 'Forceps?' she queried, 'what are they?' Dr Moffatt pressed her gently back. 'I hope we won't be needing them,' he said gently, 'but we always have them with us – just in case.' I won't need them, she thought to herself, not me. The baby will come soon, I know it will come soon.

The pains abated. She dozed. They began again. She was unaware of the concern on the doctor's face. He and the nurse half-lifted her, held the mask over her face, sponged her with cologne, talked to each other, jollied her on. She couldn't judge whether it was night or day, she seemed to have been on this rocking horse of pain and lull, pain and lull for so long that it seemed forever.

When they used the forceps, she was so tired that she did not care. Oh yes, it hurt, but they were very kind and careful and she was just so relieved to be able to rest that she'd have willingly done almost anything they'd asked of her. And Dr Moffatt showed her the baby, big and dark with thick hair and a small cut over the left eye. 'It's a girl,' he told her. She murmured and smiled and went to sleep. It was only when she woke that she realised that Paul was going to be away that night and then she wondered which night. And the nurse told her that the labour had lasted for almost thirty-six hours and what a good job Dr Moffatt had done with the forceps. Would she like to see her baby? Her husband was just coming.

When Paul came in she couldn't read his face. She thought that he looked tired and a bit shamefaced, but not disappointed.

'Are you all right?' he asked. The nurse put the baby in her arms. She looked at the baby and then at him.

'Yes,' she said. 'Look at her, isn't she lovely?'

'She's a whopper,' he said, and gave the child a finger to hold.

'She's lovely,' Joan murmured, resting her cheek on the child's warm head. 'What shall we call her?'

Paul looked at her mischievously. 'I rather like Andrew,' he said. She looked at him, too pleased to worry.

'I want to call her something like – like –' She thought for a minute. 'Lindsay,' she said.

Paul smiled approvingly. 'Lindsay.' He nodded.

Lindsay was a good baby. She ate and she slept and she grew. Paul went on working long hours, playing rugby, coaching, organising swimming galas and gym displays, teaching, arranging, drinking with the boys while Joan walked the baby in her pram and Meggy helped in the house. Joan had a sense of homecoming. She wondered, as she walked through a soft summer evening, pushing Lindsay in her pram, if perhaps Paul had been right and she had wanted this all along, because she felt, for the first time in her life, intrinsically valued and valuable. It didn't matter that her mother hadn't replied to her letter. She had managed without her.

When the school term ended and they travelled down by train to see Paul's mother, she noticed it. Mother Canning put her square hand on Joan's arm for an instant and smiled her loving smile. 'It suits you,' she said, 'being a mother.' And Joan smiled back happily. The Old Man was noticeably withdrawn and on the occasions she did have to deal with him, she found him much quieter and even conciliatory in a minor way. Paul's sisters, now married, came to visit, except for Katherine who was still living at home and teaching in the school. All in all, the summer was so pleasant that they agreed they would try to do it again the following year, and so they did, every year until the old people died, Katherine's naval surgeon was finally free to marry her and the house was sold.

13 *Joan*

Joan was enchanted by Lindsay. She loved her thick dark hair, her strongly sweet-smelling skin and her tiny beautiful ears. As a large child with well-formed limbs, mobile and inquisitive, Joan found that boy's clothes suited Lindsay better for the majority of occasions. She was slow to rise to her feet but, once up, immediately went adventuring. Paul wasn't at home any more than before so the child spent most of her time with Joan and Joan felt safe in adoring Lindsay as she had not felt safe with anyone since her father left. But as the child grew older, Joan felt that feeling of safety ebb.

She found it increasingly difficult to express the extent of her love. Might it not smother the child? First she withdrew the nonsense she muttered into the beloved temples and then the silly songs she made up and sang with her. Surely gestures didn't count for so much if there weren't words to back them up? One day she reached out her arms to enfold Lindsay as she sat on her knee and imperceptibly but definitely the child moved away. Joan opened her mouth to cry out in protest. And found no words came.

She could no longer voice her feelings to her child, in case they were overheard. She was afraid of what they might be, how all too solid and intense they'd sound if they had shape in her ears, in her mouth. She had always been wary of voicing her feelings, would not to her mother, not even to Paul. Once she might have talked in these terms to her father but he was gone and she tried not to think about him. Dwelling on him always made her cry.

Oddly, the one person she yearned for as this feeling of ineptitude grew was Guy. She felt sure that her brother would know how to help her but she couldn't understand where the idea came from. Guy didn't write, he didn't ring, he had never been married. Why, she asked herself, should I think that he would know what to do? Because he was honest about himself. He had let her know something about him.

Once or twice she nerved herself to take the step of writing to him. Perhaps on paper she would find the words to express how she had always loved him, for she felt that she must have done, and he would listen and be able to reassure her about the normality of her imperfect relationship with Paul and now with their daughter. But she could not bring herself to do it. To write down what she needed to confide was to risk lowering the defences she'd worked to build for far longer than she knew and further to make concrete what she persuaded herself in her more optimistic moments was not so.

Her marriage to Paul wasn't perfect. But it didn't have to be. No marriage was perfect. It was good and kind and affectionate. Nearly perfect. As nearly perfect as her relationship with her daughter, their daughter, with Lindsay, who just happened to be a rather self-contained little girl. And sadly the distance Lindsay began to maintain was the only thing her father commented favourably on.

It wasn't that Paul didn't want children. He did. But having got a child, he didn't know what to make of her. His absences and interests away from home kept him more apart from her than he had taken into consideration. It was sad, he thought, that Joan should have so much of herself to give to the child when the child clearly didn't want it and he could have done with that attention himself.

And then he reminded himself again that Joan was a very good-looking woman with considerable strengths and remarkable patience. She very rarely asked questions of him. She was the opposite of his sisters, all vying for his attention, each with their dramas and demands. Joan had had her troubles, he was aware of that, but none of any great moment as far as he knew since they'd been together. Oh, she'd found it rather difficult accepting the limitations of life at school but she'd been quite mature about negotiating his life and his passion for sports and physical exercise. Found her own way and got on with it. Behaved exemplarily and then been a delightful companion to him whenever he could be around. How many other women would have put up with the penury of their first years together unquestioningly? She had needed time to settle down and a baby was the obvious answer but at first she had refused and he had accepted, if not understood, her refusal, and been pleased by her eventual agreement.

And now there was Lindsay. Paul just didn't know what to make of Lindsay. He would turn round and catch her regarding him with great dark eyes. She watched him as patiently as a wild thing stalking its prey. But there was nothing acquisitive he could determine in her gaze. On the contrary, what was there was so vulnerable that Paul found it hard to face. He sometimes took her for walks. She was so busy being good that he hardly knew she was there and certainly did not know how to draw her out. And he did not read to her. Her mother did that.

Sometimes he showed her things, how a watch worked or the blades in his penknife, but again he was aware of her watching him and he felt confused by the quality of her gaze. She was waiting for him to do something, but he didn't know what it was. He praised her for being quiet. He liked it when she was biddable. What he did not like to see was the fear in her face when he lost his temper. And he did not like hearing Joan hushing her and getting her out of the way when his temper began to boil over. For it was something new, his anger, and not a good thing at all.

He was working very hard and receiving what Joan referred to as no recognition for his efforts. Which meant that although he was hailed by other physical training teachers as their best representative (and they were delighted to have the deputy director of physical education for the county on their side), that credit was not reflected in his salary. Money was very tight again and he was not advancing very fast. In fact, he wasn't advancing at all. His own answer to being stuck was to work even harder, which meant more time away from home, more duties, more responsibilities, making himself more accessible to more people. He was secretary of one voluntary group and treasurer of another, progenitor of one course of training, part-time tutor on another. He ought to be moving into a directorship of his own within another education authority, he knew that. He had sent out applications but so far none had been taken up. And so he was tired.

He explained to Joan, the first time he came home in one of the towering black rages which were to become a feature of their lives, that it wasn't anything to do with her but that she had not handled him particularly tactfully when he was desperately tired, and he really couldn't be expected to be conciliatory to a small child on top of everything else. Joan watched him as he left the kitchen and drew the white-faced Lindsay against her shoulder. Lindsay detached herself quite gently and went upstairs to her room.

Joan decided that Paul's rages were like thunderstorms. To begin with, the sky was clear and gradually, frowning clouds built up, scaring away the light and muffling the usual noises. She found that as he grew angry, she grew angry too, while Lindsay became quieter and quieter. Joan learned that Paul's rages were whole entities, almost independent of the man. They had beginnings, middles and ends, lasting anything from a day to a week, rumbling and clearing, recurring because they had not been properly cleared away. Initially, she hoped that if she learned to anticipate the beginning of them, she could avert them, but soon discovered they had patterns, plotted orbits laid down somewhere within Paul's mind and it was not possible to deviate from the allotted route.

In the midst of his rage, it was not that Paul did not want to stop but that he seemed unable to. He was like a man under the influence of a drug or a spell and she began to reach into her own armoury to fight him for himself, to help herself endure, and because she knew it alarmed Lindsay.

She found that she was as capable of being bitter as he was of being angry and that he was as shocked by her remarks and behaviour as she was outraged by his. And other things came into her range once she permitted herself to express them. She discovered that she resented sitting quietly at home with the child, waiting for him to return. She discovered that she no longer felt as she once had about Hennington and Garslake. She had not thought much in the past about where they lived, but if she had, a small market town and its nearby beauty spot had seemed ideal for the young and hopeful. But she had driven over every local inch, had walked them endlessly, first with the dogs and then with the pram, and somewhere along the way, hope had fallen from her like a handkerchief dropped out of her pocket, blown away by the wind. The narrow streets and the small stone houses had no charm for her now. They felt like a cage.

And as she didn't like where she was geographically, so she began to question where she was emotionally, to admit to herself for the first time that she thought Paul was often wrong. She saw now that much of what he did was pointless, hopeless, undirected energy and, as such, time wasted. And she admitted that she felt bitterly neglected by his absences and preoccupations, chained with the child he had said he wanted, while Paul was bewildered by her vehemence.

They were not living a life substantially different from the one they had lived together for more than ten years. She had led him to believe that she understood him, endorsed his efforts and supported his aims. What was now so different?

Perhaps Paul could have forgiven Lindsay for being a witness to all this if she had been his idea of a little girl, but she was not. Her unmovingness, her lack of suitable demonstration to her mother, her frightening attentiveness to him did not make her endearing. She was just what he did not want at this time in his marriage. She was a witness. And he could not escape the feeling that, even if she didn't understand what was going on, she was still recording it – if not the actual words, then the inflections, some sense, some essence – of what passed between Joan and himself with alarming frequency. 'It will be good when she goes to school,' he said angrily and once again left the room rather than see from the reaction in his daughter's eyes how he had hurt her.

In the winter of the year before the Duke of Kent married Princess Marina, Lindsay went to school. Two streets over and one across, Joan noted grimly. Lindsay was clever but she was shy so Joan was delighted when, a few weeks later, she asked if she could bring a friend home for tea. Rose was a very assured child, a year older than Lindsay. Her parents lived in a big house, she said, but her daddy wasn't home very much because he had business to attend to and he drove a car miles and miles and her mummy was very pretty. Well, she called them Mummy and Daddy but really they chose her, because they couldn't have children of their own, so she went home with them.

Joan, cutting bread and butter and seeing how interested Lindsay was in all this, said, 'Yes, Lindsay's father isn't at home as often as we'd like, is he, Lindsay? And what's your father's name?'

'Bernard Wootton,' said Rose. 'May I have some jam to put on the bread?'

Joan put the teapot down with exaggerated care.

'And your mother's name is Ann?'

Rose smiled. 'That's right. Her name is Ann Shand but Daddy gets cross if she calls herself that. He says Mrs Wootton is a good enough name for anyone.'

Joan put the jam into a dish and the dish before the child.

114

'Come on, Lindsay, take care of your guest. You must give your mother my best regards, Rose. We used to know each other a long time ago.' And a few days later, when she was collecting Lindsay from school, up swept Ann wearing the most becoming hat as per *Vogue* in October 1933, Rose with her hand tucked into her arm.

'So,' she said, ignoring Joan and bending towards Lindsay, 'you're the secret Joan's been keeping! Hello, I'm Ann Shand, Rose's mother,' and Lindsay smiled unhesitatingly and pleased. 'Why don't you both come to tea?' And typically she herded them off into the long, large, low-slung car which lay, moored like a ship, twenty yards down the road. Most of the first half hour was taken up with politenesses but then the girls went off so that Rose could show her room to Lindsay and Ann looked Joan over carefully.

'You look the same but different.'

Joan met her eyes squarely.

'I was thinking exactly the same about you.'

'Are there any changes?' asked Ann. 'I mean apart from the obvious one?'

Joan answered easily. 'Well, I suppose there must be, but Paul's still working too hard and life just goes on. Having the child was wonderful – ' She stopped for fear she might appear tactless.

'I'm sure,' said Ann drily, though not without humour. 'Though there are easier ways to acquire one!'

And Joan laughed. 'What made you decide to do it?'

'Well,' said Ann. 'I don't like horses. They're too big and step on one's shoes. Don't like dogs, they pant and moult. Bernard is allergic to cats. So we decided to have a kid.'

'Just as hard to housetrain,' observed Joan flippantly.

'But so much more rewarding,' opined Ann, her hands clasped in mock sentimentality against her bosom.

'More rewarding than anything,' echoed Joan.

'Certainly more rewarding than horses, dogs or cats. I mean, that child's got gifts I covet. Since she moved in, Bernard is home to dinner at least twice a week.'

Joan mugged that she was impressed, wondering in the meantime if Rose might give Lindsay lessons. Ann tapped the ash from her cigarette.

'At least you know what you've got. We'll have to wait years before we know what we're in for. Rose heard one of the teachers talking to another about her origins and now takes positive pride in telling people she might be anybody!'

Joan asked, 'Does it matter?'

Ann shook her head firmly. 'Not to me, I'll tell you. We knew we couldn't have kids, God knows we tried hard enough, but when the umpteenth doctor shook his expensive head, I was a bit shaken. Trust Bernard to come through like the good 'un I always thought he was. So we marched off to this orphanage place where they took all sorts of particulars, not to mention a bank reference, and once everybody had sworn we were decent and law-abiding, they let us look at the kids. Honestly, Joan, I could have brought home a dozen. At least, that's what I thought until I got to grips with one – which reminds me, they're awfully quiet. Hadn't we better take a look?'

Joan reflected as she followed the immaculate figure up to the nursery that it was odd to listen to Ann talk like this. But it wasn't until they had applauded the kids' efforts at dressing-up, shared a sherry and she and Lindsay had been despatched homewards in the car (for which there was now a driver) that it occurred to her that she had not mentioned Jack Riker and neither had Ann.

Lindsay enjoyed her first school, its small size being well suited to her, and she and Rose remained friends. But Joan felt constrained by the past and could not relate easily to Ann, so often the car took the children to Rose's home and brought Lindsay home in solitary state at a prearranged time.

As the days had been built round Lindsay before she went to school, so, Joan admitted to herself, they were now often structured around her return. And once the evening had been successfully negotiated, she read to her in bed. And together at the weekends they charted the hedgerows, the rabbits, the birds and the changing seasons. For Lindsay, no walk was too long, no scrap of rural information less than important. She knew she had to go to school but the countryside about her was where she felt most at home.

Just before her eighth birthday a letter arrived for Paul, which he opened and read without comment. When he left, Joan sent Lindsay to get her scarf and glanced over the typewritten page. Same old thing, she thought, and they won't even see him. How can a man have such a good work record and they won't even see him? Why won't they? People always see you, even if they're going to refuse you – unless you've some terrible professional secret, a real blot on your copybook, which Paul hasn't. Lindsay called that she was ready and Joan, snatching her coat, walked her daughter to school, the thought of Paul being refused another interview pushed into a corner of her mind but still niggling. She waved goodbye to Lindsay and continued to pick at the problem.

This wasn't the first refusal or even the tenth. Paul had been applying for jobs since Lindsay went to school or before. And nobody would even see him for interview. He'd made the transfer from teaching into the administrative side, got to the position of assistant director and there he'd stuck.

She put her key in the lock and let herself in.

Dropping her coat on a chair, she went to the desk where all their papers were kept. Paul was always taking on voluntary projects and they generated paper as if by sleight of hand. She lifted one pile after another and found the letters of application and their responses more or less together in a side drawer. She started to read them through but stopped when she realised they were all quite similar. She stood for a minute, then put them back where she'd found them and went to hang up her coat.

She made the beds, wrote a shopping list and put some clothes in to soak. She was just boiling milk for coffee when she remembered that Paul's immediate superior had always been wary of him. Paul was too active and independent for an ageing man who wanted a quiet life, a secure job and the clout of his position without the effort. And Paul, unfailingly correct, had always given his senior's name as a reference. Joan stood with the milk saucepan in her hand as if dumbstruck. But if your immediate employer declined to give you a reference, then you were stuck. As Paul was stuck. What a filthy thing to do.

When Paul came home for lunch, she sent Lindsay to wash her hands and told Paul what she suspected. He refused to believe it. It was unheard of. She pressed him to think about it. He grew quite curt. Her imagination was running away with her.

Lunch passed in silence. He went to sit down in the sitting room to drink his coffee. Lindsay helped her mother to clear the table. He came to the kitchen doorway, offering to take Lindsay to school. She rushed to get her coat. He kissed Joan's cheek. She watched them go, the girl's whole frame inclined towards the man's in unbearable inarticulate love, he very upright, pushing his bike with one hand, the other resting on Lindsay's shoulder.

The business of applying for another job was not mentioned again for some weeks. The more Joan thought about her theory, the more she was convinced that she was right. And when Paul mentioned an appropriate appointment, she asked him to show her the advertisement. He did so. 'Might as well keep trying,' he said. And later, he said that he'd write in the morning, he was tired, he was going to bed. 'I'll just finish this,' said Joan, waving her book. When she heard the bedroom floorboards creak, she scribbled the details. He was up early enough to write but she managed to persuade him to let her post it. She had hidden all the stamps. He capitulated.

That morning, when he was gone and she'd taken Lindsay to school, she opened his application, shaking at her own temerity. Firmly, in her attractive script, she rewrote his letter, exactly as it was but changing the principal reference to Robert Bower, the headmaster at Brivett House, Paul's first employer who had always had high regard for his abilities and with whom he had maintained a relationship of mutual appreciation. But supposing Robert Bower was hesitant?

She traced the number of Brivett House and asked to speak to Dr Bower, so firmly that she was put through with only the slightest delay. She told him what she suspected and asked his help. He reassured her that he would do anything he could. And unlike Paul, he did not find the idea farfetched.

'In Mackenzie's shoes, I wouldn't want to lose an assistant like Paul either,' he commented grimly and then asked after her and Lindsay.

'Yes, we're well thank you, quite well,' Joan said, finding herself flustered and her forehead positively feverish. 'Thank you so very much.'

'Any time, my dear, any time.'

She pounded the stamp into position with her fist.

Some weeks later Paul looked up from his post and announced that he would have to go to Persthorpe on Monday the 14th. He and Joan had been there once for a regional conference dinner.

'They want to interview me. They've gone right past Mackenzie and talked to Bob Bower. Somebody must know somebody, I suppose. Anyway, it's an interview. At last!' Joan burned the toast.

For the two weeks before the important Monday, Paul seemed like a man with new hope. His ire was so much less in evidence that Joan almost began to hope that it was a phase he might have grown out of. Perhaps with a new job and a slightly bigger house, leaving some of the frustrations of his work behind, the move might be a serious turn for the better. And whatever else it didn't bring, it would take them into a different area with a little more money. He returned to say that all had gone well and the board had said he would be informed directly. Within four days his appointment was confirmed and he whooped like a boy.

Lindsay was bewildered.

On the way to school that afternoon, she asked Joan what Persthorpe was like and Joan, having only been there once, tried to tell her. 'It's more of a town,' she began, 'quite a bit bigger than Hennington, further north, with lots of shops and cinemas.' She explained about Paul's job and that there was a technical college and even a theatre.

'Is it near country?' Lindsay wanted to know.

'Well, yes, quite near,' Joan told her, 'and there's a big park with an ornamental lake, where the gulls come sometimes with the ducks and swans because the town is much nearer the sea than we are here.'

Lindsay was quiet about it.

'She'll manage,' said Joan to Paul. 'When it comes to it, the move will be exciting. I expect she'll miss her friends a bit but she'll manage.'

In the room above her, Lindsay lay, her hands clasped behind her head, the pillow bunched up, her lower lip caught firmly in her teeth, tears running quietly down her face.

The house didn't help. Joan had been to see it but was so glad to be leaving the limitations of Hennington and Garslake that she came to believe that she just hadn't looked at it as closely as she should have done. But then she always thought she would make the best of everything, an optimism dented by this experience. It was dark and dingy, with windows too small for the mean rooms and fireplaces stuffed with gas fires, fires fuelled from meters which consumed shillings at a truly terrifying rate. Paul's answer to everything was that this was just to tide them over, they hadn't been able to look for anything properly because Joan wouldn't go without him and he wanted to seize the job he'd been offered and make it so inexorably his that there could never be a repetition of the preceding stalemate.

One Friday night, while he was enthusing about the job, Joan turned on him with fury. 'Oh do stop talking about the job,' she said. 'You wouldn't have the damned job if I hadn't written the letter and put Bower's name down instead of Mackenzie's.' Paul stared at her. 'You wouldn't listen to me, would you? You've got your ideas about fairness and decency and it just doesn't occur to you that not everybody else is the same. I knew Mackenzie was the fly in the ointment. He refused to give you a reference so that nobody would interview you. When I rang Robert Bower and told him what I thought and what I wanted to do, he agreed with me. He didn't tell me I was letting my imagination run away with me.' Paul left the room. Joan marched after him. 'Oh Paul, for heaven's sake. I'm sorry. It's this place, it really would depress a saint. Look, you've got the job, you've every right to be proud of it. It's just hard to be in this hole and endlessly have to hear about how happy and fulfilled you are when we're cold and cramped and stuck here.' He said nothing. She tried again. 'Paul, I'm sorry. I'm tired and I didn't think. It's just this house.' He looked at her coldly. 'Then look for another one,' he said. She opened her mouth to protest. He raised his paper. She left the room. Lindsay was sitting absolutely still, just as she had been. 'Come on, darling,' said Joan. 'Time for bed. Perhaps you'd like to go to the park tomorrow?' Lindsay looked at her mother. 'I would like,' she said steadily, 'to go to the real country.'

Paul remained silent. He listened to what Joan said to him but he did not respond, or even look her in the face. When Lindsay tried to talk to him, he cut her off with such savagery that she blenched. Joan took her to the railway station and bought two tickets. They went to the seaside, where they walked among the dunes and paddled in the freezing water, bought fish and chips and breathed great lungfuls of air which didn't smell of dirty curtains. When the sun set, they returned home, the child dozing against her mother's arm in the carriage. Too tired to talk much, Joan slept with Lindsay rather than disturb Paul. The next morning he was gone. Joan felt a flicker of panic followed by the energy of anger. He thinks he's going to get through this by frightening me, she thought. But he's wrong.

She soothed Lindsay with sandwiches and a bus trip out of town to a quiet pretty village, with ducks on the pond. By teatime they were tired and the wait for the return bus would have seemed endless but for a villager who saw them from her doorway and brought them cups of tea where they stood. 'Bus's always late on Sundays,' she said comfortably. 'Think he thinks it's his day off.'

At home that evening, Paul sat, unmoving, unblinking. Lindsay rushed in to tell him about what she'd seen and he tried to pay attention. Joan stood watching them, unbidden anger in her heart.

He doesn't like her, she thought. He doesn't like her. He'd make God knows what effort for anybody else, but with her, he can't be bothered. Gently she coaxed Lindsay away to run her a bath. For once her father's responses could not affect how happy she was to have been freed from the prison of the rented rooms. And Joan did everything she could to keep her as happy as she was until her eyes closed.

Joan went downstairs. She made tea, put a cup beside her husband and went carefully about arranging for the next day. Then she sat in the same room and drank her tea.

'Why don't you say something?' he asked her, several hours later.

'Because whatever I say it will be wrong. You don't want to understand. You only see what you see. You'll talk to me when you're ready.' The firmness of her voice surprised her.

On Monday Lindsay went to school clutching leaves and shells to show her teacher. Paul went to work and Joan set out for the bank. Fortunately the bank manager was most understanding. He gave her the names of mortgage companies, they discussed repayments in the light of her husband's salary, he even recommended an estate agent. Joan left cheered.

She found the house, a semi at the top of a suburban cul-de-sac, three weeks later. It was modest and pleasant. She painted the spare room for Lindsay and arranged their old things as best she could. She was so busy she didn't have time to notice Paul's look of respect as she organised it all. She was calm and perfectly polite but he'd said she should take charge and she had. Even Lindsay admitted it was much better than where they'd been, even if it still wasn't in the country, which would have been her first choice. Paul's moods came and went, Joan tucked her head into her chest and practised the art of making the best of it. Lindsay was removed from one school and settled into another. She bit her fingernails. Her eyes were weak and strained, she needed glasses. She put on weight. But she was doing well at school.

On 1st September 1939 Hitler invaded Poland and two days later a state of war was declared between Britain and Germany for the second time.

14 *Mercer*

So, when I met David, I wasn't thinking about being happy. I was thinking about writing. I had begun to nurse the beast. And then I met David. Now I wonder where five years went. Because I fell in love and stopped writing. And the two people who had had most to do with the most rewarding things I'd ever done in my life, Jud Chase and Harry Dent, stood among the politicos and the refugees, the telly people and the film buffs in a pub in Soho and drank our health and wished us luck. Somebody lent us a car for the weekend and then I had to come back to work on Tuesday morning, as secretary to the chairman of a public relations company, where I wore plain dresses and low-heeled patent shoes and worked like a fiend because the money I was earning was keeping me and the boy genius in the tunnel of love.

What do I remember? Not a great deal from that time. David had an ancient typewriter at which he picked with two fingers and great ferocity. I remember that when he asked me to marry him, I felt relief rather than elation. I remember that he presumed his talent to be superior to mine, although our credits were then about even, and that I didn't question him about it. I thought that the love of David would save me from the madness I carried inside me where other people carry their hearts. And I was glad he hadn't taken time to notice how imperfect I was, how unfinished. I don't think I thought even then that it was love which blinded him to these flaws in me. But when you need each other, as apparently we did, you can make it into a wedding and a honeymoon and twenty years of marriage if you've the will-power, and everybody you know will conspire with the illusion, making you prisoners of romance.

I remember shopping every lunch hour and queuing for the bus to go home at night. I remember endless films with no stories and endless stories with no ends. I remember people who came for dinner and stayed a fortnight. I remember I had a cat. I remember the shape of the rooms and the furniture and the man who owned the flat and brought his secretary to the two rooms he retained, sealed off, for a 'quickie' most lunchtimes. I remember the commander and his wife on the top floor and the rowdy ex-colonials on the middle floor and the trees in the street and how, when the house next door was for sale with its contents, the road was full of dealers in their cars while the two old women who took care of the property sat in the basement kitchen, polishing and mending and washing what went upstairs to be sold. But I don't remember being happy very often.

I know I was sometimes because there are photographs to prove that I smiled and that leads me to suspect that, like most people of my temperament, I take the good for granted and moan like hell about the rest. And as you might expect, I didn't miss writing until the gilt (or do I mean guilt?) began to wear off the gingerbread, at which time I tried again and David turned his wrath against my other interest which he rightly supposed he couldn't beat.

But that wasn't all he couldn't beat. Even giving in wasn't enough for David. You had to make him believe that you liked giving in, that it made you feel better, shriven of your incorrectitude, purged. It's a pity he wasn't religious. He'd have been so good at it.

He couldn't understand that I woke up one morning feeling hungry, as though I hadn't eaten anything for a week, but it wasn't my stomach that needed feeding. It was me. I wasn't learning anything. All I learned in offices was to do faster and better what I already knew and that offices aren't any more or less morally dubious than any other workplace. I read compulsively, though I can't remember much of what I read. Even now, I'll see a book and the title will come back to me together with the light in which I read it, huddled up in the early morning, out in the garden or crouched over my side of the bed.

I tried to write something for David as he hunted for a script that would 'take' but he said what I wrote was too linear and not cinematic enough. I didn't try again although I kept the story. It's about a girl who loves a donkey. And I wrote short stories and knew how bad they were but not how to make them better. In the last year of our marriage I began to write a commonplace book in which I documented what was happening to me, what I felt, as though the written word would give the experience some validity. Notice, by then I had not even the illusion of companionship. I wrote to breathe. I found the book when Con and I moved last time and it did not make pleasant reading.

Then Judith Chase, by now Jud because I could understand she meant to be a friend, rang me. Jud who began as a voice on the telephone and graduated to representing me when there was something to represent. Polished Jud, tough Jud, who tried to tell me I was in trouble and drank at my wedding and waited in vain to hear from me and made the occasional call or sent a note – God knows why – she rang and asked me to have lunch.

When I got there she was with another woman whom she introduced as the features editor of a magazine. We managed to talk generally all through lunch until she excused herself to a meeting and I asked Jud what was going on. She had a particular look in her eye.

'Well, I've waited for inspiration to visit you,' she said drily. 'And I thought it was time to dangle a deadline before your dazed eyes and see if you jumped.'

'I can't write features,' I protested.

'You,' said Jud firmly, 'can write anything you put your mind to.'

When I began to protest, she smiled at me grimly and suggested I wrote a short story about a marriage. It took me three weeks. I sent it to the editor I'd met with a note saying I knew it wasn't her kind of thing but perhaps she'd a colleague who might take a look at it? To begin with I waited excitedly for the mail but as time went on I forgot about it. One morning many weeks later I received a very nice note from a second person at the same magazine saying she'd liked the story, enclosing the edited version for me to see and saying that a cheque would follow in about a month.

David went to France for a week and I moved out. By then we'd had the rows and the fights and the broken glass when he threw a lamp at the floor in fury and the attempts at therapy. I moved into a little room with a bed and a table and a chair. There was a bathroom across the hall. I worked as a typist by day and I wrote at night. Well. I put words on the page. Nothing happened. I couldn't tell stories. Nothing suggested itself. I went to dinner and I went to bed, sometimes to sleep and sometimes for other diversion. I rang Midge and told her that I was O K and that leaving David was all I could do. She didn't want me to be with David but she didn't know anything about divorce. I spoke to Lindsay. It was 1974 and Paul died.

I was sad about Paul. He was like a tree that I was fond of, always there, differing from season to season but constant. And then one day the tree toppled and he wasn't there any more. He had a heart attack, started to get better, had a second and died. So I didn't have a chance to talk to him about David, who I knew was disappointing to him in just about every way that he could be. David could play rugby but he wouldn't. He made a film (Paul loved films) but it wasn't a Western. He came from Africa where nature is so large and all-encompassing that the flora and fauna of the English countryside looked pretty unexciting by comparison, no matter how Paul enthused about it. And worst of all, David only worked when he had a project to work at. Paul didn't understand that.

Paul worked until he dropped. He had retired from his job at the education authority but immediately gone back, first into private coaching and then supply teaching. By the 1970s the bravado of 'managing somehow' had become the pressure of 'making ends meet'. He didn't feel he could stop and he didn't until his heart stopped beating.

One night, in the depths of defeat, I wrote a factual piece about the sense of bereavement which comes at the end of a marriage. I couldn't think about Paul. I wasn't doing anything except following myopically, if not blindly, the line of advice which says that if you write, you must write. Talking or thinking or any other form of expression is fine but it has nothing to do with writing. To write you must write. I read it through the next morning and I looked up the name of the features editor who'd been so kind to me on Jud's behalf and rang her. She'd gone to a newspaper. I rang her there. She said no promises but send it in. I rang Jud and told her what I'd done. It took a long time but they used it.

And again, three times in the first year, then twelve the following year, more the next. I published. I only wrote at night. I lived in my clean and depressing little hideyhole, wore second-hand Jaeger to work and wrote at night.

In the second year of this divided existence, I met a man who spent eight months trying to persuade me to have his child. I must have liked listening to him but I was too ashamed to tell him how badly I wanted to be somebody's baby first. And then there was a City whizzkid, already divorced, whose plan was that I should marry him and take care of what he referred to as 'a readymade family'. And there was a writer on religious themes, a man who had been a communist, was now a twice divorced Roman Catholic with three children, who bought me books on Simone Weil. I still wrote at night.

Night became a metaphor for the stage of development I felt I'd reached. I couldn't be what I wanted to be, I couldn't get to what it was I wanted to do. I drank a bit and talked a lot and made love amiably enough, writing for three hours every night or, if there was a heavy date, for three hours before I went to work in the morning. Most of it was awful and my typing speed was demonic. I tried to write in pencil and transcribe my own work. I wrote in fountain pen and got ink on my fingers. I went back to the typewriter and stared at what I had written. I didn't know if I was writing a book, a play or a song lyric. Words poured from me and most of them meant very little. Of course I wasn't grieving for David. Damn David. I was sad about myself. I was sad about Paul.

When Paul died I learned something about Joan that I had not observed before. She was accustomed to him. His shortcomings went to the grave with him and initially she recalled only the good things. He was a habit she'd spent years establishing and she felt lost without him. What else can there be when a husband of many years dies but a hole?

The balance of power in the relationship as I had observed it led me to believe that he loved her and she stayed with him. Now I saw that it was more complicated than that and that she was in great pain. It wasn't that she couldn't write a cheque or ride a bus. Indeed, she had to. Paul left her with very little money, which is a nice, polite, well-brought-up way of saying that he left her broke, and she went back to work that winter. And if there were any business documents to be signed, she left it to Lindsay to sign them or signed where Lindsay pointed. She found the institutionalisation of domestic life – mortgage payments, death grants and so on – distasteful. I went down one weekend and Lindsay went down another and Joan my mother tried to bear up under the endlessness of the days by walking her dog and eating her supper and catching the bus to work the next day. And then she saw Giles Campion's name on a big sign for a landscaped estate.

Lindsay was at home that weekend and she told me about it.

When I asked who he was, she said, 'Oh, an architect friend of Mother's, during the war.' But when I saw Joan the following weekend, she was very low and fearful and as we were going up to bed on the Friday night, she turned in the darkness and said, 'You didn't know I had an affair during the war, did you?' I couldn't see her face in the darkness, just the outline of her head and shoulders. 'No,' I said as gently as I could. 'You never told me that.' 'Well I did,' she said, and she continued upstairs, me following until we were both on the landing. 'I loved Daddy,' she said, 'I really did, but we were away for such a long time, separated you know, because of Lindsay's reaction to the bombing, and then I met this man and –' She gasped. 'Oh dear, now you'll be shocked and hurt and you won't love me any more.' I caught her in my arms. 'I'm not hurt,' I said, 'and I'm not shocked. I'm fascinated. I'm delighted. You're my mother who I love and you're human. Do you want to talk about it?' I could feel her looking at me in the dark. 'You are a funny girl,' she said.

I asked her how she knew it was him. We were still standing in the darkness at the top of the stairs. I didn't like to move to put the light on.

'I rang him up,' she said, 'and said "guess who?" He said, "Where have you been?" I'm going to have dinner with him next week. Do you understand?'

'Yes,' I said. I didn't.

'I really loved Paul, you know,' she said again, 'but there were things that were – difficult . . .'

'He was not an easy man,' I said on cue.

'No,' she said, almost to herself. 'Not easy. But I did love him. Giles was just quite different – and the war, of course, made everything so strange.' She fell silent, then moved towards her bedroom. 'See you in the morning.'

'Goodnight,' I said. Not once had she mentioned Lindsay.

15 *Joan*

Joan's first reaction to the declaration of war was relief that Paul was too old to go and fight. And then, along with everybody else she knew, she adapted as fast as she could. She learned what she could and couldn't buy, what to hoard, what wouldn't keep. She learned to stand in queues, to carry a gas mask, to run for the shelter, to draw the blackout curtains. Lindsay learned things, too, under-standing that if she didn't do as she was told, she was in danger. But nobody could have predicted how the new noises would affect her.

If she had wept or cried out, her suffering might have been easier to understand, but as it was, she bore it all with a stunned stoicism which, Joan realised, left her, as her mother, not knowing quite how to respond. She was so distressed that she fainted repeatedly throughout the day, rarely permitting the cuddles and hugs Joan offered to soothe her and regarding her repeated, if temporary unconsciousness with such detachment that it might have been happening to somebody else. By now she had invented an imaginary friend, someone to whom she could be heard talking quite clearly, with some animation, and often, if asked how she felt, she would describe her friend's feelings instead. For Lindsay, the imaginary Margaret Johnson was more real than Lindsay herself.

They were evacuated to a vicarage, a low, pretty building a short distance from the church which was itself just outside the village, nearly sixty miles from Persthorpe. A local bus stopped opposite. The location was at once cut off and convenient. To begin with, staying in the vicarage, trying to keep her belongings separate from Mrs Ramsey's, with half their clothes and a few of their other possessions, had the quality of camping – comfortable but not quite comfortable enough. It was a time of waiting, waiting to see if Paul would telephone or write, waiting to see if there would be air-raids and, if so, how many and how often, but then time passed and, as it did, Joan found herself waiting less and doing more.

First of all, Lindsay was attending the same school as Jennifer Ramsey and they became friends so that often, if Lindsay were called and did not answer, it was not because she was hiding or even talking to her imaginary friend so much, though Margaret continued to feature in her conversations for some years to come. It was more likely that she and Jennifer were playing in the field at the back of the house or helping Mrs Ramsey to keep order among the various candles and prayer books and hassocks she felt were her sacred charge since her husband left to serve as an army padre. Or they were in the kitchen playing with flour and water, or upstairs in the attic, acting out a film or reading aloud to one another. In time they developed a nonsense language in which neither mother was proficient.

Joan tried to help in the kitchen, to become friendly with Mrs Ramsey, but the other woman remained firmly opposed to any familiarity of address and preferred to keep her kitchen as much to herself as possible. To begin with there was a certain amount of friction about who had used what from which shelf but soon Joan capitulated and deferred and stuck to the washing-up, leaving Mrs Ramsey in control. Oddly enough, once this was decided, their relationship took on a recognisable shape. To Joan it seemed odd to sit talking to a woman younger than herself and calling her by her title but as long as she did, Mrs Ramsey could be quite pleasant in small doses. The intimacy of the daughters was not emulated by their mothers.

One afternoon, Joan discovered herself at a loss, staring at her nails. She had not done this since she was adolescent, when it earned her a reproof for time-wasting. She couldn't exercise the dogs. She had parted with them to a local farmer who confided that they were far better ratters than his old cat. Mrs Ramsey might share her kitchen with other humans but definitely not with anything four-legged. Lindsay was quite happy, Paul was in regular if limited contact, and the vicarage, though bigger than any house she'd lived in, did not require serious daily housework. One of the great blessings about Mrs Ramsey was that she was no more interested in that kind of domesticity than Joan herself.

Trying to rid herself of unease, guilt and pointless defensiveness, Joan opened the local paper and, scanning it, came to the situations vacant section where a carefully displayed advertisement caught her eye. 'Municipal clerks,' she read, 'willing, good spelling, no experience – ' Even she could do that. She pinned on her hat and caught the next bus to Byrham, slightly bigger than Hennington, the near side of Garslake. The possibility of meeting Ann Shand or anybody else she knew did not occur to her. Byrham was small and drab and grey but there were enough people bustling about as Joan made her way to the town hall.

She showed the advertisement to the man at the desk who directed her to a room with a four-figure number, which made it feel as though the town hall were a good deal bigger than it looked from the outside. There were two men in the room when she got there, the older of whom asked her if she'd worked at all. 'No,' she replied, 'but I trained as a teacher.' He looked at her thoughtfully, scribbled on a piece of paper and, handing it to her, said she should go two doors down and see Mr Cole. The latter gave her a form to fill in and said he'd start her on simple filing at 9.00 sharp on Monday. At his request she wrote down her name, address and marital status and promised to bring the vicarage telephone number in when she came – at that moment she couldn't remember it. And she almost ran down the steps to the street, feeling elated, so much so that when one of the munitions factory men tried to elbow her out of her place in the bus queue, she turned on him with her most dazzling smile. 'We all work, you know,' she said, and hauled herself up on the waiting platform. Perhaps getting a job was really going to make a difference.

Lindsay was impressed by the idea of Joan with a job and, once she'd grasped the idea of her mother supplementing their small income, enthusiastic. 'We could all go out for tea!' she said. Joan nodded, brushing down her once good suit, though Monday was still four days away and she'd have to do it all over again nearer the time. When it came to it, she could have worn her gardening clothes. Simple filing was what it was.

In the bowels of the building there were scores of filing cupboards. They were originally laid out to a plan but nobody had ever written it down or confided it to anyone else outside the brotherhood of clerks so, before she could put anything away, she had to find a likely place to put it. Her head swam and she was filthy but she ploughed on. At least she wasn't sitting about, waiting for somebody else, and it gave her something to talk to Paul about when he telephoned at the weekend.

'And the money will help,' she said proudly. 'I'm taking Lindsay out to tea next week.'

'Good for you,' he said, sounding as though he meant it.

Lindsay asked if she could bring Jennifer, Mrs Ramsey declined to join them, so the three of them had tea on Friday afternoon in the town's smartest teashop and lurched happily, filled with tough scones and an edifying concoction billed as 'Maintenance Fruit Cake', on to a later bus. The weekend passed pleasantly enough, even if Mrs Ramsey was more than usually territorial about what she called 'her' kitchen, and on Monday morning Joan left for work, feeling quite an old hand.

It didn't take very long to learn the faces if not the names of the regular travellers on the bus, just as Mr Cole soon became Jim and their boss Mr Foster was 'Sir' to his face but 'Madob' behind his back because of the catchphrase he used to buck them up and urge them on – 'Must all do our bit.' Jim talked about the war, his chest, his wife's bunions, the war, the hierarchy of the town hall and whenever she flagged would encourage her by telling her, 'Joan, you've got a real gift for order. You know more about the files than anyone has for ages.'

This tribute, while sincerely meant, was not the accolade it might have been after the first two or three times, so it came as a wonderful surprise when he asked her one rainy morning if she would mind doing an errand. 'I'd go myself,' he explained, 'but my chest is so sore and what with the rain . . .' Excited at being let out (for that was how it felt) Joan insisted that she was only too glad to be of help.

'But what about the rain?' queried Jim, as if she might not have understood that he meant she'd actually have to go out in it.

'I don't mind,' said she firmly. 'I've got boots and an umbrella, I really don't mind.' So he gave her the envelope and directions.

It wasn't difficult to find though it was right over the other side of town and, when she'd pressed the bell, she stood back, looking up at a rather fine old house. The door was opened by a man. 'Look, do come in, I'm just on the telephone,' and as she nervously stepped forward into a carpeted hall, he rushed back into a room to her left to continue talking. She was dripping and he seemed to be taking a very long time but when he returned, she immediately proffered the packet. He took it from her hand as she said, 'I'm sorry, I'm making a dreadful mess on your carpet.' 'Oh, it's you,' he said. She looked at him and then half-shook her head. 'You were recruited when I was talking to old Foster about these.' He nodded at the packet. 'I'd recognise that voice anywhere.' Joan blushed. 'Come in and have a sherry. Put those wet things down.' She did.

He led her into a large room covered with papers and large drawings set out on tables with angled lights over them.

'I'm an architect,' he said, patting a chair. 'Here, sit down, I'll get you a drink.' He poured and talked so easily about his work and what she was doing, about his wife and their children, asking where Joan was living, that she was alarmed when she looked at her watch to discover that almost an hour had passed.

'I'm late,' she said, full of sherry, her clothes almost dry. 'I must get back.'

He rose at once saying, 'I'd like to say I'll take you back but there isn't enough juice in the car to get you across town. Just tell them you had to dry out a bit before you could go out in it again.'

'Isn't that a bit silly?' Joan asked as he helped her back into her battered mac.

He looked at her gravely. 'Yes, when I think about it, I suppose it is, but it's one of those perfectly reasonable excuses that everybody accepts. You have to dry out before you can face getting wet again.'

'Thank you for the sherry,' said Joan, feeling less certain than she had done a moment ago, sitting in easy conversation. He bowed slightly, she turned to go and he put his hand on her arm.

'You make the nicest messenger,' he said.

She smiled nervously and slipped quickly out of the door.

'You were a long time,' remarked Jim Cole.

'I know,' she said, 'but I had to get dry before I could face getting wet again.'

He considered the logic of this. 'You're quite right, you know, however silly it sounds. It's when I don't get properly dry that my chest plays up . . .' And Joan knew she'd hear no more about her protracted absence.

Two or three weeks later Mrs Ramsey asked Joan how she felt about letting the girls go to stay with her mother, Jennifer's granny, who had a small farm a few miles north. They discussed it and the girls were most enthusiastic. 'A real farm!' exclaimed Lindsay with delight. 'Mmm, in the real country!' replied Joan with a grin. So they packed thick sweaters and took extra towels. 'How are they going to get there?' asked Joan. 'On the bus?' 'Well, they could,' replied Mrs Ramsey, 'but if they get up early, the milk lorry will take them to the door. I know the driver, I'll have a word with him.' So at five they clambered up on the back of the lorry, surrounded by clanking empty churns.

The weekend was long without Lindsay. Joan slept until midday and idled through a bath and her washing, wearing her pyjamas under her oldest trousers and sweater. At five the telephone rang. She heard Mrs Ramsey answering and then calling for her.

'Are the girls all right?' asked Joan, coming to meet her on the stairs.

'I hope so, only it's not about the girls,' said Mrs Ramsey. 'It's a Mr Campion about your work.'

Joan started to look puzzled, then controlled her face. 'Thank you,' she said. She went down to the hall and picked up the receiver.

'Part of the war effort is keeping men in restricted occupations happy. Would you like to make me happy?'

'Yes,' she said.

'Oh good. Come to the pictures with me.'

'When?'

'Today, six-thirty. I'll come and pick you up.'

'No. I'll meet you at the Cross Keys.' This last whispered, though whether in fear of her own temerity or Mrs Ramsey's untried curiosity, she couldn't tell.

'In the lobby?'

'Yes.'

'Soonest.'

'Bye.'

She called to Mrs Ramsey, 'They've lost something I filed, I'll have to go in and sort it out.'

Mrs Ramsey appeared sympathetic. 'Oh dear, can't it wait until Monday?'

'Apparently not,' said Joan with a wry salute. 'You know, there's a war on . . .'

Mrs Ramsey sniffed, half-disapprovingly.

'I might go to the pictures,' said Joan, 'afterwards. I do hope the girls will be all right.'

Mrs Ramsey's face cleared. 'I'm sure they will be,' she said.

Joan looked at herself in the mirror. She put on a blouse and a skirt, a hat, a coat and lipstick. She left. She knew that if she stopped and thought about it, she'd never go. What if Paul rang? Mrs Ramsey would tell him she'd been summoned because something was misplaced. They'd speak tomorrow.

She ran for the bus.

He rose as soon as he saw her enter the vestibule and they began talking as if they'd known each other all their lives.

The film was enjoyable enough, although Joan couldn't remember much about it. When it was over he insisted he should take her home.

'But you can't,' she said. 'I mean, that's not what I told Mrs Ramsey I'd be doing. She thinks that I came into town to find something at the office and went to the cinema by myself.'

He put his hand over her eyes.

'Tell me the name of the film.'

She struggled to reply.

'Who was in it?'

She fumbled and stumbled.

'What was it about?' After four sentences he took his hand away. 'Somehow,' he said gravely, 'I don't think you were thinking much about the film.'

She looked at him.

'And what could be more innocent than the cause of your wasted evening bringing you home?'

'How will you get back?'

'Walk.'

She thought about it. 'I'd rather go home alone.'

He looked at her intently, as if he might never see her again.

'I'll take you to the bus.'

When Joan arrived home, there was a note from Mrs Ramsey to say that Paul had rung and would ring at six tomorrow.

Joan sat on her bed, took off her clothes and lay down.

Sleep was slow in coming.

16   *Mercer*

I have tried but I cannot imagine what it was like to live through the war. I have read books and seen films and looked at pictures but I fear that my impression of it is inadequate. It's the big things that get written about – the politics, the fire power, the death camps, the victories. But it's hard to construct from nothing an idea of what it meant for things you'd always taken for granted to vanish as if they had never existed. A French actress once wrote that she could never get used to seeing piles of oranges because her girlhood had been without them and every time she saw a fruit stall, she wanted to buy a bagful in case they vanished again.

Children quickly learned a new vocabulary of sounds: the warning siren, the relief of the all-clear, the whistle of shells, the pause before an explosion. Anxious mothers now checked that you had your gas mask as well as a clean handkerchief. Houses were demolished and people went away, not to return. And it was dirty and untidy and demoralising and the food was poor.

But I had to glean all this from books and the reminiscences of others. Within my family it was hardly mentioned.

Paul once commented that we should have listened to Churchill, that he tried to warn us that the Germans would re-arm and be back for a second crack at what they had not achieved before. Joan spoke only of her domestic experience and about Lindsay's illness ('She would get up in the morning, faint, come downstairs, faint, eat breakfast, sway again, get ready, faint, come round and go off to

135

school.' I once asked if she fainted at school. 'Not often,' Joan replied) and their removal to the country, sharing the vicarage with Mrs Ramsey and Jennifer, who was about the same age as Lindsay, of the day the vicarage roof caught fire, and dried egg.

When Paul met Joan he had already been through one war and had fewer illusions about it than many. He knew that at its best it was not heroic but brutal and ugly and funny. And at its worst it was just brutal and ugly. But on both occasions he was clear about his contribution. He was too old to fight the second time around but he joined the Air Training Corps to help train others. It was the best he could do.

I never heard Paul mention being apart from my mother and Lindsay during the war. I think he was drawn in upon himself with their absence. He did not cook very well, was not a domestic creature at all, and so rather than trying to eat with other people, he ate what there was, read and listened to the radio.

He told me when I was fourteen or fifteen, one night when he'd had a lot to drink, that he had a friend to whom he had been very close. Various people had tried to tell him (Paul) that the friend was homosexual. Paul was frightened by the idea, and repelled, but since he liked the man, he disregarded the distasteful stories about him. One day there was an air-raid. Paul's friend was not accounted for when they cleared the building. Paul went back to warn him and found him in the arms of another man. He turned and rushed out again, assuring everybody that the building had been cleared. It took a direct hit.

Joan and Paul must have spent odd times together during the seven years of the war but neither of them ever mentioned them. I knew that Joan worked as a clerk and Lindsay went to school in Byrham, where Joan worked. I surmised from a few photographs and what Joan told me that for my mother, being away from Paul's life, in the country where Lindsay was demonstrably happier, the disruption of war audibly less and the freedom of having a job was, all in all, light after a long darkness.

But after Paul died, when my mother told me, safe in some senses and standing in the dark on her way to bed, that she had had an affair during the war, what bemused me was not what she did to my father, because I had already begun to decide that they had mutually agreed the cat's cradle they were tied up in, but that she didn't mention Lindsay. She could not acknowledge that her elder daughter might know for in doing that she would have to acknowledge the role she, Joan, played in what followed.

Joan has always believed that if you don't talk about it, whatever it is, it will go away. She is not interested in the impulse towards conscious self-knowledge. Her attitude was that, if you had such an inclination, you should not admit to it, for fear that thereby someone would misappropriate your hard-won power. For her, power lay in silence, in holding everything in. That's why she admired Paul for his forbearance with his family, Lindsay for her attempts in vain to relate successfully to Paul. That's why she was uneasy from the beginning about me, not only because I wanted to know but because I was determined to find out and, having made my discovery, to talk about it. I wanted to tell.

Joan says I was enchanting as a child because I spoke well and freely, for which she must take major credit, but when I turned my search inward upon myself and began, sin of sins, to write it down, she was worried. Hadn't she herself taught me that, unless you can't avoid it, you write nothing down? If it isn't written down, it can always be denied, and she could not admit the cause of her concern. She admired me for the accomplishment of writing, because she loved to read, but distrusted me for the introspection. And when the power of that investigation came to be focussed upon her and Paul and Lindsay, when I felt I had to try to understand more about them in order to understand myself, she withdrew sharply and began sending up danger signals like a beleaguered redskin, though all I saw for many years was just a lot of smoke.

17 Joan

An affair was not discussed between Joan and Giles Campion. It was just one of those things.

Lindsay and Jennifer took to going over quite often to Mrs Ramsey's mother's farm. When they were not at the farm, they were out walking or reading together, meeting some friend or other for tea or looking round Byrham's small Woolworth's. Lindsay was very sensible. She drew comfort from Jennifer's prosaic attitude toward the sirens, the aeroplanes and even the occasional fright like the time a plane crashed in the Long Meadow and bits of falling debris briefly set alight part of the vicarage roof. She carried her gas mask, ready to use it if she had to, and sometimes she and Jennifer held hands. Jennifer understood that some people are just funny about those things.

Joan continued to work at the office. It would be unfair to say that she was indispensable but she was brighter than many of the temporary staff and, in time, found herself being asked more than once to do a bit extra or asked if she'd mind waiting or even if certain work could not be done at the weekend – for a consideration?

And Giles Campion found all sorts of ways and means to ensure that they met until one pretext was so threadbare that, having come to meet him, she found herself suddenly angry. He ordered tea and she sat down, frowning at him.

'We can't go on like this, you know.'

'Like what?' he asked.

She gestured impatiently. 'You know. You've had me in from the vicarage and yourself over to the town hall so many times. You've done just about everything except drop your handkerchief.'

His eyes met hers without hesitation.

'Good heavens,' he said. 'I thought I'd dropped that months ago.'

She sat transfixed. The waitress brought tea, offered cake. They refused it. She came back again with hot water. Joan's throat felt closed. She poured tea. He drank two cups while she watched him.

'I have a room with a view, you know, in Martins Square,' he said.

She looked down at her hands, then up to meet his eyes. He paid for tea and they left.

She followed him through the house and up the stairs. He closed the bedroom door behind them. It was all clean and fresh, there were even flowers in a jug on the dressing table.

'You were a bit sure of yourself!' she exclaimed, turning to him.

'Boy Scouts' motto,' he said. 'Be prepared.' And kissed her.

His body was smaller and finer than she was used to. He climbed upon her like a cat, seeking something, she knew he was seeking but didn't know what it was. He buried his nose in her hair, her armpit, her waist. She felt expansive, creamy, pleased that she'd done something completely apart from what she usually did, and discovered that it suited her. And then her hand flew to her mouth.

'What's the matter?' he asked.

'I – you didn't – we mustn't have a baby!' Tears of remorse and disappointment threatened to spoil her temporarily contented face.

'You won't.'

'What do you mean? You didn't use anything.'

He enfolded her, as if reassuring a favourite child.

'Mumps, darling. Very bad mumps. A sovereign and wholly aesthetic method.'

She still looked anxiously at him.

'Disbelieving woman. Ask the doctor.' He kissed her, soothed her, and soon she relaxed again.

When he put her on the bus, all she could wonder was if it showed, if what she had been doing (and worse still enjoying it) was writ, like Nathaniel Hawthorne's Scarlet Letter, large across her brow, but the occupants of the bus, several of whom she knew by sight, just laughed and teased them both about working late. A little way down the road, she checked her watch – she had covered herself. Paul knew she was sometimes on call. When she reached the vicarage, she noticed that there was a light on in the front room as well the kitchen, which was very unusual for Mrs Ramsey, and she wondered if she too might have had a more interesting day than she usually spent. But before she could put her key in the lock, the local doctor opened the door.

'Thank goodness you're here,' he said. 'Your office at the town hall doesn't answer but I suppose by then you were on your way homeward. Anyway, come in, it's nothing serious, but a nasty shock and of course she needs her mother.'

Taken aback, Joan followed him to where Lindsay lay on the sofa, pale, holding on to Jennifer as if she'd never let her go, while even Mrs Ramsey had not quite her usual ecclesiastical aplomb.

'What happened?' asked Joan, as Lindsay burst into tears and held out her arms for her mother. 'Darling, darling, there. Please will somebody – ?'

Mrs Ramsey cleared her throat. 'My mother had an unreliable fire, Mrs Canning. She left it in the room where the girls were playing. With water. Some of the water got on the fire and it shorted. Nobody was hurt but a rug caught fire and there was quite a bang. I'm very sorry. I have been trying to get my mother to get rid of it.'

Joan cuddled Lindsay and said over her head to the doctor, 'Is there anything she should take?'

He smiled wryly, closing his bag. 'No, she's all right really. Just very shaken. Your daughter was alone when it happened – '

'Jennifer went to get a cloth from the kitchen,' said Lindsay haltingly, 'and I held some water up in the jar but I slipped and it went on the fire.' Her face began to fold again and Joan put her arms round her while Jennifer sniffed sympathetically.

'There, there,' said Mrs Ramsey awkwardly. 'You were really very lucky, both of you, and when I've shown the doctor out, we shall all have a nice cup of tea.' She led the way, the doctor following. Joan got Lindsay to bed as soon as she could and she sat, holding her daughter's hand and waiting for sleep to come. Lindsay said 'I thought you were never coming. Did you have to work again?'

'Yes,' said Joan. The first lie. The first selfish grown-up lie I've ever told my daughter. And heavens, my heart is pounding.

'Poor old Mummy,' said Lindsay.

By the next day, with Jennifer's solicitude and a bit of gentle teasing, the incident shrank to less remarkable proportions and within a week they were talking about going to the farm again. Joan told Paul what had happened and the rest of their news, what little there was. The calls were ritualistic. That was what they had together, telephone calls. And meanwhile not a word from Giles Campion.

Joan went to work and came home. Mrs Ramsey cleaned out the kitchen cupboards. Not to be outdone, Joan decided to overhaul the rooms they'd been living in for months. As Joan was the very opposite of Mrs Ramsey in these matters and welcomed help, no matter how unskilled, both Jennifer and Lindsay volunteered to 'help' and they spent a tiring but rewarding day, scrubbing and shaking and washing down, while Mrs Ramsey, impressed in spite of herself, supplied refreshments and advice. When the girls suggested a game of charades after supper, Joan agreed to join in. What else was there to do, she thought, and anyway she was so tired, it was almost like being tipsy. So Mrs Ramsey said she'd play too, at which Jennifer was so taken aback that she almost started to reject the unheard-off offer. 'Good,' said Joan firmly, 'that makes two teams of two. Great stuff, symmetry. Come with me, Mrs Ramsey, while we sort ourselves out.' They tossed a coin to see who went first and chose to act out film and song titles. Mrs Ramsey quite forgot herself and enjoyed the excitement as much as any of them. They giggled a lot and eventually, still laughing, retired upstairs to their respective quarters.

On Monday morning there was a note on Joan's office desk. 'Will you have lunch with me,' it said. 'Please ring and say yes.' Joan went to the telephone box in the post office opposite at mid-morning. When Giles answered the telephone, she asked, 'What time?' He replied 'one' and she put the receiver down. She slipped back into her office, hoping that her absence would go unremarked. She worked until twelve, fidgeted for twenty minutes and set off early. Outside the house in Martins Square, she hesitated, but the door opened before she got to it and he beckoned her in. Once inside the door, he looked at her very carefully without speaking and helped her off with her coat. She didn't know what to say so she said nothing. He brought her a drink.

'Will you come and see a film with me on Saturday?' he asked.

She looked at the sherry. 'I don't think I can.'

'Perhaps we could go for a walk, Sunday's a good day for walking.'

She looked at him. 'Unless Lindsay is away for the weekend, I don't see how I can.'

'Couldn't I take you and Lindsay for a walk?' he asked.

'No.' Joan's free hand curled into a fist.

He reached over and took the glass from her. He looked at her. She stared back. He took her hand and led her upstairs.

She took off her clothes, he took off his. They lay in the cold bed very close together while he stroked her hair.

'Then,' he asked, 'how are we going to manage?'

She shook her head.

'This,' he said, placing his warm body deliberately on top of her, 'doesn't feel like a farewell. How shall I see you, beautiful?'

She swallowed. 'As and when,' she said.

'As and when?' he mocked her, sliding down her body. 'Good old as-and-when.'

She tried to ward him off. 'I'm serious,' she said.

He looked down at her. 'Good,' he said, and entered her. He pumped, rested and pumped more. Looking down at her he asked, 'Why didn't you ring me?'

She was taken aback. 'I didn't think it was up to me,' she said.

'But,' he said, moving carefully inside her, looking for something he'd only know when he found it, 'how else are we to meet? I can't plague you.'

'What about your wife?'

'My wife is in Cornwall, having a quiet war in a pretty cottage. She is not here. Nor are my children. You, on the other hand, are here.' He looked at her carefully, beginning to move again. 'Almost here.'

She looked away.

They agreed that the code for identification was 'as and when' and that barring special occasions they would meet at the house in Martins Square. Joan seemed to him to place considerable faith in her ability to lie her way out of anything but the town was small. True, there were other evacuees and true, people tended to mind their own business, but Giles felt that by confining their activities largely to the house, they would be safer. Joan had not thought about how she could be unsafe, but she agreed.

Her life with Paul seemed like a book she had read long ago, perhaps in a more archaic version of the language. She had always been, she told herself, a creature of the present and the situation of being separated, living for today because of the war, its dangers and shortages, had heightened that in her. She thought Giles was very sweet to be so concerned but she did not see how it could matter. She was very discreet in her phone calls and so was he. He made her talk and he made her laugh and he made love to her a lot, which pleased them both, though he was aware that her surrender was always qualified. Each knew how much or how little was involved and playing the game was the phrase that best expressed their experience. For provided that she spoke to Paul regularly and spent some time with Lindsay, Joan did not see that she was doing the unexpected or inappropriate. Through what happened with Giles, she could see what she had hoped for with Jack Riker, during the time she spent with Ann Shand. She didn't ask herself what that signified but was instead rather relieved to see her past behaviour as understandable.

However, as the months went by, she became aware of Lindsay watching her as patiently as she used to watch Paul. To begin with, she was afraid that the relationship with Jennifer might have failed, but Lindsay remained adamant that Jennifer was her best friend. So Joan shooed her into outside interests like the school choir or the local guide group. Lindsay went willingly enough, mostly with Jennifer, but when she was not occupied, her concentration upon her mother was considerable. Joan offered board games. Lindsay accepted and they talked while they played. But Joan couldn't feel that they were close during this time, however much Lindsay seemed to appeal to her and she to respond. It was as if Lindsay had something she wanted to say but couldn't say it. She spent time with her mother but the purpose of her proximity remained concealed. Joan found that Lindsay remained in view but was in fact hidden from her in certain moods. And trying to get through to her sometimes was infuriating. Joan felt like a woman invited to look at a view from a window only to find, upon walking up to it, that the curtains were drawn and could not be pulled back.

One day Lindsay asked Joan about her job and Joan extemporised with some fluency about filing systems, architects and the numbers of copies the town hall seemed to require of everything.

'Is Mr Campion one of the men you work for?' asked Lindsay.

Joan became careful. 'No. I work for a man called Jim Cole and his boss is Mr Foster. You remember, you've heard me talk about him? – Old "Must all do our bit". Mr Campion is one of the

143

architects in the department.'

Lindsay frowned slightly.

'Only Mrs Ramsey says he makes you work too hard.'

Joan smiled deprecatingly.

'Well, it's very kind of Mrs Ramsey to be so concerned but Mr Campion needs all the help he can get, and as I seem to be the one person in the department who can spell, he tends to give me his work in preference to anybody else. Of course that sometimes means working a bit extra but you and Jennifer get on so well that I thought you wouldn't miss that bit of me. And sometimes he takes me out for tea or a drink or something, and it's nice with Daddy back in Persthorpe, to have some company other than you and Jennifer and Mrs Ramsey.' Had she said too much?

'And Jim Cole,' said Lindsay.

'Not forgetting Jim Cole, but you know, he does rather sing one note and the war and his wife don't make for the most exciting conversational exchanges.'

Lindsay nodded gravely, then she stood up. 'I think I'll go and find Jennifer.'

'By all means,' said Joan.

She felt she had run a mile in heavy boots. Had she been seeing too much of Giles? Had she been seen with him? She tried to remember where they'd been and who could have seen them doing what. Damn Mrs Ramsey and her concern. Joan thought for a moment and then went to look for her. She was not in the kitchen, nor in the living room. But she rarely went out without lengthy explanations. Joan collected her coat and walked over to the church. As she walked, she pep-talked herself. Play it straight, she thought. Nothing is going on. If you believe that, she will. It's all innocent, isn't it? As innocent as anything is in wartime. Well then, if it's innocent, then that's the way you play it. She entered the dark of the church and looked round.

At first she didn't think there was anybody there. She walked forward. It was a friendly church, still and not too cold. She saw someone hunched over. The figure didn't move. She began to tiptoe towards it with great care, very softly.

Mrs Ramsey had obviously knelt to pray, become lost in her thoughts and fallen asleep. With her eyes closed, her face had softened and she looked less of a martinet and more like a careworn woman. Joan sat down and waited. She looked at her watch. Half an hour, she decided. Mrs Ramsey was as determined in her sleep as she was in the disposition of her waking hours. When Joan woke her, she looked up quite bewildered.

'It's all right,' said Joan. 'You were praying and you must have dropped off.'

Mrs Ramsey couldn't have looked more embarrassed.

'What must you think of me?' she demanded, pushing herself upright. 'How long have I been here? Where are the girls?'

'Lindsay went off to play with Jennifer. I expect they're in the garden or the attic. With any luck they'll have the kettle on when we get home. Come,' and she rose.

Mrs Ramsey exclaimed again about how long she'd been there, expressing her self-reproach until Joan caught her arm.

'Mrs Ramsey, we all get tired. There's a lot going on and most of it we can't do anything about.'

'Yes, yes,' agreed Mrs Ramsey, 'but you won't tell Jennifer, will you? Such an appalling example for her.'

'No,' said Joan, crossing her fingers in her coat pocket. 'And could you perhaps do something for me?'

'Of course,' said Mrs Ramsey, flustered by the directness of Joan's approach.

'Don't let Lindsay worry about me. She was asking me just today about Mr Campion. Well, you know, a lot of the things I do are for the usual reasons – a few extra pounds always come in handy – but I don't want her to worry and she is such a sensitive girl. It is confidential, the work I do, and nowadays, things are not always what they seem . . .'

Mrs Ramsey stopped and stared. 'My dear,' she said, 'I hope you don't think I'm questioning the propriety – '

'Of course not,' said Joan, 'but you know how tongues will wag and – well, I'd be very grateful for any reassurances you can give her. Subtly, of course.'

Mrs Ramsey said she understood, indeed she did, with her hand unexpectedly on Joan's own. For once in accord, they went to find their daughters.

In October, Lindsay came home terrifically excited because the school choir was going carol singing and could she go? Mrs Allnutt who taught them music would conduct and, properly escorted, they would make the rounds of every local hotel, café and meeting place, to raise money for war widows. And for once Joan could not feel what she had come to refer to privately as 'Lindsay's curtains' between them. Delighted at her daughter's animation, Joan gave

145

permission. Practice began almost at once. Jennifer too was in the choir. Joan continued to meet Giles.

She saw him less often than either of them liked but that was the offering she made to her guilt. Giles mocked her gently when she tried to explain this to him. 'You can't make a bargain with the Almighty,' he said, as she lay against the cushions on his sofa. 'It isn't any less of a sin because we do it in daylight and you never stay the night.' Joan felt foolish. 'I know it isn't and I wish I could but –' Her voice trailed away. 'Dear girl,' he said, 'we have what we have. Let's make the most of it.' She gave him her hand and he held it very tightly.

Joan cut down a coat she found at a sale for Lindsay to wear carol singing. It was a good coat, smooth cloth, and Joan sewed well. Jennifer admired it and Lindsay was thrilled. All muffled up in boots and scarves and hats, their mothers decided they would be warm enough and saw them off to school, knowing that tonight was the great carol-singing effort. At six Giles rang. 'I've got some petrol for the car. I'll come and get you. Tell Mrs Thing it's a pre-Christmas thank you for all your efforts.' Joan did. She was rewarded by a look of understanding, woman to woman, which almost made her laugh. 'She looked at me as though I were doing it for my country and did everything short of bless me,' Joan told Giles, chuckling as they drove along. It was cold and sparkling in the country and he took her to a pub for a drink and then back into the hills for another and then suggested the Cross Keys at Byrham.

'The scene of my seduction!' cried Joan, laughing.

Giles turned on her in mock reproof. 'No, no,' he said. 'If any seducing was done, you did it.'

They laughed and giggled and drove to the hotel, which was festive with streamers and holly. They ordered drinks and Joan slipped off her coat.

'I'm just going to powder my nose,' she murmured, reaching past Giles for her bag.

'Won't you powder mine too?' he said, holding her wrist for a moment. She freed herself and went to find the lavatory. It was quiet in there, with a snow scene tacked to the wall under a big red paper bow. She sat down and sighed. What would next year bring? she wondered. As she walked to the door, she could hear voices but she felt oddly weary and disinterested. Shouldn't drink any more, she thought. Silly really. No answers in that. She pushed open the door into the room and saw all the children lined up watching Mrs

146

Allnutt, who was leading them into 'O Come All Ye Faithful'. She closed the door carefully behind her. If I don't move, she won't notice me, there are so many people, but Giles stood up and waved and Joan looked from him into her daughter's eyes.

She waited until they'd finished and then went towards Lindsay, putting money in the box Jennifer held out. Still looking her daughter straight in the eye she said, 'Mr Campion brought me here as a thank you for all the work I've done.' Lindsay nodded. 'Would you like to come and say hello?' Lindsay looked at her. 'It seems only fair that you should meet.' She took Lindsay and Jennifer quickly over to meet the smiling Giles, and shepherded them back to Mrs Allnutt. They sang three more carols, Giles singing along under his breath, Joan very upright in her chair, and Lindsay's eyes stayed unblinkingly upon her mother. 'See you later, darling,' called Joan. Lindsay barely nodded. The choir left.

When she came home that night, Joan stood in the doorway and looked at her daughter's sleeping form. She wondered if Lindsay knew. Children were like animals, they picked up on things. The trouble was, she couldn't confess. It wouldn't help either of them. She would have to deal with Lindsay as she had with Mrs Ramsey. She'd have to go straight on, like a horse wearing blinkers. But suppose, suppose – the horse came to a crossroads. Her eyes filled. She closed the door. Who was it who said 'least said, soonest mended'? It sounded like something her mother would have said. She fastened her pyjamas and put out the light. Often she found the dark comforting. Tonight it made her feel very lonely.

A few days later, Paul rang to say that he had to come to the nearby county town for a course and he thought they might make a weekend of it. He was very gentle and unemphatic on the telephone and they talked about trains and times and where to meet. 'Thought we'd stay somewhere nice,' he said. 'Haven't spent a weekend together for ages.'

Joan told Lindsay about it at tea. 'Daddy just rang,' she said. 'He's coming over near here on a course and he wants me to join him for the weekend. Will you be all right here with Jennifer?'

Lindsay said she would. Jennifer said she was sure it would be all right with her mother and Mrs Ramsey, with flour on her nose, offered to take the girls to the cinema, if there was something nice on. 'How wonderful! A weekend with your own husband after all this time!' There wasn't a shadow in her voice.

Joan nodded, smiled and went upstairs. Suddenly and inexplicably she longed to see Giles. Then she went and asked the girls if they wanted to come for a walk. Lindsay hesitated but Jennifer was all for it. Within minutes they set out, booted and wrapped up, to see if they could find some eggs for Joan to take with her for Paul.

When Paul met Joan from the train, he enfolded her and she kissed his cheek. And so they stood for a long minute. Then they walked through to the hotel. To her dismay, Joan heard herself leading the conversation, while Paul listened and smoked quietly. She found him greyer, in skin and hair and manner.

'You look very tired,' she said anxiously.

He shrugged. 'Oh, I'll just be glad when it's all over. You out here, me in town. The war just seems to go on and on. You will be coming back, won't you?'

Joan met his eyes. He knows, she thought. Like father, like daughter. If I told him that, I wonder what he'd say.

'Of course,' she said.

'How's Lindsay doing?' Paul asked.

'She's always preferred the country and obviously being away from the raids has helped, but more than anything, I think it's having Jennifer, Mrs Ramsey's daughter, to play with. Lindsay needs company.' They put Joan's case in their room and went down for tea. Paul asked about Lindsay's schoolwork. Joan told him about that, and the walks and the countryside. He asked about her job. She told him about Mrs Ramsey, Jim Cole and Mr Foster.

'Sometimes,' she said, 'I'm asked to work for one of the archi-tects – Peter Mather or Giles Campion. I've done quite a lot for them, one way and another. I seem to have a rare qualification – I can spell. ' Paul smiled.

Going back on the train on Sunday night, Joan thought the weekend had been out of step with everything else. And which is real? she asked herself. Life here, without Paul, or life there, with Paul? Is life with Giles real? Oh yes, it's real enough, real all right, but it's borrowed. And if Paul knows and Lindsay knows, maybe they know more about it than me and it's time to stop. She sighed. How would it feel, she wondered, to go home to the house in Persthorpe, a house in a town, side by side with many other similar houses, with small gardens and traffic and other people and noise? And sharing a house with Paul, a bed with Paul? What would she do if Paul and Lindsay got on each other's nerves as they used to?

Three days later, she had two letters. One was from her husband, who said how much it had meant to him to see her and spend time with her, how much he was looking forward to resuming their lives together after the war. And please give his love to Lindsay because he had realised, when he saw Joan, how much he missed her too. Will ring on Sunday. And the second letter was from Giles. He said it had got to stop. It was never meant to be this serious, he wrote, but I look at the drawing board and all I see is you. Mrs Ramsey told me that you were spending the weekend with your husband. We agreed the rules and we must stick to them. Thank you for a lovely time. No more as and when. Fondly, Giles.

Trembling, Joan tore his letter into the smallest pieces and, tight-lipped, shoved them into the flames of the kitchen stove. Firmly she walked back to the stairs but, halfway back up to her room, she began to shake and whimper. She sat on the bed and cried with her head in her hands, and when Lindsay, shaken by her distress, discovered her there an hour later and asked what was the matter, she said, 'I had this lovely letter from Daddy, about how much he wants to be home and together again. He says he misses you and sends his love, and I thought of all that wasted time and it made me sad.' Lindsay sat on the bed beside her and put one arm carefully round her weeping mother. 'But if Daddy loves us,' she said, 'that's all right, then.'

18 *Joan*

Coming back to Persthorpe wasn't as difficult as Joan had thought
it would be. It might have been difficult if she had thought about it
but she was busy fighting thought. Joan didn't think of it as going
back. Under normal circumstances, she reminded herself, the situation would never have arisen. She would not have left. It was only
because of Lindsay's health that she found herself apart from Paul
and nobody had expected the war to drag on and on. Still, what had
happened, had happened. Now it was over. Life would go on. And
it did. She warned herself of what Paul would expect. He would
expect to make love to her. And he did. Of course. Infrequently, as
he had before.

It was not unpleasant. She did not feel that she wanted to cry out
or scream – she'd been afraid she might – and she felt unexpected
tenderness towards him for asking so little about their time apart
and apparently understanding, she felt, so much. She was quite
convinced that he knew there had been another man. She didn't
know why she thought this. There were few questions about their
time apart and little introspection. She decided that she wanted him
to know because if he did that barred the way to any possible
resumption of the affair or even the hope of it. If he knew and he still
wanted her back, that was a test of some sort of love, a love much
more durable than the love of a man who was inextricably married
to someone else. Perhaps she expected Paul to notice something
different about her and would have been hurt had he not. And if he

noticed a change in her, she felt, he must attribute it to something more personal than just the privation of the war years. She wanted to be marked out of ten for surviving without Paul, passing the time with somebody else and then returning to her proper place as the war ended. She didn't know why, but she did. She did not however, with equal clarity, want to have to discuss any details.

So she concentrated on getting Lindsay into school and settled, on making the best she could of what was available in terms of food, on getting used to Paul's presence again.

She found him worn by the war and the loneliness of their being apart. She was quite sure he hadn't had anybody else. Of course he didn't talk about it and neither did she but she saw what the waiting had done to him. If you wait long enough, the anticipation backfires and you lose hope.

Paul seemed without hope in those first days. But gradually, as he became used to her and made efforts towards Lindsay, they settled into some kind of harmony. And almost as she admitted to herself their new-found sense of coming to rest, she also had to admit that she felt old, older than her years. The fabulous forties, she thought wryly, staring at herself one day in the mirror, noticing that her hair had become very grey, that there were new lines round her eyes and mouth from laughing but far deeper ones between her brows. She had not thought about age and it had sneaked up on her.

She shook out her clothes, pressed her blouses very smartly and bought a new lipstick. She thought she looked better but there wasn't very much time to think about it. The house consumed her. There was so much more of it than there had been at the vicarage and that meant so much more to keep on top of. She'd never thought of herself as much of a housewife but the house was like something forgotten, as though no one had lived there. Getting it back into shape was part of her accommodation to the choice she felt she'd made.

As she shopped and cooked and dusted, beating rugs and sorting modest piles of linen for the laundry, she thought with pleasure of the municipal library which was in the process of being expanded and reorganised and from which she knew she'd get a better selection of books than at Boots in Byrham. Oddly enough, she never seemed to have much time for reading during the war – and her mind snapped back to a vision of Giles looking at her with moonlight on his face. Furious, she shook herself. She had conscientiously taught herself not to think about how she had spent so much of her time, to find explanations like – the selection of books wasn't very good. Or – we were out so much, being in the country, you know.

And she realised, too, that although Mrs Ramsey would not win any prizes for cooking, they had shared the workload. It was hard work catering for three people. Eventually she began to see, though she had rebelled against her mother's fanatical housekeeping, how much time it filled. Better still, how addictive it was, which is to say that the more you did, the more you found yourself wanting to do and once the hands were busy, the mind roamed freely, concentrating on nothing in particular, without special thoughts or deep considerations.

It was one afternoon as she was ironing that she began to debate what she would have to buy at the shops the next day and in running through the contents of various drawers and cupboards as she usually did, she realised that she had not had a period for quite a while. Perhaps she really was getting older. Was this the start of the change? Her right hand still holding the iron, she cautiously explored her waistband with her left. Was it a bit snug? She decided she should collect her thoughts and arrange to see Dr Maddern. She and Paul had perhaps anticipated the length of time it takes for the menopause to become established as a reliable method of family planning but Joan was almost sure it was supposed to be six months. Well, was it six months since she . . .? She could not think. She would have to see Dr Maddern.

When she emerged from behind the cotton screen in his surgery, he looked at her with that odd smile she'd always thought was a sneer until she got to know him.

'You're going to have a baby,' he said.

She stared at him.

'About three or four months along,' he said, putting the notes back in her folder. She sat down.

'Your husband will be rather pleased, I imagine,' he went on, still not looking at her. 'He found your separation very painful. And Lindsay? Won't she be pleased to have a brother or a sister?'

Joan said levelly, 'You haven't asked me how I feel.'

'No,' he said, after a pause, 'I haven't. I shall take it you're delighted. Believe me, this is a much more enjoyable business than the menopause.'

Joan made a little movement, almost a shrug, but then nodded. 'When do you want to see me again?' she asked.

'About every four weeks for the next few months, keep an eye on you. Not as youthful as you were. And of course if there are any problems or questions – '

Joan began buttoning up her coat. By the time she was outside, she had begun to think about how they would manage. There was the small room, next door to the main bedroom, and the doctor was probably right, this was the thing Paul needed to show him that all would be well, forever, between them.

She told him when he came home from work. He took her hands.

'Are you pleased?' she asked.

'As long as you're all right,' he replied. 'As long as you'll be all right, I'm fine.'

She nodded. He asked her if she'd told Lindsay. She shook her head. So, together, they went through to the dining room where she was doing her homework at the table.

'Mummy is going to have a baby,' said Paul.

Lindsay's eyes lit up. 'Really?'

They nodded.

'Gosh. Will it be a sister? I mean, I'd really like a sister.'

Joan smiled at her and said that she would do her best.

The months of the pregnancy passed as the months preceding it had done. Paul brought home a puppy, remembering Joan always had a soft spot for a dog, and they called him Ace. Joan took care of the house and encouraged Lindsay with her schoolwork. She planted some bulbs in the front garden and she bought three pieces of material from which she made smocks to go over the skirts she could no longer comfortably fasten. Neighbours offered books and advice but the books repelled her and the advice involved other women in whom, she had to confess to herself, she had no great interest. So she smiled and returned the books and closed her ears to the help they wanted to give her because it didn't suit her. She was eating well and sleeping well and at midnight one night, just as she'd become very bored with the idea of being pregnant and fed up with not being able to bend or see her feet without great effort, she began to feel the sensation she remembered of stretching from within.

She struggled up the stairs to wake Paul, who had gone to bed as he usually did, before her, and he called a taxi. He took her to the nursing home and came straight back to be with Lindsay. The nurses were considerate and Dr Maddern came in to encourage her. She was given gas and air and floated above it all, doing roughly what she was asked for four hours, until they put her second daughter into her arms. She looked down into a face with skin darker than her own surrounded by surprisingly strong golden curls. She smiled, a kindly nurse took the baby from her and she slept, exhausted.

There was no question that Paul was pleased with the baby and Lindsay was thrilled that she had the sister she'd wanted, but the baby herself was less than delighted to be there and cried incessantly. The whole family took it in turns to feed her and walk her up and down, singing, talking, soothing, so that they could have some rest as well. Within six weeks she was ill. The doctor thought it was a bad cold but it became diphtheria, followed by chickenpox and measles and continual colds and flu. She did not eat and she did not want to sleep and, in an effort to stay awake with her, Joan found herself reading Paul's library books as well as her own. One of these was an account of the relationship between George IV and his daughter Charlotte, whose best friend was called Mercer. 'I want to call her Mercer,' Joan told Paul the next morning. He looked puzzled until she showed him the book. 'She was such a loyal friend,' she tried to explain. Her enthusiasm for anything historical was rare, he was puzzled but pleased. But the real reason was that the name was a conversation stopper.

'Why did you call her that?' asked Joan's neighbour.

'I got it out of a book,' said Joan with a flourish and whisked the baby out of a suspected draught.

The hope was that she would outgrow her sickliness and as she grew, she seemed strong enough, though thin. But she rarely threw off a cold, it almost always became flu. And while she was remarkably patient about staying in bed and keeping warm and taking care, she was from the earliest alarmingly stubborn about what she would and wouldn't eat and wear. Part of Joan instinctively admired anybody who knew their own mind so clearly but part of her grimaced at what a burden that kind of wilfulness was going to mean. Not to Joan – she wouldn't stand for it – but to Mercer herself. She trusted her feelings towards Mercer, or at least more so than she had done with Lindsay, and Mercer was demonstrative, which was oddly comforting.

Joan was not sure why she needed comfort but there was no doubt that the offers of hugs and kisses and snuggling up which were as much a part of Mercer as her breathing made Joan feel better in some way that she refused to think about too much.

Mercer also adored Lindsay, who took her for walks and played with her but plainly suffered in the upheaval of Mercer's needs, her wilfulness, her illnesses and her ability to charm her father. For as Paul had fled in the face of Lindsay's questioning gaze and patient watchfulness, so he responded positively and warmly to Mercer's vivacity and relative fragility. Against all predictions, her hair remained gold and her skin coppery. And Paul's party piece was to get his tiny daughter to stand on his hand where she looked like a spice-coloured fairy on a very solid tree. Lindsay would go off to do her homework.

Joan went upstairs to see Lindsay one night and found her sitting on the bed, her arms round her knees, staring out of the window. Schoolbooks lay open on the table, the lights were out but Joan could sense rather than see how red and swollen Lindsay's eyes were. She sat down carefully, at the other end of the bed, and waited. Silence persisted.

'What is it?' asked Joan.

Lindsay shook her head.

'It must be something,' Joan insisted. 'You're sitting up here in the dark and you look as if you've been crying.'

Lindsay shrugged.

'Come on, sweetheart. I can't help you if I don't know what it is that's bothering you.'

Lindsay looked at her carefully.

'Why doesn't he love me like that?' she asked.

Joan frowned. 'Love who like what?'

'Daddy. He only plays with Mercer.'

Again. Joan winced inside herself and outwardly gathered the power of her logic.

'Well, that's because you're much older now and – '

'But he didn't play like that with me when I was little.'

Joan inhaled determinedly. 'No, he didn't, but you were a very different little girl from Mercer. And it was some years ago and sometimes people change when they grow older.'

Lindsay looked at her out of the pit of her pain.

'Does he love her more than he loves me?'

'No,' said Joan, probably too firmly. 'No, that's not it. He loves you differently because you are a different person. And I love you differently because I'm a different person and you love him differently from the way you love me. Because everybody's different. Everybody needs a different kind of love.'

155

Lindsay looked at her consideringly.

'But I do love you, Lindsay.'

The face before her began to fold. Joan moved forward and put her arms round her elder daughter.

'Did you have a bad day?' said Joan softly into her ear, the tiny ear half-obscured by her thick dark hair.

Lindsay nodded. She would not cry with her mother, though in extremes she would lie against her sometimes.

'What was it about?'

Lindsay pushed herself away and sat up.

'Some of the girls at school are nasty to me. They say I'm fat. Am I fat?' Without waiting for Joan to begin her carefully qualified denial in the face of the heavy body before her, Lindsay went on. 'And then I came home and played with Mercer until Daddy came in and he hardly spoke to me but he began playing with her. And you called out for me to start my homework, so I did. But I started to cry. So I sat over here until it finished.'

Joan searched her mind for something positive to say. But the things which were most positive were that Lindsay's schoolwork continued to be impressive in spite of feeling ignored by her father and diminished by her classmates, so she waited.

'I love Mercer. It's just that it seems so much easier to be Mercer than it is to be me.'

Joan sighed tiredly. 'Lindsay, it's easier to be Mercer than anybody else in this house. Babies have a good time. You're fed up with school and getting to be a big girl – more grown-up, I mean. I'm tired of broken nights and worrying about what they'll do to your schoolwork and Daddy's concentration and Daddy is tired too. We just have to get through this and the only way to do that is to do it. If I could think of a shortcut, I would use it.'

Lindsay blew her nose.

'Come on. Let's go down and see what's on the wireless and then you can have your tea and finish your homework later.'

Lindsay rose from the bed and they went downstairs.

For the first time, Joan had some sympathy for her mother. If this is what it's like with two, she thought as she sliced bread and set forth the brawn and pickles for Paul while Lindsay washed the cups and made the tea, how did she manage with four of us – and the twins when they were alive? And less money after Dad left. Well, she wouldn't have managed without Guy. But she never did like Mr Hinde. Funny how you can take a dislike to somebody. It was just that he was so fond of Guy – loved him, so Guy said – and her mother hated that. Interesting how we all thought that Mr Hinde loved Guy. I wonder whether Guy loved Mr Hinde. He sort of told me he did that day so long ago and apparently he was very upset when he died – so Cecily said. But then in her last but one letter she'd said he was marrying a woman several years younger than himself, whose father had made a lot of money out of the war, though quite how wasn't clear. Perhaps Guy just loved money best. He's certainly the only one of any of us who had much to do with making any. Joan wondered if it really mattered who you loved or whether you had to love at all, if you just had to have enough things in common to make a go of it.

She heard Ace scratching at the back door and went to let him in. Paul arrived, carrying Mercer in the crook of his arm. For once the tension which characterised so many of their mealtimes was relaxed. Lindsay was quiet, of course, but then Lindsay was often quiet. And Mercer didn't really eat, she just pushed the food around her plate. But Ace sat dreamily in front of the gas fire which imparted a comfortable warmth to the room. They didn't talk very much because Paul was reading a paper.

Later on, as she cleared the kitchen, did a bit of washing and peeled the potatoes for the next day's lunch, Joan thought again about Guy. She thought of him often, quite concentratedly, but she never got round to writing to him. And now the gap was too wide. How can you suddenly write to someone you haven't known closely for years and years, across marriage, children, the war? She used to love Guy. He was so handsome, so much in control. Rubbing her hands on the threadbare kitchen towel, she sighed. She boiled the milk for their cocoa and carried it into the living room where Paul had just put a bit more coal on the fire. He thanked her for his drink, she smiled. He went back to his book, she took up hers. Half an hour later, he stretched and said, 'I'm going up to bed, Mummy, don't be long.'

'I won't,' she murmured, her mind still on her book. He kissed her temple as he passed. Only after the door closed did she wonder about him calling her Mummy.

When she went upstairs, he was fast asleep on his side of the bed and Mercer was curled into a small ball, facing Joan's side. Neither stirred when she got into bed.

Lindsay became quite friendly with a girl called Valerie who lived nearby. Together they joined a troop of guides and sang in the school choir. Valerie's father was given to fits of rage when he was drunk but Lindsay enjoyed soothing Valerie and offering her home as a place of occasional refuge. There was no great link between Joan's daughters, how could there be? Joan sighed. The age difference was goo great.

She watched Lindsay struggling with herself and did what she could for her, spared her what energy she could from trying to find out where Mercer was and having established that, what she was doing. She thought it would be nice for Lindsay to learn to play the piano but when it came to it, they couldn't afford to buy her the instrument to keep up the necessary practice. Joan bought her a second-hand bicycle but Paul was so nervous about the traffic on the roads that even this did not bring her the freedom from them all Joan felt she needed. In the meantime, Paul began to ask Joan if Lindsay knew what she was going to do when she left school and Mercer began school, bowed down with a terrible cough, the legacy of her most recent cold.

If Lindsay was vague about the future, she made one thing absolutely clear. She would not teach. She couldn't explain why not, she just didn't want to, and when Paul's face began to darken and his mouth to set, Joan averted the obvious storm by pointing out to him that he had always claimed that teaching was a vocation so, if Lindsay didn't have that, teaching was not for her.

Unknown to either Lindsay or her mother, Paul made an appointment to see Lindsay's headmistress, who assured him that she could see nothing amiss, a good solid citizen in the making Lindsay was, but she drew his attention to his elder daughter's prowess in maths. 'In this,' said Miss Shaw, pursing her lips with pleasure, 'she is truly gifted.' If it was maths she was good at, then surely science too? Lindsay declined to be interested in science.

Paul tried again, still keeping his encounter with Miss Shaw to himself. 'What about pure maths, at university?' he asked. Lindsay replied, pulling anxiously at her fingers while her face and voice remained under control that, thank you, she didn't want to go to university. 'What are you going to do?' Paul demanded. Joan cut across them once again. 'Right now she's going to help me make the tea. Come along, Lindsay – and could you see if Mercer is still in the garden or where she's got to?' Lindsay rose obediently and stopped beside her father on her way out of the room.

'I'm sorry, Daddy, I'm trying to find something, really I am – ' He looked at her, frowning slightly, then nodded, waving her away. The subject was dropped. Their understanding was that when Lindsay found what it was she wanted to do, she'd tell them. In the meantime she worked for her exams and then she told them that she had applied for a trainee post at the Air Ministry which would take her away from home.

19 *Joan*

Paul thought having an assistant was an unnecessary frill. He didn't understand the appointment, still less feel flattered by it. He knew he was doing good work. But although he was well liked by his colleagues, the education authority refused most of his requisitions, from gym shoes for children whose families couldn't afford them to the purchase of the more modern equipment he wanted older boys to have the chance of using. And then in the same breath, so to speak, they allotted money for the salary of this young man, nice enough but hardly substantial, who trailed him everywhere, treated him with deference bordering on the fawning and whose main efforts seemed to be towards elaborate memoranda on what Mr Canning had been doing, when, where and with whom – information Paul had already painstakingly spelled out in his own reports.

Still, it was hard to be offended by Brian Toomey. He did his best, tried to be useful and was polite enough, even in the making of helpful suggestions. Paul did not introduce him to Joan. His work was his work, his home was something different. And he did not socialise with people from work either.

He read more and more and visited the Police Club, entrance secured by honorary membership after helping with their athletic club. It was a quiet place to go for a pint and a game of cards. And Paul was quite happy.

He and Joan had survived the war as a couple. It had had its effects and strains, of course, but then it had on everyone. And now they were together again. He wished powerfully that he could somehow affect Lindsay's future but they had never been close in the way that he would have liked and now she must get out and begin to live her own life, as she'd vetoed every suggestion he'd made. He was back with Joan and that was all that mattered. Mercer was an appealing little girl. He hoped she'd grow past the sickly stage because her basic personality was bright. The evenings were filled with books. Joan seemed happy enough about the second child, no matter how tiring its demands. They were all right.

He didn't know that Joan was once again beginning to feel that she was low on his list of priorities. Or that these feelings were affirmed and emphasised by the absolute lack of time there was in which to do anything, by the endless list of domestic and family tasks which absorbed her from morning till night, leaving her only longing for sleep and relentlessly unsatisfied in the morning.

Paul's apparent contentment irritated her. He had a good brain, he could do so much more with it. If he'd do a bit more – not one of those damned voluntary things he was always taking on, but a bit of paid work leading to a better-paid job – then with a little more money, there would be time for – for – she didn't know what, only that she was missing out on something.

She ran through the lists of things which preoccupied her. There was very little money to make herself look better but she reflected that she had done well to get this far looking as good as she did. The house was frankly shabby and she couldn't see that being changed in the foreseeable future. Then there was Lindsay. Was there ever a time when she wasn't worried about Lindsay? Yes, yes – there was. Before the war. Before they had to go away. Before it all happened. And that was why she worried about Lindsay.

Lindsay's schoolwork was good, gifted, even brilliant. But she didn't seem to be able to see any more than Paul could that if you didn't cash in on your gifts, there would be no rewards, no easier times, no future.

And Mercer? She was physically frail, though happy enough and growing. Mercer will be all right, Joan decided. Mercer will manage.

I wish, Joan thought suddenly, that he wouldn't call me Mummy. I know it's a sort of joke, that it's affection and that he loved his mother. But it makes me feel forgotten somehow.

And it was in very much that frame of mind, with a duster in one hand, that she answered the door to Brian Toomey and learned of his role in Paul's life.

To begin with he called on her to see if Paul was there, Paul either having given him the slip or because it was outside the hours they worked together and Brian had some item he wished to discuss with Paul. For several months, his visits were infrequent and erratic. And then he turned up on a Saturday when Paul was away, organising or refereeing, with one of his sides or clubs or teams. Lindsay had gone to a film with a girlfriend, or at least, to visit a friend. Joan hoped they had not gone to the cinema for it was unusually bright and summery. And Joan was at home alone with Mercer.

Brian asked for Paul, Joan explained his absence and offered tea. Brian declined. They discussed the weather.

'We could go to the seaside,' he said suddenly. 'It wouldn't take long in the car.'

Joan stared at him, gradually beginning to smile. Of course she could go to the seaside – why shouldn't she? She'd just leave a note for Lindsay and Paul and be home before the sun set. What she said was, 'What about Mercer?'

Toomey assured her that his plan included her and the little girl. She went to put a few things together in a basket and to pick up a cardigan. They left a few minutes later.

This was the first of several outings through the summer, exemplary in their innocence. The weather remained fine, there was just enough room for the three of them in Brian's green roadster and, as in earlier days, Paul seemed to be more pleased that she had something pleasant to be doing when he was away than perturbed that she was doing it with somebody else. Lindsay had a little more freedom and was pleased to spend time with her schoolfriends or in her own company. There were fewer outings in the autumn but there were some, to see the wintry sea or the copper leaves and colours of the moorland.

In the winter, on a rare Saturday morning when she had left Mercer with Lindsay and Paul mending a bookcase in the shed he liked to call the garage, Joan came out of the shop where she bought her stockings – half a dozen pairs at a time and nursed them for months but refused to buy any other brand, or cheaper – and met Brian Toomey. They had a cup of coffee together in the local department store. She remarked that they hadn't seen much of him lately. He seemed pleased that he'd been missed. She said he looked a bit down at the mouth. Was he all right? Yes, he said, he thought so. It was just a year ago that his wife had died. Joan muttered her apologies. Nobody had mentioned a wife.

'Were you married long?'

'No.' He shook his head.

'You never mentioned her before . . .'

'It's all so sad,' he said. 'We met in India. My family are out there, I was born there, and Aileen was very beautiful. I'd met her before when I was younger. This time it was more serious.'

And he told her, still in this unremarkable way, that they had an affair but she insisted that he should marry her, and he did so very much in the teeth of his family's disapproval because she was *chichi* – Anglo-Indian, he explained. From the beginning, they got on each other's nerves. He was quite junior in his father's firm, though with good prospects, but it wasn't enough for Aileen. No, nothing would do for Aileen but that they must put India behind them and come to England. Frightened at the thought of his untoward marriage failing before it began, he gave in.

'I'd always wanted to see a bit of home,' he said, 'and Mother's family were from the north so we came here.' Oh dear, thought Joan, I don't suppose Persthorpe was what Aileen had in mind. 'And everything got worse,' he said. What Aileen wanted, he explained, was London, or at least somewhere near enough for her to go to London when she wanted. She wanted that dream of London, made up of clothes and lights and entertainments. Instead of which, they disembarked at Southampton and passed through London on a train to go to stay with Brian's aunt, arriving in a village just outside Persthorpe on a raw November evening, when it was dark and raining. Aileen became quickly ill.

'To begin with, I thought it was a sham, a sort of malingering,' said Brian. 'But the doctor said she mustn't have anything to do with me, the intimate side, I mean. I didn't really understand.' She grew cold and punishing and revengeful because she was safe from rebut in the awfulness of some ailment which didn't respond to treatment.

'She withered before my eyes,' he said, looking at the cigarette he held. 'I should never have married her. My father was right.'

Joan picked up her coffee spoon, examined it minutely and put it down carefully.

'I think everybody who has ever been married feels like that sometimes,' she said. 'At least you had your father to blame.'

'Are you and Paul happy?' asked Brian Toomey.

'That,' said Joan primly, 'is a private matter I cannot discuss. It's just not open to question. Really . . .'

He apologised. 'You see, it's just that I've got frightfully fond of you.'

'It's only because you are lonely,' said Joan unforgivingly.

He nodded humbly. 'You're probably right.'

Joan gathered her shopping. He offered her a lift home and, though she initially hesitated, she accepted because it was a good deal quicker than waiting for a bus.

The winter stole past, with Joan mending endlessly to keep clothes going for one more season, and in the spring Brian Toomey turned up again with a bunch of flowers in one hand and invited her to lunch. Joan accepted. The car ride to a pub outside town was as good as a glass of champagne to her on a day when life had put chains round her ankles. When lunch was over and they got into the car to come back, she asked Brian to show her where he lived.

It was a quiet little house, set back from the road behind thick laurel bushes, directly between Mercer's school and home. He did not ask her if she wanted to come in but just opened the door and led her forward, and she followed. When he shut the door, he was standing so close to her that it was logical that he should kiss her and when he had shown her the downstairs, he showed her the upstairs. She noticed that he kept a photograph of his deceased wife on the chest of drawers and that he did not attempt to hide it. And she was almost surprised when he kissed her again with considerable force and they fell back on the bed.

He murmured and pressed his highly coloured face into the warmth and sweetness of her neck, while removing with more enthusiasm than expertise the garments which got in his way. She did not demur. It was all a good deal more exciting than what had been happening between her and Paul for some time. And she knew she was safe. Mercer was nearly five and she hadn't had a sign of a period since her birth. This freedom added some appetite to her lovemaking and that, coupled with Brian's recent deprivation and, as it emerged, general lack of experience, provided them with an active hour or so. But it was he who looked at his watch and gently reminded her that it was nearly three and asked what time did she have to meet Mercer?

So she straightened her hair, washed herself quickly and went to meet her younger daughter. Thrilled with school, Mercer came rushing towards her with things to say in wellingtons a size too big, tripped over an uneven paving stone and fell, raising a bump on her forehead of sufficiently serious dimensions to focus her mother's attention and restore normality without time for repining.

Later, when Mercer was soothed and listening to *Children's Hour* on the wireless, Joan laid the table for the meal they ate together in the evening and waited for Paul to come home. Brian rang and asked her if she was all right. She found herself beginning to smile as she told him about Mercer and how she hadn't thought until this moment – but yes, thank you, she was indeed all right. And so was Mercer. Was Paul home? he asked. No, not yet but he should be, any minute. Did Brian want to leave a message of some kind?

'No,' said Brian. 'I want to know if I can see you again.' His tone of voice made it quite clear what he meant.

'Yes,' she said.

'I'll ring you then,' he said. 'Bye for now.'

'Bye,' she said, putting the receiver back in its cradle, and wondered briefly how they would work it. When she'd taken Mercer to school or on the way to collect her – one or the other? Maybe both? She giggled. And then she checked the table and went in to sit with her daughter until her husband came home.

In the months that followed, she discovered that the parameters of their relationship both relieved and bored her. There was no hiding, other than being discreet about going into and coming out of the house. They had no public relationship other than the one conducted under Paul's nose or else by chance meeting. He made declarations of love, she confined herself to telling him how fond of him she was. The picture of Aileen remained on top of the chest. Once, when she was feeling irritable, Joan asked Brian why it had to be there. He was taken aback. 'Well after all, she is – was – my wife,' he said. Which made it quite clear what he thought, Joan decided, fastening her stockings. It fascinated her that no matter in how much of a hurry she dressed, she never snagged a stocking during the entire time she was seeing Brian. She felt this too was an omen, for they were so expensive, but it represented that she was meant to get through this adventure unscathed. Maybe his saying he loved her was something he felt he had to say. All she knew was that it was a great relief to go to bed with somebody more often – and not have to worry about it.

It was Paul who told her that Brian was talking about leaving.

'Oh. Why?' she asked from behind the teapot as they ended the meal together, Mercer having gone off to hunt for late raspberries.

Paul stirred his tea. 'Misses his family,' he said. 'They're all still out in India, you know.'

'I thought he had family here and that's why he came back.'

'Don't think he ever would have come back, not for more than a visit, if it hadn't been for his wife. Doesn't sound like a very happy business. Anyway, he says that he misses his people and he misses India. He's still quite a young fellow, you know, and he was born out there. It can get a grip on you that never breaks.'

Joan stood up and reached for his plate and cup. 'Has he actually resigned or is he just talking about it?'

Paul lit a cigarette, looking for an ashtray. 'He hasn't resigned yet but from the way he's talking, I think he will. Just a sort of formality to go over it with me first. I shan't mind. Nice enough bloke, but I'm much better left to myself.'

Joan smiled what she hoped was an understanding smile and began to carry the tea things towards the sink.

Paul took his cigarette and the newspaper into the back room. In the kitchen she looked unseeingly at the bubble-glass in the window. Then she began to run water into the washing-up bowl.

She deliberately didn't leave herself time to go near Brian the next day, nor for the next few, until he rang and asked if everything was all right.

'Why shouldn't it be?' asked Joan, blushing and cross.

'Why haven't I seen you?' he asked.

'There doesn't seem to be a great deal of point,' she replied, 'if you're going back to India.'

There was a silence.

'I thought you knew that I wasn't really happy here,' he said quietly.

'No, I didn't.'

'Well, I'm not. If it hadn't been for Aileen – '

'Oh yes. Aileen,' said Joan bitterly. 'Aileen and the British winter.'

'I'll write to you,' he said.

The envelope was thick, and delivered by hand. She found it a couple of days later when she returned from taking Mercer to school and doing the shopping. He had tried very hard, he said, but he had to admit, *she* had to admit, that there was no future for them and this was the second time – yes, he knew she wouldn't want to hear this, but it was nevertheless true – the second time that he faced a relationship with no future. He wrote about how he loved India, about the warmth and affection of his family. He explained that he and his parents had exchanged some very frank letters which had clarified both their regrets and his and it did seem that the way was now open for a proper reconciliation, rather than the titular one effected by Aileen's demise. And of course, because they had resolved their differences, he could go back into the family concern which gave him opportunities he simply couldn't hope for over here. The only thing which could have made him stay, he wrote, was the thought of some future together with her, but he knew that this was not to be. She had helped him to find himself again and, though he knew she would never feel for him as he felt for her, he hoped that she knew how much she had meant to him.

Well, said Joan to herself, shoving it behind the cotton box in the dresser drawer, that's that and no more silly games for you, my girl. From now on you act like a grown-up and make the best of it. And she cleaned the silver.

Some days later Paul told her that young Toomey had resigned and, as he gave every evidence of this being a hard decision, might they not have him over for a meal before he went?

Joan was aghast. 'But you never do that sort of thing,' she said.

'I know, I know,' said Paul, fingering his cigarette packet. 'But after all, he's nice enough and I've probably given him a harder ride than he deserved. It doesn't have to be grand or anything, just a meal. What do you think?'

Not fast enough to get yourself out of that one, Joan thought, listening to herself agree. And so three weeks later, Brian arrived with flowers for his hostess and a bottle of wine for Paul, who didn't like it. Brian chatted to Paul about the future and India, Paul talked of India and past days there, while Joan confined herself to the kitchen and an unusually demure silence. Lindsay was in bed reading and Mercer was staying at a neighbour's house with the neighbour's niece who was by way of being her best friend and who had mercifully come to visit at just the right time.

Priding herself on plain food, Joan turned out a simple meal, governed as much by her own unsettledness as lack of funds. Brian and Paul both complimented her on it. She gave them coffee in the living room and after a second cup, Brian took his leave. When Paul came back from seeing him off at the front door, he remarked, 'Bit quiet, Mum?'

'Head,' said Joan briefly.

'Oh, I'm sorry.'

'Just the way of things.' She shrugged. 'You don't want hot chocolate now, do you?'

He said he didn't think so, he'd just go to bed if she didn't mind. She didn't mind.

When he left the kitchen, she drank a large glass of water and took two aspirin. She sat at the kitchen table for a while after the dishes were done and wished she could cry or scream or weep, but really it was all so predictable. And what did I get out of it, she asked herself, and admitted wearily the truth of the answer – about what you put in. Bugger Aileen, she thought rudely, and went up to bed.

20 Mercer

In the house in which we lived when I was a small child, my parents slept in the large front bedroom and I slept beside them in the little one. Lindsay had the back bedroom when she was home. My earliest remembrance of my mother is of her threatening to leave. Paul said something, I don't remember what. What I do remember is her going past me, the curve of her hip in her green tweed skirt, the apron being taken off as she walked, her favourite walking shoes. She took up her old brown bag and her coat and I didn't know what she was doing but suddenly she was at the front door. 'I've had enough,' she said. 'I've had enough.' And Paul stuck in one of those gestures between appeal and appal, saying, 'But the child, Joan? What about the child?' 'Damn the child,' she said. 'You'll find someone to take care of her or she'll take care of herself.' But it was over, she was already cooling.

I've often thought that if my father had had humour as well as a sense of timing, he'd have made a great clown. It all happened too quickly for me to be upset and, anyway, it was too interesting.

That afternoon, when my father went to sleep after lunch, I took my two favourite bits of ribbon which were respectively red and gold and green and silver, left over from Christmas, and wound them round his fingers. In and out I wove them round the great hand, left hanging like a special plaything over the side of the chair. When he woke he fumbled to get at his coffee and muttered disapproval but my mother stilled him with, 'Paul, be careful.

You'll frighten her.' The only thing that really frightened me about him was how big he was. He was like some great beast with such an affinity for the place it lives that it looks to be modelled out of the same substance. When he was angry or even when he was not, and for some reason stretched himself, he appeared suddenly two or three times taller than anything else that moved round him.

I never heard my mother threaten to leave again. It must have been one of those days when the tasks are endless, the child is always around you and you're tired. For she was always doing things, no matter how tired she was, and I watched her as carefully as Lindsay watched Paul. I knew my parents had more of a relationship than I could see and Joan told me constantly that I was getting the best of it. 'He's much easier now than he was when Lindsay was little,' she'd say, half to herself, helping me on with my clothes, fastening my shoes to go shopping or pulling my boots on to take the dog for a walk. I don't remember wondering if Paul liked Lindsay or not. It wasn't a question which occurred to me. I was a happy little girl and my parents were happy too, as far as I could see, so why should my sister not be happy with them and they with her?

Sometimes I saw Paul kiss Joan. It was always gentle, hinting at continuance. Sometimes he teased and tickled her and that was very funny and they laughed. But I don't remember anything more than the kiss. The kiss became the only emblem to which I was witness that they loved each other, which was what they led me to believe. Sometimes the kiss was just what they did. I thought, they'll kiss now, and they did. Sometimes it was like an exhalation of breath, as if they'd survived this far and through all these things and now – puff – they could breathe again. Kiss. Whatever it was, I never saw or felt it false from either of them. They might be weary of all sorts of things, including their daily lives and each other, but when they kissed it seemed out of mutual respect. I liked to watch them.

When I was nine, my mother went back to work. I knew vaguely that she had had a job during the war but since the war was unreal to me, so was any idea I might have had of her working before. I understood from what I'd heard her discussing with Paul that we needed more money and accepted as children do the adaptations which had to be made so that she could fit in part-time work round my father and me. She began as a clerk in a municipal office and graduated to secretary within a year. Once, when I asked her what difference her working had made, she took me round the house pointing out what was new – new loose covers in the living room, new bedside rugs in her room, our bedrooms redecorated, various clothes – 'And we're going on holiday!' she announced triumphantly.

I had not missed holidays. I thought they were when you saw your friends and read at breakfast and we usually went to the seaside a few times. But this time we stayed in a chalet in a holiday village just outside a seaside town on the south coast where one day we got lost and covered with prickles fighting our way through a gorse common. If I don't remember more, I don't think it means anything bad.

I was a kid. I had older parents and a big sister who lived away from home. There were days when it rained and days when it shone and my parents made me laugh more than they made me cry. I knew I had been ill as a small child, which was why colds were so dreaded and I was put to bed with rum in my hot milk. I still occasionally climbed into their bed.

When I was smaller I was put to bed in my own room but routinely transferred to fall asleep in my parents' every night. They tried to decide whether I should be put back in my own bed at the risk of waking me or allowed to stay which would effectively separate them. Although I gradually did it less, I slept in their bed until I was nine or ten. Their bed had an eiderdown and it was warm and deep and something to nestle into. I remember that long after Paul died Joan let me spend a night in that bed with David and I was appalled at how uncomfortable it was.

I wonder when Lindsay decided that sisters were all very well but the age difference was insurmountable and what she needed was a friend? I'm sure it's true, that she said she wanted a sister for all the usual reasons and so that there was a seal on her parents' relationship, showing that it would last. That what she hoped she didn't have to know about her mother could now be expunged from memory and called a mistake.

But she had had her parents to herself and now she had to share them. And that wouldn't have been so bad except that they were so pleased with this new child of theirs. Although it cried and was often ill and stubborn and a show-off, it could do little wrong. Her mother, whom she had doubted but always loved, gave her small sister unstinting love and attention.

Her father, whom she loved deeply but had never known, because he would never let her, was pleased by the child and permitted it tender liberties she had not dreamed of. What could Lindsay have thought of me other than these things? I was brought along as a supporting player and proceeded to hog the limelight.

After she left school and got her job, she lived miles away. Both my parents seemed disappointed by her job and I remember Joan sighing and saying that she hoped it would make use of her maths skills. We went to visit her once when I was very young and she showed me the teleprinter room and made the machine talk back to me. She said her work was interesting. She said she was all right. She also said that she was cold in her digs and that the canteen wasn't wonderful. But she stuck to it. I haven't thought of it until now but I wonder why she stayed. And I have never asked her.

Perhaps she was afraid to give it up in case she couldn't think of anything else. Perhaps she thought that succeeding at something so different from what Paul and Joan had wanted for her would gain her their respect. Or perhaps she was afraid to look for work anywhere where anybody would look at her, because by now she was both tall and hefty, with far from becoming spectacles, and she knew that my parents couldn't keep her, even though they offered, at least for a while, because there was only so much money and then there was their dependant – me.

I remember Lindsay came home once and I looked at her curiously because she seemed changed, but I couldn't have explained the nature of the difference. I hung about her as I always did and when, after tea, she went upstairs to unpack her case, I went with her. She took out a parcel for me, wrapped in many layers of tissue paper, and I was naturally excited. It contained a dress, a perfect little girl's striped dress, brightly patterned with a white frilly collar and cuffs. I can see the hands coming towards me, she loves me, I know she bought it for love of me, and I hate it. I leave the room. I couldn't at the age of eight begin to explain to Lindsay that it was hard for me to believe that anyone who loved me would want me to wear such a thing.

Joan came looking for me. She said it was a nice dress. I looked up into her face. She was not joking, she was firm, clear, serious. Lindsay bought it with her own money, hard-won, from the job she kept saying was all right but which seemed to be full of wrong things like unexpected duties, cold rooms, not enough time off and disappointing food. Her own money. I hear, I know, I understand. Of course I understand how important money is. It's one of those things grown-ups talk about quite a lot and their voices almost always alter after they've been talking for a bit, as if they'd felt sick or something. Or the money had run away. And again my mother says, 'Her own money. So you will try and like it, won't you Mercer?' I look at my mother and if I had known the then-phrases of teenage, I'd have asked if she was kidding. I stare. 'Just try,' she says, very gently.

I know that if you grow very fast, you can grow out of things very quickly. I resolve to grow so fast that the dress will be a non-issue.

When we have tea, I see the shadows in Lindsay's eyes. The ones *in* her eyes are quite different from the shadows under them, which are fine and brown, or the shadows which are always there, like light on the moving surface of a brown river. These are new ones. I have crossed some line I did not even know was drawn. I have refused her gift. Joan may not see it as such, but Lindsay knows.

Was I, I ask now, a truculent little girl? Was it not handled appropriately? It is embarrassing when a child takes a liking to something unsuitable or, as in this case, rejects something perfectly suitable. And I could not explain to Joan that I had already seen her direct her disowning look at me. For sometimes Joan looked at me as if she didn't know where I'd come from, as though I were a thought made flesh, a dream, a challenge, but not a child. I'd caught the sense of it once or twice when I was out of favour and thought it had to do with her being angry, but I had almost immediately begun to realise that being naughty was irrelevant.

She could not answer me and instead of confronting me with the strength of her ignorance, which would have reassured me of her love, she began to doubt me. What I was, what I thought, my clarity. Why wouldn't I wear the new dress? And I could never answer except to say that it wasn't right, it really wasn't, and I'm sorry, Mummy, I'm sorry, I'm sorry but it's not. So I offered equally abject apology and adamant refusal but the weight of the apology never affected the depth of the conviction to refuse.

21 *Joan*

The job Lindsay had chosen was attached to the subsidiary of a ministry and so Joan could refer to it as 'civil service, sort of', which she did with some pleasure. She doubted that Paul ever thought how hard it was not fitting in all the time, and then she wondered at herself because it had been like that for so many years and it was odd to reflect how it still bothered her. Both Paul and she accepted that it was time for Lindsay to get out of the nest. They hoped collectively, if without discussion, that her flight would be successful. That she would be so far from home was not what they might have hoped for, but she chose it and they capitulated without further argument.

In her absence Joan discovered the joys of her younger daughter for Mercer, given that she still resembled a stick figure and became ill alarmingly easily, was quick and bright and tough and extrovert. If anybody teased Mercer about being thin, as they had Lindsay about her bulk, Joan didn't hear of it.

Mercer's only complaint about school was that nobody read as much as she did, so it was difficult to find a best friend.

'Oh, but why?' asked Joan, amused at the fierce consideration upon the little girl's face.

'Well,' explained Mercer, 'you can't really have a best friend who doesn't understand you when you talk about the thing you like best in the world and I like books best.'

'Why do you think that is?' asked Joan, over her shoulder from the sink.

Mercer thought for a moment and then replied, 'Because anything can happen in books, and they don't go away. I didn't like it when Lindsay went away.'

Joan explained that when you grow up you can choose to study or work away from home, adding that they would still see Lindsay. Mercer went off to play pirates with Ace the dog.

Then the letters began to arrive. Lindsay wrote often and fluently. There were complaints, of course – mostly about getting used to shift work – but no misgivings. She wrote of meeting Tony, four years her senior, an only son. She said she thought she loved him but they had talked about it and he had told her she was too young for marriage yet. She thought he was wonderfully considerate. One morning, putting Lindsay's letter aside, Paul commented that she seemed to have settled down quite well.

Joan, bringing toast in from the kitchen, agreed. Soon after this, Lindsay wrote that she simply could not hope to wash things in the billets, there was no space to dry more than her underwear. Could she please send things home for washing? And Joan agreed. And so the parcels began to arrive. Mercer was fascinated to see things unpacked, crumpled and messy, and see them repacked, clean and folded, packed around spice cakes or gingerbread, for though Joan never made any fuss about it, she was a great maker of cakes, throwing in the ingredients, never measuring them, adding marmalade when she ran out of dried fruit and somehow always managing to make something delicious.

When Lindsay came home on leave, she brought still other things to be cleaned and small gifts and much excitement. Getting Lindsay's room ready was one of Mercer's favourite games, for she was allowed to help Joan and arrange things on the dressing table and then to sleep in Lindsay's sheets when she returned to work, sheets which smelled faintly acrid but infinitely comforting.

Mercer did not like going to see Lindsay off at the station. She would dance or sing or do anything rather than say the terrible word 'goodbye', for no amount of reassurance from Joan could convince her that she would ever see Lindsay again. And then the letters would resume and the odd clothes parcels would arrive to be transformed and Mercer would become again an only child with a daddy whose knee she sat upon and a mummy who read her stories. Joan, who had not sewn other than to mend for many years, found herself spending an afternoon during the winter making shoes for Mercer's doll. She was surprised at how much she enjoyed it and secretly proud of her daughter for wanting to show them to everybody and boast about them. Meanwhile Paul took her with him, a willing accomplice, to schoolboy boxing, to watch displays of gymnastics or swimming competitions. Joan could no longer pretend to be interested in these extensions of his work, though she always asked how they had gone and encouraged him to talk about them when he came home. Mercer loved seeing her father so big and knowledgeable, the centre of attention and admiration, some of which, she felt sure, must reflect on her. And Paul delighted in the smile of his little daughter, only a child, so pretty and keen, surrounded by men and boys, who enjoyed whatever sport it was on that particular occasion.

One day Joan discovered Mercer sitting on the front step with the big scissors from the cotton box, cutting off every golden curl. After she'd been shaken and punished, Joan went to shove the scissors into the back of the drawer where they were kept and found Brian Toomey's last letter, which she pulled out and took out of its envelope, intending to throw it away. Still in the envelope, separately, was a small card with his address in India printed on it and when she turned it over, she saw that he had written, 'If you should need me'. She studied it wryly for a moment, then pushed it into her pocket and tore up the rest. Calling Mercer upstairs, she brushed what remained of her hair and they went to the shops.

During the second year of Lindsay's job Paul sent Joan and Mercer up to stay nearby. He couldn't get away himself, he said, and it would be nice for the three of them to be together. They lodged in a modest guest house and walked about and looked at the shops and went up into the local mountains for a picnic or two. Lindsay told Joan that her feelings for Tony had grown, though of course she went out with other people. 'But darling, you are young yet,' said Joan. 'There's plenty of time.' And Lindsay agreed, though she looked wistful.

The sun shone and they came home quite brown.

Paul seemed to come more into his own in the months that followed, almost enjoying what Joan still saw as the limitations of his work and their life. And yet Joan too was seized less frequently by the impatience which had first enveloped her when Mercer was a baby. If only Lindsay is happy, thought Joan.

Lindsay's letters gave evidence of nothing else. She came home for Christmas, and maybe twice during the year. One year she couldn't afford the fare and neither could they and she hitchhiked home. Paul was furious. She talked about a promotion, she still spoke of Tony, outings with the girls in her section; of Nat King Cole and dances at the nearby US Airforce base. There was wonderful music and she'd bought a circular felt skirt. She'd bought some wool, too, she was knitting – 'I seem to be quite good at it,' she wrote. She and Iris were going out with Jim and Billy from the base. And then one week there was no letter.

'Have we heard from Lindsay yet?' asked Paul, home for his evening meal on Thursday.

'No,' said Joan. 'Perhaps she's been tired or missed the post – I don't know. I'm sure we'll hear tomorrow.'

But Friday brought no letter and Joan thought the safest thing to do was to ring the number Lindsay had told her the office only permitted to be used in case of emergency. In Joan's mind a week's silence from Lindsay, normally a reliable correspondent, constituted just that. The slightly officious voice on the other end asked her to wait and then she was put through to another voice which said, 'Yes?' so quietly and humbly she could hardly hear it.

'Lindsay?'

Another murmured assent.

'Lindsay, it's Mummy. Are you all right?'

Silence.

'Lindsay – '

'I can't talk now. I'll ring you straight back.'

'Are you all right, because – '

'I'll ring you back directly. Bye.'

Joan stared at the telephone as if it had bitten her and replaced the receiver.

She wandered into the kitchen and sat down. Then with a sigh, she got up and began to peel vegetables for the stew. The telephone rang. It was Lindsay from another telephone.

'Hello, Mummy. I'm sorry that I worried you – '

'It's all right, I don't mind if you're really all right. But Lindsay, you do sound – '

'Mummy, I'm pregnant. I have tried not to be but I am.'

Joan said the first thing which came into her head.

'You can't come home.'

'Oh,' said Lindsay.

'How did this happen?' Silly question, thought Joan, as if I didn't know.

Lindsay hesitated. 'Tony and I had a fight,' she explained haltingly. 'He made me so angry. When I came off duty, I met Iris and another girl and we went to the service club where I met a chap I've seen around. I drank too much. We went to bed together.'

Joan drew in her breath so hard that her nostrils narrowed.

'Have you and Tony been involved – physically, I mean?' she asked.

'Oh no,' Lindsay said, 'no. Mummy, this was the first time.'

'I see,' said Joan, unyielding. 'What about this man? Are you fond of him?'

'I hardly know him.'

'Oh my God – '

'And he's married.' Lindsay's voice was monotonous.

'How old is he?' asked Joan.

'I don't know.'

'But older than you?'

'Yes,' said Lindsay, sounding bewildered. 'He must be – well his children are twelve and fourteen, some age like that.'

'Then you'd better go and see him,' said Joan, 'and you'd better tell him that you're going to have a baby and ask him what he's going to do about it. Has he got any money?'

'He's a pilot,' said Lindsay. 'They earn quite well.'

'Good,' said Joan. 'Well then, you tell him that if he doesn't offer you the money to support you while you have the baby, you will see his wife, or I'll see him and then his wife. We can't help you, Lindsay. The money isn't here. He's got it – you get it from him.'

'Yes, Mummy,' said Lindsay.

'I'll be up at the weekend. I shan't tell your father. He doesn't need to know. Try and sort it out and I'll come up at the weekend and we'll see what's to be done.'

'Yes,' said Lindsay.

'And you'll have to tell the personnel officer or welfare or something so that they hold your job for you or make arrangements for absence or whatever it is.'

'Yes,' said Lindsay.

'But you can't come home. Daddy's got a public position. There isn't room. I don't know what you're going to do about the baby. How do you feel?'

'All right. I am sorry – '

'Never mind. It will just have to be dealt with. Now you go and see this person – what's his name?'

'Robert MacLinnie – they call him Linnie.'

'I can think of other things to call him,' said Joan grimly. 'Taking advantage of a tipsy girl half his age – '

'Mummy, at least some of it was my fault.'

'I'm sure it was,' said Joan, 'but men don't get pregnant. Women do. He's got a wife and a family to think of, he's older than you, he should know better. He's got a responsible job. Tell him that if he doesn't pay up, he's going to be in trouble.'

'Yes,' said Lindsay.

'Now, take care. I'll see you on Saturday and I'll drop you a note to tell you which train I'll be on.'

Joan sat and looked at the telephone. Silly girl, she thought. Poor kid. Money for the journey. That night, elaborately casual, Joan said she thought she might surprise Lindsay by going up for the weekend. Paul was a bit puzzled.

'Will you take Mercer?' he asked.

'I don't think so,' said Joan, confidentially. 'You know how sensitive Lindsay can be. I think a weekend with just me would be a great treat for both of us. You can manage Mercer, can't you?'

Paul agreed. Joan didn't know how she had pulled it off. She kept waiting for Paul to ask her more questions but he did not. She took the money out of her savings account and went to see Lindsay on the train. Lindsay was pale and tired and defeated. She told her mother that Linnie had agreed to pay the money for her to have the baby in a private mother and baby home in London which had been suggested by the welfare officer, who knew the place from her previous job. Lindsay would be granted three months' leave only. Joan nodded.

'But Mummy,' said Lindsay, 'that means it'll show. I shall be in the office and everybody will know.'

'I'm sorry,' said Joan, and put her arm round her daughter.

Lindsay drew away.

They walked a bit and talked a bit and Lindsay introduced her mother to Iris, who'd been away when Joan and Mercer visited before. Iris was a tall, plain woman who unsettled Joan by the directness of her gaze and made no bones about being squarely on Lindsay's side and not thinking much of the way Joan had responded.

179

Joan withdrew into glacial dignity. She stayed overnight at the station hotel, expecting to have lunch with Lindsay the next day, but found a note from her daughter waiting for her when she came down to breakfast.

'Dear Mummy – I'm sorry, but I've been asked to cover for one of the girls on duty this morning and so I won't be around until late afternoon. I'm sure you'll want to get back so I'll write next week. I'm truly sorry about the mess I've made. I don't think it would have happened if only I could have persuaded Tony how much I love him, but that's no excuse. You know I will do nothing to embarrass you and Daddy further. Give Mercer a big hug from her big sister. Much love, Lindsay.'

Joan pushed a piece of toast down, swallowed some coffee, packed her bag and caught the next train home.

The next letter talked about the weather, her friend Iris's experiments with dyeing a dress and what she was reading. Joan wrote back about the weather, Ace the dog stealing a joint of mutton and bringing it home, how proud he was, how embarrassed she was but how she'd finally washed it in vinegar and water and cooked it, having asked all round the block and failed to discover the neighbour from whom he had taken it.

Paul added a note about the athletics display he was organising with blind and partially sighted students in the area, keep well, let's have your news soon, much love – Daddy.

And so the next five months or so passed. Within that time Joan managed to fit in four more visits, the money scrimped out of housekeeping, using the coach because although it took longer it was cheaper, still totally evading any explanation to Paul. Where in the past she had chafed and complained about his outside interests, she seemed now to positively encourage them. One night he asked her suddenly if Lindsay was all right.

'Yes, fine. Why do you ask?' replied Joan brightly, her heart constricted momentarily in her chest.

'Just wondering,' said Paul carefully. 'Are there any problems?'

'Well, I think she's still very fond of Tony, but of course she is still very young and he's that bit older and has tried to make her see that she mustn't try to rush things,' babbled Joan, wondering which way this conversation was going.

'No, very sensible.' Paul paused and carefully lit another cigarette. 'Is work all right?'

'Well, Paul,' said Joan, trying to control the edge that she could hear creeping into her voice, 'I only know what you know. She seems to be happy enough. Nobody's job is exactly what they want it to be. She chose it and she's making the best of it. It might not be everything she wants but she chose it and she's making the best of it.'

Paul nodded, smoking thoughtfully.

'She's made one or two friends, she's more sociable than she used to be,' Joan went on, 'and her girlfriends seem particularly loyal.' I'm not going to tell you, she thought. If you ask me, that's one thing, but I'm not going to tell you. Think what you like. I won't tell you. Paul looked at her. She met his gaze. After a moment or two he went back to his book and she to hers.

A few days later Lindsay rang her mother and told her that she was going down to London to stay in the residential home where she would have her baby. The welfare officer had recommended that she left the following week, thus extending her leave. She gave her mother the address and telephone number.

'I'll try to come and see you,' said Joan.

'If you can,' said Lindsay wistfully.

That night Paul announced that he had been thinking about it and he would really like to go and see Lindsay to reassure himself that everything was all right.

'But you can't,' said Joan.

'Why not?'

'I thought you were busy,' she said.

Paul shrugged. 'I think something's wrong and I want to see her and make sure.'

Joan's mouth dried. 'She's not there' she said.

'Where is she?' asked Paul calmly.

Joan swallowed. 'She's in London.'

'Why London?'

Joan couldn't think any further so she told the truth. 'She's staying at a home for unmarried mothers. She's going to have a baby.'

There was a long silence. Joan braced herself.

Eventually Paul asked, 'When?'

'In a few weeks.'

'Who is the father?'

Joan told him the story.

He remained absolutely calm. He asked if she had Lindsay's

address. She nodded.

'Write it out for me,' he said. 'I'm going down to see her tomorrow. I'll call the office and leave as soon as I've explained.'

'What do you mean – explained?' said Joan, her voice suddenly shrill. 'I've moved heaven and earth to keep this quiet and now you –'

'I shall simply say that I have family business to attend to,' said Paul. 'I understand what you've done and why you've done it. I just want to see my daughter.'

Joan began to cry. Paul went and put his arms round her while she wept and then he said quietly, 'I think I'll do without the cocoa tonight, Mummy. I'll just go to bed.'

She nodded and he went up, leaving her to put out the lights and follow him soon afterwards.

22 *Mercer*

When I was about twelve and she was twenty-four, Lindsay got engaged. She brought her fiancé home to meet us at Christmas and then went to spend the rest of the holiday with his family. Tony was big and round and sweet-faced, with dark curly hair and spectacles. He was taller and heavier than Lindsay and they laughed a lot and danced well together and I'd never seen her look so pretty. She shone and twinkled as though I'd spread frost flakes all over her instead of the bottom of the Christmas tree. Tony made everything and everybody easy. Lindsay was easy and Joan was easy and Paul took Lindsay's hand and told her he was proud of her.

In the summer they came with us for two weeks to a guest house on the south coast and everything went right. The sun was warm, the food was good and the rose garden smelled so lovely that Tony persuaded the landlady to lend us a card table and tried to teach us canasta in the velvet summer evenings.

In the autumn, the leaves chased each other before the hard winds and the memory of the two weeks in the sun when everyone had been so happy became as bright as coloured slides with strong light behind them. The winter came. Lindsay had a new posting south and told my parents that she could not get leave to come home for Christmas. She was disappointed, naturally, but since she and Tony planned to marry in the spring, she felt you couldn't have everything, and she'd just have to make the best of it. I was sorry, too, because I'd never seen Lindsay and my parents so happy and, having had all that once in the summer, it seemed a pity we couldn't have another dose of the same in the winter. But I expect I got used to the idea because I had moved on to a new and more demanding school and there was a lot of homework. Joan was now doing the odd evening sessions as part of the same job and Paul was spending more time in the garage, where he had begun carving wood.

As the end of the winter term and my school Christmas party came up, Joan walked all over town with me to find the golden sandals I'd set my heart on wearing at it. She bought them in a shop she'd never liked because they were the only ones that fitted and when we left the shop she said, 'I bet you wear them all of twice.' She was right. By the time the party was over, I hated the sight of them.

Christmas Day fell on a Saturday. We had no television but had ordered the Christmas editions of the *Illustrated London News*, *The Spectator*, *Tatler*, *Punch* and *Holly Leaves*. And the Sunday papers would be printed as usual, we'd heard, so Monday would be Boxing Day proper. We sat about and read, listened to the radio and talked a bit. Ace went missing. He went out as usual and didn't return. My father walked round the neighbouring streets, calling and calling, but he didn't respond. Perhaps he'd come back in the morning. He'd done that before, returning triumphant in the success of his adventures and still very much in one piece.

It was very cold. During the night, the temperature dropped further and I huddled in my bed at first light, the covers pulled up over my nose. Then I got up and crept into my parents' room to my mother's side of the bed to see if she was awake. She motioned me to climb in for a cuddle and to get warm. We talked in whispers until my father woke and then he elected to go and make tea, a rare treat for my mother.

He called up to tell us that Ace still wasn't back and that the heater in the kitchen didn't seem to be working, so he was going to get the coal fire in the living room going as quickly as he could. While he moved back and forth between the hearth and the coal cellar, which was just a big cupboard set in the wall outside the back door, we heard the paperboy deliver the Sunday editions. A few minutes after that, Paul appeared at the top of the stairs with a newspaper in his hand. 'Joan, oh Joan,' he said, 'Tony's been killed.'

Joan pushed herself out of bed and pulled on her dressing gown. He showed her the paper and then she walked away towards the bathroom, then back to begin walking down the stairs while he stood helplessly clutching the paper. 'Where are you going?' he asked. 'We must ring Lindsay,' she said. I got out of bed very quietly and watched them go down the stairs, heard them go to the telephone in the back room. I noticed that I was shaking and pulled on my dressing gown, too. I could hear them dialling, then speaking. Their voices bubbled against the silence like a trickle of water under thick ice. Joan called to me, asking if I wanted to speak to Lindsay. I shook my head. She called again, almost angrily. I ran to the back room. 'Tell her I'm sorry,' I whispered. She nodded and turned her back on me, all her attention on the telephone.

Paul wandered into the kitchen and sat down holding his head in his hands. My mother stood in the doorway. I heard scratching at the back door and let Ace in. I poured the tea Paul had made, I offered to make Joan toast but she said she couldn't eat it. They wept and I watched them, frightened. Ace sat at Joan's feet, pushing his head into her lap. Awed by the desolation, I went back into the hall and picked up the rest of the papers. There had been a major car accident on the way down through England. Eight people were in hospital, five were dead. Their names were listed and I stared at Tony's.

Joan went down to see Lindsay and she came home at New Year. Nobody knew what to say. Tony had gone to see his widowed mother to whom he was very close and then left her to try to fit in a flying visit to Lindsay. He was killed outright in the collision. I don't remember feeling that I wanted to comfort my sister. It didn't seem possible to offer comfort in the face of what had happened. It wasn't so much hopes cast down as walls thrown up, the end, and I couldn't work out why. She was not yet twenty-five. How could this be her last chance? But that's how it felt, and how we all treated it.

She had some time off work. She spent some with us, some with other friends. She apparently accepted that life was for the living but we conspired to ignore, whether out of embarrassment or ineptitude, that although she was breathing, she was not among us. She was gentle, polite, willing but insubstantial. I felt that if I hugged her too hard, she would collapse like a big bundle of cobwebs. She said things and did things but what she said had no resonance and what she did didn't matter. She was gone, almost as much as Tony. And Paul and Joan acted as if they were unaware of it.

Once she went back to work, phone calls from Lindsay were rare. Joan rang her, once a week. She had decided to change her job. A friend introduced her to a woman with money called Kay who also had a large house in the country and inexplicable faith in a gifted engineer, Stuart. They planned to start a small business and Lindsay would be the administrator.

Lindsay wrote letters to my parents. The letters were long, with strange writing, half-sprawled, half-looped, formed in a memorable way. Distinctive, unyielding. Retaining what? It was clear that these letters did not bring glad tidings. My mother would read them and pass them to Paul. Paul would read them, his jaw hardening before he drank his coffee and made for the door. Sometimes they would discuss the letters but never when I was supposed to hear. Occasionally Joan would put a letter in a less than obvious place in the kitchen in the hope that Paul wouldn't spot it before it was time to go.

I did not read these letters. They contained messages for me, love sent to me, but they were for my parents. Once or twice Paul read them first and lost his temper. Joan would send me out of the room to get dressed (we ate breakfast in our dressing gowns) or wash my hands or read a book, anything rather than continue to argue about Lindsay's letters in front of me. Joan resigned herself to reading the letters first so that she could contain the situation and avert Paul's rage. She would rush from the kitchen to the hall, scoop up the letter, ripping it open as she walked back to the kitchen, reading it while the toast burned and the coffee boiled, so that when Paul flung down the pages and raised his eyes wearily to hers, she could say firmly, 'We'll talk about it later, dear.'

Four years passed. For four years, we visited Lindsay and her friends, each year in a different hired house at the southern end of England, always an enormous house with grounds and orchards and workmen and dogs. For four years she came home and spent the Christmas holiday with us and everything had to be just right, like appeasing the gods, so that she and Paul would not fight, so that Christmas would not be spoiled, so that the family would seem to be united.

I cannot begin to think of the strain this must have been on Joan and I did not begin to think until relatively recently of why she did it. She had made her bed and she was lying on it. She had stayed in the marriage to Paul, she had a daughter whom they both loved but had failed in different ways, whose 'terrible luck' (her phrase) bound them together, and she could voice nothing of how all this felt to her for fear of breaking her own code of silence and bringing on more trouble. She didn't so much keep up appearances as cobble together the dreams she had had. She tried so hard for everything to be cordial that Paul responded to this wish of hers and of course I did because they both set me up for it. But all was not well.

Lindsay's friend Kay was running out of money, there was nothing to show for what she'd spent and her engineer chum had proved to be better at spending money than making it, indeed better at using up every kind of resource but not what you'd call a getter of anything. And Joan was terribly worried about Lindsay, worried that she worked too hard and had too little money, worried about the statutes of the business in which she was involved, worried about the nature of the relationship between Lindsay and Stuart, the engineer, what it was and was not, for he was a divorced man, an undischarged bankrupt and not someone in whom she, Joan, reposed any confidence at all.

Once in the middle of that four years we arrived to meet Lindsay after a very long car journey during which my parents apparently forgot that I was there at all and discussed their feelings about Lindsay and the people she was involved with in bewildering and angry detail. I listened. Both Paul and Joan had things they wanted to say, things they agreed to say. They knew they were out of their depth. They couldn't see how the triumvirate of Lindsay, Kay and Stuart worked, where the money came from, where it was going to, what was being created, what constituted the business, constantly referred to. They were aware of the strain of all this upon them and how helpless they felt in the face of what Lindsay was doing to herself. For hour upon hour the road rolled south and I interrupted only to tell Paul where to turn and which road to take in accordance with the elaborately plotted navigational schedule he had drawn up for me.

When we arrived, we were shooed into the dining room to eat something light – which turned out to be an unheard-of extravagance in the form of salmon. We stumbled through a meal, my father resigned like a patient elephant to the weight he'd become accustomed to on his back, the tendons in my sister's throat and my mother's so tight they could hardly swallow. When we went out into the hall, it was to talk about a walk, and I burst out that we had not come through England to go for a walk and talk polite nothings. My sister was on the stairs, some distance from us, my mother looked uncomfortable. Lindsay asked most politely what I was talking about.

'Why don't you ask them what I'm talking about?' I yelled, stung by the forbearing demeanour of my elders after all those hours of talk in the car.

'Perhaps this isn't the time – ' began Midge. My sister looked at us carefully.

'Mercer is a bit overwrought,' she suggested.

'Maybe,' said Paul.

My mother went towards Lindsay and Paul gently propelled me to the front door and out into the darkening garden.

Paul and I began to walk. It was pleasant to move through the air after so much sitting. He asked me why I had shouted. I told him how awful it had been listening to him and Midge in the car. I told him about her grabbing the letters, me listening to their voices, hoping this would be a letter that wouldn't cause too much trouble.

'Why don't you talk to Lindsay?' I asked. 'It's almost as if you're afraid of her. If I upset you, you'd tell me how you felt.' He was silent. 'Wouldn't you?' He nodded. 'Yes. Yes I probably would, but you and Lindsay are very different, Mercer. Entirely different people, and I can't talk to her as I might to you.' I wanted to ask him why I was so different, what could happen that two people in a family should be so different, but I waited. 'Do you love your mother?' he asked me suddenly. 'Yes,' I said. 'And Lindsay?' 'Yes,' I said. He nodded. 'And I love you too,' I said, unsolicited, into the dark. He smiled at me with great tenderness. 'Little friend of all the world,' he said, 'the keeper of dreams.' He walked on for a few paces. 'We'll just have to wait and see.'

Nothing changed. Midge took on several teaching sessions as well as her other work, Paul went out early, came home for tea and went out again. I went to school. Sometimes when Midge was working he would talk to me about the past, his mother and sisters, his soldiering days in India, what he read, what he believed. It was not always what he said that caught me as much as the way he said it. And he would never call me down to talk until I had finished my homework.

In the summer before I joined the repertory company for my first job, Lindsay and I went away on holiday. We stayed in bed and breakfast hotels in the West Country, drove and walked and swam. She borrowed a van with bunks in it and a stove, and we talked together quite easily, without Midge or Paul around. She knew that I wanted to act, she knew that this was the year I'd be pushing for it and she asked me what I knew about men. I didn't feel the need to confide in her so I said, 'Not much.'

'And birth control?'

My dignity was ruffled. 'Well, I know it's important, if that's what you mean.'

'Good,' she said quietly, spreading potted shrimps on fresh bread for supper. 'Because I didn't and I don't want you to have to go through what happened to me.' And while I sat staring at her, for once unquestionably in charge, she told me about the baby she had conceived and Joan's response, how she had kept the whole business from Paul until the baby was due and that when he heard, he rushed down to London and offered to adopt it, if that was what she wanted. But that she couldn't let him do that.

'Wasn't that what you wanted?' I asked, puzzled.

'I didn't know what I wanted,' said Lindsay, patiently explaining as to a child.

To begin with I cried, more out of confusion than sympathy. And unbidden the memory of her magnificent twenty-first birthday cake, which my mother had had professionally iced, swam before my eyes. I don't remember anything else about the holiday except that I was fascinated by the omission of all this from my life.

When I came home – Lindsay put me on the train for Persthorpe and I read *Jane Eyre* all the way – when we'd finished discussing where we went, and the beds, and the weather, I asked why I had never been told about Lindsay's baby. My father sat very still but Midge got up and crossed the room to the door in disgust.

'For heaven's sake,' she said with razor blades in her voice. 'Why do we have to go through all that again when we went to such trouble to keep it quiet?'

Paul still didn't move.

'In any case,' her eyes came to rest on me, 'there wasn't anything to tell you. You always knew.'

I protested. 'But I didn't, really I didn't – '

Paul, still unmoving, caught Joan's eye.

'What are we doing?' he asked quietly. 'What have we done?'

23 *Mercer*

Once, when I was first living in London, Lindsay rescued me. I had had a couple of acting jobs in terrible plays with mediocre acting companies and there wasn't anything else immediately available but I didn't want to go back to Persthorpe. Joan had never been keen on Persthorpe, and had grown to hate it. It was her third world war. She disliked the accents and the tacky shops and the factories whose filth stained the air. But she could live in it. Well, she was with Paul and he lived there. I, her younger daughter, the child of her hard-won wisdom and her determination, was going to get out of it. Of course I was. It was as obvious as her knowing that once my golden curls were cut at the age of nine, I'd grow darker and darker and more like what she remembered of her father.

Of course I was going to get out of Persthorpe. She always wanted me to, but Paul said nothing. Lindsay had already left home. Paul was wary about my wanting to be an actress. Midge was exhilarated by it. For Lindsay, it was just the evidence of how different we were, and she wasn't impressed or disapproving or any other concrete emotion. I was going to do something which didn't interest her.

So I tried. I stayed in London. And after that first couple of jobs, I began to take shorthand and typing classes because I was working in a bar and hating it. By the time I could type worth a damn, I had also worked in a shop, and I didn't like that either. In an office, I decided, I could play at being a secretary, I could be neat and sweet and relatively safe. I didn't ask myself what I needed to be safe from. Anyway, earning the money to get the classes paid for took a bit off the bit I'd got and there wasn't much there to start with, so I didn't eat very much. All right, I didn't eat at all. But this wasn't anything interesting and revealing like anorexia. I just starved. At most, I drank black coffee and ate an orange for breakfast, had a roll and more black coffee for lunch, prayed to be taken out to dinner or else a boiled egg. Six eggs for six days.

Then there was a really nasty strain of flu that winter and I lay in a heap in my bedsitter, waiting to feel better, while the world retreated into murkiness and the shadows grew like equatorial flowers around me. Suddenly the bell rang, my bell, the bell for my room.

My dressing gown was an ancient towelling robe left by whoever relieved me of the brand-new wool one Midge had bought for me before I left home. I shuddered in its fraying depths as I went along the hall and down the stairs, trying to think. It can't be anyone from work because there isn't any work and I can't owe any money because I haven't got any money. The door was one of these would-be grand entrances with patterns on the windows. I opened it and there stood Lindsay in one of her better suits.

'Hello darling,' she said. Well, she doesn't say it. She sort of sings it. This cadence, this trill at the moment only conveyed familiarity. I had flu. She sounded kind. I fell on her.

She took me upstairs, murmuring and crooning as she did. She filled the kettle and put it on the little two-burner stove I had in the corner of my room, a room with no shape and no colour other than my books and a bright china teacup I bought in Portobello market. She explained that she had to come to town to see to various things connected with work and that she'd rung my last number. When they said I'd left, she came round to the address she and Midge had for me. 'You look awful, you poor kid,' she said.

She made tea. She talked about the dogs. No matter how bad everything else was, there were always dogs. They had three usually – Stuart's German shepherd, Kay's West Highland white and Lindsay's mutt – otherwise respectively known as Wolf, Lulu and Mug. She told me that the state of the business was somewhat problematic but that prospects were good. Paul had once drily remarked that Lindsay's business had crises twice a year, midsummer and Christmas, and that otherwise they had problems. I remember being very impressed by this because Paul always said he knew nothing about business and in case he ever forgot his ignorance on this score, my mother was there to remind him.

Lindsay told me to stay in bed and then changed her mind. 'Would going out to lunch cheer you up?' she asked. I said I thought it might but that I hadn't any money. 'We'll manage,' she said. Lindsay was used to that. So I went off to have a bath and put on my warmest clothes. When I came back, she was sitting by the window, smoking.

I don't remember where we went except that it was not far from where I lived. And I don't remember what we ate. I do remember that she talked throughout the meal and I can't recall a word because I was so fascinated that she had come. It was such luck that she had arrived when I was feeling so awful and now I was eating something hot and it wasn't eggs.

I remember that I was grateful for something familiar, something that reminded me of home. She used words in ways I'd already begun to forget, family turns of phrase which made me feel less lonely and less light-headed. And eventually I confessed that I didn't know if I could stick being in London alone, that I had called Midge and burst into tears all over her only a few weeks before, but she had told me not to come back to Persthorpe, there was nothing for me there.

'I hate London,' said Lindsay. And then she stirred her tea deliberately and said that Midge was probably right. 'Once the flu's gone, it won't seem so impossible. You must go back in and try again.' One of the great tenets of family faith. A cross between 'if at first you don't succeed . . .' and 'We Shall Overcome, Lord.' And she paid for the meal.

But she was right. Because, within twenty-four hours, I rose and stopped feeling grey and Midge sent me a five-pound note. So I went out and bought rump steak for supper. And I got a temporary job at a bottling factory where I typed invoices and answered the enormous switchboard (once somebody had shown me how to use it) and ran errands and they liked me and I stayed for six weeks.

But when Lindsay and I met like that again, it was another two years down the line and I'd been home and had my grand affair with Hugh and come back to try my hand and heart and back at London and acting again. I was neither ill nor grateful for being rescued. We met on a Saturday, again for lunch, in a slightly better place still near where I lived in my little amoeba room, so colourless that when I think back to it, I remember there was a window but can barely recall where it was in relation to the door.

Of course I'd seen Lindsay in the meantime. We went home to see my parents for Christmas and in summer at least, whenever we could. Holidays were for the rich or at least for people richer than us. We went home, washed up and told stories, and walked the dog – by now no longer Ace but his successor Gyp.

And once or twice I had been to stay at one of the large houses in the country which she still shared with Kay and Stuart and the children from Stuart's marriage if they were on holiday and the dogs and the men in the workshop. Though apart from a great deal of talk about prototypes and safety standards I never saw anything tangible that they made. When I asked they told me they were in light engineering.

I saw how Lindsay lived. She was first up and last to bed. I saw how she catered for and catered to. The children liked her, their father, Stuart, both needed her to admire him and despised her for doing it. He didn't return whatever affection she had for him. Lindsay told me once, in her most controlled voice, that he had told her that he was very fond of her but not attracted to her. On another occasion, she sat on the side of the bath, while I cleaned my teeth or something, and told me that he occasionally slept with her but had always told her that she was no good in bed and that he knew about these things, so she presumed him to be right and more or less gave up. What I saw at first-hand were the entanglements, emotional and physical, of that household.

There was Kay, whom nobody really liked or wanted except that she had the chequebook with the cheques that didn't bounce and she was kind to animals. There was Lindsay who quite liked Kay but wasn't sure if Kay liked her. But Lindsay liked, was drawn to, maybe even once in a full moon loved Stuart and, if called to choose between the two, would always have sided with him. But of course Kay would never put Lindsay in that position because Kay too was used to being unloved, rejected, unsuccessful on the casting couch for leading lady that Stuart seemed to run. So she too kept her head down and made the best of a bad job and played the role required of her while Stuart demonstrated something he called his manhood.

If a human erection is a man, then Stuart was a man, because he certainly had erections. He talked about them, worried about their occasional non-appearance and cherished them when they materialised. He was generous with them in the sense that as long as he found somewhere warm and comfortable to put them, he did not much mind who was the owner of that pretty place. His wife had borne him two children and left him. She took them with her but they visited. There were girlfriends who worked for the company, girlfriends past, present and hopeful, old friends, new friends, and Lindsay's kid sister. Me, impressionable me.

I thought I had never met a man like Stuart because I was only in my late teens, didn't know very much about men and was in the process of finding out. I began by being flattered that he talked to me, paid me compliments, held my hand and flirted. I enjoyed the secret thrust of power that lurked in his shabby tweed trousers. I thought his power was something to do with my own. And then I saw how his constant demonstrations, over me, over Kay, over anybody, hurt Lindsay. How reined-in her voice became, like a wind running under rice paper held down with steel pins. How she looked in any other direction, down, away – anything rather than witness what he did. And, bruising to the ego, I saw how indiscriminate was his drive.

It was like something that itched. It itched physically and he scratched it mentally or physically. Sometimes he just played with the idea of what he could do, what he might do and sometimes he followed through – with Kay, with Lindsay, with Jubby who came for the weekend or Anita who did the filing. And I never knew if he did what he said he did or just wished he had had the chance or had actually had the chance and been refused. But the combination of his sexual aimlessness and the ache in Lindsay's throat which I could feel if I looked at her when he was talking about it was enough to put me off.

I kissed him passionately on the landing but when he tried to take it further I evaded him. Stuart showed me that like and dislike are as close as love and hate. My fascinated curiosity was defeated by some sense of self-preservation I didn't know I had. The menu was more interesting than the meal. And so many other people were offered and had had a bite.

But Stuart unwillingly admired Lindsay because of her willingness to try, try, try again, even when there wasn't any money and the profit margins on the machine parts they made was so thin that any success they had must be reckoned in paper rather than cash. He admired her because she cared for his children. And made tea for the boys in the workshop. And in between the requirements of housekeeping, wrote up the books and kept the creditors at bay. I once did a drawing of Stuart with a balloon over his head in which he is

194

thinking '. . . if only she was desirable' – not that he let that stop him when the itch was making itself felt and there was no better offer in sight.

Lindsay and I did not discuss this much when I was at the big house. She was in a role. She was my elder sister, my hostess, my benefactor even, and all she required of me was that I be pleasant, help out, wash my hands before meals and keep a still tongue in my head. In her scheme of things, I was too young to be able to say anything that might help her and she was no keener than Paul had been years before to have a witness to what was going wrong.

When we met at home, we were also in roles. She was the firstborn and I was the afterthought. We must not rock the boat or upset the applecart. Joan required it because she needed to be reinforced in the knowledge that the decision she had made to stay was right, and Paul because if 'the girls' fought, it showed disrespect for their mother whom he still loved deeply, erroneously but deeply. Talking there was more along the lines of deliberately superficial discussion. We received the party line on Lindsay's life and times. Joan and Paul debated it between themselves and sometimes I had a conversation with one or the other of them alone. Talking to Joan about Lindsay, even if she initiated the subject, always resulted in her rationalising whatever was under discussion, from the shape of her elder daughter's spectacles to her involvement with Stuart. Joan made me feel that if I understood Lindsay, I would accept her. It was unthinkable to her that I should understand my sister and decline to accept her.

But Paul let me talk. He did not criticise or justify Lindsay. He asked occasional questions, we debated the subject matter rather than the person concerned. And one afternoon when I had remarked with some bitterness that Joan was always reminding me Lindsay was my elder sister, Paul said quietly, 'Only chronologically.' I stopped dead. 'She was born first,' he said. 'In every other way you are the older child and you always will be.' I sat silent for a moment, the trust seeping into my skin like water in a parched garden. And then we talked about other things.

So I went about my own way of acquiring wisdom, wisdom to protect the dreams I was keeper of, and the wisdom I sought was about the world. I wanted to know what made people the way they were, why did they behave and perform, what freed them, what inhibited them. For these were the answers to all the questions I had not articulated but which slid from side to side in my brain, like

195

heavy luggage in a fast train. I didn't set out to be approved or disapproved of. Indeed, I spent no time that I can recall wondering how the fallout from my actions would affect anyone else.

So the next time that Lindsay and I had lunch, the second time only in all these years, I was unwilling to remain in my allotted role of younger sister and the temperature of our conversation escalated through sullen flashes to a verbal electrical storm until, my eyes wet with self-pity and my face red with irritation, I heard her say that she could not come to terms with my wild life. The injustice of it stung me far more than any implied criticism of my conduct. How could I have a wild life, I thought, when all I wanted to do (then) was barred to me, I hadn't any money to spare, when I didn't know any other way to do it but to just go ahead and pick up the pieces later?

And I looked at her, at the anxious shoulders held rigidly under a sweater in a particularly trying shade of cyclamen which only she could wear successfully. Better all kinds of adventures with no more conclusions than that life was varied and interesting than hanging about with a man who despised you for caring about him when he didn't care about you. And who the hell was she anyway?

I said none of this, fortunately, but I pointed out that I didn't need or want her criticisms, having perfectly good parents, and I felt it was up to them to tell me whether what I was doing was acceptable or not, not her – safe as I was in the knowledge that, from that distance, they could only know the censored version of events I was prepared to let them in on.

'They're getting older,' she reminded me. 'They don't want fights, they don't want to alienate you.'

'They are my parents,' I said, hardening my jaw. 'It is for them to criticise me, not you.'

'Darling,' she exhaled with that familiar cadence, at once beseeching and exasperated, that mixture of do be reasonable and don't be difficult. 'I'm only trying to help you.'

'Maybe,' I said, heroine of my very own B-movie, 'and maybe I don't want to be helped.'

I grabbed my bag and marched down the street to the phone box in the corner of the post office, where I rang Joan with great despatch and demanded that she tell her elder daughter that I had a family, thank you, parents, and I didn't need her to manage me and tell me what to do. Outrage is total when you're nineteen. By the time Lindsay arrived I was in tears and my mother was enquiring what the hell was going on and we were both trying to soothe her and Lindsay to soothe me. The sense of unfairness remained.

In that moment, I wanted to tell her how my parents already thought she was the chosen one, that there was nothing I could do, nothing, which would bring them to focus all their attention upon me because part of it was always focussed upon her. I wanted to tell her how I had gone to church the year after Tony died and prayed that God would take me so that my parents could have her back again because they were so out of their depth in the face of her bereavement and loved her with such helplessness. I also prayed (while I was at it) for stigmata, not because I wanted to be a saint but because that would be real evidence, because I felt that only by showing them how much I hurt could I show them how much I cared and then perhaps they would stop talking about her, stop taking so much notice of her and talk to me and if they would do that, I could afford to be generous, wanted to be generous and help her.

I wanted to tell her that I was tired of being alone and trying so hard for a prize that lurked about my head and out of my reach like a golden netball, while all the crowd chanted 'Take it! Take it!' and I still didn't know what it was or how to catch or where to run. I wanted to tell her that my childhood had been full of the echoes of other voices endlessly talking about her. I wanted to tell her how much I hated the dress she'd bought for me when I was eight. I wanted to tell her how sorry I was that Tony had died. I wanted to ask her why she'd accepted that as the end of everything. I wanted to kill Stuart for her. I wanted to be acknowledged for having done something to move us on from this place that we were all locked into. I said nothing. She kissed my cheek goodbye. I went for a walk and looked at the park and wondered if I'd ever be any good at anything.

24 Mercer

In the weeks after Paul's death, Midge and I spent more time together than in recent years. But it wasn't a matter of comforting. Neither of us honestly knew what to do with each other. We wished to be of use to each other and we desperately didn't want to offend but we didn't know what to do other than to be gentle and polite and there.

I returned to the hoarded photographs. They were a kind of consolation to me, evidence of the existence of people I knew and loved, like Paul and others I never knew or didn't remember. My mother would sit there while I went through the hoarded envelopes.

'Isn't this Brian Toomey?' I asked one afternoon.

'Yes, that's right.'

I thought for a minute. 'He had red hair.'

She nodded. 'He was married, to a beautiful Anglo-Indian girl. Made his life hell. He came to be Daddy's assistant.' She handed the picture back. 'He was a nice boy. He had a car.'

I wanted to ask her why this was important but of course I knew. Joan seemed to regard cars wistfully, as if they were almost magical, but if I asked her why she never learned to drive she would say that there was never enough money, and that in any case Paul didn't want her to. And I didn't feel I could push her any further.

Later that same afternoon, she remarked that Brian had been very fond of her. I said that I was not surprised. I remembered riding in his car.

'You can't really remember that, can you?' she asked. 'You were very small then.'

And then once, when we were talking about a wife's infidelity in something we'd seen, some play on television, she laughed drily and said, 'Oh Lord, I remember that – stockings over the chair back and a rush home with a lump in your throat. Bit strenuous in the long term.' But I wasn't sure if I was supposed to hear, if she knew what I wondered, what was inferred. Was she shocked and so not thinking? Did she care – or was she testing? I left it.

Brian Toomey had a moustache and smelt of vegetable water. His sports car was green and I did not like the idea of lying in my pram – or for that matter on the back seat – while my mother had her bi-weekly extramarital constitutional with Brian Toomey. Yet she somehow managed to suggest that Paul not only knew but would have understood.

'I remember once he said – after we got back together again, after the war – that the one thing you really own is your own body,' she told me. 'It was quite a shock to me. I wondered if he knew what it meant. And then I thought – right.' But not in the town that was too small to hold Lindsay's pregnancy, where Paul held a cherished public position? Not with his sidekick? I thought it was unfortunately all too human to say that what you don't want is untenable while what you do want, in exactly the same circumstances, becomes magically possible.

Several months later it occurred to me to ask her if she'd ever gone to her dinner with Giles Campion. 'Of course not,' she said. 'I rang up and cancelled it.'

There didn't seem any more to be said.

I sat up in bed with a book that night but I didn't read. I was glad, I thought, that Paul had come to the theatre to see my play, glad that he understood about the writing, sorry that I hadn't had time to explain more about David, glad that I didn't have to, glad I was his daughter, that Paul and Mercer was different from Paul and Joan or Paul and Lindsay. And I was glad to get on the train and return to London at the earliest decent hour the following day.

In the meantime my agent, Jud Chase, had been putting busy fingers into new pies for me and in consequence I was invited to go to New York for a new production of my first play. I wanted very much to go, of course I did, and Joan felt that I should not hesitate. Feeling embarrassed, I approached Lindsay. 'Mother will manage,' she affirmed, 'and I'll get down every weekend I can.' I said I thought that seemed rather a burden. 'But, darling,' she replied, running vocal fingers over these syllables – harp strings? heart strings? – I couldn't tell, 'of course you must go. It's such a compliment. We'll miss you, but we'll manage.'

To begin with, I was to be there for six weeks, maybe two months but not more, to sit in on and contribute to this new version of *The Cradle*. And the foreignness of New York was soothing because it was so strange. I learned quickly to eat different things at different times, to ask for exactly what I wanted and that meeting the management, actors and producer was all much the same as before. Except that Jud had set up some sort of reputation for me. They expected me to be odd, to be sensitive, to be difficult. And so I was and they were not disappointed. At least I thought I was, but they kept telling me, all of them, singly and in groups, how amazingly easy and thoughtful I was, how truly wonderful to work with. Just great.

And I saw the play differently. It was old to me – I could see the holes in it, less clearly the power and conviction I'd had when I wrote it. In the ten years in between there had been other battles and other losses – David, the marriage, the divorce. Paul's death, the long, long pause without writing. So for the first time in my life I was quiet and certain.

I thought a lot about Paul. He would have hated New York. The strange night and the unsleeping city were not for him. They weren't really for Joan, either, although the adventure of it would have appealed, the adventure of being anywhere. But she wouldn't have liked living there, which daily seemed more attractive to me. And I knew why.

It was far away from everything. From Lindsay, from the failure with David, from the death of Paul. From Joan, about whom I felt for the first time distaste. And reminded myself that I was not in a position to judge. I did not, could not know the whole story, and I'd had more than two affairs in the course of my marriage and anyway, the only indication that she'd had an affair with Brian Toomey was my nasty mind and a turn of phrase I'd leaped upon like Sherlock Holmes finding the crucial clue. But clue to what? An affair in wartime was one thing. An affair under my father's nose was something else. Even if I had the courage to admit that I didn't like some of what my mother did, my love for her remained unshadowed. Didn't it? Wasn't it? Shouldn't it be?

One night I walked through midtown, looking at the shop

windows, past the big hotels when from one of them hurried a man who almost tripped over me, or I him, as our paths crossed. He apologised and helped me right myself. The voice was English and I was suddenly homesick. I had already been away for nearly five months, staying free in an apartment owned by one of Jud's friends who was on psychic sabbatical in Colorado, spending time with the actors, the management, their friends, lying without compunction about the need to stay there. Time alone, time unknown.

I'd sent off three pieces to various publications, I'd used the telephone and facilities in the offices of Jud's American associates. I had some money, I spent very little. I was very interested in feeling this young and this free and this viable again after so long. But the man's voice made me feel as if I were playing games with myself. What can you ever be in a foreign city but a professional expatriate? I didn't belong here. I could only hide out until I ran out of money or the furies caught up with me in some other way. Always quit when you're ahead, said Joan's voice in my ear.

But I didn't want to go back and start visiting her and risk hearing anything else I didn't really want to hear. At this distance I could hide behind the cost of phone calls and I've always been a poor correspondent. Perhaps it's because I can only write when I'm being paid for it. Writing and paying for it isn't my kind of equation at all.

So I told my new-found acquaintance that I was leaving next week. And I told my mother and sister I had the opportunity to go with the show on tour and I would be very nearly uncontactable for a further – eight weeks. I could be absent for two more months, couldn't I? And the following Monday I flew home to England and hid in a large seaside town where I found a bed and breakfast place and rang Jud.

'It's your fault,' I said. 'I've been living in a way to which I could easily have become accustomed.'

'So,' said Jud calmly, 'why didn't you stay in America?'

I hesitated.

'They were very enthusiastic about you.'

'Enthusiasm doesn't pay bills,' I replied, ever my mother's daughter. 'And anyway, I haven't got the right papers.'

Jud sighed. 'Are you writing anything new?'

'Well, I did those things when I was there – "Britain on Broaday" for Milly and some stuff for Pat and the Black Prince.' She was usually appreciative of my nicknames but this time she didn't respond.

'Anything else?'

'Not now, no. I've only just got back.'

'Well, God knows what you're going to write from there,' she said wearily. 'How long will you stay?'

'I don't know.'

'Anything in mind?'

'Yes,' I said. 'Yes, I have but it isn't there yet.'

'When will it be?'

'Jud, you know I'll call –'

She paused. 'You got enough money?'

'For now? Yes.'

'Why don't you call me on Monday?'

'But that's less than a week. I've only just got back.'

'Yes, Mercer, Think about it and call me on Monday. Mind out for sea breezes. Talk to you.'

Agents and water diviners have a lot in common.

That night I went for a late walk, marvelling at how differently enchanting were the harbour lights on British water from the store lights on Fifth Avenue. There was a man sitting on a bench. When I came back past him he remarked that it was getting cooler.

'It's not that,' I said, 'it's just that I'm tired.'

'Sea air,' he said.

I opened my mouth to tell him that it wasn't, it was jet lag, and now my bloody agent wants me to get down to work and I haven't even had time to sort it, the idea, through, but I thought very fast.

'Do you find it tiring?' I asked.

'No,' he said. 'Peaceful.'

I wanted to ask him why he needed peace, he seemed so quiet and self-contained, sitting there in the almost darkness. But I didn't, I just waited and then began to walk away again, not back to my room but out along the front again. He caught up with me. He was much taller than I and we walked some way in silence before he said, 'Where were you in the States?'

I stared at him.

'You pick up accents quickly,' he said with a grin.

And we started to talk. About travelling – he seemed to have been to many places. About books. He didn't like the theatre.

'Married?' I asked him.

'I was.'

'Me too.'

By one o'clock we'd walked the front and the streets leading to it and, apart from a couple going home, feeding each other fish and chips and an old man with a dog, we saw no one.

'I'm going to bed,' I said, 'I'm tired.'

As he walked me to my door, I wondered briefly if he might be a mad axeman or a rapist on a day return. But he just wished me good-night.

The next day I got up and confronted the typewriter. But I couldn't settle. I went to find the landlady to explain that I wanted to write something. At first she frowned and looked doubtful but when she understood that it wasn't a letter and that I had a typewriter, she became quite excited.

'Are you a writer, then?' she enquired.

'Sort of – more of a journalist really. This is just background stuff I need to type up. You know, like research.'

She nodded, visibly impressed.

'So you won't mind the typewriter?'

She was quick to reassure me. 'Bang away all you like,' she said cheerfully. And as she was out all day she gave me a key.

I saw him again that evening. We had a drink and went for another long amiable walk. He didn't ask me any questions that I could regard as leading. We had established that we were both alone, so how or why didn't seem to matter. He didn't tell me what he did. I told him I was writing and that I had written a couple of plays, which was how I'd come to be in New York. He said his name was Constantine.

'Constantine?' I almost laughed. 'Why?'

He shrugged. 'Father was more interested in cricket than Mother. Call me Con. And you're?'

'Mercer.'

'Where did that come from?' he asked, implying I hadn't done any better in the name stakes than he had. I told him it was the name of the best friend of the Prince Regent's daughter and my mother said she'd got it out of a book.

'Is it ever shortened?'

'Sometimes.'

'You don't mind?'

I shook my head.

He looked out across the sea and talked about Cornwall.

By the fourth day we had a routine. I wrote and bought a paper and read and wrote and had a sandwich and washed my underwear and wrote. Mrs Gates came in from work and we had another cup of tea and I dressed carefully, a little lipstick, a pair of earrings, and I met Con on the front by the benches. I had a pile of stuff written and was wondering if I shouldn't ring Jud now, to tell her I was working. But I didn't. On the sixth day he wasn't there. I felt terribly disappointed. It was hard to realise how alone and vulnerable and silly I felt, at the thought of dinner alone and the evening alone and the walk alone. So I set off briskly reminding myself that, as a woman of the world, worse things have happened and undoubtedly will again. I didn't want to get up on the seventh day and I was picking moodily through my papers at ten-thirty, eyeing my previously most comfortable narrow bed with dissatisfaction, so I went and bought a large envelope and sent everything off to Jud, telling her I'd be home in a few days, but as far as my family were concerned I was still in America. Lindsay could always telephone Jud on the understanding that Jud could call me in the States if Joan was taken suddenly ill. And I went back to tell Mrs Gates that I would be leaving on Monday. I never have liked Mondays.

I was sitting at the station reading a book about the Red Indians teaching a missionary how to die when Con cast his shadow over my page and I looked up and saw how delighted and white and determined and real his face was. The most real face, as if all the other faces had been imaginary, or printouts from the memory. And I stood up with my arms so wide that I dropped the book and he wrapped his arms round me and the train came in.

'I'll see you in London,' he said, tucking something into my pocket.

I closed the door behind me and looked down at him.

'The address and everything – it's all in there,' he said.

'Will it be all right?' I asked him. Why am I on this train with my bag and my typewriter if he's not?

'Yes, of course it will,' he said. 'I love you.'

I stared at him.

'I could get off the train,' I offered.

He smiled and shook his head.

'It'll be all right,' he promised. 'You read the letter. I'll see you in a couple of days.'

The train began to move.

'I hate goodbyes,' I said.

'So, say hello.' He hadn't kissed me. He didn't know if I was any good in bed. He didn't know about my writing, how bad-tempered I could be. He hadn't met my family. They hadn't met him. He still looked very large and solid. Maybe this is it, I thought.

'Hello, Con,' I said. And I yelled it as the train pulled out. 'Hello, Con.'

25   *Mercer*

When I got back to London, I returned to an hotel and a great deal of telephoning. Eventually I found a room with a woman who'd been somebody's secretary at the BBC and was a friend of a friend, two or three times removed. She wanted income and no fuss. So I moved in, leaving a lot of my stuff in left luggage while I looked for somewhere more permanent to stay.

And who should I meet in the street but an editor friend of David's who just happened to know a director going out to Africa on an extended project who wanted to let his flat for a year. He took me back to his office and I rang from there. His friend said he'd be back at the flat at six, so by ten the following morning I was in the process of lining up my suitcases and boxes of books in the hall of a large flat, sized not so much in numbers of rooms but proportions, with a place to settle for twelve whole months. And a week later I left Our Lady of the Pursestrings and moved in. And then I rang Jud.

'Where are you?' she asked, and I told her.

'You sound terribly happy,' she said suspiciously.

I began to laugh. 'What do you think of the stuff I sent you?'

'It's OK, it's good even. When will you begin?' she asked.

So I told her in the morning, explained about the flat and she exclaimed. Then I said, 'Oh, and I met somebody.'

'Good.'

'It's important.'

'Good.'

'But I'm broke.'

I could hear Jud pursing her lips. 'Hasn't he got any money?'

'Probably, but it's a bit soon for that.'

'How much do you need?'

'Five hundred and a job.'

'OK. Start writing and I'll be in touch. Cheque in the post.'

'I'll pay you back as soon as I can.'

'I know,' she said. She was grinning at the end of the phone.

I sat on the side of the bed and took Con's letter out of my pocket. It told me that he was leaving for Manila in the morning, that was the day after he left me on the train, and that he would be away for two weeks, flying from one place to another. He listed a whole string of cities I'd never heard of and had to buy an atlas to locate. He would not telephone. He would be back in London on the 18th. Please would I ring him at 6.00 p.m. that day? I thought that you couldn't get any more organised than that. There was no explanation, no account. But it was still five days away, so I started typing.

In the morning, I made telephone calls, explained where I'd been, trawled for jobs and got nowhere. In the afternoon, I wrote. Slowly the idea began to take shape. I wanted to try for television and I thought I had a good chance with this. The next morning I made more calls, drew more blanks. And wrote all afternoon. Jud's cheque arrived and I banked it. I was back in a routine, familiar but different. I wasn't exactly waiting for the 18th but I kept hoping it would happen soon.

And when it did I was terrified. We knew so little about each other. Suppose he tells me it was a put-up job, I thought, a cover for something else he had to do or be seen to do? Suppose he's in the garment trade? I couldn't think of any other reason for going to Manila. I had looked at every pore of my skin twice. My hair would never satisfy me and I had applied cologne, liberally, three times. I rang the number. He sounded as if he was sorry he'd be a bit late home for dinner. We agreed to meet at eight. I got there early and found him waiting. He kissed me. I sat down blushing to the roots of my hair. I had three drinks and I don't remember anything I ate. He took me home and stayed with me. I asked him why Manila and he said he would tell me, he promised he would, but not now. And we went to bed.

He stroked every inch of me. I felt incredibly beautiful, as if my beauty should affect where I was, like causing glass to melt or walls to fall down. He remained inside me for so long that I forgot where I

207

ended and he began and began to feel linked to him by some vital limb. And all those spurious thoughts about one-night stands and great sex and where do we go from here didn't surface, much less have to be pushed away. It was quite unlike anything else that had ever happened to me and I felt that my life had been saved.

As dawn came up, he spread himself above me like an enormously powerful but wholly benign animal and I was covered in every way for the first time that I remember. And I felt marked and changed specially, for which there is no language because the only explanations for such sensations are expounded at the other end of the scale, having to do with fantasy and male domination, which was nothing to do with what was going on. I was not alone.

In the daylight he told me that he was a bodyguard to an immensely rich man who was a member of one of the leading families in a small Indonesian state, a Mr Parah. Or at least, he said that he had started out as that and had graduated to becoming his business troubleshooter because, apart from being very big and strong, he was also 'quite sharp' and good at figures. He said that he had been in the services and waited for me to ask more. I knew that I should not. All I knew about that was that once you were involved you were likely to stay involved, which didn't seem to augur well for the future. And yet, what he said felt honest. 'One day I'll explain,' he said. I looked at him. He looked at me. I knew he wasn't going to tell me any more. He smiled and nodded.

When he travelled, he travelled at the drop of a hat for the period of time required. It might be a few days, it might be a few weeks. He had been everywhere, at least once. He didn't ask me if I could cope with it.

I told him that I was trying to write a play for television. He was encouraging. He asked about the flat. Would I mind if we met here rather than at his place? I didn't mind but I asked why. He said it was more private. 'Eavesdroppers?' I asked, curious but not wanting to say any more than he felt he could respond to, sensing something withheld, waiting to be confronted, wanting him to know that I understood and that even if I didn't, I accepted.

'Intrigue,' he said.

'Will you be all right?' I asked.

He nodded.

'I'm serious,' I said.

'I promise,' he replied.

He stayed for three days. When I next saw him, he asked me what I was living on and when I said my agent, he put a large wad of bills on top of the fridge.

'Don't be short,' he said. I was taken aback. I protested. He watched me while I said that I couldn't possibly and even if I did, how would I repay him, and he told me that it was common among people who were serious about each other to take care of your partner. And I began to cry. And when I'd cried and he'd taken me to bed and we'd eaten supper, he told me that he'd be leaving for Australia at the end of the week.

'When will you be back?'

And he supplied the date and we agreed the time, and although it was very odd and novelettish, it was also just the way it was. So I got on with it.

In the meantime my mother announced that she couldn't continue to live in the house in which Paul died. That he didn't die in the house but at a local hospital was academic. What she meant was that she had never liked it and now she wanted to be out of it and, anyway, Lindsay couldn't continue to commute and was going to give Stuart and his business ventures one last go so they were selling the family house and going to buy a house together, had in fact already looked at one in Aising, on the Sussex borders. Perhaps, my mother suggested, if things between Lindsay and Stuart were on more of a business footing, things would work out better between them.

I did not tell my mother and sister about Con. I couldn't explain what he did, his absences or the state of play between us. I wouldn't have had to explain to Paul. He would have known from the way that I talked, from what was said and not said. I would have kissed him and he would have grunted and I'd turn to go and he'd catch my hand and say, 'Remember, if you step on to a highwire, don't waste time looking down. Just concentrate on how you're going to get to the other side.' The memory made my eyes fill. I don't remember Paul putting his arms round me a lot, but I missed him then. I thought I could smell him. And I wished I could tell him about Con, because he was a lot of the things that Paul wanted for me. A lot of the things that Paul was not able to be. I had other arms to run to and I wished I could share it with somebody.

Lindsay rang to make it clear to me that she didn't feel Joan could continue to live alone. I forbore to point out that without her, she wouldn't be able to move back from Stuart. It would be unkind to salt the emotional GBH he'd already done her.

So the house was sold and Midge spent weeks tearing up the papers Paul had hoarded. 'There's every gas bill from 1929,' she exclaimed in exasperation, 'and wads of stuff from all that voluntary work he would do. Nothing to show for it but paper and he kept every darned sheet of it.' I wondered if I was supposed to offer to help and the more I thought about it, the more I felt I should, praying meantime that she wouldn't accept my offer.

In fact, she declined it rather diffidently, and when I pushed and made it clear that if she really needed me, of course I would come, she explained that she didn't want me to be hurt but actually she didn't want either of us around. 'It's funny,' she said, 'uncovering all this stuff from years ago, photographs and so on. Like looking back at your life, and it isn't all pleasant. Do you know, the other day I found a whole bunch of letters his father wrote to Paul and Paul wrote to his father about the Old Man's gambling debts. It was years ago now, when we were first married. The Old Man got into trouble and came to his eldest son to bail him out and Paul did, for years, and then told him he could never come to him for help again. I remember him telling me about it. But Mercer, the letters were awful. They were so bitter. I only read one or two and then I put the whole lot on the fire.'

So I left her to it, with suitable expressions of conciliation, and went back to my typewriter which, if not steaming, was at least maintaining a degree of noticeable heat while I plunged on with the idea with which I'd begun. Only it seemed to swing between two developments – either a play or a series. The idea of a series terrified me but eventually I rang Jud and we agreed I should work at the play as the first segment and try to go on from there.

'Try calling it a pilot instead of a play,' said Jud drily. 'You'll see, it'll clear your head to get on with it.'

She was right.

When I saw Con, writing ceased because he was never there for long and we had to spend time together when we could, but the rent was paid and I was eating and keeping meticulous notes about what I spent his money on, hoarding unspent chunks of it in a ginger jar on the kitchen shelf so that I could have time to stop looking for other work. He had insisted that I repay Jud as soon as possible so, in my mind, I was stuck in the most awful debt to this person whom I thought I loved, and wondered what I would do if I stopped loving him or, more likely, if he stopped loving me. So I kept an account book and tried to be frugal. I was quite good at being frugal about everything except books. And magazines. And haircuts and lipstick and soap. And olive oil. And – it became embarrassing. To me, that is. He accepted it without debate. But I continued to explain, justify and, if asked for the slightest explanation, defend. He spent a lot of energy defusing my defending, did Con.

Every time he arrived, he was noticeably pale. Whether we met at one of the places we now called ours or at home (cross fingers behind your back, Mercer: nearly eight months to go before the owner comes back and we have to think about the next stage), he was pale. It was not white and washed-out but rather as if he was holding so many things in that the flow of blood to his skin was impeded. And I noticed, too, that after half an hour or so, his skin warmed and his mouth had shape. One day I mentioned it to him.

'You do the same thing,' he said.

'Do I?'

'Yep. You arrive looking like a ghost and somewhere between twenty and thirty minutes later, you begin to look like you.'

'But you have reasons, don't you, for looking so taut?' I asked carefully.

'True, but so do you. This is not what I planned. I promised myself nobody ever again, except for fun, casually.'

'And I'm not casual?'

He looked at me so hard I felt it. 'No.'

'Are things going wrong? Between us?'

'No, not those things, but others may do. The point is, things are ending. There will be changes.'

'Do you need money?' I asked immediately, my mind flying to the ginger jar and the accounts book.

'Mercer, money is not the problem. I have money, stashed away. What I give you, I give you because you need it. I want you to have it. It's not a loan, it doesn't have to be repaid. It's not an investment either. It's just money. No, I don't need money.' He hadn't raised his voice, it had no edge. He wasn't angry, I wasn't shaking. All this had to be said. How did he know that?

'Right. What do you need?' I asked. It was a nice enough restaurant we were sitting in, there was space in between the tables and the lavatory was clean.

'I need to know you'll be there. I need to know you can hang on till I'm ready to tell you what's happening.'

'I'm here,' I said. 'Besides, I'm in such awful fucking debt to you that I'll never be able to pay it and leave.'

Con's smile is the opposite of the one psychologists tell you you should control because it's appeasing and you'll lose points. His smile starts in his eyes and works down his face like a thaw over a winter landscape. It has many component parts but appeasement is not one of them and even in four months I had discovered that his sense of humour is as black as I will allow mine to be.

'Fucking debt, indeed,' he said.

It was a great night. They all were. They still are.

Lindsay and my mother found a house. The first of my scripts became a pilot. Midge held back nothing from the purchase except a few hundred pounds which she said would be my share, which both embarrassed me and made me proud. The television company decided they liked the pilot and would buy the series. On the strength of that, Jud got me to a features editor I'd never met on a new women's magazine and we agreed on a rolling column on life before and behind the camera, using as the springboard my series and every other one I could gain entry to. I began to put money regularly into the bank and offered Midge a monthly allowance. She said that the last thing she wanted was to be a burden to her daughters. I said that we had to face it, Paul hadn't left her any money, she couldn't go back to work at her age and it wasn't fair that Lindsay should have to pay for everything.

I deliberately told her that I was not offering her the biggest sum of money in the world but that this was a sum I could maintain, through thick and thin. 'Well, it's only extras,' she said. 'I mean, the house is almost paid for and I've got my pension.' It still sounded pretty slender to me but you can't talk about London money to someone who doesn't live there. Midge valued her independence and so it seemed that a modest amount of money would make me happy because I could keep it up and her happy because it was just that. And a little allowance would not rock the financial boat around Lindsay, who was always thin-skinned on the subject of money, probably because she believed what everybody said about what they had and what they spent, but never had any herself. Plus the fact that I never talked about money with Lindsay in case Stuart got wind of it.

Con told me he was going to have to go away. When I asked for how long, he said several weeks, maybe a couple of months. I asked if he was in trouble. He said no. He couldn't tell me anything. He didn't beg or ask me to understand. I asked when he would be leaving. He said in three days. I wanted to ask for a ring or a present, a written promise, a talisman. I wanted to give him a keepsake or a loveletter. 'Nothing special,' he said, as if he'd read my mind. 'I'm coming back.' He accepted without apparent misgiving my regular attendance at studio meetings. The offer for the series had been finalised, it was real, but I had not yet begun to write more than notes so I would write when I could and spend the rest of the time with him. He would leave for several hours and I would fall on the typewriter. He returned and I would ask what we'd do now?

'What time do you have to leave?'

He said eight in the morning. It was a Monday.

Usually I kissed him goodbye at the door and, if I watched, I hid behind the curtains. I couldn't watch till he was out of sight. It might break the luck. But this morning, I watched him till I couldn't see him any more without waving. And then I went to work.

I rang Jud, who picked up instantly on my tone of voice and said we should meet for lunch, and I hit the typewriter as if both our lives depended upon it. I rang my mother. If I'd known his mother's number I'd have rung her. Midge said the house was coming on nicely, things seemed to be working out rather better at Lindsay's work and I asked, as I always did, how was Lindsay?

'More cheerful than I've seen her for ages,' said Midge. 'Of course you know she's been seeing this man, Bob.'

I fished around in the memory files and said yes, I thought I remembered.

'Seems quite keen,' said Midge. 'Still, we shall have to wait and see.'

I asked if she needed anything. She said no. I said I'd call later in the week.

I drank three glasses of red wine with lunch and Jud remarked, 'Tough patch?'

I nodded and, when lunch was over, I thought I'd better get into a cab and go home. She asked if I was due anywhere. I said no, but I should be writing.

'You can have a day off, Mercer,' she said wisely.

I protested that I had had lots of days off.

'But this is different,' she said.

'He's gone away,' I said, my eyes filling.

'He'll be back,' said Judith Chase, God bless her.

Meetings appeared out of the wall. Copy had to be produced for the magazine. New ideas had to be discussed, debated, rejected and raised from the dead. Actors had to be auditioned, working teams had to be established and the scripts had to be written, written and written again. Days passed and I was not looking at the calendar. I lit a candle for Con every night, on my mantelpiece. It burned from the time I went to bed, all through the night. I had found the right size candles in a local ironmonger's.

And then Lindsay rang to tell me that she was getting married. I think, I hope I said all the right things. She was marrying Bob. Would I come down one weekend soon and meet him? They were being married in a month. I said I would come as soon as she invited me. We agreed to make it the forthcoming weekend. Bob was tall, grey-haired and smelt unmistakably of nylon-shirted armpit. He talked all the time in a very loud voice, knew more than everybody about everything and, when he didn't, subdued the speaker by sheer volume. His fingernails were long, like talons.

The weekend was not a success. And I kept looking at Midge, my snobbish mother, the woman who had told me at intervals down the years that it was easier for women, they could always marry 'up', and wondering, what is this? Are we desperate? Are we blind? Where oh where is the transforming nature of love – my God, it'll have its hands full here – and drinking yet another cup of tea. So much tea. Tea the cure-all, balm to the spirit but rough on the digestion. When they went for a walk in the afternoon, I shut the door with relief and said to Joan that the silence was truly golden.

'Lindsay's very happy,' she said defensively.

'And good luck to Lindsay,' I said, collecting the current set of cups for washing. Bob drank as much instant coffee as we had drunk tea.

'Well, she is your sister. She is entitled to her happiness.'

'Of course she is,' I said, fighting rising impatience. This was the woman I'd seen wincing every few minutes for the past three hours and here she is treating me as if I'm the Bad Fairy at the longed-for baptism of my sister into the world of real women, complete with proposal, husband and hearth. 'I just hope she stocks up on earplugs.'

'You must be more tactful,' said Midge, sounding less and less like my Midge and more and more like the sort of Vinegar Nell with embroidered guest towels she's always dreaded becoming. 'Lindsay isn't you. Her choices aren't as wide, she's not as young as you and Bob makes her happy.'

'Good,' I said, carrying cups purposefully into the kitchen.

'He knows about her and he accepts her. He isn't married and he doesn't just want her to live with him. It means she'll have a house of her own. Isn't that something you want for her?'

I'd never thought about what I wanted or didn't want for Lindsay. Her life was the burden of mine. She had never had very good taste in men and Bob didn't seem to be any exception. I thanked God Con wasn't with me. I opened the kitchen window. And before I could say anything, my mother used a phrase in which she took refuge when she couldn't find anything more pleasant to say. 'Bob has a lot of good points.'

'I'm sure he has,' I said. 'It's just that I'd prefer to discover them with the volume down a bit.'

'Lindsay says he's very insecure. He never had a father, you know.'

'I see,' I said.

I didn't feel sympathetic. I didn't really care. If Con were here, he'd say, 'a bastard in more ways than one', his voice uninflected, daring me to laugh. I washed up the cups. I thought of Con twice that whole afternoon. When Lindsay and Bob returned, we drank another cup of tea and she drove me to the station. She told me they were looking for a house and asked me particularly to come to the wedding. She didn't enquire about my attachments or lack of them and I offered no information. I went to sleep on the way home and once there had a bath and slept more. I go to sleep like that when I'm tired – or depressed.

26 *Mercer*

Lindsay married Bob just before Con came back from the last protracted trip for Mr Parah. She married in mauve at a registry office with the two children of Bob's previous marriage, Midge and me in attendance. Her employers – she had finally split from Stuart and Kay and was working for estate agents – thoughtfully gave her some superior champagne and we all behaved impeccably. I lent Bob and Lindsay my flat for the weekend because they couldn't afford a honeymoon, and I stayed with Midge. As we walked the dog and ate little meals and talked, I became aware that she was ageing. I hadn't noticed it before.

She was not as interested in anything as she had been, almost deliberately non-committal, and I heard myself pushing the conversation, trying to entertain her, to get her to react. I don't know whether I thought that was what I ought to do – it was more or less how I'd related to her for years, talking about my life as if it were a performance – or whether I did it because she expected me to, or both, or what. Perhaps I was diffident about what I did for a living, and her not understanding it. But I would like to have talked to her about Con and I didn't feel free to.

She talked about how Lindsay had finally come to leave Stuart, who used to employ Bob and of course was jealous of him. She made references to the financial difficulties of Lindsay's showdown with Stuart, which had to do with his status as an undischarged bankrupt and her culpability in the business. She mentioned solicitors and counsel in chambers. 'She's much better off where she is now,' Midge said. 'They're getting a council house near where she works and Bob's looking for a better job.' She did not ask about my scripts. She did ask about the magazine and I told her funny stories about that, though she still didn't seem very responsive. But she did tell me that her brother Guy had died and left her seven thousand pounds which was, she said, the most incredible windfall. And she talked about the colour scheme Lindsay was thinking of for the bathroom, what the Princess was wearing in Bermuda and how her dog Johnny was going to have to go on a diet. Against such a backdrop, I couldn't start talking about a man whose background was nothing if not dramatic, in her terms at least.

So I left it. And Con rang one evening when it was late and had been raining. He said he would like to come over in a couple of hours and I agreed, thinking with pleasure of the key I'd had cut for him. When he arrived he was almost puffy with tiredness and we were awkward and unable to speak to each other. He asked for a cup of tea and, while I made it, stood behind me in the kitchen, his arms wrapped round me. He sat in the living room holding my hand and waited for his tea to cool.

When he came inside me, I said, 'Welcome home,' and he went to sleep on my shoulder.

I woke up at five and he was looking at me.

'Can I talk to you?' he asked. I said that I wished he would, so he explained that Mr Parah had enemies. Everybody with that kind of clout in that kind of country had political connections and so Mr Parah had enemies. They had decided that he, Con, was the perfect way to get at the boss and so there had been an attempt on his life. When he caught up with Mr Parah in Rome, Con had asked him about it. He denied all knowledge, expressed shock, offered guards but for some reason Con wasn't convinced. The showdown came when Con realised that Mr Parah's enemies had persuaded him that Con was plotting against him.

'What happened?' I asked.

'They blew up my room while I was in the pool,' he said. 'When I went back in to find out what was going on, I saw Parah going out of a side door. I went back and told the chauffeur to give him a message and then I reported to security, saw the police and all the rest of it. I met him four days later at his request. He beat about the bush a bit but finally told me that he knew I was plotting against him and had decided to teach me a lesson. I lost my temper.'

'What did you do?'

'Told him who he was really up against, threw him through a plate-glass window and walked out.'

I swallowed. 'Are you safe?'

He hadn't raised his voice. He lay back against the pillows.

'Oh yes, by now he's checked, found out that I was on the level. He tried to get me to come back but I'm not going.'

'What will you do now?'

He shrugged. 'Sleep a bit and then sort out something. Can I stay here?'

'I wish you would,' I said, and I got out of bed to get him the key I'd had cut.

At eight I put a folded blanket under the typewriter, drank juice and left him alone. He was still asleep when I left at midday so I wrote a note telling him I'd be back at six or so. I returned somewhat nervously, clutching steak and salad and wine. He was a tired man, I a woman who should be taking care of him – he came rushing to the door, grinning from ear to ear, and I was embraced, talked to, given a drink and led into the kitchen to tell him how I'd like my steak. He'd already been shopping.

That night he told me that much of the money he'd saved was now lost. I said I had money. And he was going to see an old friend about a job in the morning.

'What job?' I asked.

'I'm going to drive a minicab until I get sorted out,' he said.

'And Mr Parah?'

'Finished,' he said.

'He won't come after you?'

He shook his head.

'Can you just stop, just like that?'

He looked at me calmly. 'Don't ask me about this, Mercer. I can't tell you any more. But I promise you, it's over.'

'And I suppose you want a nice house in suburbia with a wife to come home to?'

'I hate suburbia. You have to work, you're good, and you'll go mad if you don't work. I think we should look for a flat – how long have you still got on this place? – and then we'll get married.'

I began to laugh. I looked at his long face and his long hands and his long legs and I thought that I couldn't have dreamed him up, that he was the best thing that ever happened to me, and I went and put my arms round him.

'When are you next going to see your mother?' he asked.

I said I supposed in a couple of weeks and he suggested that he drove me down.

We did a great deal of talking from then on. He went to work and I went to work and we made supper and talked and woke with the dawn and made love all over again and talked some more. And then we drove down and met my mother and of course Lindsay was there.

I was very nervous about Con meeting my sister and my mother. It wasn't so much that Con was different from anybody else I'd ever been involved with – though, thank God, he was – but rather that I knew no matter how polite he would be, he would not only tell the truth about what he thought but would also refuse to play conversational games with them. He would say please and thank you, all right, and make conversation about trivialities if he had to, but there were no special dispensations available to either of them. My own feelings of security with him were very much based on knowing that I could ask anything, say anything, and that my work was accepted rather than tolerated. With Con I felt whole for the first time, a whole person. But I thought the meeting went well. Lindsay was a bit hearty but otherwise agreeable enough, and Midge was impressed by him. So she said.

We weren't there long, and Con meeting them, my meeting his parents and family a bit later on took care of the formalities. Bob wasn't in attendance on that occasion but he was the next time we visited and Con suddenly suggested that he'd like a drink, very pointedly didn't invite anybody to join us, do you need a jacket Mercer, and swept me out of the door. Both of us hate pubs so we walked up the road away from the house in silence and then I asked what we were doing. 'Getting the hell out of there,' he said, grimacing. 'Wait till we get to the pub.'

It was a seedy grey building with a formica bar, the kind of place that puts squash in drinks requiring juice. We sat down and he asked me what I thought was the story between Lindsay and Bob.

'Middle-class lady of a certain age gets tired of being alone.'

'Mother approves?' he queried.

'Apparently. It will give Lindsay, quote, a home of her own. Her options, quote, aren't as good as mine.'

He nodded.

'Does your mother realise what a strain Lindsay is under?'

'I don't know.'

He looked at me. I didn't know, or at least, know anything new.

'My mother and my sister have a different relationship from the one I have with my mother.'

'How much do you have to do with the financing of your mother's life?'

I explained about the allowance. He nodded. We walked back to the house. The afternoon passed. We both had headaches when we left.

Within the week I had a letter from Lindsay which pointed out that she couldn't very well pay for the upkeep of two homes and as she and Bob would need all they could muster for their own home, she hated to ask me but did I think I could take over the mortgage of Midge's house? The sum wasn't enormous, so I agreed. She rang me back to explain that the mortgage was in her name, Midge being too old to have been considered eligible for one. So I set up a standing order to go into Lindsay's bank account for the sum of money she indicated as being appropriate, plus a contribution to the rates. Midge immediately rang to see if I could manage this. I said that I could. She said it was very good of me. I said that they were my family, things were going well with me, with us and I was glad they were good for Lindsay too. Midge agreed that they were. Con's name wasn't mentioned.

When I told him about it, he suggested with tact that I should check with solicitors. When I mentioned it to Jud Chase on the phone, she said shortly, 'And what do you get out of this?'

I asked what she meant.

She spoke very patiently. 'Mercer, you pay your mother an allowance? Admirable. Your sister gets married from the house in which she has lived with your mother, a house bought with the cash your mother brought from the sale of her last home, the family home but upon which she raised the mortgage – right? So they couldn't have done it one without the other. Your sister hadn't got the cash and your mother couldn't have signed the documents. Now, your sister marries and moves out and you take over paying the mortgage.'

'It seems only fair,' I said. 'I am much younger, I do earn more money.'

Jud sighed. 'Have you seen the mortgage form?'

'Jud, for heaven's sake, this is my family –'

'So,' she said, shaking out her cuffs in that gesture I knew so well – I could just imagine her. 'And since when have families become such a sunshine institution in your little world? Mercer, I'm not saying don't do it – I'm only respectfully suggesting you cover your arse. Don't talk to me. I'm partisan. I represent you. But please, talk to a solicitor. See mine. He's a sweetheart and he's no fool.'

So, between them, they persuaded me to spend an afternoon with Mr Abrahams, a strong-faced Scottish Jew who listened patiently and then asked what my share of the house was. I said that I thought, my mother had always given me to understand, that it would be left to me and my sister equally. He asked if I had a written agreement to that effect. I said I had not. He said that he agreed that if I were to pay these sums I must do so informally so as not to jeopardise my own standing in the matter of a future mortgage I might want, but he felt that he must point out to me that as things stood I was completely unprotected.

I tried very hard not to be annoyed. He was doing his job.

I couldn't go back and ask for my share from a woman who was living on tuppence farthing. I did not want to confront my mother and ask her what my share was. How could I ask her to set up a will? It was like mentioning her death. She shrank from these things and so did I. Besides, besides, they were my family. They knew that, even if I came good all the way home to the Bank of England, how hard I had worked, how I had waited. They would be fair to me. There was no reason they would not be fair to me.

Mr Abrahams said that he would draft an agreement for my consideration. When it arrived, I took a deep breath and sent it on, with a letter of explanation. Midge rang soon after it was received and told me how much I had upset Lindsay by even suggesting that either of them would do me out of anything. I said that I was sorry they had been upset but I had taken advice and so on.

'You know you'll get half of everything,' said Midge, hurt. 'You must know that neither of us would ever knowingly do you down.'

I said I did know that, of course I did, but unfortunately the legal advice required some sort of written agreement and I had sent the one they'd put together for me as a starting point, against which Lindsay might reasonably have her own suggestions to make.

Mr Abrahams read the new draft Lindsay had sent me with a frown.

'Well, whatever you do,' he said calmly, 'don't sign that. It may represent your sister's interests in the matter but it certainly doesn't represent yours. What was her response to the letter I drafted?'

'She didn't like it,' I said.

He nodded.

'My mother felt it was offensive to her – my sister's, I mean – intentions.'

'It probably was,' said dear Mr Abrahams. 'The law doesn't deal in intentions, Miss Canning. It deals in facts. And what you have to be sure of is that you have enough facts on your side to adequately represent your case. If that makes your sister or your mother unhappy, you must ask yourself why.'

So we left it there. At least, I took meetings no further with Mr Abrahams. Nor did I sign Lindsay's draft agreement. I just continued paying mother into her bank every month and Lindsay into her bank every month for the mortgage. And I rang Jud and thanked her for introducing me to Mr Abrahams.

It took a year for Con to climb into a position of financial security in his own terms and then he worked for a housing trust. He did not earn wonderfully there but he learned, all over again, that his mind was attuned to both people and business. For my part, the television scripts looked likely to go to a second series, the magazine and newspaper pieces were rolling in and out of the door with blessed regularity and we were both being sensible beyond our wildest dreams.

It was in the purchase of our flat that I discovered that Con could not only read the kind of documents which made my eyes swim before the words could register in my mind but that he understood them and could ask intelligent questions about them. And so we wound up with a friendly mortgage broker through whom we acquired a very attractive flat with a garden. And we got married. And I shamelessly contrived to keep Lindsay away because I couldn't invite Lindsay without Bob and I couldn't face Bob over a wedding breakfast. I did not think that perhaps he might have felt as violently about me. Midge came and was as charming as Midge can be on these occasions, with a sort of social ease which Con has, too, though his grace lies in knowing exactly who he is and what he can do while in Midge it's to do with smiling the situation into submission, subduing it with movements as precise as a matador's cloak and finally just as concealing.

But I did not think very complex thoughts on my wedding day. The sun shone and we were married at midday, with Jud and my mother and Con's oldest friends – none of whom meant a great deal to me that day, for all I saw was him. I did not think that perhaps in marrying a man she couldn't categorise I had defeated my mother's plan for me.

I didn't think that perhaps in daring to be happy in both work and relationship terms I had removed myself from my mother's orbit, never to return, and so would be punished for that escape.

I did not think about David or Con's earlier wife.

I did not think about Lindsay and Bob. I thought briefly about Paul, but then if he'd lived it would have been different yet again, though I didn't think then that the hole left by his death would draw Midge and Lindsay into such an impenetrable alliance. Perhaps I was stupid. I should have thought more. I was just busy being happy.

I suppose just how indissolubly Midge and Lindsay were linked together and what I felt about it was best illustrated when Josh was born.

Con and I talked about having a baby. I told him about the abortion I'd had when I was younger. He told me about the doctor who'd told him he was sterile. We talked about miscarriage, stillbirth and cot-death, infertility, tubal pregnancy and post-puerperal depression. We talked about everything like this, in gory detail. It may have verged on the obsessional but it was, overall, very reassuring. Having Josh was only ever as complicated as talking about it. After a year Con thought it would be nice to try. So we tried and we got pregnant. He was by now earning a great deal of money in a private security consultancy and I didn't think we should wait any longer. The gods were smiling on us, weren't they? Why wait?

When I told Midge that we were pregnant, she was delighted. She said Lindsay was delighted too. We went down to see her that weekend when, for some reason, Lindsay and Bob couldn't join us. I had noticed that they joined us, either Lindsay or Bob and Lindsay, every single weekend we went to visit Midge but had not known how to indicate to my mother that perhaps we'd like to see her alone some time. However, they were not there this time so we took her out for lunch and went back to the cottage for tea, when she remarked, 'Do you realise, this is my first grandchild? You can't count that thing of Lindsay's.' I went to call Con from the garden where he was playing with her aged terrier Johnny and as I walked I wondered – that isn't very nice, or am I just getting soppy because I'm having a baby? No, she can't have said that to Lindsay. I hope she hasn't, and if she hasn't, does that make it any better? If that's what she's thought but not what she's said? So why did she say it at all? Wasn't it the wrong time to be warning me or reminding me of an unhappy past about which I could do nothing?

I called Con, we drank our tea and on the way home in the car I began to cry. When he asked me what was the matter, I tried to tell him, afraid that he would think I was overreacting, afraid of being silly, of being accounted a foolish woman. But being Con he talked about it, about the imbalance of all the relationships, about the money, about my mother's relationship with Paul which he'd never seen, about Lindsay's past relationship with Stuart which we'd talked about before, about the baby and Tony's death, and the miles slid by and I was able to become calm again under the endless discussion of people whom I did not often trust but in whom I was endlessly interested.

There were several more visits when I was pregnant and then I went into hospital to have Josh. It wasn't a horrible delivery, but nor was it without its strains, and in the end I just wanted to rest and get used to the new person in the cradle beside me. Con kept my mother away for two days and then warned me she was coming that afternoon. I didn't see harm in what he'd done or malice in delaying her arrival but I wanted him to know that I was all right now, so I patted his sleeve and then, later, began to weave silly dreams about how Midge would look and what she'd say – except that she didn't say any of these things for, as I walked down the ward that afternoon, she and Lindsay came towards me out of the lift and I was torn between saying, 'Oh damn, not her!' just like the brat I'd always known I was, irritation at my mother's lack of judgement, and being struck by the disciplined blank pain, like a child with a mortal illness, which Lindsay wore on her ostensibly welcoming face.

27 *Mercer*

When Midge came to stay the first Christmas after we had Josh, I was very excited. She was, after all, coming to stay for a time that I could never remember being less than special, and having my mother to stay with my husband and son for Christmas really was very important. She was tired when she arrived, with the devoted Johnny at her heels, but she enjoyed it all. I gave her cashmere and she gloated over it. Con was expansive, friends dropped in and Josh smiled even if he didn't sleep too much.

For some reason I've never been able to understand, I insisted we had candles on the tree. Somewhere in the recesses of my mind, I decided that my mother was just about old enough to remember a tree that way and that she must have it again in my home. I wanted Josh to see them too but it took Josh a little longer to master the refinements of Christmas. I'm very glad I found those candles and their holders and made it happen because by March of the following year Joan, who had read every night of her life that she could remember, had only residual eyesight left. The light just faded out of her eyes which critically reduced what I could talk to her about, as my life was entirely bound up with words and images.

She was chillingly brave about it. The forbearance I'd read about in older people was there in spades and she adapted with amazing speed to talking books, the taped works provided for the blind.

But she continued to wish to live alone, although Lindsay grew more and more worried about her. I didn't worry about her. I rang regularly, asked how she was doing, emphasised that if she was unhappy about anything – anything at all – she should tell me, but if she insisted that she was all right, I presumed she was telling the truth. She was self-sufficient, she always had been, and she admitted that she didn't tire easily of her own company. She walked her dog, she ate properly. I was only a telephone call away, Lindsay came to see her at least once a week. We saw her less frequently, much less frequently, but then we could never see her without Lindsay and Bob.

As Midge grew older, she grew deafer, and Lindsay's voice seemed to spiral upwards in patterns like old chainstitch, monotonously embroidered, and Bob always had a new project or scheme for making money, always a shortcut, ill-conceived and impractical. Whatever it was, he always wanted to talk to Con about it, though he was always displeased by Con's reaction. Con, fastidiously repelled by the physical reality of a man so charmless, was sorely tried by anybody wanting money without realising they'd have to work for it and without any understanding of business. And Lindsay didn't like Con. She responded to him because of his calm, his ability to go straight to the heart of confusion, distress or any other emotion without bias. But knowing he understood her dilemmas didn't make her feel warm towards him. She felt transparent in his presence and resented him for it. And somehow Midge refused to see all this, refused to hear it. Not because her eyesight was dim and her hearing impaired but on the same basis that she had controlled things in the past. If she refused to acknowledge what was happening, then it didn't happen. She set her considerable will against what was there to make it disappear. So I continued to try to please her in my way and Lindsay continued to try to please her in her way.

That my mother should spend Christmas with Lindsay and that we would all get together on Boxing Day was an accommodation on everyone's part. It left Con and me free to have Christmas with Josh and the small number of people we held dear. It left Midge free to minister to Lindsay who was even now beginning to acknowledge that she wasn't as happy as she had hoped she might be. It made Lindsay feel needed, for Midge was no longer young and the elderly must have Christmas provided for them as must the children.

I wasn't unwilling to spend part of Christmas with Lindsay and Bob theoretically speaking, being as much imbued with the traditional familial ideals of Christmas as anybody else. But I couldn't find a way of suggesting to Midge that perhaps she might not always have Lindsay there when we were. Once I decided that instead of being polite, I should just ask. 'Well Mercer,' she shot back firmly in a clear, slightly martial voice, just short of expostulation, 'I know you aren't keen on seeing Lindsay and Bob but Lindsay does leave him behind as much as she can. And I can't forbid Lindsay the house. It is after all her home.' Indeed.

I went down once or twice with Josh in his buggy, midweek, unannounced, and we all enjoyed each other. But Lindsay and Midge had now become a hydra-headed entity called my mother-and-sister and it obviously suited them and, since I had so much else in my life which suited me, they expected me to get on with it.

I tried to but I cried. I cried with Con in the car or in the kitchen when Josh had gone to bed, once I'd recognised that his mummy crying every time we left granny's wasn't a very positive image for a child as bright as mine, or come to that, any child. I went over and over the past, what I knew of my sister's earlier life and my mother's life with her and before her, with Con, with Jud, with my friends, with any intelligent and reasonably thoughtful person I knew. I talked about my father and my mother as a couple and independently, I discussed the affair my mother had had during the war, the possibility of a second – not because they were in them-selves such terrible things but because of what they indicated, what they might indicate and what I might learn from them. I wasn't looking to judge but to resolve. My work was established, I had a husband I loved who loved me and a son we adored. I wanted to share this with my mother. The way I was brought up led me to think that that was what you did with good fortune. You shared it, you let your little light shine.

Perhaps I was foolish. I should have understood before Con had to say it to me that I had too much, so much that my mother could not enjoy it for feeling guilty that my sister, by comparison, had so little. But even when I understood this intellectually, I couldn't make sense of it emotionally because emotionally I was being punished. I was being denied the next phase of my relationship with my mother because she didn't feel I ought to need her any more. And yet when I attempted to break further away from her, to see her less, she was angry, as if I were omitting some part of a tribute she felt she had the right to exact from me and I, because I had Con and Josh and work that I loved and friends and a life of comparatively infinite horizons, felt that I must use all these good things for strength to continue as we were.

There were incidents which highlighted to me how far adrift we were but on the few occasions that I attempted to itemise and analyse what I believed to be awry, I was met by a system of defence which NATO would envy. And my mother had me on toast. I did not see her as often as Lindsay, I didn't live as near, I didn't telephone daily. Lindsay did, usually twice a day. I could not and would not pretend to feel about Bob other than I did, which was that he was a boor, another exploitative man, one of a number my sister had selected for reasons which at the time I had not begun to consider. I found him hard to bear and whenever possible refused to bear him. And Con, behind his impassivity, nursed acute watchfulness towards Bob and Lindsay and how they behaved towards each other, inasmuch as it directly influenced how they behaved towards my mother. He did not try to keep me away from Midge but he did point out that something was happening and that the atmosphere was always loaded.

When Lindsay attempted to persuade Midge to sell the house and go and live with her and Bob, what fascinated me was that she couldn't just say no. She would have done so to me without a second thought. And when I asked her about it, she replied placatingly, implying that I, with all my ability, of all people should understand, it was quite simple really, with, 'Oh Mercer, you and Lindsay are very different people.' I was sorely tempted to retort 'Thank God!'

In some sense I tried to withdraw, because it's very hard to go through things which once meant a great deal to you as if they now meant nothing more beyond the form you observe. I don't like rote, I have fought against it. Life is for living, not moving through blindly, as if there were no choice. And I'm not socially graceful. How could I go down and pretend all was well when it wasn't? But neither could I quite stay away. I was told that Bob wasn't working, that Midge had made Lindsay a loan. I was told that Lindsay's job just wasn't enough for them to live on because Bob insisted on running his own car. Con was told that Midge paid Lindsay's weekly bills and all sorts of bits and pieces. I knew that when Lindsay took Midge away on holiday, Midge paid for everything. And Lindsay told Con that Bob had borrowed an unsecured loan from the bank to start up a home-selling job but that he hadn't seen any return on it. It's amazing how much people who haven't got any money talk about it.

Then Lindsay said that she couldn't do everything that needed doing in Midge's house. She was eligible for a home-help but she wouldn't have one. And before I could screw up my puny nerve and process that any further, Midge found herself a woman with time on her hands, who liked housework and didn't need money and became her tame old lady, her quasi-mother and a friend. I upped her allowance and she settled once more into enjoying her independence.

Somehow or other the business of the will came up again and I seized the time and asked Midge if she and I and Lindsay could get together and go through it, to make sure it was all squared away. She agreed, so Con drove Josh and me down there and he played with Josh in the garden while my mother and sister and I shut ourselves in my mother's bedroom, each of us initially edgy and embarrassed, but it turned out to be the happiest afternoon that the three of us had spent together for ages. We made jokes, we teased each other, we went through the contents of each room and encouraged each other to ask and to say. There was an hour of peace, without shadows. I remember it tenderly. And then Midge asked to have a word with Con.

In the car going home, I was quiet, enjoying the setting sun, and Josh went to sleep in the back. Con asked if the will was fair; I said I thought so and he told me that Midge had wanted to leave her wedding ring in trust for Josh. She had opted firmly for cremation and had heard terrible stories about rings being stolen from the bodies awaiting disposal. I was touched. Con nodded thoughtfully.

Months passed. I was deep in a play for television. Josh had settled into a new school. Con's working days still lasted too long. I had ceased to try to call Midge more than every few days. She was worried about Lindsay, about her job and how much was demanded of her, about Bob and how unsatisfactory their domestic life seemed to be, about how far she had to drive to work, about how tired Lindsay was, about what the future might hold if she stayed with Bob who hadn't worked for a year. She even mentioned the unmentionable, that maybe Lindsay and Bob would not, could not stay together. And what did she want to hear from me?

How Josh was advancing at school, readers' praise for my articles, the success Con had scored with his latest contract. And when I ran out of good news, she wanted entertainment, something to take her out of herself and stop her worrying about what was going to happen to Lindsay. It became harder, less appropriate to call her by a pet name that had always been my name for her. What was she to me? I began to call her Joan – it seemed more in keeping with our distance and the strange formality of our relationship. I sent her flowers to cheer her up, brought small gifts with me whenever I came and made her cakes, tributes to the ones I remembered from my childhood. Sometimes I made the effort when I was feeling good to ring and tell her things. But the harder I tried, the less relevant I became. I was cast as her success and her time was devoted to her less successful daughter.

It was no good both of us pursuing from opposite ends of the spectrum the same deadly intent about internalising. She wanted me around as part of a family she couldn't afford to see division in. I could see the division, all right, and if I could see it, I had to decide whether to ignore it and press on or to acknowledge it and move back a bit. The former was her way. I practised the latter.

I received an unexpected letter from Lindsay, saying that she was in terrible financial trouble – three mortgages on the house, pressure from the bank, other loans. She said that Bob was going to pursue his selling ideas abroad and that she had agreed that she would see him off and then sell the house. 'The only thing I can see myself doing at the moment,' she wrote and I could hear her voice saying it as I read, 'is moving back in with Mother.' She also asked if she could talk to Con about her financial problems, 'because he obviously has the best business head.'

I showed the letter to Con when he came in. He said quite quietly and matter-of-factly that he would ring her. He went upstairs to see Josh and then bathed him while I got supper ready. We rang Lindsay after the *Nine O'Clock News*. I spoke to her initially, she was as she ever was. She said that she was going to muster all the money she could so that Bob had something to start with. I asked if she intended to join him. She said not, that she didn't want to live in Spain, this was his idea. I didn't want to push but I did want to know. 'Is this the parting of the ways?' I asked. 'Seems so,' she replied. I passed the telephone over to Con and left the room. Midge always left the room if there was a personal conversation in progress to which she was not directly party.

I went upstairs. Josh was sleeping peacefully, his large forehead and little nose ridiculously dignified, his arms outflung imperially. I went back to the kitchen. I could hear nothing from the living room. I put the dishes in the washer, wiped the table down. When I went through to the other room, Con was standing, looking out of the window.

'You know she wants to sell up and go and live with your mother?'

'Yes, so she said. She's apparently in the most awful financial trouble.'

He nodded.

'And Bob's going off to Spain?'

He nodded again.

'I've asked her to send me a schedule of her borrowings and debts,' he said. 'And then we'll see.'

'I'm sorry you had to get into this,' I said.

'I'm not,' said Con, with a little smile that flicked round his lips like a lizard and then was gone. 'And don't forget, when the going gets tough, you've got it in writing – your sister wrote to you to ask if I would get into it.' He put his hand briefly on my shoulder, then against my face as he passed. 'We haven't heard the whole story yet.'

I put my sister's last letter firmly into the file I had made up about mother's will.

The next morning Joan rang.

'I gather you spoke to Lindsay last night,' she said, 'and Con said he would try to help her sort things out. You know she's going to have to sell the house? It's all that bloody man and his grand ideas – '

'Bob, you mean?'

'Bob, Bob and his big ideas, big ideas and no money to pay for them and guess whose name the overdraft is in?'

I didn't exactly have to guess.

'She wants to come and move in with me for a bit, once he's gone off to Spain. That's all right, isn't it?'

'It's your house,' I said. 'But I can't help wondering – is Lindsay going to get a divorce?'

'Don't think she wants one. She's talking about a separation but I mean, if he's in Spain and she's here, that's the end of it, surely?'

'He could always come back from Spain,' I pointed out, 'and if he's stuck he'll come to her for help. And you know what Lindsay's like. And if she's living with you where does that leave you? With Lindsay and Bob in your little house?'

'No thank you,' said Midge.

231

'Then she'd better go for divorce.'

Did anybody say that to me when David and I broke up all those weary years ago? Yes. My mother did. She said, 'If you're together, you're together, and if you're not, far better make a clean break of it. Better for everybody.' Quite right, Joan, one of the wisest things you ever said to me.

When the next letter arrived from Lindsay it was addressed to Con, who opened it that night after he came in, which was late because he'd been to a meeting. When he'd read the papers, he went through them again and then he asked me to get a pad and a pencil and note down some figures. And so we sat while he called out numbers and did sums on his calculator and asked me to write amounts down and then used them in different ways. Eventually he asked me if I still gave my mother an allowance. I said that I did. He asked me if I made any other contributions to the house in Aising. So I said that I did, an amount which was paid directly into Lindsay's bank. He asked me why it was paid that way. I said, at the solicitor's suggestion so that it wouldn't interfere with my standing in relation to a mortgage of my own. He asked me what this amount represented. I said the mortgage payment plus a contribution towards the rates. How long, he asked, had I paid it? For ten years, I replied. The room was very still. The beam from the central light was thin and we both looked very tired.

Con stood up, still with the papers Lindsay had sent him in his hand.

'Well, those figures aren't here,' he said, gesturing towards the sheets he held.

I looked at him and frowned.

'She must have been overwrought, she's very upset. She's missed them off by mistake.'

He looked at me carefully.

'Everything else is listed,' he said. 'Every miserable thing. There was more going out of that house than there was coming in and she's never thought how she's going to pay it back. There is nothing here relating to a mortgage payment on the house at Aising.'

I didn't move.

'There is, however,' said Con very quietly, with his eyes fixed on mine, 'an endowment policy in the names of Lindsay and Bob Durlin, which has been in operation for ten years. When did you say they were married?'

I shook my head.

'Ten years ago?'

I nodded.

'Well-organised wedding gift.' He sighed. 'I'll have to ask Lindsay to let me see the papers.'

I should like to be able to report that my sister's misdealings appeared to me to be just one more little problem in a troubled world, that with the help of my husband I was able to restore order to the affair, to sweep and tidy in these matters much as I did in the home. I wish I could say that but the truth of it is I was very shaken.

28 Joan

As she grew older, Joan found that the past became both clearer and more important than the present. She had time to let her mind wander and it did as she sat with her dog on her lap and let it.

She had always admired the force with which Mercer committed herself to the idea of acting. She thought of nothing else for years, refusing to be put off by the difficulty of getting acting jobs, indomitable in the face of the other duller, more routine occupations she took up in between. Perhaps knowing that that was what she could fall into if she ever gave up the dream of something else was what kept her trying so hard. But she certainly did try. Classes in voice production and dancing and scene study. Pub theatre, travelling companies that seemed to last only a few weeks before they were gone and never paid, so that before Joan could get used to what she was doing, she had stopped doing it and was back in some office or other, working away to get the money to pay for the next experiment.

For all that she read, Joan didn't think much about writing. She thought about writing in a book being good or bad, pleasing or less than pleasing, but how it was done or what made you do it never crossed her mind. She had been somewhat surprised therefore to receive a letter from Mercer which indicated that not only had she written a play but that it was being put on. The theatre was one unknown to Joan but she felt that she ought to be there to see it even if Paul declined to go. He had always disliked the theatre. His idea

of entertainment was a Western. But Paul announced that they
would both go. Joan was startled.

'But I don't think it's that important,' she said. Paul looked at her
piercingly over the top of his paper. She knew how ungracious she
sounded. 'Well, of course, it's important to Mercer,' she qualified,
'but I don't know anything about the theatre, I've never heard of it.'

'The home of Britain's experimental theatre,' said Paul, still
looking at her. 'It's famous for tryouts, new talent, plays that
nobody understands but wish they did.'

'Oh,' said Joan, discomfited.

'In the paper often,' said Paul, going back to his reading.

In the darkness of the theatre, Joan had wished that he wasn't
there, that she wasn't there. She remembered wondering why on
earth Mercer had to go and write a play about some poor girl
getting rid of a baby? Still, it had been quite well written with a
beginning, a middle and an end, which was more than a lot of the
stuff you saw on television these days. Mercer had looked very
small and white when they met her afterwards. She had taken them
to a restaurant before putting them back, at their request, on a late
train to the next stop up the line from home which was where they'd
left the car. Joan asked to see the reviews Mercer had mentioned to
her and, while she was looking at them, Paul put his index finger
gently against his younger daughter's arm.

'Tired?' he asked.

She nodded.

'Quite a life you live.' He spread the rest of his fingers carefully
out on her forearm. 'Hard work, writing,' he said. 'But worth it, I'd
say.'

She almost smiled at him.

Well, thought Joan, moving the dog into a more comfortable
position between her side and the arm of the chair, Mercer certainly
stuck to writing. They hadn't gone to see the next play, she'd almost
seemed not to want them to, and then they decided against it
anyway. And then she married David. She stopped writing when
she was married to him, just to keep him going. And then she went
back to it and Paul died. Felled like a tree. Gone. I miss him yet, Joan
thought, although he was soft about money and never had the guts
to challenge me, or maybe he thought he didn't have to because I'd
never leave him anyway. He did the best he could, she thought, and I
thought he was there forever.

She got up and walked through to put the kettle on. She

remembered how Mercer had hated saying goodbye to Lindsay at the train. Mercer, she thought, saw us all in relation to herself and was not at all pleased when things began to change. Once she was grown up, she wanted continuity, but she didn't know how to provide it. She was so up and down. Perhaps it wasn't her fault, perhaps it was just the way she was made. Just like a kid, Mercer. She wanted to run away and dress up and hide but she thought we'd still be here, waiting for her when she'd finished playing. She wanted it all to be the same without putting in any of the upkeep. But all that changed when her father died. She was already out on her own but that made it clear that she wouldn't be coming back. So off she went to America and began writing again. And then Lindsay began to see the awful Stuart for what he was. Well, she wouldn't have done that, thought Joan as she waited for the tea to brew, if she hadn't had me behind her, me to consider. I was one excuse she could use and stick by.

To begin with, Joan knew that she kept house for Lindsay but as she grew older she accepted that Lindsay kept a house that she and Lindsay lived in. It was to be expected. Slowing down was inevitable. She hadn't the energy she'd once had and was quite grateful that Lindsay took her dog to work with her. He was the gentlest dog in the world but he was a bit large for an elderly lady whose loyalties were centred on the much smaller Johnny who trotted everywhere sedately at her heels. She had admitted to herself that she was truly frightened of Johnny dying before she did. And it was just as natural that she should spend her time worrying about Lindsay rather than Mercer.

First of all, it had seemed as if Lindsay would never marry, and then she met Bob. Bob wasn't everything Joan would have chosen for Lindsay by a long chalk, but when you've wasted as much time on a bad 'un as Lindsay had, you're jolly glad when somebody asks you to marry him. He was nice enough, Bob, if a bit loud, and nothing like as bright as Lindsay. But she said she was happy with him and if she was happy, that was all there was to it. Joan never had any intention of living with them. She would stay where she was.

Mercer had been very good about money, she was always good about money. Maybe being short of it herself for so long had made her understand, and Con was very good at those things. She didn't make a fuss about it, she didn't even jib when Lindsay asked her if she'd take over the mortgage payments on the house at Aising. Of course she knew she'd get her half in the end. Though Joan thought she was quite brave to have brought up the will. Lindsay would always fight shy of something like that in case it upset Joan. Neither of them get it quite right, thought Joan. Mercer's so direct it gives me a headache and Lindsay wants me to be a little old lady, to be run round and fetched and carried for. Well, I'm not quite ready for all that yet.

And I do miss my books.

She couldn't remember when she first knew that Lindsay wasn't happy. Was less happy than usual. Was worried. Lindsay wouldn't tell her unless she was pushed. Joan applied herself to pushing. Lindsay confessed that she was worried about the way Bob spent money. They had a talk about it and Joan pressed her to accept a cheque, a cheque she could, she said proudly, well afford since her late brother had generously provided her with a bit of a lump sum. And that year when Lindsay volunteered to take her away for a few days, she accepted gratefully and paid all the expenses.

Joan watched Lindsay try with Bob. Lindsay, Joan knew, was used to trying. Trying and making the best of it and keeping the lid on and slogging on. The trouble with Bob was nothing was within his means. To cheer Lindsay up he'd take her out to dinner but it would always cost a bit too much. 'Now was it really a bit too much or just a bit more than you thought it should be?' Joan asked her older daughter wisely. 'After all, dear, he *is* trying.' So the tide of their affections flowed in and flowed out again, sometimes over sand, sometimes over shale and sometimes over sharper things, and the daily friction of living between a man who never listened and a woman who couldn't hear began to eat at Lindsay's vocal cords, pitched higher and higher and harsher to make themselves heard and register over the other things that claimed her mother's attention and her husband's interest.

Joan became more dependent upon Lindsay when her eyes dimmed. And then they dimmed a bit more after that so that she could sort of see if there was a car coming round the corner when she walked the dog and could distinguish between light and dark on the television but nothing else very much that could be relied upon. So she must give somebody power of attorney. It was obvious that that would be Lindsay. She lived too far away not to grumble about being tired when she drove over during the week, but she was nearer and more regularly seen than Mercer. She told Mercer herself. All perfectly matter-of-fact. And Mercer agreed.

Joan thought Mercer had married well, considering how highly strung she was and how committed to this writing business. But there was something in Con that always evaded her. She couldn't quite put her finger upon it. He was always courteous, sometimes friendly. He clearly loved both Mercer and Josh. The size of him, the sheer physical bulk reminded her of Paul but he was a great deal more subtle and powerful than Paul had ever been. And yet his rages were of the same intensity, if quite a different heat. She supposed that the reason she was never quite at ease with him was because even when he was being kind, she always felt that he had outman-oeuvred her and this feeling was both unusual and uncomfortable. Often as she grew older she dismissed it. She listened to Mercer singing his praises and thought, well, at least one of them's happy, but the very fact that it was so, that there was somebody there she couldn't add up, irritated her.

She tried in every way she could to get Lindsay to talk to her. Lindsay did sometimes and sometimes she regretted it. But she must talk to somebody, Joan pointed out. 'When things are bad, you can't just lock it up in your head.' And this would inevitably lead into another outpouring of emotional mismanagement and financial woe and the writing of another cheque, another gift, another offer of help, another suggestion, and Lindsay would be on the telephone the next day, twice a day most days now because she felt that her mother should not be left alone and that she, Lindsay, must offer something in return for what she was getting.

Lindsay explained to Joan that she and Bob had agreed that they couldn't go on together and he was leaving for Spain.

'I'm sorry,' said Joan, 'but I expect it's for the best really, isn't it?'

Lindsay said she thought it probably was but she explained that this left her in considerable difficulties. The most sensible thing seemed to be to sell off their house and to discharge her debts so that she could start again with a clean sheet.

'Do you think I could come and stay with you for a while, until I get things sorted out?'

Joan said she couldn't see why not. She was sorry it had come to this. Was there really no other way?

'Not that I can see,' replied Lindsay.

'And will you and Bob divorce?' enquired Joan.

Lindsay was opposed to that. Joan left the matter. Over the next few weeks, Lindsay stored and sold furniture, consulted with her solicitors and moved back into the bedroom she'd had before she married, to the house she still thought of as her mother's. Then Mercer rang and, recapping on Lindsay's contact with Con for advice, said that they would like to come down that weekend. There were some problems which needed sorting out. Joan agreed that they should come.

When they arrived she was a little surprised that they had not brought Josh but, once they were all in the living room, she soon understood why. Mercer hardly spoke and Con spoke to Lindsay as if she were an errant employee. He asked questions about Bob's absence and Lindsay explained he had gone to Spain. It had been mutually agreed between them.

'Does your mother know that you not only gave him money to go with but that you have assumed the responsibility of paying all his outstanding debts?'

Lindsay replied primly that she understood her own responsibilities and had not thought that she should burden her mother with them.

'If you divorced him, you wouldn't be responsible for them,' said Con directly, but politely.

'I should still be morally responsible. I borrowed the money.' Lindsay sat like a witness at the dock.

'Did you borrow the money from your mother's mortgage?' asked Con.

Lindsay looked puzzled.

'Was converting your mother's mortgage from something that would benefit you and Mercer into an endowment which would be in Bob's interest and your own, his idea?'

Lindsay said that she did not know what he was talking about.

So he explained. He explained that the mortgage money was paid into Lindsay's bank by Mercer, had been since Lindsay and Bob married. When Lindsay asked for his help to try to straighten out her dishevelled finances, there was no mortgage on the schedule of repayments. There was, however, an endowment policy to benefit Lindsay and Bob. 'The premium on that policy was a good deal more than the premium on the mortgage for this house could ever have been, twice, maybe three times as much. I assume you put the surplus to good use.'

Joan stood up and went into the kitchen to put the kettle on. She stood for a second by the kitchen window. Con came in and stood in the doorway.

'I'm sorry, Mother,' he said.

'I couldn't understand why Mercer was still paying that mortgage,' said Joan. 'I put everything I had into this house at the time. Lindsay and I agreed I should hold on to a couple of thousand for absolute emergencies and if Guy hadn't died when he did and bequeathed me a bit more, that's what there'd be. But the house only cost £8,000 to start with and if I put down £5,000 and Lindsay raised a mortgage for the other three, including a bit of building work, what's Mercer been paying off for the last ten years?' She shook her head and reached for the teapot. 'The trouble with me, Con,' she went on, 'is that I've always been a bit feckless. Do you know what I mean? I don't understand business, I never have, and I depended first on Paul and then on Lindsay.'

Con nodded.

She left him with the teapot and went to look for Mercer whom she found sitting quietly by the window in the spare room. She made no movement towards her mother. Joan got on her knees beside Mercer. She could see a bit of her face that way, through one of the shafts of light which sometimes lit up her blank eyes from a curious angle.

'Mercer,' she said. 'I ask you to believe that Lindsay would do nothing knowingly to hurt you.'

Her younger daughter's face turned towards her.

'Oh, Mother,' she said, 'you can't afford to believe anything else. Look, I know you love her but you've got to face it. Forms do not transform themselves. They have to be altered. Somebody has to do it.'

'I do not believe that she did this to harm you,' said Joan, and rose and went away.

She was very glad she was deaf, very glad that she couldn't hear all of it and was unwilling to understand what she could hear. She had never known Mercer so quiet. Mercer was always the noisy one. She spoke once that afternoon, to urge Lindsay to get a divorce, and it seemed to Joan that Lindsay eventually unwillingly agreed. Con spoke most of the time, Lindsay sometimes answered him so quietly that Joan couldn't hear. She didn't want to ask for anything to be repeated. Con and Mercer left at just after four o'clock.

She asked Lindsay what had happened and Lindsay said that of course Con was on Mercer's side and that Mercer seemed to want to believe that she, Lindsay, would trick her own sister out of money.

'But you had altered the documents,' said Joan.

240

'Of course I altered them,' said Lindsay. 'It was a much better way for Bob and me to get our share.'

A couple of days later Mercer rang and said that she and Con must again come down to put an end to all this business. She said it affected the will. And again Mercer was unusually quiet. Con did most of the speaking. I must be very deaf, thought Joan, because I can't hear half of what he's saying. It's too formal for me to keep saying, what's that, what do you mean, could you say that again? So she sat there, brows knitted, watching.

Suddenly Mercer leaned forward almost into her face and asked her, 'You meant the will to be divided straight down the middle, didn't you?'

'Yes,' Joan answered clearly, 'except for the £800 which was your share from the sale of the family home.'

'Then,' said Mercer, every word clear-cut and unequivocal, 'that's what I want. Draw it like that. Right?' and she swooped towards Lindsay, who said something Joan didn't catch.

The house was very quiet after they'd gone but after all the house was often quiet if you were deaf, there might be things happening all around you and you'd never know. Joan sat and dozed in her chair.

Later she and Lindsay attempted some conversation over supper. Lindsay said that the trouble with Mercer was, she'd got too big for her boots. And Con! Well, of course, the trouble with Con was that he was such a know-it-all.

'I don't understand why you're so angry,' said Joan, a little plaintively. And out came a stream of stuff from between Lindsay's lips which hissed and snarled, terms from the mortgage and terms from the will.

'You know I'm not very good with legal terminology,' said Joan. 'Mercer – '

'Damn Mercer!' cried Lindsay.

Hm, thought Joan. I'm too old for all this, tomorrow is another day.

29 *Mercer*

I went down to the first confrontation between my mother and Lindsay and me with a beating heart. I was scared, though I couldn't have told you what of. Perhaps I was superstitious. Perhaps I thought I'd got too much, too much of everything, too much happiness, too much peace. Too much with Con and Josh and the work that I loved. Perhaps I thought that now I had to pay for it. It wasn't pretty watching Lindsay wriggling on the point of the questions Con asked her. But he had to ask. We were still, as far as I was concerned, dealing with a sleight of hand I don't understand, in a language which might as well have been Chinese. I knew that Joan was only getting about half of what was said and I knew that she wouldn't ask for anything she couldn't hear to be clarified. In a funny way I could sympathise with that. This was not what she wanted to hear.

When we left that time, Con said, 'You know we're going to have to go back there, we still haven't got to the bottom of it –' and before I could nod he went on. 'And I want to consult with solicitors before we go any further. I want to know what the legal grounds are and once we know that, if you want to go on and try to contain it within the family, all right. But you must know what you're dealing with first.'

Between the time he saw our solicitors, who had been his before he knew me, and who represented his business and my business and the house and everything, and getting ready to go down for the weekend, Lindsay sent him a copy of the original mortgage agreement made on the Aising house. It was clear from that that Joan had never held a half share in the house, although she put up most of the money for it. She owned somewhere between a third and a quarter and so, when she made her will, she left half her portion to each of us.

On the way to our second meeting, Con told me that he would stop being pleasant if he had to, that Joan must accept that not only had Lindsay done me out of money but that she had quite matter-of-factly defrauded her mother.

'Joan won't accept that,' I said.

'Why not?'

'Because it's not part of the scheme. You don't understand, Con – the game is called Poor Old Lindsay. If Lindsay has done this, then it is either by default or under pressure from her wicked husband –'

'The mortgage on the Aising house was drawn before Lindsay ever met Bob –'

'But she did meet Bob and he has let her down. She has lost the only home she's ever owned and she's not young and Mother is actually quite old and we don't need any large, tough, stroppy men coming in here and upsetting our applecart, so loaded with bruised apples as it already is.'

'Go on,' he said.

'Say what you like, Con. I give you permission, and I will too. But let's have no mention of courts and cases because that's a rich man's game and there's not enough money in all this to be worth that, even given the rate of inflation and the property boom. You see, I know what I'm supposed to do, I'm supposed to shut up and go away and leave them to get on with it, except when I bring her grandson for tea and can behave nicely. That's the pattern. But I want my money – I never thought I'd ever say that in my life – but I do. If Lindsay has taken money from Joan by one means or another, that's between them. She's got power of attorney, God knows what she can do. I want half the sale price of that house, that's all.'

Con permitted himself one of his black smiles.

'Quite reasonable really,' he agreed, 'considering you've bought the bloody thing twice over.'

And so we came to round two. And at the end of round two all I had heard Lindsay do was omit or evade or deny or refuse to confirm, but she had started divorce proceedings and she agreed to the house being assigned to my mother, to what was outstanding on the mortgage being settled so that this could go through (Joan paid Lindsay's half so that she shouldn't feel outflanked) and the will re-written and re-entered.

In the car going home, I felt almost peaceful. At least this wasn't boxing with shadows. This was real. All the explanations and interpretations in the world couldn't make this unreal. It was no longer a question of what I thought or felt, but what I had seen, what I knew. And I remembered Con asking me once, when Josh was asleep in the back of the car and I was choked with tears and bitterness, 'How will you feel when she dies?' And I had answered, 'I'd like to think that I will remember the good things, the happy times when I was younger. But if it's a bad day, all I'm going to think is good, that's "x" a month that won't have to be found.'

And Lindsay? Lindsay was like one of those girls I never liked at school. I kept looking for things to like but I never did and I can't make any pretences about loving her, either, because you can't love somebody who has just methodically stitched you up and would never have admitted it unless the going got tough. Con said she wanted to be found out. I don't know what to think.

I didn't ring my mother. I didn't ring my sister. I didn't have to make an effort to stop myself, either. I didn't want to. My mother rang me twice and took me through the whole weary business all over again, what I had said and what Lindsay had said, allowances to be made and understanding to be offered. I tried very hard to be polite and stay calm but the second telephone call was extremely painful because all I could hear was my mother asking me to agree to play the game of 'this is not so and now we can all go on as before'. And where oh where is it written that if there are more of them than you, they *must* be right? I had stopped writing my play. I couldn't write a shopping list. But interestingly it did not occur to me to wonder why Lindsay had chosen me as her target. I don't think there was much question about that. It wasn't even personal. I was just there.

A long envelope arrived through the post. It contained a codicil to Joan's will cancelling the sum she had said she always hung on to as my share from the last house she owned with Paul. I didn't know what to think. I knew that Lindsay could have asked her to sign without telling her what it was but somebody would have had to instigate the preparation of the document with solicitors. I couldn't ring Joan. She was blind. I rang Lindsay. She said that I had plainly stated that if I got half the house, I would quite happily forfeit any special bequests. I said that I did not remember saying this. She reiterated that I had insisted that the deal was strictly fifty/fifty. Joan was only doing as I had instructed her.

'All right, I hear you,' I said. 'I don't remember it that way but you do and I'm tired of fighting. So, fine. I'll sign the damned thing and that's the end of it.'

'You sound terrible,' said Lindsay, her voice sliding into a mixture of concerned elder sister and bossy nurse. 'I think you should talk to me.'

'No, thank you,' I answered and replaced the telephone.

Con had to go out that night. As he kissed me goodbye, he said, 'Do one thing for me. If you ring your mother tonight, say everything. Don't hold back or try to be considerate. Say the lot.' I nodded and off he went. So, of course, I didn't ring her. How could I? All my resentments were piling up like flames in the boiler of an old steam train and I would crush anybody who got in the way of my wheels. So I didn't ring.

But there was a god or a gremlin in the machine that night because she rang me. And she began in that tone that had first told me something had changed, that I had first noticed when I was afraid that David would leave me all those years ago and had dismissed as an aberrant mood, and had continued to dismiss until I couldn't, until it was noticeable to more than me and Con finally told me that she might be my mother but she wasn't my friend any more. She sounded like a mixture of Queen Victoria and Mother Teresa, slightly bored and sorely tried. And the rage came up from so deep inside me that it never occurred to me to deny it.

I shut the living-room door in case the noise I made woke Josh and I told her she could not speak to me that way ever again. I said that I had loved and respected her all my life and that she had no idea what the last few months had cost me. I told her about crying in the street and feeling that I had lost everything I had once believed to be mine. And she fought back.

First she played, 'I am your mother', level voice, controlled tone. And then she did, 'For goodness' sake, I'm over eighty', with a little expostulatory sob at the end of the phrase. In a more conciliatory vein, she tried, 'You are my younger daughter, I can discuss anything with you'. And when that didn't work, she reverted into, 'You're making me feel so guilty'. And I called her on all these

245

games, never having done so before, never having wanted to before, those so efficient and effective word patterns and emotional ploys with which she had contained me and bound me to her for years without seeing or wishing to see what was under my nose. I couldn't depend on her to take care of me. I had to take care of myself.

I said that I understood why she behaved as she did with Lindsay. She said we couldn't go into that now.

'Then,' I said, 'we will never go into it.' I said that I wouldn't play games with her any more.

'What games?' she asked, as if dumbstruck.

'You have ways of controlling people,' I said. 'We all do. But in your case they have been directed for some time at Lindsay and at me. And they work with Lindsay because you have something on Lindsay and Lindsay has something on you. Because Lindsay is the firstborn, the one you learned on, the one you failed with. And just as at eighty you still talk about how your father asked you to go with him and you didn't and you've regretted it all your life, so you failed Lindsay when she most needed you and you've danced round each other ever since. What you call devotion, I call unhealthy dependence. Did you know Paul and I discussed Lindsay needing professional help before he died?'

She didn't understand the phrase.

'Help,' I said, 'as in counselling, psychiatry.'

'Paul didn't believe in psychiatry,' she said disdainfully.

'Well then, he may not have done, but he changed. He changed enough to discuss it with me.'

'In any case,' she said, 'Lindsay hasn't done you out of as much money as you said.'

'Mother, for God's sake, are we talking about amounts or are we talking about principles? She did me and she is family, the family you're always banging on about, the family I didn't think I had to protect my back against. Don't you understand that this is a dereliction of everything I know, everything I absorbed from my father and you and all of you down all these years, and you expect me to put it to one side and pretend it never happened, that I'll come down and have tea and we'll all go on as before?'

'But what about Josh?' she said.

'Leave Josh out of this!' I shouted. 'Josh is free of all this and he stays free of it. You shouted at him once and frightened him because he was getting more attention than you and you'll never do that again. You've got Lindsay and you've had me but you'll never have Josh.'

'But how shall we go on?' she asked.

'I don't know,' I said, and there was silence.

'I don't think Lindsay meant to do it,' she said.

'Midge,' I said, 'for God's sake. There are three charges of criminal fraud I can bring against your elder daughter and the Revenue will bring a fourth. Is that what you want? We'll go to court.'

And she caught her breath. Seconds out.

'What do we do now?' she asked.

'Make a cup of tea, I expect,' I said wearily.

'And then?'

'And then – what?' I asked.

'When shall we have a reasonable conversation?'

'Oh, Mother,' I said, 'I give you full marks. I don't know. I don't feel what you call reasonable. If the price of being reasonable is as high as this, I may not want to be reasonable. I may want to stay unreasonable.'

'You make me sound so tough,' she complained.

'You are tough, Mother,' I said. 'You're as tough as old boots.'

'So,' she said. 'When shall we speak again?'

And I told her grimly, 'In the words of the agents, Mother – don't call us, we'll call you.'

I sat in my pleasant living room, blue and book-lined, and shook. And then I wept and waited for regret, but it didn't come. And I wished that I had taped it all so that I could know what was said and how it was said, in what order, and what it meant from her end and from mine, so that I would have a record of the day of reckoning, to remind me that I had heard and I had understood but I was still allowed to breathe. And that the umbilical cord was finally cut.

The solicitors went to work, forms came and were signed and went. The house was now my mother's, and she left it equally to both of us. I got my share plus the bequest and I suppose she and Lindsay went on sorting out a version of events they could agree upon.

I did not telephone either of them. There was no point in writing to my mother and I doubted if I'd ever write another letter to Lindsay without lodging a copy with the solicitor. But I couldn't work. I began reading books about parenting, the effect of abnormal upbringing on children, child psychology. I think I wanted to discover that apart from my temper, it was I who was abnormal and at fault. I chewed what had happened over and over with both Con

247

and Jud, with other friends, and I nestled deep into my son's neck for comfort every night he'd have me. I knew that my not ringing Lindsay and Joan was putting the onus on them to contact me and I knew that they hadn't the stomach for it and that was fine, because I needed time to get used to a universe in which they were reduced in stature and importance. If I had wanted to get in touch, I would have done. I didn't want to.

And then there was a terrible storm. Trees were uprooted and roofs blown off and the morning after that I reminded myself that my mother was old and rang to see if she was all right.

We managed a courteous enough conversation about nothing very much in particular. It did not lift my heart or cast it down. She was an old lady and I was her daughter. Filial consideration ran to a telephone call if no further. But I declined to go down at Christmas, or before it, or on Boxing Day. Joan clearly thought this was excessive but I didn't.

We didn't speak again until the spring and then Lindsay rang me to tell me that Joan was in bed, quite dazed and unlike herself, and the doctor thought it was a stroke.

Three days later Lindsay told me that she was no better and that Johnny, her little dog, had been failing so badly that she thought the kindest thing to do was to have him destroyed.

'Have you told Mother about it?' I asked.

'Yes, well – she came round for a bit this afternoon and I told her I'd had him put to sleep. She was quite lucid and seemed to understand. It wouldn't have been so bad except his bowels were going, and he was quite desperate, poor thing.'

'And how's Mother?'

'She's just not interested in anything,' said Lindsay, 'and I'm going to have to go to work tomorrow so Amy Whitford's coming in to sit with her and the doctor's coming.'

Within three more days she was in hospital and, though conscious from time to time, refused to eat or drink. Lindsay visited her every night in hospital, coaxing her with chocolate, trying to get her to sip tea. I was not asked to come and I did not offer. Lindsay loved the drama of it all and I hated it. Why couldn't my mother die in her own bed? Johnny had gone and she had always drummed into Lindsay and me that you could skip a meal if you had to but you must drink.

The next thing I heard was that she was being fed on a drip because the hospital was worried about how low she was getting, but they soon gave that up and then it was saline. Lindsay says that she called me at two one morning when it looked as if the end was near, but the telephone never rang.

Perhaps I hoped that I would be let off the hook, that she would die in the night and that would be that. But she lingered and two weeks later, when Con asked me if I would like to go and see her, I said that I thought I would. He said he would drive me down. What I didn't want was a cosy chat over my mother's recumbent body with Lindsay in her favourite role as the good daughter. I just wanted to say goodbye.

I looked at the low red-brick building which comprised the hospital, at the tired walls and the shabby flooring. It didn't mean anything very much to me that she was here, not any more than it would have meant had she been anywhere. She couldn't see it or hear it or feel it and she couldn't care less. She was beyond all that now.

I identified myself to a nurse and she asked if I realised the extent of her deterioration. I said I did. She indicated a partially curtained end bed and Con walked beside me to where the little husk that had been my mother lay.

He went away almost immediately to find a doctor.

I stood and looked at what she had become and knew she would have hated it. It was the only time the word 'helpless' had any meaning in connection with my mother. And I was very sad. Her hair was still thick and pretty, not old lady hair except that it was white, and the lines of her nostrils and her shoulders were as pure as ever. I was the same age now as she was when I was born. And I wondered if it was an acceptable definition of love not to feel guilt at difference but only lasting respect and sorrow. I stroked her forearm, said goodbye and forbore to pity her. Con put his hand on my shoulder.

'Don't ever let that happen to me,' I whispered.

'Pillow over the face,' he said tenderly, 'I promise.'

We saw the doctor. He said it was only a matter of time. Did we know about strokes? He was very kind. I wished I could stop thinking about a description of starvation I had read, one phrase repeated in my mind like a record stuck in a groove . . . and the chest collapses, and the chest collapses.

As we left, I turned back quickly, went once more to stand beside her, to wonder what she had desired? Not that it mattered. She couldn't have it now. And I began to weep. But then I often weep when I've just seen my mother.